SPECIAL MESSAGE TO READERS

THE ULVERSCROFT FOUNDATION
(registered UK charity number 264873)
was established in 1972 to provide funds for
research, diagnosis and treatment of eye diseases.
Examples of major projects funded by
the Ulverscroft Foundation are:-

- The Children's Eye Unit at Moorfields Eye Hospital, London
- The Ulverscroft Children's Eye Unit at Great Ormond Street Hospital for Sick Children
- Funding research into eye diseases and treatment at the Department of Ophthalmology, University of Leicester
- The Ulverscroft Vision Research Group, Institute of Child Health
- Twin operating theatres at the Western Ophthalmic Hospital, London
- The Chair of Ophthalmology at the Royal Australian College of Ophthalmologists

You can help further the work of the Foundation
by making a donation or leaving a legacy.
Every contribution is gratefully received. If you
would like to help support the Foundation or
require further information, please contact:

THE ULVERSCROFT FOUNDATION
The Green, Bradgate Road, Anstey
Leicester LE7 7FU, England
Tel: (0116) 236 4325

website: www.foundation.ulverscroft.com

John Kenney has worked as a copywriter in New York City for many years. He has also been a contributor to the *New Yorker* magazine since 1999. He lives in Brooklyn.

TRUTH IN ADVERTISING

Finbar Dolan is lost and lonely — except he doesn't know it. Despite escaping his blue-collar upbringing to carve out a mildly successful career at an advertising agency, he's a bit of a mess and closing in on forty. He's recently called off his wedding; and now, a few days before Christmas, he's forced to cancel a vacation in order to write, produce, and edit a Super Bowl commercial for his diaper account in record time. Then he learns that his long-estranged and once-abusive father has fallen ill, and that neither his brothers nor his sister intend to visit. It's a wake-up call for Fin to reevaluate the choices he's made, admit that he's falling for coworker Phoebe, question the importance of diapers in his life, and finally tell the truth about his past . . .

JOHN KENNEY

TRUTH IN ADVERTISING

Complete and Unabridged

CHARNWOOD
Leicester

First published in Great Britain in 2016 by
Corsair
An imprint of
Little, Brown Book Group
London

First Charnwood Edition
published 2017
by arrangement with
Little, Brown Book Group
An Hachette UK Company
London

The moral right of the author has been asserted

A catalogue record for this book is available
from the British Library.

ISBN 978–1–4448–3356–0

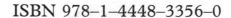

Published by
F. A. Thorpe (Publishing)
Anstey, Leicestershire
Set by Words & Graphics Ltd.
Anstey, Leicestershire
Printed and bound in Great Britain by
T. J. International Ltd., Padstow, Cornwall

This book is printed on acid-free paper

For Lissa

In the world of advertising there's no such thing as a lie, there's only the expedient exaggeration.

— Advertising executive Roger Thornhill, played by Cary Grant in *North by Northwest*

NEVER BORE THE AUDIENCE

Paul Murphy was a Vietnam veteran whose legs had been blown off at the battle of Da Nang and who now lived in one of the Veterans Administration hospitals in Boston. I met him in my senior year of high school when I had to write a term paper for a modern-history class. A large part of the assignment involved our ability not merely to research but also to interview people.

I spent many days interviewing doctors and nurses and orderlies, which eventually led me to Paul. Paul was skeptical at first, but I was able to put him at ease, mostly by bringing him cigarettes and once a bottle of vodka. One day, while I was visiting him in his hospital room, a place that smelled of disinfectant and sometimes of urine, I asked Paul Murphy about a book that we had read in class called *Born on the Fourth of July* by Ron Kovic, who would, years later, be played by Tom Cruise in the movie of Kovic's life.

'Have I read it?' Murphy asked, rhetorically, between drags on a Marlboro. 'I *am* it.'

'Were you born on the Fourth of July?' I asked.

'No,' he said. 'April twenty-seventh.'

'I see.'

'I wonder if you do,' he said, lighting another

1

cigarette off the one he'd already lit.

Paul Murphy was an angry man. But he was learning to deal with his anger. Once a week he read to inner-city children and the blind. He loved bowling and was in a league. They bowled and drank beer and laughed and had team shirts. He was seeing a woman who worked at the hospital, a young woman who had great compassion. Her name was Phyllis and she wrote letters to the governor about the need for more handicapped ramps in and around Boston. They got tattoos of each other's names on their buttocks. Paul said they had to be creative during their private time, 'on account of the fact I'm a limp dick.' I put all of this in my paper, which I titled *A Living Death*. I received an A.

My history teacher, Mr. Stevens, said in his brief evaluation:

Fin, this is a paper of great maturity and unusual sensitivity. I was deeply moved at times. You should be proud of this work. Nice job.

And I was proud. The only problem was that I had fabricated every aspect of the paper, including the person of Paul Murphy. Not one ounce of it was true, not his name or his smoking or anger or missing limbs or his passion for bowling. I invented everything. I said that he had been a star soccer player in high school in Ashtabula, Ohio, because I liked the sound of the word *Ashtabula*. I said that if he could stand he would have been 6′ 2″. I said that his penis didn't work properly because I wanted to work the word *penis* into the story because it made me laugh when I saw it in print.

2

It's not that I didn't try to do the assignment. I did, in a half-assed way. I spoke with a friend of mine's older brother, Larry Gallagher, who'd been in Vietnam. He was the assistant manager of the bowling alley, Parkway Lanes, though mostly he sold nickel bags of pot in the back. I interviewed him there, if by interview you mean ask him a few questions while he sprayed disinfectant into the bowling shoes. I asked Larry to tell me about Vietnam and the scars it had left him with. Larry said it didn't leave him with any scars except for where he cut his leg once on a jeep door when he was drunk. I asked him to tell me about the lasting pain of it all. He said it wasn't very painful but it was boring a lot of the time. He said it was fun firing his machine gun and that 'R&R was great because Vietnamese girls really know how to screw.' I thanked him for his time and then he let me bowl two frames for free but charged me for the shoes.

Alfred Hitchcock said that drama was life with all the boring bits taken out. I believed that in creating Paul Murphy, who surely must have existed in some form somewhere in the United States, that's all I had done. I wasn't interested in unearthing the truth so much as creating a truth I wanted to believe, that I knew others would believe. Because it *seemed* true.

Maybe it's not entirely surprising that I ended up in advertising.

AND ... ACTION

Fade in.

Close-up of a man's face. Mine.

A little internal voice. Also mine.

'Psst. Hey, Gary. Gary? You suck.' (My name isn't Gary, but the little internal voice knows I have an unnatural dislike of the name Gary and calls me that to annoy me.) 'You suck, Gary. You're a fraud and a phony and a hack and also did I mention that you suck? You lack soul and depth and intelligence. You've gone about it all wrong. You've wasted your life. Strong words. Think about them. Oh, except I forgot. You don't think about words. You use them like you use paper towels. Without thought or care. Can I say something else, now that I have your attention? Can I ask you to think about the fact that you got a three-ninety on your math SATs? Why do you leave the house in the morning?'

Cut to a short film, a reinterpretation of the seminal moment in *Sophie's Choice* when Sophie, just off the train at Auschwitz, must choose who lives, her son or her daughter. Except here Sophie is my mother. She must choose between me and ... nothing. The SS guard shouts at her: 'What will it be?!' She looks at me on one side. She looks at nothing on the other. She chooses nothing. The camera moves in for an extreme close-up of my confused little

4

expression as we cut to my mother, who shrugs, as if to say 'Sorry.' Pull back to reveal the expression of the SS guard, who also shrugs, something you rarely (ever?) see in the SS in particular and Nazis in general.

Raphael is speaking and has been speaking for some time, though I don't know what he has said because I haven't been listening — I've been in Auschwitz. But I should have been listening because we are about to roll film. And that means we are spending money, many hundreds of thousands of dollars, as is reflected by the number of people (nine) listening to Raphael, the director of the commercial. Also by the presence of Gwyneth Paltrow.

'So what are we talking about here?' Raphael says to Gwyneth. He then looks to the floor, clearly a man reflecting deeply (albeit about his own question). 'We're talking about life. Yes? I mean, that's what we're talking about. We're talking about motherhood. Is there anything more precious, more beautiful? You, the giver of life. You made this life, this child.'

Raphael is twenty-nine, with creative facial hair and no deficit of self-love. He is far too intense. Jack Black on coke. Watching him is a group that consists of five client representatives, as well as my art director partner, Ian, our producer, Pam, the director's producer (or line producer), and me. We stand in the middle of a set that looks exactly like a child's bedroom on a soundstage in Queens. We are not supposed to be in Queens. We are supposed to be in Pasadena, California, in a lovely Arts and Crafts

5

home that a production company chose after scouting close to seventy-five other homes in and around Pasadena, Santa Monica, and Laguna Beach. The home, per the client's verbatim direction, should feel 'suburban but not too new and not too old and not too far from a city center but by no means urban, i.e., New York City and its general 'smart-alecky' sensibility, which often tests poorly in market research.'

We did this in large part because Gwyneth was going to be in Los Angeles on vacation with her family and we wanted to (were forced to) accommodate her. Except it turned out that Gwyneth was no longer going to be in Los Angeles at the time of the shoot. She was going to be in New York for meetings and a partial vacation and could we find a location there, please? At which point the New York office of the production company scouted suburban but not too (see above) homes in Scarsdale, the Upper West Side, and Brooklyn Heights. All of which Gwyneth's assistant was fine with ('Scarsdale's not really New York, though, is it? Bit of a drive and we hate driving.'), but all of which the client hated. At which point the New York office of the production company hired the set director from the former Broadway smash hit *Mamma Mia!* to design a child's bedroom to the client's specifications, which was then built by union carpenters, at a cost of $135,000. All before rolling a single foot of film.

Raphael says, 'That's what we're talking about here. Life. You, mother Gwyneth. And your womb. Your *vagina*.'

6

He pauses to let this sink in. Which it does, whether she wants it to or not.

Raphael continues. 'The Latin word for *sheath*. Say it with me. *Vagin* . . . '

'I wish you'd stop saying that,' Gwyneth says with a smile, trying very hard. I give her credit. She's much nicer than I imagined from my casual reading of *Us Weekly*.

'The way Raphael sees this shot . . . '

'I'm so sorry,' Gwyneth says. 'Who's Raphael?'

'That would be me,' Raphael says, his titanium ego unfazed.

'Huh. Okay.'

He barrels along, a clueless man-boy dressed in jeans that are dangerously close to falling down and a T-shirt emblazoned with the words FRITOS ARE LIFE. 'Raphael sees that baby is naked, afraid. So he looks to you for everything. Now, let us consider your breasts.' And with that he moves his hand to mime the shape of Mrs. Coldplay's diminutive yet shapely bosom.

Gwyneth is by far the highest profile super-mom that we've shot for our almost-award-winning campaign, 'Snugglies Moms and Snugglies Babies: Together as One.' To date we've shot Rachel Weisz, Rebecca Romijn, and Kelly Ripa (whom I saw, briefly, in her underpants). Gwyneth at first refused to do it, saying through an agent that she 'didn't care for advertising, though she made no aspersions toward either the brand or the agency, though she was not familiar with either.' Initially Gwyneth was not on the consideration list, as both the agency and the client felt she'd never do it. There had been a great deal of discussion — in-person meetings as well as conference calls involving dozens of personalities — as to who best represented the brand, as well as who would do it for the money. (I am not at liberty to disclose that figure but it was between $299,000 and $301,000.) Names like Madonna and Angelina were short-listed but ultimately the client feared that they were seen as 'baby thieves' (the client's words). Nicole Kidman was considered, but was labeled 'weird and scary.' (We had a large board in a conference room with names and corresponding traits.) President Obama's mother-in-law, Marian Robinson, was added to the list but was also ultimately nixed because, as our senior client, Jan, said on a conference call to general acclaim, 'This is about the mother-child bond, not the nana-child bond. Though we would like to see more women of color.' Which is when a midlevel client responded, suggesting Victoria Beckham (aka Posh Spice). Which is when we informed the client that Mrs. Spice-Beckham was not, in fact, a woman of color but just a woman colored, perpetually tanned, often deeply so.

We launched the campaign in 2007. The initial focus group testing results had been very good. But the economic downturn found a far different attitude toward extremely rich, unusually beautiful, oddly thin mothers who, according to groups in a number of cities around the country, 'probably had twenty-four-hour-a-day help' (Chicago) and 'sure as hell ain't using the drive-through window at McDonald's to shut the little bastards up' (Houston). Gwyneth is our last super-mom in the campaign.

'Breast milk,' Raphael begins.

'Maybe let's move on,' Gwyneth says, the radiant smile somehow still in place. She appears to have no pores on her face.

'Also clothing,' he continues. 'You have to ask yourself this question — what diaper will you place on his precious bottom?'

One senses a collective 'Give-me-a-fucking-break' coming from the assemblage. But then one notices the five clients. They are mesmerized. They're buying it. Which is both good and bad, as they now think Raphael (who, it turns out, is named Richard Dinklage. That's right, Dick Dinklage) is a genius.

He slowly, dramatically, raises a diaper.

'Will it be any old diaper, or will it be . . . a Snugglie?'

Pam elbows me and whispers, 'Say something. Now. We are *way* behind schedule.'

I say, 'I think what . . . ' I realize I can't say his fake name, so I simply gesture to him instead. 'I think what the director is saying is that this is one of those nothing little moments that actually mean a lot to a parent, when you're changing your baby and they're smiling and there's that connection. The whole idea is that nothing is more important than being a mother.'

Gwyneth speaks to me and smiles, and I instantly understand why some people are stars. 'Cool. That's great. I like that. Are we starting now? Because I'd love to use the ladies' room.'

The crowd disperses. Pam, Ian, and I walk to

9

the craft services table for coffee.

Craft services is the odd name given to the food service area on a shoot. It's not, as first-time-to-a-shoot clients and neophyte creatives often mistake it, a place to buy handmade knitwear and driftwood art.

Pam says, 'She is so much better looking than a regular person. She's like a different species. I look like ass next to her. And, in case you haven't noticed, the client's pissed.'

I say, 'Why? They looked happy to me.'

Pam says, 'They say we're not following the storyboard. And the purple liquid thing. They want blue.'

Ian says, 'Where the hell is Alan? Where's Jill?'

Alan and Jill are our colleagues. They are account executives and their responsibility is to shepherd the client, act as liaison between client and agency, help devise a strategy, understand the client's business as well as the client, understand the creative's job, smooth the process. It is an important and powerful job. The relationship between client and agency rests upon it. Both Alan and Jill attended graduate business schools of the Ivy League persuasion. Currently, they're on the neighboring sound-stage, trying to sneak in to watch the filming of an episode of *Law & Order*.

Ian says, 'It's really like he has no idea what he's doing, like he's in film school.'

Pam says, 'He's one of the hottest commercial directors in the world.'

Ian says, 'He keeps using the word *profanity*. Only he's using it wrong.'

I say, 'I noticed that. He thinks it means *spacious*.'

Ian says, 'I heard him say to the set designer that he wanted the baby's room to be more profanity.'

Pam says, 'He makes $30,000 a day.'

Ian looks at his iPhone. 'He's tweeting about the shoot.'

Pam says, 'Who?'

Ian holds up his phone, shows Raphael's Twitter account. 'Cecil B. DeMille.'

Pam says, 'Please tell me he didn't tweet about her vagina.'

I say, 'Tweet about her vagina sounds wrong to me. Do you tweet?'

Pam says, 'What do I look like, Kim fucking Kardashian?'

I say, 'I don't tweet. Should I tweet? Maybe I should be tweeting, be more of a tweeting presence in the digital world.'

Ian says, 'What would you tweet about?'

I say, 'Thoughts. Ideas. I have ideas about things that I think people would like to hear and follow. I think I'd have a lot of followers. Like Jesus.'

Pam says, 'Tweet this, Facebook that, LinkedIn my ass. C'mon. I mean, what the fuck?'

I say, 'There are times when you don't strike me as someone named Pam.'

Ian says, 'Clients want it, though. It's magic to them. Gotta be on Facebook. Gotta tweet about the new campaign. Go viral. Big phrase these days. Go viral. This spot will have its own Facebook page.'

11

I say, 'And the world will be a better place for it.'

At last count the three of us have made twenty-three commercials together over seven years.

Ian says, 'God bless that clever Mark Zuckerberg.' He looks down at his phone. 'Raphael just tweeted again saying people should go to his Facebook page to see new photos of him with Gwyneth.' He looks up at me. 'By the way, Merry Christmas, Tiny Fin.'

Christmas is three days away.

Pam says, 'Seriously, though, where the fuck are Alan and Jill?'

We make our way back to video village, that place on every TV commercial shoot where the client and agency sit and watch the action on a monitor.

I see Jan, our senior client, and know immediately by the large smile on her face that there is a problem. Diapers are to Jan a kind of religious calling.

Before we move on, a word about Snugglies. Snugglies and Stay-Ups and Nite-Nites and Tadpoles (for swimming). We are the agency of record for the largest manufacturer of diapers in the world. *Snugglies babies are happy babies*. I know that because I wrote that line. You will never see an unhappy baby in one of our commercials. Other companies show unhappy babies. This is a mistake.

'Jan,' I say. 'It's going well, don't you think?'

Jan says, 'I do, Fin. Really well.'

I say, 'Raphael.'

Jan says, 'He's brilliant. He gets the brand. He gets the brief.'

Her colleagues nod and smile like lunatics.

One says, 'Has he read the manifesto?'

I say, 'I'm . . . I'm not sure. But I doubt it.'

Her colleagues are suddenly chirping like birds.

'He *has* to read the manifesto,' says one. 'How is that possible?' says another. Yet a third makes odd noises and contorted facial expressions, as if she just found out that her favorite woman wasn't given a rose on *The Bachelor*.

Jan remains calm. 'Let's get him a copy. Immerse him in the brand. Perhaps Gwyneth would like to look at it as well.'

I'm sure the Academy Award winner would love nothing more than to review the Snugglies manifesto.

And what *is* a manifesto, you might ask?

You may have a vague notion from history class that a manifesto once referred to the soul of a revolution: blood, sweat, and tears on paper, codifying women's rights, civil rights, human rights, economic justice, religious freedom. Today, it's about diapers. Or cars. Or refrigerators. Or gas grills. Or dental floss. In advertising, a manifesto is something that sums up a brand, one page, maybe two hundred words. Name the product and my people will write the manifesto for it. Superlative claims, a badly skewed world view, sentences like, 'Because let's be honest — what's more important at the end of your day than your family . . . and their enjoyment of grilled meats?'

13

The Snugglies manifesto is particularly awful. I know. I wrote it.

I lie and say, 'We'll get copies to Raphael and Gwyneth. Otherwise, though, I think we're in a good place with the spot.'

Jan says, 'It's real, honest, artful.'

Ian says, 'It's what we wanted.'

Everyone smiles and nods. This is very good. We're about to turn and go when Jan says, 'Except . . . is it *too* artful, Fin?'

★ ★ ★

There are two kinds of creative people in advertising. Those who think they're smarter than the client and those who are successful. To say that the client is unreasonable is to say that death is unreasonable. Death *is*. Deal with it. Deal with it by making the client (death) your friend. Respect them, despite what they say. Advertising is a language and they do not speak that language. We say things like 'It's original' or 'It's a big idea.' Wrong. Picasso's style of painting was original. Penicillin was a big idea. They call us *creative*. Baloney. The inventor of the corkscrew was creative. The irony of advertising — a communications business — is that we treat words with little respect, often devaluing their meaning. The *all-new* Ford Taurus. Really? Five wheels this time? *Great for any occasion*. I saw these words on a large sign in front of a national chain of cupcake shops. *Any* occasion? Doctor: 'Mr. Dolan, the test results are back and I'm afraid you have an inoperable brain tumor. Cupcake?'

I do not think I am smarter than the client. Instead, I simply try to put myself in their sensible shoes, when, say, the long process that is the making of a commercial begins. Watch their furrowed brows and puzzled expressions as they listen to us present ideas. Watch as they sneak a peek at a colleague to see if they understand what the hell we are talking about. *Were we working from the same brief?!* they wonder. Watch as they listen to the agency reference movies and shots in movies that they, themselves, have never seen nor in some cases even *heard* of ('We'll shoot it like that great tracking shot in *The Bicycle Thief.*'). Song and band references that might as well be in Farsi.

Inside, the client screams, *What does any of this have to do with our toothpaste?* Outside, they nod, slowly, letting their own insecurities build. *I never wanted to be in marketing for a toothpaste/diaper/paper towel/ soda manufacturer,* they think for the eleven millionth time. *A frat buddy/ sorority sister/parole officer suggested the job, after a long, pride-deadening search in other fields, a bit lost at age twenty-eight, wondering what to do with my life. I wanted to be a poet/a drummer/a porn star/a machinist.*

Give me your tired, your poor, your great teeming masses of middle managers who are unable to move the process forward or make a decision! The Carols and Maries and Trents and Tracys and Carls! Give me your resentful and angry, your worried and deeply frightened, your petrified of the next round of layoffs, of those insufferable human resources women with their easy detachment and heartless smiles. *You're eligible for Cobra and the family plan is just $1800 a month.* The afterlife for HR people is a *Clockwork Orange* — like reel of everyone they've ever fired, playing over and over and over.

This is life in advertising and marketing and public relations today, largely superfluous service-sector jobs in the great economic crisis where homes are worth less than we paid for them, job security no longer exists, college tuition is $40 million, and the future is a thing that parents sit up nights trembling about. Fulfilled by your job? Who the fuck cares. *Have* a job? Then do whatever you can to hang on to it. This is business today. This is *America* today. A land of fear. Fear of things that cannot be proven with focus-group testing. Fear of layoffs and large mortgages, education costs and penniless retirements, fear of terrorists and planes that fly too low.

★ ★ ★

Jan is staring at me, waiting for an answer. As is her team. What was the question?

'How do you mean, Jan?' I say.

Jan says, 'Is this the brand?'

I say, 'I think it is. I think it's very much the brand. Ian?'

I write the copy. Ian does the pictures. He's much smarter than I am and a champion talker.

Ian says, 'Emotion. The mother-child bond. Life. This is the DNA of your brand.'

If you can speak like this with a straight face,

16

you can make a very good living in advertising.

Jan says, 'Agreed.'

Her colleagues nod. It's as if they're wired to Jan. Almost all are texting, talking on wireless headsets, tapping an iPad. Unless you are connected you are not alive. Earlier I heard one of the clients in the toilet on a conference call, his voice strained at times from peristaltic exertion.

Jan says again, 'But is this *too* artsy for our brand?'

I say, 'I'm hearing you say you think it might be too artsy.'

Jan says, 'I think that's what I'm saying, yes.'

I say, 'How so?'

Jan says, 'The camera is moving around quite a bit. I'm not seeing the product.'

I say, 'Well, we're trying to focus on Gwyneth and the baby, but, as we discussed in the pre-production meeting, we wanted hip, cool, and edgy along with the brand attributes of safe, homespun, and conservative.'

Jan says, 'Agreed. But Gwyneth and the baby aren't the product, Fin. The product is a Snugglie, the finest diaper in the world.' You wait for the punch line but it never comes. People speak like this.

I say, 'Absolutely. No question. But the baby is *wearing* the diaper.'

Jan sighs deeply. It is a signal to one of her drones. In this case, Cindy, a bubbly twenty-eight-year-old Jan wannabe. Cindy says, 'As infants grow and become more active, our job is to create a diapering experience that fits their

17

lives . . . and the lives of their moms. We aspire to do nothing less than let them be the best babies they can be. Largely dry and free of diaper rash. Though legally we can't guarantee this.'

Now, as if it's the final scene of a high school musical, others jump in. Chet, late thirties, also extremely eager. Chet says, 'I.e., new Snugglies Diaper Pants. The ultimate in flexibility for babies on the go. Explore. Be free. Be dry. New mommies love this. Focus groups bear this out.'

I say, 'Are you fucking crazy talking like that? This is a diaper. C'mon. Let's all get drunk and get laid.'

Except I don't say that at all. I nod and say, 'Understood.' Because Jan knows, as do Cindy and Chet, that it is 2009 and the agency I work for will do anything to keep the sizable fee that this brand brings in. Jan could say, *Fin, I need you to climb up on that rafter, take down your pants, shave your ball sack, and jump into a Dixie cup full of curdled beef fat*, and she knows I'd do it.

'One more thing,' Jan says. 'Purple.'

Her colleagues nod.

'Purple?' I ask with a smile.

Jan nods. 'The liquid in the demo shot rehearsal looked purple to us. We'd like blue. A deep, deep blue. Like the brand.'

Cindy adds helpfully, 'According to recent focus group testing, the color purple often connotes homosexuality, and homosexuality, according to our testing, tested poorly.'

Ian can't resist. 'Maybe you're just giving the wrong kind of test.'

18

Jan says, 'We good, Fin?'

I manage a nod, smiling. 'We can fix it in post.' The great go-to line on a shoot. Post being post-production: editing, color correction, audio mixing.

Then I turn and walk away, leaving what's left of my scrotum on the floor.

We walk back toward the craft services table. On the way we pass dozens of crew, some of whom help to set the shot, position Gwyneth, tend to her hair and makeup, many of whom stand around and check their iPhones.

Ian says, 'I thought that went well.'

Pam looks at me and says, 'You're pathetic.'

Ian pours coffees. Pam eats a donut. I rub Purell on my hands.

Ian says, 'It was genius on paper.'

It's a thing we say on every shoot when we realize the spot isn't going to be any more than average.

Ian asks Pam what she's doing for Christmas.

Pam says, 'Family. Pittsburgh. Vodka. Cigarettes. You?'

Ian says, 'Dinner for friends. Jews, atheists, fellow homos, the great unwashed. People who have no family or family they don't want to go home to. Tons of food and wine. No store-bought gifts. Everything has to be handmade. Could be music or a video, whatever. It's amazing. We've been doing it for about five years.'

Pam says, 'That's so gay.' She looks at me. 'You?'

I say, 'Mexico.'

'Family?'

'Not so much.'

'Friends?'

I say, 'Alone. Going alone.'

Pam says, 'That's weird.'

'Is it?'

'Weird and sad. No family? Of any kind?'

'We're not that close.'

Pam says, 'I hate most of my family. I can understand. But you seem reasonably normal. Why alone? Bring that cute little assistant of yours. Half the men in the agency would divorce their wives for her.'

I say, 'Phoebe? Don't be ridiculous.'

Ian raises his eyebrows. Pam does the same.

I say, 'We're just friends. We're good friends. She's my assistant.'

Ian says, 'She's not *your* assistant. She's the creative department assistant.'

Pam says, 'She's your office wife.'

I say, 'What does that mean?'

Ian says, 'Everyone has an office husband or wife. I have both.'

I say, 'Who's your office husband?'

Ian says, 'I'll never tell.'

Pam says, 'But you have to be careful of the power-struggle thing. They can't report to you. Does Phoebe report to you?'

I say, 'No. Why?'

Pam says, 'Good. Eliminates the sexual-harassment thing, which I myself had to deal with when I was screwing a production intern last summer. Poor thing left in tears.'

I say, 'You're a romantic.'

Pam says, 'At least I'm not going on Christmas vacation alone.'

I say, 'It's a last-minute thing. An interim

vacation. I'm planning a big trip for after the New Year. February. Possibly March.'

Ian says to Pam, 'My dear friend Mr. Dolan has been saying this for a while. He calls it the big trip. That's his name for it. He's a copywriter.'

I say, 'The big trip is going to be amazing. Life-changing. I just can't figure out where to go, though. It's complicated.'

Pam says, 'What's complicated about it?'

I say, 'I have these two tickets to anywhere in the world. Two first-class tickets.'

Ian says, 'Very expensive tickets.'

Pam says, 'I thought you said Mexico.'

I say, 'I did.'

Ian says, 'It's complicated.'

Pam says, 'You have two first-class tickets to anywhere in the world and you're going to Mexico? No offense to Mexico, but are you high?'

I say, 'No. I'm not using them for Mexico. They're for the big trip. After Mexico.'

Pam says, 'So, wait. You have two first-class tickets anywhere in the world and instead of using them, you've bought *another* ticket to Mexico.'

I say, 'Yes.'

Ian says, 'It's complicated.'

Finally I say, 'They're the honeymoon tickets.'

Pam says, 'The what?'

I nod slowly, waiting for her to do the math.

Pam says, 'Shit. The honeymoon tickets.'

I say, 'The honeymoon tickets.'

Pam says, 'Yikes. Sorry.'

I say, 'So it's complicated because I don't just want to use them for a trip to Mexico.'

Pam says, 'Do you ever hear from her?'

21

'Not so much.'

Did I mention I canceled my wedding? I probably should have mentioned that. I was supposed to get married last May. I was engaged to a really wonderful woman. Amy Deacon. But then I got a very bad case of cold feet. More like frostbitten feet, where they turn black and your toes fall off and you think you're going to die. That's the kind of cold feet I had. We canceled six weeks before the wedding was to take place. We were going to go to Italy on our honeymoon. I've been trying to take a vacation ever since then, trying to use the tickets. In the past eight months I've planned three trips, canceling two because of work and one for a reason that escapes me. To be honest I feel that the tickets hold power. The tickets urge me to find the right destination, to figure out where they want me to go. This place will be the place that assures me happiness. It doesn't say this on the tickets, unfortunately. Mostly it just talks about the restrictions. The problem is that the tickets expire in three months. And I can't get the obscene amount of money I paid for them back. So I have these tickets.

My cell phone rings. It's Phoebe, our aforementioned group's assistant.

I say, 'Stop bothering me. I'm an important executive.'

Phoebe says, 'How's Gwyneth?'

'Gwyneth who?'

Phoebe says, 'Tell me!'

'Honestly? She's heavy. Bad skin. She keeps hitting on me.'

'Shut up.'

I say, 'What's up?'

'Nothing. I'm bored with you and Ian gone. And Carlson wants you to call him.'

Martin Carlson, my boss, executive creative director of the agency.

I say, 'Why can't he call me himself?'

Phoebe says, 'He's too important. He said it's urgent. And that he wants you in a new business meeting Thursday.'

'Thursday. As in *this* Thursday? Christmas Eve? Not possible. I'm going on vacation that day. He knows that.'

'I know that.'

'Did you tell him that?'

'Did I tell him that he knows you're going on vacation Thursday?'

'Yes.'

'No.'

'Why not?'

'Is this a logic test?'

'I'm not canceling another vacation.'

Phoebe snorts. 'You mean unless he asks you to.'

'Exactly.'

Seconds go by. I can tell she's reading an e-mail, looking at her computer. I stare at a key grip's ass crack as he adjusts the base of a lighting stand.

I say, 'Do you tweet?'

'Sometimes. I follow some people.'

I say, 'Do you have a lot of friends on Facebook?'

'Not really. Not compared to some people I know.'

'I have one hundred and nine, but there're

about twenty I've never met.'

Phoebe says, 'Oh.'

I say, 'What? How many do you have?'

'About twelve hundred, I think. Maybe more.'

I say, 'I'm feeling great inadequacy right now.'

Phoebe says, 'Run with that.'

The key grip stands and turns to see me staring at his ass crack and gives me a look that suggests he might do physical harm to me.

Phoebe says, 'Also your brother Edward called. Is he the one in San Francisco?'

'No,' I say. 'That's Kevin. Eddie's in Boston.'

'He left his number.'

I say nothing.

'Fin?'

'Yeah.'

'Do you want his number?'

'No. What did he say?'

'He said, 'Tell him it's about his father.''

How nice. Hi, Daddy!

One word, one blink, and I am back in the basement of Saint Joseph's Rectory. A winter night. I am in the Cub Scouts. I am eight years old and I wear a dark blue Cub Scout shirt and yellow kerchief and military-style enlistedman's cap. Tonight is the Pinewood Derby, for which they give you a small block of wood and plastic wheels and ask you to carve it into a car. Kids spend weeks with these things, mostly with their fathers. He'll show you how to whittle, say, or paint, or put the wheels on. He'll gently ruffle your hair the way they do in TV shows from the sixties or present-day commercials. An experience you will always remember, that perhaps you

24

will one day share with your own son. Tonight, on a small wooden track, they will have a race for the fastest car. Happy fathers and excited sons. Lots of prizes and trophies. Everyone goes home with something. And then there's my father, who's just screamed at my mother and made her cry, and who stormed out of the house with me in tow, the silent drive to Saint Joe's. I'm holding a Stride-Rite shoebox with my pathetic excuse for a car in it, confused as to whether to be more terrified of my father in one of his moods or of the reaction of my fellow Cub Scouts when they see my car, which my father has not helped me with, and which, as I have no affinity for carpentry, is still largely a block of wood, except for the paint I put on it. I don't want to go. That was what the fight was about. My mother said I didn't have to go. I told her about my lame car. But my father said I had to go, that I was wimping out, that I should have worked harder. I briefly imagined a storybook ending (the budding copywriter), wherein my hideous, misshapen block-like car thing would somehow speed to victory in record time, stunning the crowd of vastly superior Scouts. Reality was crueler. I came in second to last, just besting Tommy Flynn, whose wheels fell off. He burst into tears, his father holding him. And my father? My father said, 'Well, that was a waste of time, wasn't it?'

He's dead. He must have died. That's the only reason Eddie would call me about 'my' father. And since when did he start calling himself Edward?

Phoebe says, 'I hope everything's okay.'

25

I say, 'I'll call him.' But I won't. And maybe Phoebe senses that from my voice.

Phoebe says, 'Do you have his number?'

'Yes.'

She says, 'You're lying. What is it?'

'There's a seven in it.'

'I'm texting it to you. Call your brother. Also he may be calling you since I gave him your cell. And call Carlson. Can I come to the shoot this afternoon?'

'You'd be bored. It just looks exciting. Like the circus. Or a strip club. So I've heard.'

Phoebe says, 'I want to meet Gwyneth. I think we could be friends.'

'I'm hanging up.'

Phoebe says, 'Say something nice.'

I say, 'You're prettier than she is.'

'Yeah, right.'

'I'm not kidding.'

And she knows from the tone of my voice I mean it.

Three or four long seconds. Never awkward, though. Not with her.

Phoebe says, 'Call me later, okay?'

Her text arrives. *Edward's number*.

Did I mention that I have family? Eddie's the oldest and for years acted that way. Maura left a job in finance to raise her kids. They're both up in Boston. At least they were the last time we spoke. Kevin is in San Francisco. If Ian's the gay brother I never had, Kevin would be the gay brother I actually have. Some families grow closer. Others are Irish.

I delete the text.

A twenty-five-ish production assistant jogs up to Ian, Pam, and me.

She says, sternly, 'Raphael wants to roll immediately.'

Pam says, 'We'll be two minutes.'

The PA says, 'Umm, he said to tell you he wants to roll immediately.'

I wince and see Ian do the same.

Pam's face breaks into a big smile. 'What's your name?'

The PA says, 'Saffron.'

Pam says, 'Saffron. Wow. I'm going to guess southern California or, wait, Boulder.'

Saffron says, 'Boulder. That's amazing!'

Pam says, 'I want you to listen to me, okay? There are two things I know to be true. One is that there's no difference between good flan and bad flan. What movie is that from?'

Saffron stares at Pam, clueless, only now sensing, perhaps, that she's made a terrible mistake.

Pam says, 'Disappointed. *Wag the Dog*. Classic Mamet line. Not sure what you're doing in this business if you don't love film. Two, we roll when I say we roll. And if dick-breath has a problem with that you have him come see me because this is my show. Okay?'

Saffron is wide-eyed and stunned and scared and nodding slowly.

Pam says, 'One more thing. I don't like your name. So I'm going to call you Barbara for the rest of the shoot. Now go away and tell Raphael to learn what an F-stop is.'

Saffron scurries away.

Another woman walks up to Pam and has what appears to be a massive amount of baby spit-up on her shirt.

Ian says, 'I have bad news for you about your blouse.'

Pam says, 'Who are you?'

The woman says, 'The baby wrangler. We have a problem.'

Ian says, 'We got that part.'

The woman says, 'The baby's puking like crazy.'

Pam says, 'What about the backup baby? So far we've only shot this one from behind.'

'Yeah, I know,' the wrangler says. 'But there was a bit of a screwup and the casting agency sent . . . they sent a black baby.'

I say, 'Chris Martin is not going to like this.'

Pam doesn't blink twice. She takes out her cell phone and calls the casting agency. Into the phone she says, 'It's Pam Marston for Sandy.' Away from the phone: 'Barbara!' Saffron comes running, wide-eyed, an eager, terrified little Marine ready to follow Pam's orders into battle.

Alan and Jill, our account execs, finally reappear.

Alan says skittishly, 'You want the good news or the bad news?'

No one says anything.

Alan says, 'Okay, that's good because there is no good news. So I'll move right to the bad. We're using the wrong diapers.'

Pam stares at Alan in a way that could not be mistaken for friendly.

Alan says, 'These diapers are for infants. We need the Diaper Pants for toddlers.'

Ian covers his face. I look to the ceiling, in hopes of a ladder being lowered from a waiting helicopter.

Pam says, 'We've been shooting since 7:46 A.M. It's 11:32. Do you know how much film we've shot?'

Alan says, 'A lot?'

'A lot, Alan? We're shooting thirty-five-millimeter film, haircut. One-thousand-foot mags. Eleven minutes a mag. Two dollars a foot to process. That doesn't include transferring or color correcting. We've blown through eight mags so far today. That's eight thousand feet of film that's useless.'

Alan says, 'I missed a lot of that.'

Pam says, 'Try this. The client just spent thirty-six thousand dollars on nothing.'

Alan says, 'That's very bad.'

Pam says, 'Wait. Are the diapers we've been using that much different? How different-looking can diapers be?'

Jill says, 'Dramatically different, Pam. That's the Snugglies touch.'

Pam says, 'Jill. Say another word and I will drown you in a toilet.'

Pam puts the phone to her ear. 'Sandy. Pam. I have a black baby.'

A woman approaches, one of Gwyneth's assistants.

'That's so beautiful,' the assistant says. 'I wish more people would break down the color barrier. Are you Pam?'

Pam nods and says into the phone, 'Sandy, I'm going to call you back in sixty seconds.'

Gwyneth's assistant says, with a big fake smile,

29

'I think there might be some mistake. We see here on the schedule that this is a two-day shoot?' She slowly shakes her head no. 'We were under the impression it was just one day.'

Pam says, 'What? No. No, no. No, it's definitely two. We need her for two. We went over all of this with you guys. Like, twenty times.'

The assistant, still smiling, says, 'I know, but that's not going to work because she's on a plane tonight to Berlin. The new M. Night movie.'

Ian says, 'Is it about diapers?'

The assistant says, 'Sorry.' But she's not sorry at all. She turns and walks away. Everyone stares at Pam.

Pam says, 'There are so many filthy, filthy words I want to say right now.'

She turns to Alan. 'Talk to the client. Fix this blue-purple-gay thing. Do *not* tell them about the scheduling thing. Go.'

He snaps into action, and Jill follows him.

Pam turns to Saffron. 'White baby, then M. Night. Ian. Come with me.'

I stand alone as three people attend to Gwyneth's hair and makeup. I watch the director of photography and the second assistant camera loader change lenses. Gaffers adjust huge lights nimbly, quickly. I appear to be the only person on the set with nothing to do.

My phone rings. The display reads *Martin Carlson*.

Martin is English and famous in the advertising world and came to our agency about eighteen months ago and changed what was a wonderful place to work, if by work you mean *not work very much*, into a place where you have to work, if by work you mean *work*, a lot, nights, weekends. Martin loves meeting on Sunday afternoons to review work. His arrival has not gone over well.

Our previous creative director was a legend in the business. Ron Spasky. Ron lived in what was most certainly one of the heydays of advertising. Budgets were large, clients listened, you could scream at people and still keep your job. Who's to say what caused his downfall. A misfire in the synapses, too much stress, bad wiring. Or just too many years of repugnant living. Like so many cliches in the business — men nearing fifty who dress far younger than their years, keep guitars they do not play in their expansive offices, wear bizarrely large wristwatches — Ron's real downfall began with his hair, which seemed to have a direct line to his penis. The more hair he lost, the younger the women he dated, to the point where he began dating a twenty-four-year-old junior producer, the unfortunately named Fiona Finkel. Fiona was a curvy woman, a woman who knew the power of her sexuality over men of a certain age, an age when the supple elasticity of young female flesh can be mind-altering. She was promoted, rather abruptly, much to the dismay of others who had worked far longer and knew much more. One thing led to another, the other being working late with Ron, the odd late-night drink, a ride home in his car service, dinner at out-of-the-way places where coworkers — or anyone else, really — might not see them. During those late dinners way downtown and sometimes on

31

Arthur Avenue in the Bronx ('Why are we up here?') she would, using her foot, play with his Cialis-assisted erection through his trousers under the table. She had never before seen an American Express Black Card.

Later, Ron left his wife of many years, his wife who had increasingly found herself alone late at night, wondering when her husband was going to get home from the office, leaving him a little something on the counter, a note under the plate, Saran Wrap protecting the sandwich, the chicken leg, the piece of homemade cake. *I miss you*. Surely his wife's mind drifted during the boring sitcoms that she watched after the children were fed and bathed and read to. Wandered from her quotidian life in Katonah to his exciting one in the city, in the company of young, interesting, attractive people. She wondered why he never invited her to join him for the occasional event. She could get a sitter, she'd told him. You'd be bored, he'd told her. They say she was on antidepressants for some time, her heart and ability to trust a kind of roadkill now. They say Ron found himself a particularly vicious divorce attorney, left her with very little, and certainly without pride.

Powerful Ron and curvy Fee (her preferred name, the irony simply too rich) wed on a beach somewhere. Friends from the city, from advertising. Great sums of money were spent. Small, fancy hotels. They'd called the island's only helicopter service late one night because they wanted a tour under the full moon.

But that little black card does not come cheap.

And so it was that one day a few years ago, in the agency's main conference room, Ron stood up in a meeting and began removing his clothes, not saying a word, not changing an iota, one witness said, the smile on his face. I'm told he continued presenting the idea (I believe it was for batteries). Later, when the police arrived, he refused to get dressed and was led out of the building and into a waiting police car on Sixth Avenue wearing around his buttocks and manhood his secretary's canary-yellow cardigan, the one she kept on the back of her chair for summer days when the building's air conditioning was too cold. She urged him to keep it.

Now, one hears stories of Ron and Fee's rocky marriage, of her forward ways on television commercial shoots with young men who are rising in the agency, while her formerly powerful husband is at home, surrounded by specially made soft gardening implements, where he tends to their tomato plants and, on good days, is allowed to walk the dog. In the afternoons he is given cookies.

Since Martin's arrival I have tried to show my worth by enacting what I like to call The Finbar Dolan Campaign for Creative Director, Long-Term Success, and Renewed Self-Esteem. (A long and not particularly interesting title, to be sure, especially from someone who's supposed to be good at writing exactly these kinds of things.) How have I enacted The Plan? I have done this by getting in at 9:30-but-closer-to-10 and leaving around six, with a midday pause for a long lunch. Also by acting as a respected mentor to

33

the other creatives in my group, which is not technically my group, nor do they really see me as a mentor or even listen to me. My great hope (as I believe is reflected in the clever titling of my plan) is to be promoted this year to creative director. It is an important milestone in one's advertising career. You go from merely creating ads — concepting, writing, art directing — to overseeing, critiquing, criticizing, and most often shooting them down. It is something I feel I could be good at. It would also be a bump in salary. It would mean the respect of others at the agency. Which is not to say I don't have enormously high self-esteem or that I rely on the opinion of others. (I don't and I do.)

I say, 'Martin.'

'Fin.'

'Martin.'

Martin says, 'How goes it on the coast?'

'We're in Queens, actually. Which is certainly a coast, but not the one you were thinking of.'

Martin says, 'And Gwyneth, Fin? Stunning?'

'Stunning,' I say.

Martin says, 'Met her once. She might remember me.'

'I mentioned you to her,' I lie. 'She remembered.'

Martin cackles. 'I *knew* it. Did she say where that was?'

'She didn't. You sound strange, Martin.'

'Yoga, Fin. Standing on my head at the moment. Secret to life. Releases tension. Have you tried it?'

'No, but I masturbate a lot. Does wonders.'

Martin says, without a hint of a laugh, 'Humor. Very good. Hearing reports of black babies, Fin, of unhappy clients.'

How does he know these things?

'Just rumors, Martin,' I say. 'We had some issues earlier but things are better now.'

'Good to hear. Creative directors take care of these things. Bull by the horns.'

Creative directors.

Martin says, 'I have some excellent news of my own, Fin. Big oil.'

I say, 'That's great. Except I'm not sure what you're talking about.'

'Petroleon, Fin. Head man's an old chum — we were at Eton together. Not happy with their current agency. Want to avoid a formal pitch. Meet and greet, see if the chemistry's there. Oh, Christ.'

I hear a thud and then moaning.

'Martin?' I say.

Muffled, somewhat at a distance, I hear, 'These *bastard* walls!'

I hear a hand grabbing the phone, rubbing the mouthpiece.

'Martin?' I say again. 'You okay?'

'I don't feel pain, Fin. Anyway. He's only in town a short time. I'd like to bring in one of our top creatives.'

This is turning out better than I had hoped.

Martin says, 'Except none of them will be around Thursday because of the holiday.'

'Oh,' I reply cleverly.

'I'm joking, Fin. I think you could be the man for this. Might be a nice change from diapers.'

'You said 'change' and 'diapers.' That's funny.'
'Are you available Thursday?'
'This Thursday?'
'Yes.'
'My flight leaves Thursday, Martin.'
'Morning or afternoon.'
'Afternoon,' I say, sensing my mistake immediately.

'No worries, then. Knew I could count on you. You, me, Frank, Dodge. Top brass, Fin. The big leagues. Win this and write your own ticket.'

I say, 'Wait. Isn't Petroleon the one responsible for the big spill in Alaska awhile back?'

'And you're perfect, I suppose? Don't mention the spill. Very sensitive about it.'

'Are they doing anything about it?'

Martin says, 'About what?'

'The spill.'

'Of course. Deeply committed to change. That's why they're hiring a new agency.'

I say, 'Excellent.'

Martin says, 'Snugglies client happy?'

I say, 'I guess.'

Martin says, 'Don't guess, Fin. Make sure. Keep them happy. Keep your job. Humor.'

The line goes dead.

A twenty-two-year-old from craft services with spiked hair walks up with a tray of small paper cups of coffee.

'Mocha cappuccino?'

I say, 'I have a degree in English literature.'

The kid stares at me.

I say, 'My thesis was on Eliot's 'The Love Song of J. Alfred Prufrock.' I won an award for it.

That's a lie. I almost won an award for it. Or would have, perhaps, if I'd finished it and submitted it, which I didn't.'

The kid continues staring.

I say, ''Let us go then, you and I, when the evening is spread out against the sky, like a patient etherized upon a table.''

I say, 'I wanted to write. I wanted to write poetry. To touch people's hearts and open their minds. I wanted to live by the sea, England perhaps, teach at an old college, wear heavy sweaters, and have sex with my full-breasted female students.'

The kid stares some more, his mouth open a bit now.

I say, ''Do I dare to eat a peach?''

The kid says, 'Um, I don't think we have any peaches. But I could make you a fruit smoothie.'

I hear Raphael shouting, 'I want to film something! Ms. Paltrow and I are waiting!' There's a pause. 'Why is this child black?'

THE LAND OF MISFIT TOYS

Did I mention that I am a copywriter at a Manhattan advertising agency? I am. You might recognize the name. Lauderbeck, Kline & Vanderhosen. It's been around for decades. We have offices in New York, Los Angeles, London, Amsterdam, and, as of January of this year, Tokyo. We were acquired many years ago, like so many once-independent agencies, by a multinational PR firm. That firm was acquired earlier this year by a Japanese shipping company, though I have no idea why a shipping company — or a Japanese one at that — would buy an American ad agency, except that I've heard rumors that the shipping company owner's son, apparently a spectacular moron, was given the agency as a pet project by his father. Anything to keep the kid away from large vessels holding millions of dollars' worth of cargo.

Why did I, Fin Dolan, choose advertising, you might ask? Why not law or medicine or the fine arts? Because of bad grades, fear of blood, and no artistic talent of any kind. Was it a passion, something that simply overtook me, the way famous people on television speak of their careers as a passion? No. Did it dawn on me at a young age that advertising was my life's work, the way it dawned on Mohandas K. Gandhi, after he was thrown off that train in South

Africa, that wearing a dhoti, carrying a stick, and changing India would be his life's work? No. Was it more of a calling? Did I try the priesthood first, spending several years in contemplative study with the Jesuits/Mormons/Buddhists before coming to the realization that God wanted me to serve Him by creating television commercials for Pop-Tarts? No (nor have I worked on the Pop-Tart account, though I would be open to it). Did I do it because I was kicked out of the Morgan Stanley training program after three days, the recruiter saying these words to me with a contorted face: 'It's as if . . . I mean . . . seriously, pal . . . it's as if you have no understanding of mathematics at all.' Yes. Definitely yes.

And what is it that I actually do? How does one find oneself on the set of a fake bedroom that is not attached to a real home on a sound-stage in Queens with a group of people who are bizarrely serious about a diaper?

It starts this way. A small office, a cubicle, a place of unopenable windows and bad lighting. People with colds. A cafeteria that smells of warm cheese. An assignment. Let's make a TV commercial! Teams of people trying to come up with ideas that will resonate with a mother holding a child whilst on the phone preparing dinner with the TV on. Get to work, Finbar Dolan! Maybe I work. But maybe I don't. Maybe, instead, I search the Web for information on Pompeii or hiking boots or the Tour de France or the history of the luge or Churchill's speeches or why people have dermatitis. I write down a terrible idea for a commercial that seems like a great idea at the time (its terribleness will make itself apparent in a day or two), then write down an equally terrible idea for a screenplay or TV pilot that I will never write. I leaf through a magazine. I go out for coffee. I call Air France and put a hold on a ticket I will never buy. I wonder if anyone would catch me masturbating. I enter the word *assface* into the search bar just to see what comes up. I play air drums to Barry White songs playing on my iTunes. This is my job.

Indeed, this is also the job of the other fifty-four creatives at the agency. Copywriters and art directors. They are artists. They are misunderstood. They are impulsive, brilliant, difficult, short-tempered, divorced, heavy drinkers, smokers, recreational drug users, malcontents, sexual deviants. It is the land of misfit toys. Every one of them deep believers in their individuality, their Mr. Rogers 'You-Are-Special'-ness. And yet so very much alike in wardrobe, attitude, world view, background, humor; readers of HuffPo, Gawker, Agency Spy, people who quote *Monty Python, Spinal Tap, Waiting for Guffman*, who speak in movie-line references over and over, who like Wilco, Paul Westerberg, Eddie Izzard. Fast talkers, people who no longer tuck in their shirts, overly confident people with low self-esteem, people with British friends, people who know about good hotels and airport business lounges, people who are *working on* a screenplay/ novel/ documentary, watchers of HBO and *The Daily Show*, politically liberal, late to marry, one-child households, the women more than likely to have had an abortion, to have slept with their male copywriter or art director partner, the men having had sex with at least one coworker and probably more, half having once experimented or are now experimenting with facial hair. Everyone wears blue jeans all the time.

These are my people. These creators of oft-times indelible images for massive, far-reaching corporations. We are so much alike, sitting in a cubicle, in an office that is rarely large or impressive, the copywriters most likely working on an Apple PowerBook, typing in Palatino or Courier or Helvetica twelve-point, the art directors staring at comically large screens, who, from God-only-knows where, find an idea that will define a company, that will reach millions of people.

There are three kinds of creative people in advertising, according to my exceptionally un-scientific point of view. There are the remarkably talented, the people who create the commercials you see and think, *Holy* shit, *that's cool!* They create the commercials everyone talks about: the sneakers, the computers, the high-end cars, the soft drinks, the fast food. Then there are the pretty darned talented who take the seemingly bland accounts and make them interesting: your credit cards, your energy companies, your insurance firms. Smart, solid work from smart, solid people who could easily get jobs writing speeches or managing a political campaign. Then there's the rest of us. Me and my coworkers. We do diapers. We do little chocolate candies. We do detergent and dishwashing liquid and air fresheners and toilet paper and paper towels and

41

prescription drugs. Our commercials have cartoon animals or talking germs. It's the stuff you see and think, *Blessed mother of God, what idiot did that?* That idiot would be me. I make the commercials wherein you turn the sound down or run to the toilet.

If there is a hierarchy in advertising products, surely a small plastic bag that holds poo and won't degrade for hundreds of years is well toward the bottom. You might think my colleagues and I would be discouraged by this. You would be partially correct, but only partially, as I myself find the idea of working on Nike or Apple or BMW so daunting as to be frightening. Whereas diapers, to my mind, are a tabula rasa. (I try to share this thought with the troops from time to time but it often falls on deaf ears.)

Within these three groups are various factions.

Some love it. They love the work, love talking about it, thinking about it, being friends with other advertising people. They love the exciting travel, the five-star hotels, the expense-account meals and expensive wine. And they have a point. It's tough to beat. But more than that, they are believers (like the senior partners at my agency, whom you shall meet in a moment). They believe advertising matters, that it is important, that it can be a force for good. Depending upon the day and my mood, I dabble in this camp.

Some merely like it, as it beats most jobs, but feel a sense of . . . longing. Longing for something better, more substantial, more important. True, advertising helps drive the economy,

42

but, these people sometimes ask, 'Is this the best I can do?' This sometimes colors their view of others, so they often feel a need to crap on any work they or their friends haven't personally done. (Except for the crapping-on-other-people's-work part, I can also be found in this camp at times.)

Some see advertising as a path to Hollywood greatness. They feel that they are as-yet-undiscovered scriptwriters and budding directors and that if someone at CAA or UTA would just take a careful *look* at their new Taco Bell/I-Can't-Believe-It's-Not-Butter/Tampax Light campaign they would *see*. As such, they are often frustrated (bordering on angry), eager to emulate Hollywood movies/scripts/dialogue, hire famous directors for spots. I once worked with a man who was obsessed with David Mamet dialogue. Every commercial he wrote sounded like a bad Mamet film.

MAN 1: The thing.
MAN 2: What thing?
MAN 1: The thing. This is what the man said.
MAN 2: The man said the thing?
MAN 1: This is what I'm saying.
MAN 2: What thing? What did the man say?
MAN 1: He said Bounty is the Quicker Picker-Upper.

Still others are simply too good for advertising. We have a couple of guys (every agency does, and they're always guys) who fancy themselves 'real writers,' guys who are always starting commercials by quoting Hemingway or Kafka or

43

some deep thought of their own, lines that sound great when read in a really deep slow voice but that don't mean anything (*If life is about living, then maybe living . . . is about life . . . long pause . . . Introducing new Stouffer's Cheesy Bread.*). The problem is it's a commercial, not literature, and at some point you have to get to the product. These guys are always working on a novel. And God love them for it. They're better (and certainly more driven) men than I. They can't quite believe that they're forty-ish ad guys, when the plan twenty years before was to be on the third novel, the previous two having been optioned for screenplays, which they themselves would have written. They also use the phrase *selling my soul* a lot. They say this in a poor-me kind of way. It's charming. Not to me. But it's charming to the young account girls, who are often wooed by these grizzled writers, men who carry books and sometimes read them, who drink too much, who bed these impressionable lovelies. But here's the thing with the selling-your-soul business. People who work for tobacco companies and hide proof that cigarettes cause cancer sell their souls. Pharma companies that test drugs on African kids sell their soul. Oil companies who cut safety and environmental corners sell their soul. But ad guys? People who make cereal commercials? Client changes that ruin your *art?* Grow up.

And finally there is the silent majority, the daily grinders. They have grown tired of advertising's early allure and are now restless. Unfulfilled. Despondent. They want to be doing something else. But they don't know what to do.

44

Work on the client side? Start a café? Run drugs for a Mexican cartel? They possess that hybrid of confusion and sadness at having awoken, well past their prime, married (or just as often divorced), with two children and a mortgage on a house in Larchmont/Wilton/Montclair and thinking, *How did this* happen? They never really figured out what it was they wanted to do with their lives, and so life took over, marriage came along, children, a home, massive amounts of 'good' debt, and, after mediocre sex on Sunday night, they lie awake and think about how much damage it would cause if they left their wife and traveled around the south of France for the summer fucking twenty-one-year-olds. And as they are thinking this, their child awakens from a bad dream, calling out. They go to their child, walking naked through the quiet house with the new Restoration Hardware furniture, tramping quickly through the hallway to their perfect daughter's room, pulling on a pair of boxer shorts and almost breaking their neck doing it.

'What is it, pumpkin?' they coo.

'A dream, Daddy. A bad man chasing me.'

'There's no bad man, honey. You're here with Mommy and Daddy and Chuckie,' they say, referring to the filthy dog who farts and slobbers all over the furniture, bought on credit. They hold her, this three-year-old bundle of loveliness, caress her silky-soft downy hair, pat her tiny back, and say, 'Shhhh. Shhhh. Do you know how much Daddy loves you?' as they lay her down and pull the covers up to her chin. They kiss her cheeks again and again and hear her say, laughing, 'Stop it, Daddy, you're silly,' and know that she is all right, know that she will sleep, know that she will wake in the morning with no recollection of what has gone on here tonight in these two minutes, know that they themselves will never forget it, know that they will never leave this child and go to France, know that they will never again fuck a twenty-one-year-old, know that they will show up for work bright and early at the job they hate because of this girl.

I should admit that some of what I just wrote in the previous paragraph was from a spot I did for life insurance a few years ago. I apologize. I get carried away sometimes. But that's my job. And Lauderbeck, Kline & Vanderhosen is one of the premiere agencies in the world to do that job. At least, that's what we always say in our press releases and in our presentations. We use the word *premiere* because it tested well with focus groups.

Let's meet the team.

FRANK LAUDERBECK (SENIOR AND JUNIOR)

'I want to die on my way to a client meeting,' Frank's fond of saying, usually to the horror of his audience. Frank's father, Frank Sr., started the agency in the late forties. Apparently Frank Sr.'s war duty (due to flat feet and horrendous vision) included a stateside posting to the War Department, where he wrote and edited newsreels on the war's progress. They say he was a whiz. There he met Walter Kline, an MIT grad who was an early adopter of market research, number crunching, unearthing trends through the sifting of massive amounts of data. They built an impressive agency during the post-war boom years. Frank Sr. groomed his oldest son for the job. Groton, Yale, summer internships at the agency. The man-boy showed zero aptitude for the creative side of the business, but took to account service like a Swiss to fondue. He loved the schmoozing and the golf and the martinis and the pleasing. But he wanted the keys. He had his own ideas. It would be years before the old man finally ceded control, which he did one summer afternoon, the office half empty, the old fellow at his desk, apparently concentrating hard on a memo in front of him. It would be several hours before the cleaning staff found him dead at his desk, a number-two pencil frozen in his gnarled hand, halfway through editing a print ad for Froot Loops.

They say brainy Walter Kline never cared for young Frank, whose easy charm had morphed over the years into cockiness. Walter did the worst thing he could do to Frank: he left him on his own, disappearing one day, leaving his wealth to his family and taking a single suitcase to a Trappist monastery in the French Alps.

The agency faltered. The work turned bad. Clients dropped off. They couldn't win a new business pitch if they were the only ones in the room. Frank went through a few creative partners until a fortuitous meeting in the bar at Grand Central one evening with his old Groton roommate, Dodge Vanderhosen. Dodge had been known as someone with a decidedly artistic bent at boarding school. A diminutive man, he had been asked to be a coxswain but kept falling out of the boat. Instead, he put his prodigious efforts into arts and entertainment, editing the school newspaper (he did the drawings and photography), heading up the cheerleading squad (he wrote the Groton fight song, 'Let's Try Not to Lose Today'), and was big in the musical theater departments of both Groton and, later, Williams. That evening, Frank, already well lubricated from a long lunch, and Dodge, in the dumps after another day of failed Broadway auditions and orders from his parents to 'find a job that doesn't require a costume or we'll cut you off,' formed a partnership. They bumbled their way into new business and never looked back.

Today, Frank (like Dodge) is a largely ceremonial figure, the heavy lifting of account services and creative being deftly handled by younger, smarter, faster, MBA-sporting versions. Now, with his driver and sleek Range Rover, his sartorial splendor, Frank is a man with little to do except share the details of his life of wealth. I once heard him say to a junior art director who happened to mention that she was going to the Hamptons with friends for the weekend, 'Do you take a helicopter? It's a must.' To which the junior art director responded, after Frank had gotten off the elevator before her, but still very much within earshot, 'Douchebag.' He is, as the one grandmother I knew would say, a nincompoop.

Frank on advertising: 'It's my religion, my personal Jesus. And yet it's also incredibly profitable. Can I refresh your drink?'

DODGE VANDERHOSEN

Dodge is the creative one of the duo — or was, as he has nothing to do with the creative product anymore. A late-life crisis a few years back resulted in a dramatic change of wardrobe for Dodge. Whereas once he wore sensible Brooks Brothers suits and bow ties, now he appears to have come upon a large trove of clothes from Chess King. Check pants, shoes with a substantial heel (Dodge is 5'4" on a good day), open-collared dress shirts, revealing shockingly white skin, the kind that one imagines might have appeared in Michael Jackson's dreams. It is not uncommon to hear Bobby Short singing Cole Porter songs on the iPod in Dodge's office, Dodge singing along in a tinny falsetto.

During my interview with Dodge several years ago, he complimented my work and then asked me if I danced.

'I'm sorry?' I said.

'Dance. Do you dance? Just curious.'

'Ahhh . . . not . . . I mean, not really.'

'Stand up.'

'I'd rather not.'

'It'll be fun.'

I stood up and he held my hands and we danced around his office for several seconds. When we finished, he applauded and said,

'Wasn't that wonderful?'

Dodge on advertising: 'It's an art form. As surely as mime, the Irish jig, and rap. In one thousand years people will look at commercials as the pinnacle of our society's best artistic efforts. Or possibly TV shows like *ER* and *The Good Wife*.'

But here's the thing about Frank and Dodge. They're believers. They believe in the power of advertising, in the importance of myth, in the malleability of fact, the invention of truth, the happiness at the end of a dollar. They are businessmen and they are very good at it. The secret of their success is not a vital service offered — the crafting of a lasting message in a loud and crowded world — but rather the relentless pursuit of supplication, to borrow from Lexus. There is nothing they won't do for a prospective client. That said, they also provide a good wage and health insurance for hundreds of people every week, myself included. And I happily accept it. Surely this says more about me than them.

Let's meet the rest of the cast, shall we?

MARTIN CARLSON, EXECUTIVE CREATIVE DIRECTOR

Martin is the worldwide chief creative officer, which is impressive for a man of forty-two. On paper, Martin reports to Dodge. In reality, Martin reports to no one. Dodge fears Martin, as do most people. The simple truth is that

50

Martin runs the agency.

Martin started his career in London, rose through the ranks of one of the finest agencies there. He ran our agency's London office before taking this job. Tall, trim, beautifully dressed, he is undeniably talented. But he also has an English accent, which makes anything he says sound thirty percent more intelligent to American clients. I've seen it in meetings.

A daffy client: 'What do *you* think, Martin?'

'Me?' Martin says, blinky and Hugh Grant — charming. 'Right. Well, *I* think you're a ponce and a fool and frankly wonder why you exist. One man's opinion, of course.'

The client, nodding: 'I think that's exactly right.'

I sense that Martin feels that I do not immerse myself enough in the business, in nurturing my teams, in doing what it takes to get to the next level. I sense this because these were the exact words Martin used at my review last year. I'm due for one early in the New Year and hope to be promoted to creative director, an important difference and one *The New York Times* would no doubt lead with in my obituary. The chances of the promotion are slim to none.

Martin on advertising: 'All clients are geniuses. We merely execute their vision. I'm sorry, I thought this was going to be posted on the agency website. No? In that case, clients are largely frightened and undereducated. Creatives are difficult and not nearly as talented as they believe themselves to be. Management is old and foolish. And yet, I look forward to going to work each morning. Strange, I know.'

IAN HICKS, SENIOR ART DIRECTOR, MY PARTNER

You met him on the shoot. He is my art director partner and, along with Phoebe, my closest friend. He is the brother I never had. Unless you count the two brothers I do have who I almost never speak with. I trust two people in the world. Ian is one of them. He grew up in Montana in a place that was not particularly accepting of homosexuality. He left after high school and put himself through NYU. There he studied photography. At one point after he graduated he had three jobs just to make a livable wage. He continues to take pictures and has had three gallery showings of his work and once had a photo in *The Sunday Times Magazine*. It hangs in my office.

Ian on advertising: 'It's a job. Once in a while we get to make something good. I've cleaned stables, been a dishwasher, done flooring, worked as a mover. It beats most jobs on the planet.'

PHOEBE KNOWLES, CREATIVE DEPARTMENT ASSISTANT

You met her briefly on the phone. Twenty-eight years old, from Boston, of Knowles & Knowles Attorneys at Law (Boston, London, Frankfurt, Hong Kong). The youngest of three, her two older brothers already at the family firm, Phoebe has no interest in law. She moved to Paris after graduation, where her father knew someone who knew someone who was the editor of French *Vogue*. Phoebe was a junior editor there for a few years. Physically, she is nothing special, unless you find heart-stopping beauty special. Men become foolish around her. She followed an older man back to New York from Paris, a Frenchman, who broke her heart. She doesn't speak of it.

PAM MARSTON, AGENCY BROAD-CAST PRODUCER

Pam is a producer. She's one of eight or ten producers at the agency. Her job is to make the production happen. It is a complex and thankless task, usually underpaid. Too often the creatives expect to be treated like babies, their producer-mothers procuring their airline tickets, upgrades, car services, corner rooms, smoothies, lattes, dinner reservations, and usually the check after dinner. (Though I should point out that Ian and I always make our own plane reservations.) Why this is, I don't know. When one thinks of the name 'Pam,' one tends to think (I feel empirical evidence would back me up here) of a perky, upbeat, generally optimistic woman; perhaps one with an athletic build, small of breast, who ran track in high school and now makes time in the evening for 'projects,' which might include making her own stationery or mini-muffins. Not so with our Pam. Our Pam smokes and drinks hard and generally hates — and scares — most everyone she meets. I don't know how old she is (I'd guess forty-five) as she refuses to give her age because, as she herself says, 'Go fuck yourself and I hate birthdays.' Her hair is unusually long, a shiny, silky black. Most days she wears it in a ponytail, pulled back severely from her pale face. She's fond of Frye boots (the heel gives her 5′ 2″ frame a lift), long skirts, and sweaters that conceal her ample chest. I've never known her to have a boyfriend (though Ian said she married and divorced young), but a certain kind of man is definitely attracted to her. She treats men the way the worst kind of a man treats women. For some reason I've never been able to figure out if she likes me.

Pam on advertising: 'Fuck off.'

STEFANO & PAULIE, ART DIRECTOR AND COPYWRITER

Stefano was born in Spain to an Italian and a Spaniard and, so I've heard, moved to New York twelve years ago, where he took a number of design jobs, retooling the look of many well-known magazines. He speaks five languages, though English must surely be his worst. He likes to use colloquialisms at every chance, often inappropriately. His accent remains heavy. I don't know how old Stefano is. He looks to be a few years older than me. A man far more European than American when it comes to matters of the gym, of exercise, of anything, actually. He claims that it is impossible to find edible bread in North America and that coffee here is largely undrinkable, though he drinks between five and eight cups a day. Similarly, he quit smoking a year ago but still smokes several cigarettes a day. He claims that this doesn't count.

Paulie is a copywriter and a wisp of a fellow, maybe 5′ 5″, 130 pounds. At lunch sometimes, or when he's bored, he goes to the fifteenth floor, where the agency's telephone operators are located, and answers calls. He says he likes to give the other operators a break, time for a smoke or a coffee. Ask him an employee's extension and eight out of ten times he knows it immediately. There was a period, before he met his wife, when he had a band and would play shows at small clubs around the city. He'd be out until four in the morning. It made weekday mornings tough for him, and for anyone close enough to smell the liquor seeping through his skin. On some of these mornings he would come into my office, particularly hung over, close the door, and nap for a time on my couch while I quietly typed at my computer. I would often unplug my phone, so the ring wouldn't disturb him.

Paulie on advertising: 'There's the yin and yang of it, Fin D. You get to travel and stay in great hotels and eat great meals and drink expensive wine and be treated like someone on a movie set. Yet it's not art and deep down we want it to be. We need it to be beautiful. We need it to mean something. And it does, for the first twenty-three seconds of the spot. Then the voice-over comes in and talks about chicken tenders.'

Stefano on advertising: 'I don't care for it. And would prefer to say this: Do you know what I think every morning when I wake up? I ask myself, 'How can I seduce my wife today?''

MALCOLM & RAJIT, ART DIRECTOR AND COPYWRITER

Malcolm and Rajit came over a few years ago from the Y&R office in Sydney. They claim that, for several months, the Sydney office didn't realize they were gone and continued paying them. They once presented ideas over the phone — from our very offices — to a gathering in Sydney, saying they were both home with a stomach bug. Malcolm wears his dark blond hair long, often in a ponytail, and has unusually large, gleaming white teeth. He has the easygoing, worry-free demeanor one associates with Australians. You can't help but like him, smile back at him, as he casually says something in his heavy accent, like, 'I was adopted as a child.' To which you find yourself responding with an equally large smile, 'That's great.' He says 'Hey' before saying my name, which makes my name sound like 'Hyphen.' He would be the ideal companion to be lost at sea with on the famed Sydney-to-Hobart sailing race. He's single and often spends his weekends with Rajit and his wife (they live in the same building in DUMBO).

Rajit — Raj to most — is his diminutive, portly writing partner. Raj is also Australian, born of Indian parents. Raj himself will be the first to tell you this, though it is unlikely you will understand what he is saying as his accent is so dense as to cause most listeners to wonder what language he is speaking. Malcolm has no problem understanding him and often translates. Raj is a very good writer but is perhaps the least driven man I have ever met. If he's near a computer with a video game, he's happy. Malcolm and Raj smoke. A lot. They smoke in the building even though you can't. They have been reprimanded many times, brought before human resources, threatened with dismissal. The problem is they are so kind to everyone they meet that it's almost impossible to stay mad at them. Human resources finally suggested, after several meetings that began as reprimands and turned into long, laughing lovefests, that at the very least they dismantle the smoke detector in their office and place a wet towel at the base of their door.

Malcolm on advertising: 'I can't believe I get paid to do this. And I was adopted as a child.'

Rajit on advertising: unintelligible. Malcolm says, 'The people are lovely.'

~~Finbar Dolan is the greatest copywriter who has ever lived. Despite never winning a single major advertising award, peers see him as a legend. His keen mind, razor-sharp wit, and deft prose leave industry giants and suburban housewives breathless. The words *Now with 20% more absorbency* hang in the Guggenheim with his name on it. As if that's not enough, he is a~~

~~powerfully built man in his late thirties and can~~
~~bench-press four times his body weight. He is a~~
~~scaler of great heights, a poet, a marksman, a~~
~~man skilled in the art of close hand-to-hand~~
~~combat. Of the roughly 6,500 languages spoken~~
~~on the planet, there are only four in which he~~
~~cannot read and write.~~

What do you say about yourself? How do you describe yourself when people ask? Height? Weight? Fine. I'm 6′ 2″ but appear taller as I'm thin. I can't seem to gain weight, can't get past 170 or so. I slouch. I feel my ears are too large. I wear the uniform of the new urban landscape, the service economy, post-Apple. Jeans, sweaters, work boots. It's all part of the new irony, where college-educated, white-collar workers dress as if they were blue-collar workers, liberal guilt at cushy jobs that require zero physical labor. Where once the subway was filled at the day's end with men in soiled work clothes, carrying hard hats and lunch pails, perhaps canvas bags with tools, the smell of honest-to-God sweat, now it is peopled to a greater extent (and certainly on the L train to Brooklyn) with those who are terminally hip and under the mistaken impression that life is supposed to be easy, wearing $300 pairs of jeans made to look old, vintage-inspired eyeglass frames, waxed canvas bags from Jack Spade holding Apple computers/iPhones/iPads/iPods, reeking of Jo Malone Lime Basil & Mandarin for Him. What accounts for this new breed of creative man? The fickle mistress of fashion, certainly. But I would also suggest — from my own close observation — that this inchoate man is also confused and adrift in a world where the generational gap is wider than ever. And who sometimes feels the need to use the word *inchoate* when *not fully formed* would have worked just fine. Pulled down by a rip-tide of hair products and spin classes, white wine and *feelings*, my generation of late-to-marry city dwellers lost any connection with their change-the-car-oil-on-Saturday-afternoon-with-a-couple-cans-of-Carling-Black-Label fathers. They bear little resemblance in income, hobbies, out-look, number of sexual partners. Men good with their fists versus men who take yoga. Men who understood how life worked versus man-boys who give long thought/reading/classes/trips to India to allay their confusion about the meaning of life. Who complain that they're not happy.

I worry that I have a kind of retardation having to do with romantic relationships (thirty-nine and single), marriage (see the aforementioned cancellation of wedding), children (enjoy holding and smelling them, fear being responsible role model for them). My day is spent in diapers (has to be a better way to say that) and yet I, myself, have never changed one.

There are hundreds of me out there. Thousands. We look alike and think alike and come up with almost identical ideas because we approach life from the same perspective. We roam the streets of New York and Los Angeles, San Francisco, Minneapolis, London, and Amsterdam. The less reflective among us whine that we're not 'more.' Haven't done more, achieved more, made more. The smarter ones thank God every morn-ing for the world of advertising. Most days I enjoy going to work and am quite fond of my coworkers. The bad days are the days when I wonder what might have been had I tried something else or when I read about someone doing something that took courage and talent, neither of which I possess.

Me on advertising: 'Is there any way I can get an extension on this?'

★ ★ ★

We are all here. The beautiful twenty-six-year-old girls who work in media and enjoy the perks of free tickets to anything in town they want, who will be married within three years and entirely out of the industry within six. The thirty-eight-year-old producers, almost all women, almost all single, having pursued the career in the hopes of switching from commercials to Hollywood films but who never made the transition, who know far more about the complex job of making television spots than clueless young creatives ('Yeah, but why *can't* we use a helicopter for that one shot?') and who now bring a bitterness to the job in large part because they put off marriage and children in the hopes of achieving something professionally. The account people, jackets and ties, smart skirts and tops, the front line in client services ('I get to work with creative people *and* I get to work with business people. It's really the perfect balance.'). The skinny Asian boys with bad skin who run the computer help desk and who laugh aggressively at inside jokes, hidden away somewhere in the subbasement

60

('Um, like, is that *really* how you set up your desktop menu?'). The fit, handsome, gay designers, gym bags at the ready, shirts tucked in, black belts cinched a hole too tight. The accounting department, thin men who blink a lot and bite their nails, and heavy-set women, most of whom are black, who leave at five-thirty on the dot every afternoon. Human resources, socially conscious people who put up flyers near the elevators (LEUKEMIA WALK SATURDAY!). The art buyers, twenty-eight-year-old women, chunky shoes, multiple piercings, amateur photographers, fine arts degrees that translate into nothing in the real world, body art at the base of their spine (and often, for a fashion reason beyond my ken, the top portion of their ass crack), revealed when they spread a photographer's portfolio on the carpet and shake their head and use the word *derivative*.

So another day begins at Lauderbeck, Kline & Vanderhosen, a subsidiary of Tomo, Japan's largest shipping company and third largest in the world. Almost five hundred people looking for a paycheck, a dental plan, and an intangible something that will give us a sense of purpose at the end of the day. Most often we settle for free soda in the refrigerators.

Ian and Pam take a car service from the shoot back into the city, but I get carsick in a parking lot, so I take the subway whenever I can. I make my way to Corner Bistro, where I find a seat at the bar. I eat a cheeseburger, drink a couple of beers, and read the *Times*, though often I stare at the TVs, which show a hockey game, a cable show with what appears to be a panel of eight people yelling at one another, and, for some reason, *The Sound of Music*. None of the TVs have sound.

★ ★ ★

I call Phoebe on my way home.

She says, 'What if I had a guy over and was involved in an intimate moment?'

I say, 'But you're in bed, sort of reading, sort of watching *The Bachelor*.'

'That's just weird that you know that,' she says. 'Where are you?'

'Walking home.'

'I was reading a story in *Vanity Fair* about Johnny Depp. He owns an island.'

'Like I don't?'

'Then I started reading that Billy Collins book you gave me.'

'Which one?'

'*Picnic, Lightning.*'

'I like a funny poet. Why are so many poets depressed? It's always dead people and dead mothers and dead soldiers. Grecian urns. Epic poems. Why not a poem to donuts? To canned tuna?'

Phoebe says, 'I loved Sylvia Plath in college. I loved Emily Dickinson.'

I say, 'I've tried to read Emily Dickinson and I have no idea what she's talking about. Love is the thing without feathers? That's like a password in a spy novel. And then your contact says, 'Yes. And Belgium is lovely in springtime.' You stopped listening.'

'I was watching that new iPad commercial. They're so good. How come we don't do ads like that?'

'Those are done by the talented people. We do diapers.'

'You excited about Mexico?'

'Yes. No. I'm wondering if I should have picked someplace else.'

'You always do this. At some point you have to make a decision and actually take a vacation.'

'Why? I enjoy the planning.'

'You'll cancel. I know you. You'll end up home alone cooking a chicken.'

'Keats was twenty-five when he died. Byron, Shelley, Tennyson.'

'What's your point?'

'I was just seeing if I could name some poets.'

Phoebe says, 'How was the rest of the shoot?'

'Fine. We got what we needed. Barely. I don't know how, considering the director, the client, and the agency.'

Phoebe says, 'It always works out. You worry too much.'

I wait at the light and watch as a cab goes by with three guys in their twenties in the back, one of whom has pulled down his pants and is sticking his ass out the window.

I say, 'One beautiful thing.'

Phoebe says, 'I've got a good one.'

It's a thing we do. Every day — well, most days — we have to describe a beautiful thing we saw that day, one beautiful human interaction. It was her idea, something her parents used to do with her when she was little.

She says, 'So this kid gets on the train. Tough looking. Wearing this baggy suit. He sits across from a dandyish guy. You get the sense the kid has a job interview or something. He has a tie around his neck. He starts trying to tie it. But it's obvious the kid has no idea how to do it. The dandy's watching the kid. Says something to him in Spanish. I'm thinking there's gonna be a fight. Only, the kid says something back, sort of . . . meek. The dandy says something and the kid hands him the tie. The guy ties it, talking the whole time. Undoes it, ties it again, then hands it to the kid. Dandy got off at the next stop. I love New York.'

'That's really nice.'

Phoebe says, 'You?'

'I can't think of anything.'

'That's not the game. The game is that there's at least one beautiful thing that happens to you every day.'

'I can't think of anything.'

'Think harder.'

It takes me several seconds, but it comes to me sharp and clear.

'I was walking to the subway this morning. Early. Like five thirty. To get to the shoot. And there's one of those guys, the Ready, Willing and Able guys. Former homeless people, guys just out of prison. You know these guys? The city puts them to work sweeping and cleaning. Anyway, he's swapping out a huge bag of trash and putting in a new empty bag, and there's this homeless guy sleeping in a corner, by a subway grate. The heat from them, right? This homeless guy is curled into a ball. The cleaning guy walks up to him. I'm sure he's going to wake him up, tell him to move on. Except . . . he takes his jacket off. This uniform jacket. And puts it over the guy.'

Phoebe says, 'I like that. See, you just have to look. Beauty is everywhere.'

'Thank you, Oprah. Now go to sleep.'

'Don't tell me what to do. Did you call your brother?'

'Yes.'

'You're lying.'

'I'll call him tomorrow.'

★　★　★

It's early the next morning and the office is quiet.

Someone has put up politically correct holiday decorations, limited — by an agency committee comprised of deeply serious human resources

65

people — to snowflakes, snowpeople, and sleds. Except at Denise Muniari's desk, which looks like a mini Rockefeller Center around the holidays. She has a small tree in front of her desk with lights and ornaments on it. She also has a miniature manger, with tiny figurines of Mary, Joseph, the three Wise Men, animals, and, of course, the birthday boy. Denise is the creative department's manager and believes, as she once told me, 'It's Merry *fucking* Christmas, not Happy *fucking* Holidays. I have the utmost respect for Jews, Fin. God knows they've been through a lot. But don't rain on my baby Jesus birthday parade.'

I hear music, faintly. It gets louder the closer I get to my office. I stop outside the office, in the hallway, and listen as Paulie plays the guitar and sings.

I stand at the door. Paulie looks up and smiles.

Paulie says, 'Fin D. What up, my brother?'

'Hey, Paulie.'

'How was L.A.?'

'Didn't go. Shot at Silvercup instead.'

'Bummer. Who wants to go to Queens in December?'

'Who wants to go to Queens ever?'

'I thought you took the red-eye back. I love the red-eye, Fin D.'

'Really? Can't stand it myself.'

'No, man. I love the idea of going to sleep on one coast and waking up on another. Check this out. It took the Donner party five months from Springfield, Illinois, to reach the foot of the Sierra Nevadas. Imagine that. Five months. And yet we traverse the continent, with a nice glass of tomato juice and a magazine, in under six hours.'

I say, 'The modern world is an amazing place, Paulie.'

'I guess,' Paulie says, still smiling. 'Mostly it's just louder and faster.'

'You're in early.'

'Can't sleep lately. Plus I like it here when it's quiet. So how was Gwyneth?'

'Couldn't be nicer. Couldn't be lovelier. She's rich and beautiful and successful and happy. Like all of us.'

I turn to leave and Paulie says, 'Oh, hey, Fin man, I almost forgot. That NVD spot is up for an award. We found out from the account team.' He chuckles. 'You bastards.'

About a year ago Ian and I helped Paulie and Stefano out with a project. Our group also works on a pharmaceutical account (indigestion pill and depression/anxiety medication). The company had a new drug that helped relieve what the account team referred to in meetings and e-mails as 'NVD,' which I soon found out was pharma-speak for the family of symptoms known as nausea-vomiting-diarrhea. So Ian and I thought it would be interesting to personify them. We'd cast guys who looked like they might *be* nausea or vomiting or diarrhea. The amazing thing was how many actors in New York and Los Angeles actually look like nausea, vomiting, and diarrhea.

In our imagined commercial, the NVD would stand together, in what looked like a stomach, and talk to the camera about how horrible it was to be them. We'd use grotesque sound effects. We thought it was funny in an incredibly childish way. We thought the client might laugh and say, 'Okay, where are the real ideas?' Except they loved it. They thought we were serious. They thought we'd found a window into the 'soul of the brand.'

At the presentation, the head client leaned across the table, all but reaching out for our hands.

'You get it. No one wants to be nausea or vomiting or — God forbid — diarrhea. But they are. And we can help.'

The problems arose during casting. Nausea and vomiting were relatively easy to find. And the client loved our casting suggestions. Nausea (perhaps not surprisingly) was a balding, stocky guy with a mustache and very hairy arms. Vomiting was a tall, incredibly pasty guy with the most pronounced Adam's apple I'd ever seen. His mouth hung open and he had bad teeth. He was also balding. Diarrhea had a full head of slicked-back hair and an unnaturally yellow tint to his skin. He was an oddly shaped man, like a pear, and he wore his pants quite high. Joey Beetie was his name. 'No one beatie Joey Beetie, huh?!' he'd say, and then laugh like a hyena. 'C'mon!' He hit on almost every woman at the casting session (including Pam, who simply stared him down). He was physically and emotionally repugnant. He was, to our minds, the perfect embodiment of diarrhea.

Except the client didn't like him. I know their exact words because I've saved the e-mails.

'While we like Nausea and Vomiting very

much, we're having a problem with Diarrhea. We feel strongly that Diarrhea simply isn't aspirational enough for the brand.'

The account team responded.

'Our understanding of Diarrhea was that he should be repulsive. Obviously we'll continue to cast, if you feel strongly about it, but creatively we feel like we really have Diarrhea.'

The client e-mailed back.

'We feel you're missing the point of Diarrhea. While repulsive, Diarrhea is also very much part of the brand. Much like a family black sheep that is still embraced. Diarrhea is bad but Diarrhea is the reason for the brand. In that way, people should *aspire* to the brand. Thus Diarrhea should be aspirational.'

Agency: 'Could you suggest guidelines as to what aspirational Diarrhea might look like?'

Client: 'Young (thirties), clean-shaven, not too tall, wears sneakers maybe. If he weren't Diarrhea he might be in a beer commercial playing the part of the friend. We feel strongly that the audience should like Diarrhea as *an idea more than an actual symptom*. What about someone with a lisp or a harelip? You feel sorry for them in a small way, perhaps, as if being Diarrhea isn't necessarily their fault. Looking forward to seeing options.'

In the end, the client chose a boy-next-door type, bit pudgy, perennially lost look on his face, the kind of guy you see on a street corner in New York in the summer, looking down at a map, then up, then back down. Matt someone-or-other was his name. Nice guy. I asked him what

69

he thought Diarrhea's character might say if he could speak. The client was standing with me. Matt thought for a moment, as if I'd just asked him if he believed in the afterlife.

He said, 'Well, like, if I were Diarrhea? I think I'd, like, say, 'Uh-oh.''

The client turned to me, smiled, and nodded. We knew then we had Diarrhea.

I tell Paulie it would be the highlight of my career to win an award for that spot.

Paulie says, 'Hey, Fin man. You have to talk to Stefano. He's turning forty next month and he's wiggin' out. Maybe it's an Italian thing. Thinks it's the end of his manhood. He has this plan.'

'Why am I sure this is going to be a very bad idea?'

'He wants to break the four-minute mile.'

'Makes sense for an overweight smoker.'

Paulie puts his guitar down. 'Have you decided on the vacation thing?'

'Mexico. Christmas Eve. Very excited. How about you?' I ask. 'Where are you going for the holidays?'

'Wife's family in Westchester.'

I nod to his guitar and say, 'Sounds really good, Paulie. Nick Drake?'

Paulie says, 'You got that right.'

'Tortured soul.'

Paulie shakes his head slowly. 'He felt too much, Fin. Saw beauty everywhere. Too overwhelming, ya know?'

I say, 'I'm not that deep, Paulie.'

* * *

70

In my office, I open up *The New York Times*, turn to the obituaries. Whole lives, right there, in three hundred words. Full, rich lives. Exciting lives. Sad lives. Lives lived through war, depression, children, success, failure, ridicule, public embarrassment, famous patents, Nobel Prizes, moon landings, prison, Academy Awards, the invention of tubing, coils, rheostats, anti-lock brakes, the Kelvinator, the pilot light, lived in Paris/Taos/Mill Valley, supported passage of civil rights, textile imports, Holocaust survivor, Cold War spy, OSS. It's all there. A modern Shakespearean drama.

Also there, on the next page, is a gravy boat. It's in an ad for Bloomingdale's, for their fancy dinner plate collection. For the holidays. For families who get together and set the table with fine china. And who use a gravy boat. Or *sauce* boat, as I learned they are called. We got a sauce boat, Amy and I. For our engagement. We promised each other we wouldn't do the usual thing: the round of parties, the formal invitations, the registry. But we ended up doing all of it because Amy wanted it. And so did her mother. Amy said we had to register. I said we didn't need anything. She said I didn't understand, that people wanted to show us their love by buying us an ice cream scoop from Crate & Barrel. I said I found that hard to believe. We argued but mostly ended up laughing about it. Especially the gravy boat. She had registered for an eight-piece fancy dinner set, complete with gravy boat. She said it was essential to have a gravy boat. I asked her if she often made gravy, because I'd never seen the results. She finally admitted that she'd never actually made gravy but was eager to try. She said it felt old-fashioned, a thing married couples do. The more I ridiculed her about gravy and its accompanying vessel, the more I found I wanted it. Once set up, we followed the registry online, like a kind of video game, watching as the things she'd chosen were ticked off. We waited for 'sauce boat — quantity 1' to disappear. I'd suggested we ask for ten. It all seemed unreal to me. But not to her. Amy could see the dinner parties we were going to have. With gravy.

Then there was the engagement party. This was about eighteen months ago. Amy's mother's apartment, Brooklyn Heights. A swanky neighborhood just over the Brooklyn Bridge. Looks like a movie set of old New York. The family bought their townhouse in 1980 for the then-princely sum of $275,000. I would never ask how much it's worth now. But I don't have to with Zillow.com, which says it's worth $4.5 million. Amy grew up there. Went to Saint Ann's, played squash at the Heights Casino. She could see us living there, she said. See raising our children there. Grace Church School had a wonderful preschool program. Two hours a day, two days a week, for just $7,000. And then either Saint Ann's or Packer or Brooklyn Friends, each running about $30,000 a year from age five on. This wasn't taking college into account, mind you. A quick tabulation had the education bill, per child, at $500,000. Good. Excellent. All made perfect sense. I nodded and smiled. But who was she talking about? Who was this man named Fin who would be the father and do the things fathers do? Surely not me. Didn't she know I wasn't that man, that I would never be that man?

Amy's parents, Linda and Syd. Divorced, but friendly. He's a hedge-fund guy, she's a landscape architect for rich people. Amy's sisters, Cassie, short for Cassidy (God only knows why), and Celia. Cassie's a producer at Warner Brothers in L.A., and Celia is in 'transition,' bouncing from job to job, trying to be a singer in a band, a model, an actress, and most recently (after seeing the Sean Penn/Nicole Kidman film *The Interpreter*) an interpreter. She flirts and feels the need to exude sexuality. She also drinks too much.

Despite the fact that it all seemed unreal to me, that it was as if I was watching myself in this tableau, there was something quite real and lovely happening. Amy's family and friends, happy people who knew one another, shared each other's birthdays and bar mitzvahs and first communions, soccer leagues and dance recitals. Big hugs, real smiles. I watched it all, not part of it. Watched Amy, the center of attention, radiant in a clingy black dress and boots. Me, next to her, a seemingly normal man, a decent job, no body art or criminal record. One after another I was introduced to Phil and Alice, 'our old neighbors,' Glen and Miriam, 'whose daughter Tammy was my best friend growing up,' Lindsay from the Heights Casino squash league, 'who was bulimic and slept with everyone.' Presents

73

piled up in a corner, large, beautifully wrapped decanters and flatware, blenders and All-Clad pans. And one gravy boat.

Then the toasts started. Amy's father first, lauding his ex-wife, who was standing across the room holding back tears as he talked about what a great mother she was, how Amy possessed her goodness, her relentless love of life and people. Then Amy's mother, telling stories of Amy as a girl, willful, confident, kind. How she was an early sharer, how she helped others. Cassie next, talking about what a great big sister Amy was, Celia at her side smiling, three too many gin-and-tonics. They meant it. Every word. A round of applause to Amy.

And then the pregnant silence when it was over as people looked around, waiting for my family to say a few things, share a few insights, tell the story of my life. I could feel myself turning red, smiling like a fool. I was about to say something that would have no doubt only added to my embarrassment when someone started talking.

'I have to apologize for being late,' Ian said, Jack Kennedy — charming. He was in the back of the living room where we'd gathered, near the front door. I hadn't seen him come in. I don't know how long he'd been there, but long enough to take in what was happening. He was shrugging his overcoat off, his boyfriend, Scott, taking it from him. They looked over at me, handsome, smiling faces, lifeguards swimming to a drowning man.

Ian said, 'I was putting the final touches on my

talk. But I was under the impression this was a roast, not a toast.'

Smiles and laughs all around as people craned to see him. Others near the doorway made space and he took a few steps toward the center of the room.

'So, hi. My name is Ian Hicks, and I am . . . ' He pulled a face, looked over at me. 'What am I to you, Fin?'

Scott jumped in. 'You better not say boyfriend.'

Everyone laughed.

Ian said, 'We won't go there. No. Finbar Dolan is my copywriter partner at work. But mostly Fin is the brother I never had. I don't mean to treat this as a therapy session, but when you grow up gay in Montana, you pray that there are people and places that are . . . different. Better. Accepting. That's what brought me to New York. And when I first met Fin, when I got partnered up with him, I thought, 'Oh, Christ. A fag-hater.'' A couple of uncomfortable, polite coughs from the crowd. 'I'm sorry, but I judged him on his bad clothes, which I've tried hard to fix. Except I was the one who judged. Because here was this remarkable person, this loving, funny, amazingly kind person.'

He talked for a few more minutes. I stopped listening, though, merely took in the tone, the reaction on the faces, laughing in the right places, moved at the right times. I thought of my family — Eddie, Kevin, Maura — whom I'd invited. Granted, it was a half-assed invitation, giving them an out if they wanted, saying I

75

understood that it was a long way to come — especially for Kevin — for just a few hours on a Sunday night in Brooklyn. I said there was always the wedding. As it turned out, they all had plans that would have been tough to break. And I really didn't expect them to come.

Much later, after we canceled the wedding, we had to return the gifts. It took an entire day, Amy's mother coming with us. We spoke almost not at all. The clerks would inevitably ask if there was any reason for the return. 'We've canceled our wedding,' Amy would say simply.

Late in the day, with one gift to return, Amy reached her limit. I told her I'd do it. I would have walked to Tierra del Fuego on my hands if it would have changed the expression on her face, lifted the gloom. All day I'd opened doors and gotten water and coffee, carried boxes and tried to smile, waited on them both like a beaten servant. And I was happy to play the role. I kept saying sorry.

We were standing on Fifty-seventh and Lex and it was getting dark. I wanted a movie moment, a smile, a hug. I wanted forgiveness. Her mother stood a few feet away, examining her hands.

I said, 'I'll call you, okay?'

Amy stared. 'No, Fin. You won't.'

I said, 'I'm sorry, I didn't mean anything by it.'

Amy, with too much edge, her patience spent: 'Stop saying you're *sorry*, Fin.'

It was loud on the street. Cabs honking their horns, a car alarm not far away. City noise wears on you sometimes. It had been a long day. Not enough food, too much coffee. I hadn't been sleeping well. The thing is, I'm not someone who raises their voice. It came on fast, out of control.

I said, 'I didn't *plan* this! Okay?! The idea wasn't to *hurt* you! You think I like this? Hurting you? I don't! I'm just so fucking sorry, okay?'

My throat closed up and my eyes welled and my hands were shaking and I was pretty sure I was going to vomit. I bent forward, hands on my knees, like I was in a huddle, and a strange sound emanated from me, a kind of primal moan.

And just that fast whatever anger was there was gone, and in its place an overwhelming regret that I had created all of this. I stood up and put my hands on my hips, trying to catch my breath, my heart beating like I just ran the hundred-yard dash. I think in that moment, for the first time in weeks, Amy saw me differently. If the look on her face was any indication — though how can one ever know these things for sure? — I think she saw that she wasn't the only one in pain. Which is why she then sobbed harder than she had the night I said I couldn't do it, wailing away a block from Bloomingdale's.

The point is that I never made it to Simon Pearce that day to return our last engagement party gift. Nor any day after that. I kept it. I do not know why, exactly, but I needed to hold on to it, even if only for the imaginary dinner party I would have with my imaginary wife, where one needs an obscenely expensive gravy boat.

★ ★ ★

The phone startles me. I see the display, the area code before the number. 617. Boston. It's Eddie. It has to be. I watch myself watch the phone ring, like someone in a movie, and think, as I do when I'm watching a movie like that, *Answer the phone!* A tingling in my stomach, in my palms. *Answer the phone, it's your brother, for God's sake.* But I continue to hesitate. Because it's Eddie. Because of who Eddie's become. Because it's about my father. And maybe he's alive and maybe he's dead and there's a one in a million chance he's come back to beg forgiveness but I'm sorry, old fella, there's a statute of limitations on forgiveness. At least with the Irish.

The ringing stops.

I go back to the obits and read about a pioneer in DNA research who won a Nobel Prize. I read of an economist who was noted for his 'mathematical rigor.' I read of the inventor of the Bundt pan. Unlike the other two men, there is no photo of him. Instead, there is a photo of a Bundt pan. He was eighty-six. This is how he is remembered to the world. I wait for the red light on my phone that signals a message but it never appears.

* * *

An e-mail informs me that there is a problem with Doodles.

Doodles are a chocolate candy with toffee in the center. They are one of the oldest candies in America. Chances are good that you have eaten them. We have been their ad agency for many,

78

many years. Doodles and Chew-gees and Gooshy Gum. One of the company's newer products, Joy-Jellies, which is selling very well, is handled by an agency across town. We would very much like that business. Last year alone, those four products earned two-point-eight billion dollars worldwide. The Chinese love Doodles and they love Joy-Jellies but they detest Gooshy Gum, whose name, we learned not long ago, is roughly the equivalent to the Chinese word *shit*. People here take Doodles very seriously. The company needs a new rip. (A rip is a rip-off of video footage from other TV commercials and sometimes movies that we share with the client at the start of the production process as a guide to the kind of thing you'd like to shoot for them, or sometimes just to make them happy: '*Hey, look! We stole these images from an award-winning Nike commercial and from* Mission: Impossible III, *among many, many others to show you how great your candy is.*' We also steal music we could never, ever use. U2, Coldplay, The Rolling Stones. It's akin to me sharing *The Great Gatsby* with someone as a guide to my writing.)

Another e-mail — agency-wide — reminds us about the holiday party, which this year is being held . . . next year! In another time, in a far different economy, long, long ago, the company holiday party was a special affair. Not so this year. My admittedly unscientific poll has shown that people have laughed it off but one gets the sense they're hurt. People work hard. There are many people here for whom a party is a nice thing, a special thing, a thing to get excited about, perhaps an excuse to wear a pretty dress. It shows that the company you work for — that you invest so much of your life in — cares just a little bit. I do not generally think of a Tuesday morning as a great time for a holiday party, but our parent company does. There are several reasons they think this way. One is because the cost of renting a greasy-smelling banquet hall in a Times Square hotel at this time slot is far less. Another is fewer people will drink at a party at 10:00 A.M., limiting any potential liability when, say, a male employee, perhaps after six too many Stoli-and-tonics, 'accidentally' pulls his penis out of his pants and runs around screaming, as was the case last year. Less alcohol means less cost (a theme?). And, perhaps most importantly, fewer people calling in sick the next day. The e-mail reminds us that the party begins at 10:00 A.M. with speeches by Frank, Dodge, Martin, and a special keynote by Keita Nagori, the aforementioned son of the agency's new owner. Brunch and dancing to follow.

★　★　★

Later in the morning the office fills with the hum of the workday: the R2-D2 of electronic phones, the light tapping of laptop keyboards, the quiet buzz saw of copiers and printers, conversations muted by the carpeting. Light days today and tomorrow, the agency closing at noon on Christmas Eve.

Phoebe comes into my office with two coffees,

something she does most days. I am hard at work. I'd begun, but did not complete, my expense report, as I got distracted by a Google search for information about Mexico but somehow find myself reading a long story about Brett Favre's childhood.

'There's a new receptionist on nine,' she says.

'This is not a great lead sentence,' I say. '"Call me Ishmael' is a great lead sentence. 'Mother died today. Or maybe it was yesterday' is a great lead sentence. 'There's a new receptionist on nine' needs work.'

'She's a former Miss Black Deaf America.'

I say, 'Much better.'

'I'm serious.'

'I don't know what that means.'

'It means she's deaf and beautiful.'

I say, 'Would you rather be deaf or beautiful?'

'Neither. Wait. Beautiful.'

'The other four senses of the deaf are far more highly attuned than the average person.'

'Is that true?'

'I have no idea. I hear perfectly well.'

Phoebe asks, 'What sense would you lose?'

'Touch.'

'You say that very quickly. You're sure? Never feel softness, texture?'

'Touch is overrated,' I say.

Phoebe says, 'You'd give up touching the curve of a woman's hip?'

'Okay. I see what you did there. Umm . . . hearing.'

Phoebe says, 'No music?'

'I want all my senses, but I also want that

81

thing where your other senses are more highly attuned because you can't see or hear.'

Phoebe looks at me and says, 'Stop.' She says it gently.

I'm touching my scar, the small one along my jawline. I got it when I was a kid. I'm self-conscious of it. Phoebe knows that.

She says, 'Did you hear about Tom Pope?'

'Tell me.'

Tom is an associate creative director who sits a few offices away.

'I heard from Jackie who was out with Erica at what's-it-called across the street that Tom was at the bar with that new account girl.'

'The stunning one?'

'The stunning one.'

'Not his wife, in other words.'

'Definitely not his wife. They were making out. At the bar. Like openly making out. This is across the street! Tom gets so drunk that he puts his head on the bar and the stunning one strokes it. People are watching them now. He puts his hand up the back of her blouse. He gets up and walks into the hostess stand, almost knocking it over. The hostess picks him up, asks if he's all right. He says he's fine. Then he walks out onto the street and in full view of the entire restaurant, pukes onto the sidewalk.'

Why is there a part of me that secretly enjoys hearing about this? Why is there a tingle of excitement at someone else's misfortune, poor decision, emotional duress? Is it because somewhere in my own psyche I understand poor, sad Tom Pope's actions, his need for attention from an attractive young woman as he grows older? Is it because I recognize this as a cry for help, a longing for something that's clearly not happening at home? Or is it because it's just plain funny when a grown man makes a horse's ass of himself in public and then vomits freely?

Phoebe says, 'Promise me you'll never be like that.'

I say, 'If he keeps this up he could be a partner in no time.'

Then Phoebe says, 'Would you miss me if I left?'

'You mean, like, left my office?'

'Left. Quit.'

'You thinking of leaving?'

'Yes. No. Maybe. I'm getting a little bored.'

Ian has stuck his head into my office and says, 'Can I come with you? I'm bored, too.'

I say, 'The entire agency may come with you.'

Ian says, 'I'm headed to Chubby Feet.'

This is not an insult by Ian. Nor is it a form of Tourette's. This is the name of the company where we color-correct commercials. After you've shot the commercial, edited the commercial, you then primp it for air. This takes place at highly specialized companies in New York and Los Angeles, usually in formerly industrial buildings in TriBeCa or West Hollywood or Santa Monica. Often they are simple raw spaces, open concrete floors and walls with modern sculpture, an array of death masks perhaps, a flat-screen TV that shows nothing but waves hitting the beach. In the middle of the room there is almost always a

Ping-Pong table. Soviet-era posters might adorn the walls. Sleepy-looking young people wander the halls, their hair unwashed and bedraggled, their pants low on their hips, ironic writing on their T-shirts (I'M NOT GAY BUT MY BOYFRIEND IS). And in the semi-darkness of the editing suites with their double-paned sound-proof glass doors, there sit exceptionally expensive computers and software systems manned by industry-famous men with one name. Luke. Rush. Anton. They provide exceptional lunches.

The companies have uniformly bizarre names that bear no relation to the business they are in. No Stan Whaley's Plumbing and Heating Supplies here. Instead, Chubby Feet, Hey Gary!, Ham Sandwich, and Super Happy Good Time. The receptionist at this last one, a perpetually fatigued-looking young woman named Petrol, must say the company name hundreds of times a day. Often she answers the phone by saying, in a voice that suggests otherwise, 'Super Happy.'

Who's to say why they choose these names. It is, I think, in the worlds of advertising/ entertainment, the almost manic pursuit of hip. This is crucial. Who's hip, who's cool, who's *the guy*? The problem is that by the time I've heard who's hip/cool/the guy, they're no longer hip/cool/the guy. They're mainstream/accepted/ cliché. The key is to be just ahead of the hip curve, which I have never ever once been. Where does one go to learn of this hipness and coolness? My father wore zip-front cardigan sweaters. Not cool. Kurt Cobain wore zip-front cardigan sweaters. Cool. Why? Could be his use of heroin and his playing of the guitar. But what *is* cool? What is *hip?* My sense, after a lot of thought, is that if you have to ask, you'll never know. Also, it would be gauche and profoundly *uncool* to ask how these post-production houses came up with their clever names or why they simply didn't call themselves Alan's Post-Production Services. When I'm there I say things like 'Hey, man' and 'Hey, dude,' even though I don't use the words *man* or *dude* in normal conversation. In this way, along with my uniform of blue jeans, Blundstone's, and short-sleeve T-shirt over long-sleeve T-shirt over short-sleeve T-shirt over a life vest, I believe I can be seen as cool.

Ian says, 'Come over if you want lunch. I doubt I'll be back. Or call me later if you need. Also . . . I'm hearing rumors of another round of layoffs.'

Phoebe says, 'I've heard them, too.'

'All rumors are true,' I say.

'Who said that?' Phoebe says.

'I did. Just now.'

'I thought so,' she says. 'It doesn't make any sense.'

'I know. But it sounds good.'

Ian says, 'Did you hear about Tom Pope?'

We nod and Ian shakes his head and leaves.

I turn to Phoebe and say, 'So wait. She's deaf *and* she's a receptionist? She answers phones?'

'No. Just greets people. She speaks. Like Marlee Matlin.'

'We hired a person who can't speak well to

greet people and we're a multinational communications company?'

'Well, now that you put it that way.'

I say, 'Is she beautiful?'

'Who?'

'Miss Deaf Black America?'

'Gorgeous.'

'Does she look deaf?'

'You're an idiot.'

'The blind look blind,' I say. 'I'm just wondering if she appears particularly oblivious to sound.'

Phoebe has stopped listening. She's leafing through an *Us Weekly* while I casually scan CNN.com.

I say, 'So, you heading to Boston?'

Phoebe says to *Us Weekly*, 'Yeah. Taking the train Thursday.'

'You excited?' I say to my computer screen, which is currently displaying a story about the Fox channel premiering a show called *Naked Housewives*.

'I love Christmas. On Christmas Eve, if it's cold enough, we all go skating. There's a pond at my dad's country club with a hut and they build this big fire and there's hot chocolate and, because it's all WASPs, there's also gin and beer. And then we have dinner at the club and go to midnight mass. In the morning my mom and I go to a women's shelter in the city and hand out gifts, help serve breakfast. Then later we have dinner at our house and open presents.'

'Same here. Almost exactly. But without the skating. Or the family part. Or the dinners. Or the volunteering. Or the getting-together parts. But the gin and beer is identical.'

'Did you call your brother?'

'Yes.'

'You lie.'

'Only to clients.'

★　★　★

Late in the afternoon, Jill, the Snugglies account exec, calls.

She says, 'There is a serious problem with the Old MacDonald animatic.'

She and Alan have me on speakerphone. They ask if they can come down to my office. I call Ian. Fifteen minutes later we all sit in my office. Jill closes the door.

An animatic is one of the last stops along the long, painful conveyor belt to approval — from brief to creation to internal review to client presentation to revisions to re-presentation to additional presentation to more senior clients to additional revision based upon senior client feedback to animatic to focus-group testing. In an animatic, a voice-over reads the idea as the focus group looks at hand-drawn pictures. It's the kind of thing you might have seen in a high school phys ed class in the sixties about avoiding syphilis or the dangers of Western culture as told by state agencies in Pyongyang today. An animatic has about the same relationship to an actual commercial that Orangina has to orange juice.

I say, 'What's the problem?'

Jill looks to Alan. Alan says, 'The problem is cock.'

Ian says, 'I'm all ears.'

Alan says, 'This isn't funny.'

I say, 'Ian doesn't joke about cock.'

Jill says, 'You guys. Seriously. The client is really upset. And the Young MacDonald launch is a huge deal for them.'

The Young MacDonald launch is a new line of diapers that have animals on them. This may not seem like a big deal as there are plenty of diapers with animals on them. In fact, it's unlikely that you can buy diapers without animals on them. But these aren't ordinary animals. Our client signed an exclusive deal with Pixar (translation: Snugglies paid Pixar an exorbitant fee for the right to use the cartoon animals) and is launching the animal diapers in concert with the opening of a movie using the same characters in January. We were awaiting focus group testing and footage from Pixar before editing the spot. The movie is about a cartoon teenager who grows up on a farm (his grandfather is Old MacDonald, his father is simply MacDonald) and who doesn't want to be a farmer — he wants to be a hedge-fund manager. Though he eventually realizes he wants to stay on the farm. Throughout the spot we'd see babies (wearing only Snugglies diapers) crawling around, playing with cuddly stuffed animals, as we hear children singing 'Old MacDonald,' which Pixar has contracted with Beyoncé to re-record. The challenge was finding a way to seamlessly integrate the movie into the spot. How would the babies see it on a farm? Several ideas were tossed around. One involved showing the movie on the side of the barn. Another had the movie reflected in a puddle in the pigpen (both the client and Pixar reacted angrily to this, misconstruing our creativity for an indictment of the film). Yet a third had a drive-in movie theater next to the farm, but the concern there was that children would have absolutely no idea what a drive-in was. In the end, we eventually decided the babies would sit in front of a large flat-screen TV (the client's input via a co-branding deal with Sony's flat-screen division), where they would watch a partial trailer for the movie.

I say, 'But what's the problem? And please don't say 'cock' again.'

Jill says, 'In the script you use a cow, a pig, and a rooster.'

I say, 'Of course I did. I'm a professional writer.'

Jill says, 'Sing the song for me.'

I look at Ian. This is a trap. I say, 'I won't sing. But I'll talk it.'

Jill says, 'Whatever. Just do it.'

I say, 'Old MacDonald had a farm. E-I-E-I-O.'

Ian says, 'I feel like this is how Christopher Walken sang to his children.'

Jill says, '*Shh*. Keep going.'

I say, 'And on this farm he had a cow. E-I-E-I-O. With a *moo-moo* here and a *moo-moo* there, here a *moo*, there a *moo*, everywhere a *moo-moo*.'

Jill says, 'Jump ahead to the rooster part.'

I say, 'And on this farm he had a rooster.

E-I-E-I-O. With a . . . oh, shit.'

Ian says, 'With a *cock-cock* here and a *cock-cock* there, here a *cock*, there a *cock*, everywhere a *cock-cock*. Where is this farm? I want to live there.'

Jill says, 'We need to get on a call.'

Ian says, 'So you're saying this is a huge cock problem.'

I say, 'Can't we just lose the rooster? Cow, pig, chicken.'

Alan says, 'There's a problem with the cow and the pig. They didn't test well. People were offended by the pig. They thought it was demeaning to heavy-set mothers. They thought we were calling people fat cows and fat pigs. The client's really upset.'

Somewhere, not far from these offices, surgeons are saving lives, social workers are helping the poor, the clergy are ministering to the forgotten, scientists are on the edge of breakthroughs that will improve the human experience, artists are writing plays, novels, painting masterpieces. I want to know if Miss Deaf Black America looks deaf, and I have a cock problem. Truth be told, this is not an unusual day at Lauderbeck, Kline & Vanderhosen.

IT'S INCREDIBLY STUPID. I LOVE IT.

'Fin. How nice.' It's Martin's assistant, Emma, whom he brought with him from London. She's called and asked if I could stop by Martin's office. He'd like a word.

Martin's office sits in a corner of the building with spectacular views of Bryant Park. I wait in an anteroom. I hear voices from his office and recognize them as the soda guys, Glen and Barry. They are brothers, twins from Florida. They went to school for advertising, received actual degrees, apparently. I would think advertising would be more of a course than a degree, more like a week's bartending program or CPR or omelet-making. The twins were recruited to work here, having come from a far superior agency known for its award-winning work. They love advertising. They study the business, read the industry periodicals, know the names of the best copywriters and art directors, the best agencies, which account has moved where. They know the directors. They watch reels of commercials from around the world for hours at a time. They are true believers and they will one day run this place. Or someplace like it. They bear an uncanny resemblance to Elmer Fudd.

They run the fizzy orange drink account. The fizzy orange drink is preferred by the African-American community. The fizzy orange drink is very important to the agency. The agency hopes to parlay our success (as-yet unproved) to the fizzy orange drink's parent company, based in Atlanta. From the sound of it, Glen and Barry are very excited about their idea.

Glen (or maybe Barry) says, 'Youth-oriented. Hip. Street.'

The other one says, 'Jay-Z, Young Jeezy, Lil Wayne.'

Which is when they say their idea is a small black doll that talks.

I peek my head in and see that Barry and Glen are each holding a rubber doll about a foot high, presenting it to Martin and a few others.

Babs Moss, management supervisor on the account, says, 'Do the thing, guys. Talk like them.'

Glen talks as if he were the doll. 'What up, yo?'

Babs says, 'No, the other thing. The funny thing.'

Glen says, 'Blast is so *right*, yo. Fresh.' Blast is the fizzy orange drink.

Babs squeals with delight.

Barry says, 'I find it quite refreshing.' He says this in a posh English accent.

Martin sits, hands in a contemplative tent over his nose, a deep thinker, a man listening to a new idea for peace in the Middle East.

Martin says, 'So they're two puppets who talk.'

Glen and Barry nod.

Babs says, 'I think that's right, Martin. I think that's *exactly* right.'

Martin says, 'Aren't they similar to what Nike

did some time ago with Lil Penny?'

Nike used Chris Rock as the voice for an inanimate little doll that was former NBA great Penny Hardaway's alter ego. It was funny, in no small part because it was Chris Rock and not Glen and Barry.

Babs says, 'They most certainly did, Martin. But we feel this idea is very different.'

Martin says, 'How is it different?'

Glen says, 'We have two, not one.'

Babs says, 'I think that's a crucial difference. Also one's white.'

Martin says, 'Why is one English?'

Barry says, 'It's just funny.'

Martin says, 'Is it?'

Babs says, 'It's certainly not classically funny, Martin. Not laugh *loud* funny. It's a chuckle. A smile. A half-grin.' Babs makes a half-grin face.

Martin turns to Glen and Barry. 'Did you do two because you're twins and they're twins?'

Glen says, 'That was part of it.'

Babs jumps in with the intensity of a hostage negotiator. 'Martin, the target is African-American teens, thirteen to seventeen, hip-hop culture, NBA-focused, single-parent homes, at-risk kids who consume on average two to three bottles of our product a day. Our projections want that closer to seven to ten bottles a day. We think the doll will reach them, and the client is putting major money behind it. NBA playoffs, MTV Music Awards, and Bling Thing.'

Martin says, 'Bling Thing?'

Babs doesn't miss a beat. 'It's the inner-city anti-violence initiative sponsored by Iced La-Táy, the rap star who was shot two weeks ago.'

Martin says, 'Interesting. Part of me thinks it's funny. Part of me thinks it's one of the dumbest things I've ever seen.'

Babs says, 'That was the brief exactly. It almost makes you wish you were African-American. Not literally African-American, of course, but you know what I mean.'

Barry says, 'It's stupid, right? That's what I love about it. It's just so stupid.'

Martin says, 'I love their pants. They're very baggy.'

Babs says, 'Should they have little belts?'

Glen says, 'That wouldn't be true to street.'

A junior account guy says, 'That's true. I've seen them. Always pulling up their pants.'

It dawns on me that everyone in the room is white.

Martin says, 'When's the meeting?'

Babs says, 'Thursday in Atlanta.'

Martin says, 'Knock 'em dead. If you don't come back having sold it, kill yourself.'

Babs laughs, but she's not entirely sure Martin is joking.

'Fin!' Babs says as she walks out of Martin's office smiling, her lips disappearing. I heard a rumor that her husband left her recently. Three children.

'Hey, Babs. How are you?'

Babs begins crying for no reason I can discern.

I say, 'Are you okay?'

And just as quickly she stops crying. Eyes wide, lunatic smile. 'Sure am, Fin.' Machine-gun

94

laugh out of nowhere, then gone.

Babs says, 'Did you hear we're trying to get the Dalai Lama for Crest White Strips?'

'Wow. Does he do advertising?'

'Who the fuck knows?!' she says, a giant smile still plastered on her face. I feel like she might explode.

'Sounds like a great meeting in there.'

Babs says, 'A great meeting. A *great* meeting. Leaving for Atlanta in about an hour. *Hotlanta*, they call it down there. More like *Shitlanta*. What a dump. Need to talk with you first thing after the New Year about the Doodles thing.' Her cell phone is ringing and she's readjusting the folio she is holding to her birdlike chest in order to answer it.

'Barbara Moss,' she says into the phone, nodding to me, smiling.

I nod and smile.

Merry Christmas, she mouths, and she's off, a trauma surgeon heading toward the ER.

'Good luck,' I shout, and see her bony arm come up and wave as she disappears down the hallway. God love her.

'Fin,' Martin says, from inside his office.

There's a Christmas morning atmosphere in Martin's office. Boughs with white lights adorn his window with a view to Bryant Park and the skating rink below. Gifts from clients, vendors, editorial companies, music companies, production companies. New Patagonia jackets here, an engraved bottle of Johnnie Walker Blue Label there. This is my future. This office. This is what I've been working for. Though the chances of me

95

ever getting here are comically slim. The simple truth is that there are far more talented people all around me. They possess a drive and passion for advertising that I lack. It's not that I don't work hard. I do. I enjoy work, enjoy accomplishing something, solving a problem, completing a thing. It's just that, for me, lately (and more and more often) there is always another voice competing with my own internal monologue. One that questions and laughs a lot and makes comical grimacing faces at the work, the gravitas, the inanity of it. Take Glen and Barry's idea, for example. I like it. It's something I couldn't come up with. It's exactly the kind of thing — done right — that will garner five million hits on YouTube in a two-week span. It's the kind of idea I used to get very excited about. But then the voice creeps in and says, '*Psst*. Hey, pal. Are you out of your fucking mind? That's the dumbest idea since the Chia Pet.' Cynicism is very dangerous in advertising. You must be a believer. If you stray, if you start questioning its worth and validity, its credibility, you are in for a very long day.

This voice is not present, I am sure of it, in the heads of the other creatives who've achieved far more than I have. Take the team that just launched the 'What's the Question Because the Answer Is Soup' campaign for Campbell's. The client called it 'breathtaking.' I happen to know that each team member received a bonus and an expensive, handmade Italian bicycle. When I talk with them, when I run into them in the hallway or the cafeteria or at a company event, they speak with great intensity about their work, an intensity and intelligence I admire, as well as their wardrobes and hair. I feel inferior to them and their awards, their quiet cool. Inevitably they ask about my work in voices of thinly veiled condescension. 'Missed you at Cannes this year,' they say, referring to the French city where the premiere annual advertising award show takes place. I often have a remarkably cutting comeback, such as, 'Oh, yeah? Well . . . that's because I wasn't there.'

There are bookshelves in Martin's office holding an impressive array of books, some on advertising, some on writing, and several volumes of the OED, which look to be quite old. Also a collection by Philip Larkin and three by Seamus Heaney. Mostly there are awards, dozens and dozens of awards, oddly shaped things, blocks of Lucite, gold-colored pencils, a winged lady, Greek-inspired surely, holding a globe overhead. Clios, Effies, Andys, Chuckies, Chippies. (I made up the last two.) The Clio is the big one. The name comes by way of Greek mythology, which seems right to me, as the essence of what we do is create and foster myth.

Martin is on his iPad. Emma brings in tea.

'Fin. Have a seat. Just finishing something up. Help yourself,' he adds, nodding to the pot of tea. It is a ritual of his, each afternoon around four. He has a large pot of tea and a tray of scones brought in from Tea & Sympathy in the Village.

It has crossed my mind that I may be here to learn the news of my impending (and much sought after) promotion to creative director. Considering the bloodbath of the past year (three rounds of layoffs) and the continued grim economic news, I can't imagine this chat is about a bonus.

Emma leaves and Martin turns to face me. 'Christmas has come early, Fin.'

I smile my fake smile. 'Really?'

'Indeed.'

My palms begin to tingle and perspire. I feel my promotion/bonus/ life-changing career moment coming, and I believe that I am an exceptional predictor of the future (though empirical data disproves this).

'I've just received a call from Brad,' Martin says.

Brad is the CMO of Snugglies, a division of General Corp., makers of baby diapers, adult diapers, soap, shampoo, cereal, candy, car tires, jet engines, diesel locomotives, and guidance systems for Tomahawk missiles.

Maybe Brad called Martin about me. Brad saw — helped Martin see — my worth, my uniqueness, my way not merely with words ('Does *your* diaper do this?'), but with people, how I inspire them, how, if I died tomorrow, the line for the wake would wrap around the block, the *Times* would publish the obit, I would be remembered. I mattered. Which is when Terry Gross begins to interview me for the many wondrous achievements of my storied career.

TERRY: This is *Fresh Air*. I'm Terry Gross. I'm talking with world-famous copywriter and poet Finbar Dolan. Your first book, *Me, How Wonderful*, a collection of poems and an international bestseller, is being made into a film directed by Ang Lee and starring both Brad Pitt and George Clooney as you at different times in your life. You've been asked to act in it and to write the screenplay. Is it hard to write a screenplay for a book of poems?

FIN: It is, Terry. But I was able to do it in a day.

TERRY: You chose to live in Paris for much of the writing. Why was that?

FIN: It's one of my favorite cities. I bought a home there. And, of course, I speak the language without any trace of an accent.

TERRY: You're the youngest member ever to be elected to *L'Academie française*.

FIN: Oui.

TERRY: That's an incredible accomplishment.

FIN: Thank you, Terry.

TERRY: You once landed a 747 safely after the pilot passed out. How did you know how to do that?

FIN: Luck. And of course a great deal of skill.

TERRY: You're far better looking in person than on your book jacket photo.

FIN: (*embarrassed*) That's very kind.

TERRY: You recently played against Roger Federer in a charity tennis tournament and beat him. Left-handed.

FIN: Roger's a sweet kid.

TERRY: What's the capital of Nevada?

FIN: Carson City.

TERRY: At what temperature are Fahrenheit

and Celsius exactly the same?

FIN: Minus forty.

TERRY: Marshal Phillipe Pétain oversaw Vichy France during World War Two. What color were his eyes?

FIN: Blue. A startling blue.

TERRY: This is *Fresh Air*. I'm Terry Gross. If you're just joining us, my guest is Finbar Dolan, copywriter, poet, hero. You mentioned climbing K2 without pants last year.

FIN: I wanted a challenge.

TERRY: What's sex like with Miss France?

FIN: Nice. Really pleasant. We had fun.

TERRY: How tall are you?

FIN: I'm six-five.

TERRY: Are most people happy?

FIN: That's a great question. I don't think so.

TERRY: Why?

FIN: They lack fulfillment in either love or work.

TERRY: You have a lovely speaking voice. How much can you bench-press?

FIN: Ohhh, I'm not sure, really. Two hundred and twenty-five pounds.

TERRY: You broke your former fiancée's heart.

FIN: Excuse me?

TERRY: You broke her heart. You embarrassed her and yourself. You called off a wedding with a month to go.

FIN: I . . .

TERRY: Your mother died.

FIN: Please don't . . .

TERRY: Your mother died when you were

young. Tell us about that.

FIN: Please don't do that.

TERRY: Are you close with your father?

FIN: Why are you . . .

TERRY: You have family. You have a sister and two brothers. Are you close? Do you keep in touch?

FIN: No. We, ahh . . . no. We kind of lost touch and . . .

TERRY: Your brother Eddie called you and asked that you call him back. Your brother. And yet you can't pick up the phone to call him. That seems sad and pathetic. You make no effort to keep in touch with these people, your siblings, your flesh and blood. Your family. You're a terrible person. What are your plans for Christmas?

*　*　*

'Fin?' It's Martin. 'I said, what are your plans for Christmas?'

I'm blinking quickly. I'm touching the scar on my face. I sip tea and spill some on my shirt.

'I'm going to Mexico.' I smile.

'Right. You mentioned that.' Martin leans forward in his chair, looks toward the door as if he is about to share nuclear codes with me. Quieter voice now.

'What if I told you that Snugglies was in possession of the world's first eco-friendly, one-hundred-percent biodegradable diaper that can be *flushed* down a toilet, not thrown into a landfill?'

His eyes are wide, his shock a mirror, he palpably hopes, of the shock and facial expression I will soon experience. He lets the news sit in the refined air. Then, right elbow on desk, he separates his thumb and forefinger, slowly rotating his wrist, as if carefully imparting a biblical insight: 'Redefining disposable diapers.' Eyebrows still raised (they look stuck up there at this point), Martin sits back and says, 'What d'ya think?'

Here is what I think, in an amount of time that perhaps only NASA could measure.

I think, I love when a hockey team pulls its goalie in the final minute of the game, down a goal. I think, I hate the word *panty*. I think, do I have an average, above average, or below average-sized penis? I think, where's the punch line to what Martin just said, because there has to be a punch line because I'm pretty sure I'm on a reality TV show and there's a camera filming my face and somewhere, behind the scenes, people are laughing at me. I think, this is one of those rare occasions where I have let the question, 'What do I do for a living?' come to the fore, where I question things, which is never a productive exercise for me. I think, my father's going to die and none of us care. I think, keep going, keep moving, keep smiling.

I say, 'Wow.'

Martin nods slowly and says, 'Wow in*deed*. I'm glad you see it that way. Brad said they've reconsidered the launch of this. Had planned on the Academy Awards in March but are excited and worried that Procter & Gamble have an identical product. Corporate espionage, Fin. So I think you know what that means.'

My expression suggests that I have no idea what that means. Is he asking me if I know what corporate espionage means?

Martin says, 'It means they want to launch on the Super Bowl.'

'Which Super Bowl?'

'The one in six weeks.'

'You're talking about the famous one. The football one. With the commercials.'

'Yes.'

'That's not possible.'

'Of course it is,' Martin says. 'I told them it is. Which means it is.'

'So, wait. Come up with a Super Bowl-worthy idea. Get it approved. Find a director. Prep it. Shoot it. Edit it. Mix it. Score music to it. Six weeks, with Christmas and New Year's in between.'

'Exactly.'

I say, 'Have I offended you in some way?'

'This is a great opportunity, Fin. I think you're the right man for the job. Truly.'

'How many other writers did you ask before me?'

'Two.'

'At five I would have been offended. So wait. You're asking me to cancel another vacation?'

'Absolutely not. How long's your vacation?'

'Seven days.'

'You should definitely go. Enjoy yourself. Relax. Forget work completely. But only for two days. A long weekend.'

'A regular weekend.'

'Two days. Much deserved. And maybe jot down a few ideas while you're there and send them to me. Each day. Then hop on a plane, come back, and work the week. What fun. The city's quiet, so is the office.'

'That's because everyone's on vacation.'

Martin says, 'We need to show ideas January second, in production first week of January, shooting second week of January. That means working over the break, I'm afraid. Exciting, though, Fin. You and Ian, Stefano and Paulie, Malcolm and Rajit. I chose only the single people. No families.'

'Stefano and Paulie and Rajit are all married,' I say.

'No children, though.'

'Paulie has two children.'

Martin blinks several times. 'I wanted to tell you first as I'd like you to lead the charge on this end, as I'll be away.'

'Where are you going?'

'Vacation. It's Christmas. Meeting to tell the teams in a bit. More tea?'

The lucky ones have a passion. The other ninety-eight percent of us end up doing something we kind-of, sort-of like-ish. The place where you show up for work each day for five, ten, twenty years is who you are. Isn't it? And yet, from time to time, there is that small voice that screams, 'Leave. Go. This isn't what you want.' Except that other voice, the one that calls you Gary, whispers, 'But where would you go? And what would you do?'

Two and a half hours later, two days before Christmas, one day before the agency closes until the day after New Year's, fourteen people sit grim-faced in a conference room ready to be briefed on a revolutionary diaper.

Ian, myself, Malcolm and Raj, Stefano and Paulie, Pam, Jill, Alan, Martin, and four people I've never seen before in my life, all of whom appear to be twenty-eight and taking notes, despite the fact that the meeting hasn't started. All have beautiful hair and sparkling white teeth.

One of the perfect-hair people hands out copies of the assignment, or what we call the 'brief.' Despite its name, it is six pages long, single-spaced, twelve-point Futura (the agency's typeface). Every brief aspires to answer the same questions: background, challenge, marketplace, problem we are solving for.

Alan says, 'Okay. Everyone? Let's get started, please. I know this is not what any of us had in mind for the holidays, but I think you'll see, after we've gone over the brief, that this is a special product and a special chance to make a difference.'

There are groans, almost exclusively from the creatives.

Paulie says, 'Like the Peace Corps.'

Everyone laughs. Except Martin.

Martin's voice is never loud. He has the ability to break through noise and be heard.

Martin says, 'The average baby goes through five thousand diapers before being potty-trained.

Because ninety-five percent of these diaper changes are disposable diapers, most of them end up in landfills. Fifty million of them get thrown away each day. Each one takes up to five hundred years to biodegrade.'

Everyone is listening. He is looking around the room, making eye contact. He's talking without notes.

He says, 'Disposable diapers are the third largest contributors to landfills in the world and yet only five percent of the population uses them. Diapers in landfills in underdeveloped countries are especially problematic because they often aren't properly disposed, and excrement leaks into the local water supply. No diaper — not even biodegradable ones — can break down in an airtight landfill. How many people in this room have children?' Forty percent of the room raises its hand. 'How many of you *plan* to have children?' Another forty percent goes up.

Martin says, 'Diapers? Soda? Candy? Toilet paper? Disparage it, make fun of it, call it dull, but never, ever say the products that touch the lives of billions of people every day don't make a difference. And what we're asking of you here today is to speak to the world. There are worse ways to make a living.'

He lets the silence play out and then turns back to Alan. 'Alan. You were saying?'

Alan continues. 'Okay. What business problem-slash-opportunity is the campaign designed to address?'

He walks through the document, Jill jumping in to help. They read almost word for word

106

what's on the page, skipping parts that are included on every Snugglies brief, such as 'Tone and Manner' (fun, informative, positive, upbeat, inspirational, unique, hopeful, anthemic, break-through).

Martin's phone rings and he steps out of the room.

Jill says, 'The point we're trying to communicate: New Snugglies Planet Changers are the first one-hundred-percent biodegradable, flush-able diapers.'

Alan says, 'This is nothing short of a revolution in disposable diapers. It is a breakthrough of epic proportions. It could change the world. And no, we can't use the Beatles song 'Revolution' because it costs too much and because the mayonnaise group used it last year for their new low-calorie mayo launch.'

Raj says something. Malcolm says, 'He says what do you mean by the word *toxic* on the last page?'

I hadn't seen it, as I hadn't really been paying attention. But there, on the last page, at the bottom, in smaller type, is a paragraph with the word *toxic*. In fact, the word *toxic* appears several times in the paragraph.

Ian says, 'Oh, goody. The fun part.'

Alan says, 'Malcolm, thank you for pointing that out. I was coming to that.'

Jill smiles. 'Good catch.'

Alan says, 'Let's talk about the mechanics of the diaper for a second. What makes them work is super-absorbent polymers.'

Raj says, 'SAP.'

Malcolm says, 'SAP.'

Alan says, 'SAP is the gel you find in disposable diapers and it's a miracle. It can absorb something like three hundred times its own weight. Chemicals, polymers, the genius of American innovation, right?'

No one so much as nods. Jill says, 'Absolutely.'

Alan says, 'Of course, no product is perfect. In *certain* studies, SAP has been linked to an increase in childhood asthma and a decrease in sperm count among boys.'

Stefano says, 'Unfortunate.'

Alan says, 'Most of you are too young to remember this, but SAP was removed from tampons in 1985 because of its link to toxic shock syndrome.'

Paulie says, 'Can we mention that in the spot?'

Alan ignores him. 'The industry did studies and found no connection to toxic shock in outerwear, including diapers, incontinence products, and feminine napkins, which all contain SAP.'

Ian says, 'The industry study found it was safe?'

Alan says, 'They hired independent researchers.'

Paulie says, 'I'm sure it was completely unbiased.'

Alan says, 'Am I sensing sarcasm within the ranks?'

Ian says, 'Alan. Light of my life, fire of my loins. You just told us Christmas is canceled for a world-beating product that lowers sperm count. I think we're all just processing this information.'

Alan says, 'Totally understood. And we're here to help.'

Paulie slips a piece of paper in front of me. It says, *Know what'd be a good name for a TV show? My Dad Is the Pope.*

My cell phone rings. The screen reads *Unknown.* I'm eager to step out of the briefing, so I answer as I get up and walk out of the room.

'Fin. It's Eddie.' My brother. Shit.

'Eddie. Hey.' I'm not sure when we last spoke. Three years? More?

'I called you a few times, left messages,' he says, sounding annoyed.

'I'm sorry. Completely my fault. Work's been busy.'

'Yeah.'

I say, 'So how are you?'

Eddie has no time or interest in answering. 'I got a call two days ago. He's in a hospital on the Cape.' Cape Cod. Last I'd heard he was in Florida.

Eddie says, 'You there?'

'Yeah.'

'Apparently it's bad.'

His voice is flat, cold, distant. He's been waiting to deliver this news his whole life but it's just not coming out like he's imagined. I think of my green bike. It appears with startling force. I see it, lying on its side on the grass in the yard by the back stairs. No kickstand. It had been Eddie's and then Kevin's, and there was no mud flap fender and when it rained there was always a stain from the muddy water along the back of your shirt.

I say, 'How did they find you? I mean, what made them contact you?'

'He's been in a nursing home. Gave them my name, apparently.'

How strange to think of him so close to Boston. How strange to think of him at all.

Eddie says, 'Anyway. Thought you'd want to know. I talked with Maura. Left a message for Kevin.' Our sister and brother. We share a last name, the four of us. We share a history. We share this dying man. But we share almost nothing else, not, say, the names of our friends and coworkers, details of our last vacations, the funny thing that happened the other day at the dry cleaner/the gym/Starbucks. We don't call to check in, to say *hi*. Eddie knows nothing of my day-to-day life, of who I've become. I know nothing about him, very little about his children. I'm not quite sure how it came to be that way. But I do know that once it happened it was far too easy to let it continue, to drift further and further away. You change what you want to change.

But here's the thing: The way I see it, there are maybe five or six really important things that happen in your life. Big things, I mean. Five or six things that define you, that stay with you. You were teased mercilessly in third grade because of a stutter, say; you had an uncontrollable erection (hypothetically) at age fourteen on a bus and had to go five stops past your stop before it was safe to alight; you were witness to an act of violence that never leaves you. Events that act as markers along the way, that change you, that may not

110

appear so obviously each day but that inform your actions, your outlook, your narrative. To date, for me, Eddie has been there with me for almost every one.

'Are you going?' I ask, knowing the answer.

'No.'

'Are you asking me to go?'

Silence. He was my best friend once.

He says, 'Look. Okay. I can't go. I've got . . . things. The kids. I'm just saying, all right? He's in the hospital.'

'Okay, then,' I say.

'Yeah,' Eddie says.

I hang up.

I go back into the room, take my seat. Jill's still talking about the brief. I can see that people are fading, doodling, texting. I also notice that someone has defaced a small corner of the large, expensive conference table. Someone has drawn a tiny picture of a turd. He is a turd man, with eyes and arms and little legs. Steam comes off his little turd head. He leans forward, as if atop a precipice, and from his little turd fist drops smaller turds — several of them are in mid-flight — into a basket below marked IDEAS.

WHERE ARE YOU GOING TODAY, MR. DOLAN?

Frank is speaking. My sense is that he's been speaking for some time now, though I don't know for how long or, for that matter, what he's talking about. It's the day before Christmas, and what says Christmas better than kissing the asses of several oil company marketing executives?

We are gathered — Frank, Dodge, Martin, myself — in the midtown offices of Petroleon, the ninth largest corporation in the world, with headquarters in either Dallas, London, or Dubai (they refuse to say which). Their New York offices occupy one of the greenest, most ecologically friendly buildings in the world, a tribute to renewable architecture and design, and a breathtaking public relations coup, high above the East River, just south of the United Nations. ' 'Green' isn't simply a wonderful marketing ploy for us, Fin,' one of the marketing people had said to me while we were all shaking hands. He kept shaking my hand as we spoke. 'We absolutely believe in it, as is reflected in our sizeable marketing budget. People say, 'Hey, aren't you guys an oil company?' No. We're an *energy* company. Even though technically ninety-one percent of our profits are derived from oil. *Oil* is an exceptionally dirty word, as focus group testing both quantitatively and qualitatively proves out in spades. Energy is clean. We're the good guys. Try the Danish. They're insane.'

There seemed to be very few humans in the halls — blond wood, glass, steel, plush carpeting — except for the receptionist and two armed guards. One is escorted everywhere at Petroleon — keycards, punched numbers, heavy steel doors. A humorless woman named Claire acted as our guide and took us to the conference room we're in now, asking that we sit anywhere, as long as it wasn't in the center of the table, north side, since that's where Mr. Cameron, Petroleon's CEO, sits.

Directly underneath the table at that seat, Claire said, is a panic button. Previous privileged guests to Petroleon, she tells us, not having had the advantage of Claire's direction, have sat in that seat and silently kneed the button. To their great surprise, approximately eighteen seconds later, an insistent knock had come at the door. The conferees did not answer correctly (a one-word password from Mr. Cameron to let the guards know he's not in a hostage situation) and six extremely serious men (three former SAS, two former Mossad, one former Navy SEAL) burst into the room, fingers on the triggers of short-barreled Heckler & Koch assault rifles. One of the conferees that day, a Stanford geologist giving a presentation on the composition of subocean mafic rock, wet himself. Claire tells this story in a quiet voice, a slim, knowing smile. 'One can't be too careful these days. Certain constituencies have taken offense to the work of Petroleon. You can't please everyone, can you?' Certainly not the indigenous people of Honduras, Liberia, and northern Brazil, where Petroleon has decimated groundwater supplies, been linked to absurdly high cancer rates, spilled millions of gallons of heavy crude, and, according to human rights organizations, hired mercenaries to murder protestors. You certainly can't please everyone, Claire. Especially if you're trying to kill them.

'It's an honor and a privilege to be in this room with you today,' Frank says with the gravity of an archbishop. In the car on the way over, Martin had coached Frank on his opening remarks.

'These are serious people,' Martin had said, mostly for Frank's benefit. Frank was focused on a grilled cheese sandwich at the time. 'They don't muck about. This isn't soda and it's not toothpaste. To do what they do they spend a billion dollars a month. Also, let's be very careful not to mention the spill of a few months ago.'

Martin says this because Frank has a bad habit of not being able to stop speaking when he doesn't know what he's talking about or is lying, two things he does often. He is a nervous speaker. This is due in part to severe self-esteem issues, causing him to both love and loathe himself in alternating moments. He can't believe he has the job he does, the money, the *stuff*. He feels he deserves it and, in the same moment, feels like a fraud. It makes for interesting meetings. He pops Xanax like Tic Tacs.

Frank says, 'What spill?' He has a blob of cheese on his chin.

Martin says, 'Third largest oil spill in U.S. history. Destroyed eight hundred miles of Alaskan coastline. Fishing, polar bear habitats, seal, otter, sea lion. They've offered money. But these things happen in a world hungry for oil, don't they?'

Frank says, 'Should I mention that?'

Martin says, 'No, Frank!'

Frank's job is simply the setup. 'It's the day before Christmas and all over this city agencies are closed, employees are gone, but we're here. Christ himself couldn't get us to Bethlehem to miss this opportunity to meet with you today.' He feigns a laugh. No one else so much as grins. Mostly they drop their heads out of embarrassment, pretend to make a note or check their BlackBerry.

Frank continues. 'Your company is a towering monument to what is good about this country. We love you. We don't want to leave. We never want to leave.'

I catch Martin making a small head motion to the senior client, a 'not-to-worry-we-will-leave-the-building-at-some-point' motion.

Frank hands it over to Martin, who deftly walks through the agency's credentials, showing a PowerPoint slide with the logos of our many internationally known brands — diapers, packaged goods, candy, fast food, soda . . . oil? Martin talks about our 'remarkable growth' during the 'nightmarish global recession,' but does not get around to saying exactly how we achieved that remarkable growth (we cut our fee after most of our clients demanded that we cut our fee, laid off 129 people, and imposed an across-the-board pay cut of five percent, all of which achieved remarkable growth).

A quick scan of the room suggests that someone appears to have dabbed a tiny, yet pungent speck of poo under their collective noses, if their expressions are any indication. Though, in casually turning to my left, I notice what may be the cause of their poo expressions. Dodge is sitting next to me, asleep. Martin has seen Dodge's sleeping visage a fraction of a second before I have and now appears to be sending me a signal with his eyes, as he is widening them to an unnatural state, one that looks painful. He is sending me a signal, I am sure of it, and that signal is to wake Dodge because Martin — I know this from the agenda in front of me, in front of all of us — is about to introduce Dodge, who, after rambling about God only knows what, will then introduce me, and I will impress the ninth largest company in the world by showing them a reel of commercials about diapers and candy.

And then, with his eyes closed, Dodge says, 'I was just thinking.'

It's somewhat difficult to believe he was daydreaming and not sound asleep, as he's curled his slight, boneless-breast-of-chicken body into a sideways ball in the chair.

'I often do that with my eyes closed,' he says, eyes open now, trying to find the focus, casually righting himself, as if he's just awoken from a lazy afternoon doze.

He continues, sounding oddly like Mr. Rogers.

'I was just thinking that it takes courage to make mistakes, doesn't it?'

Everyone is confused now, but he has their attention, this wee, curiously dressed man. He leans forward, arms splayed out on the polished table, and looks around, the confidence of a Harvard Business School grad. This is Dodge's genius. This is why he is a rich man.

Dodge says, 'I was told not to mention the spill. But I'm going to mention the spill, because to ignore it is to ignore an ugly pimple on the tip of your nose. Everyone knows it's there. And what you have is a big ugly pimple on your oily, oily nose.'

I'm excited because I can see that both Frank and Martin are terrified. I'm excited because Dodge is finally going to flame out, not be able to pull up from his bullshit nosedive. It is his Christmas bonus to me.

The reaction of the oily-nosed clients suggests profound confusion. In fact, it looks like one of them is on the cusp of saying something. But Dodge gets there first.

Dodge says, 'You're Babe Ruth. That's right. I just said Babe Ruth. We all know he hit the most home runs' — Dodge is unfamiliar with Barry Bonds — 'but do you want to know a little something else about the Babe? He also holds the record for most strike-outs. Now I'm not saying you've struck out or that you're a portly, cigar-smoking, dead baseball player. I'm saying that you get up there every day and swing the bat, do amazing things, and sometimes miss. Let's celebrate that. Let's celebrate the courage

117

of *effort*, the nobility of *trying*. Some fish died. They died in a noble cause. Some beaches were soiled. They were soiled in an effort — granted, a failed one — to bring the world energy. Think about that. To bring the world energy. To make it run. To make *lives* better. What's wrong with that? Can someone please tell me what's wrong with that?'

And just like that, as if someone threw a switch, Dodge loses his energy, sits back in his chair. The silence roars. It's the moment at the end of the car chase where the car is hanging off the edge of a cliff. Will it fall?

One of the senior executives says, 'I think that is a remarkable perspective.' And he smiles.

Frank is a giddy schoolgirl. 'That's why I love this man. If I weren't happily married . . . '

Martin cuts him off. Then he reels it in.

'Television. Print. Social media. We can envision a sweeping campaign. A campaign about Petroleon's courage.'

Look at their faces. You can see it all.

* * *

'What are you doing with your life, Mr. Dolan?' I hear the woman behind the American Airlines counter at JFK ask me.

'I beg your pardon?' I say.

'Where are we going today, Mr. Dolan?' the woman behind the American Airlines counter at JFK actually asks me.

'Well, Betty,' I say, looking at her nametag, 'we're going to Bhutan, to the Kingdom of

Bhutan. Have you heard of it? They have something called the Gross National Happiness. They measure people's happiness, not just their productivity.'

Betty gives me a fake smile. 'Says here you're going to Cancún.'

'Must be some mistake. Come with me, Betty. Do you have plans for the holiday? We'll pop over, try some local food, feel the happiness. It'll be great.'

She types quickly and hands me my boarding pass.

'I'd go, but I've got these family plans.' She smiles again. 'Gate forty-six. You're all set. Merry Christmas.'

'Merry Christmas, Betty,' I say.

I make my way to the Admirals Club and wait. I am one of the only people left, I think — certainly after 9/11 — who still enjoy airports. Airports to me — after the near strip search and often less-than-confidence-inspiring security staff — are places of possibility, of new beginnings. You've got a ticket on the red-eye to New York. Or do you? What about walking up to the ticket counter at British Airways and buying a ticket to London instead? What about connecting through London for service to Marrakech? What about LAX-Johannesburg, Johannesburg-Mumbai? Imagine waking up in Mumbai! Because it's possible. Because you *can*. I'm convinced, possibly by the glossy photos I see and the persuasive copy I read (photos and copy manufactured by my very own colleagues), that in these places — these St. Barths, these Kenyan safaris, these Bali beaches, these happy-obsessed Kingdoms — are the keys, the experiences, the visual and emotional stimuli that would bring happiness. I'm sure of this. And airports are the gateway. Don't think of a flight delay as a hassle. Think of it as an opportunity.

Have I myself done it? Have I found myself killing time in JFK or OHR or CDG, leafing through a swimsuit issue, drinking a coffee, staring at the crowds, and then changing my trip, my destination, my future? No. Never. Only a crazy person would do that. I'm just saying it's possible. Because I have these two tickets. These two first-class tickets, and I can go anywhere.

My phone rings.

'Hi,' I say.

'You're a jerk,' Phoebe says.

'Merry Christmas.'

'That was really sweet,' she says. 'Thank you.'

I put a gift on her chair before I left today. A hat and scarf from Barneys. It sounds boring but they're cashmere and she's been talking about wanting a new hat.

'Your fashionable warmth is my concern.'

Phoebe says, 'Where are you?'

'Airport.'

'You excited about your lonely trip?'

'Lonely? Maybe you're unaware that most of my relatives are Mexican?'

She says, 'You're an odd man.'

'Where are you?'

'On the Acela to Boston. I just got a beer. I'm wearing my new hat and scarf. I'm very happy.'

Three, four seconds of silence. I think about telling her about Eddie's call, about my father.

120

I say, 'Okay, then.'

Phoebe says, 'You good?'

'Never better.'

'Don't miss me too much, okay?'

'I'll try not to.'

I leave the Admirals Club and walk through the airport toward my gate. Businessmen hustle past awkwardly, holding briefcases, garment bags, pulling wheelie suitcases that won't stay steady. Families camp out eating makeshift dinners. I look for a seat alone but the gates are crowded with holiday travelers. I sit against the corridor wall and watch people pass. The wardrobes of many people strike me as aggressively casual. Teenage girls wear pajama bottoms and UGGs and oversized sweaters, pulling the sleeves down to cover their hands. They walk in pairs, laughing, bad posture, unsure of their bodies. A wave of sadness sweeps over me watching them, and I call home. My phone number growing up in Boston. I have done this a few times over the years. I usually get an answering machine but twice I've had to hang up on a real person.

A woman answers. 'Hey, did your cell phone die?'

I say nothing, confused for a moment.

She says, 'Steve?'

I'm about to hang up when I say, 'Is Fin there, please?'

It's my house. I can picture her, where she's standing, if the phone is at the same jack. The small kitchen with the windows looking out onto our small backyard. She's in my house. I should have asked for my mother. A quick word. What time's dinner? Is Dad home?

'Who?' she says.

'Fin Dolan. He used to live there.'

'No, I'm sorry, there's no one here by that name. You've got the wrong number.'

It's not the blatant, drunken screamer who does the real damage. Give me the father who beats you, who's always angry, any day of the week. At least I can learn to hate him. At least you know where you stand. It's the mood shifter who's the real danger. He's your friend, the mood shifter. *How was your day, dear? Really? No pork chops at the market? Oh, well. Hot dogs and beans is just as nice, isn't it, Finny? Maura? How's that homework coming?* She tiptoes through a mine field with harmless answers, my mother. She can see the other side, safety. It's going to be a good night. She can feel it. I'm sitting there. It's almost dinnertime. Maura is at the dining room table, in the next room, doing her homework. I can see her. We all feel it. All is calm. Except then he opens the cupboard and sees that we're out of Barry's Tea. His favorite. The only tea he drinks. No coffee. Never coffee. Tea. Barry's Tea. Two bags, two sugars, a lot of milk. Big cup. His hands are searching for it, moving packages and boxes, Saltines, Jiffy Corn Muffin Mix, baking powder, peanut butter. The hands moving faster now, violent hands no longer just moving things but knocking them over. He's mumbling, 'Where's the Barry's Tea? Where is the . . . it has to be here. We *have* to have Barry's Tea. I asked you for the Barry's Tea, this morning, before I left.

What was the *one* thing I asked before I left the goddamned *house* this morning before I went to work and put on a bulletproof vest for this family?! I asked you to get some Barry's *Tea!*' I turn to Maura, who's put her hands over her ears, to my mother, who's trying to say something — that she forgot, that she can go now, that she can be back in ten minutes, that it's okay. But it's not okay, he says, his voice louder. It's not okay. Kevin at the back door, just having gotten home, staring in at the scene.

I try to remember a specific Christmas Eve but it's a Thanksgiving that comes to me. Him blind drunk, trying to take the turkey out of the oven, falling, the bird skidding across the kitchen floor, Kevin and Eddie carrying him up to his room. My mother putting us in the car, stopping at a convenience store for turkey sandwiches and chips, driving in silence through 'rich' neighborhoods west of Boston, big houses set back from the road behind tall old trees and stone walls, no one drunk, no turkeys skating across the floor, everyone happy, heads bowed before the feast, giving thanks for life's riches.

They're calling a flight to Honolulu. They're calling a flight to Tokyo. They're calling a flight to Sydney. They're calling my flight to Cancún, where a car service will be waiting to whisk me an hour south to a small hotel on the beach. Twenty rooms. Clean white sheets. Highs of seventy degrees during the day, cool breezes at night. A fireplace in every room. Ocean waves lull you to sleep. Santa comes this evening bearing gifts. And I, in the great Christian tradition, head to Mexico alone. Just a few hours ago this plan seemed cool and independent and exciting. It suddenly seems pathetic, sad, and lonely. It's time to go. But I don't move. And it's then I know I'm not getting on that plane. I don't know when I decided it. It comes as a bit of a surprise to me as I stand a few yards from the gate, listen as they make the final boarding call, watch a few stragglers hustle past me, hand the gate agent their tickets. The two agents say good-bye to each other, safe flight, Merry Christmas, and one walks down the jetway while the other closes and locks the door with a key. I watch as the plane pulls back from the gate, turns, and taxis out toward the runway, to the line of waiting planes going to wonderful, exciting, exotic locations around the globe, as well as Cleveland, Minneapolis, and Muncie.

I turn to see the empty waiting area. The LCD sign above the check-in desk at the gate has changed from CANCÚN to SÃO PAULO. That flight's not leaving for three hours, though. I picture Phoebe on the train, a camera dollying down the aisle to find her staring out the window at the Connecticut coastline. She does this thing where she bunches her hair up and pushes it back, but it falls right back to the front of her face again. I picture Ian at home with Scott, getting ready to host their big dinner tomorrow. Paulie with his wife in Mamaroneck, putting the kids down so he can put toys together. Stefano and his wife in the West Village, making dinner. He mentioned that his mother was flying in from Italy today for the holidays. Malcolm, as always, spending the holidays with Raj and his wife. I pick up my laptop bag and my knapsack and start walking. There's a part of me that wants to go home but it would be empty and sad, too much of Amy left there in the silence. I walk hundreds of yards through the airport, past Sunglass Hut (two of them), past Cinnabon, past Sbarro, where a man looks at me for a long time, having just taken a massive bite of pizza, a comical look that says he wants to harm me, past a woman slowly mopping the floor, to the gate for the flight to Hyannis, Massachusetts, with brief layovers in Nantucket and Martha's Vineyard. I buy a ticket on a half-empty flight to spend Christmas with my father, a stranger I have not seen in twenty-five years.

★ ★ ★

He's dead.

This is what I think when I look at him from the doorway of his hospital room. His eyes are closed and he's not moving and his face and hands are an unnatural color for a human. It looks like him but it doesn't. I can't believe he's dead. Except he's not. The sheets are pulled tight around him and you can see his chest rise and fall slowly, hear the beeps and blips of the machines that signify he's alive.

And just that quickly I wish I hadn't come. Why am I here? It's not for him. It's for the idea that it seemed like the right and noble thing to do. It's something one might see in a commercial: *Open. An airport. Night. Tired businessman about to board a flight when his cell phone rings. 'Hello?' Long pause. 'Where? No, it's just . . . we haven't seen each other in a while. No. Okay. Thanks.'*

He walks to the jetway, is about to hand the ticket to the attendant, when he turns and runs.

Cut to him pulling up to the hospital in a cab.

Cut to him in his father's room.

Cut to a tight shot of him holding his father's hand.

Cut to a nurse, buxom, leaning over the bed . . . wait . . . lose the nurse.

Cut to his father opening his eyes, the surprised look. 'Fin. I'm sorry,' he whispers, voice hoarse. 'Don't leave me.'

United Airlines.

I like it. It works. It works because we can imagine it, because we've seen it or something like it hundreds of times. It's emotional comfort food, a known narrative, like the ABC Sunday Night Movie or Leno jokes.

Except here, now, someone's not following the script. My father's not waking up to say his lines. Even if he did I wouldn't really care. I want to leave and head as fast as possible to New York, to the Ear Inn, to the White Horse Tavern, to Corner Bistro. I want to call Ian, call Phoebe, call someone. Yes. I will do that. I do not want to be here. It's Christmas Eve, for Christ's sake. I want to be home. Or at the very least on a plane to Mexico. I don't know whether to stand or sit.

'Can I help you?'

A nurse appears beside me. She looks like a nurse. I wonder if I look like a copywriter in my

126

blue jeans, boots, and $300 James Perse sweater that Ian and Phoebe made me buy.

'I'm Fin Dolan.'

'His son. Of course. I'm Margaret Nash.'

His son? Legally, I guess.

We shake hands and I think of the proximity her hands have to death and disease. Where does anatomical waste go? (According to an article in *Harper's* some time ago, it goes primarily to one of three places: New Jersey, Staten Island, or Delaware. What is it, exactly, about these places that willingly accept ill-functioning kidneys, spleens, and bloody, viscous tissue?)

'I'm so sorry,' Margaret Nash says. 'This must be very difficult for you.'

'It is, yes,' I say with a pained look, as if I'm a character on a soap opera.

'He's stable now. It's a matter of time, of course, until we know something. The doctor should be around shortly.'

'Thank you,' I say to Margaret, who may be forty-eight or may be sixty-two. She has short, shiny silver hair. She's a healthy woman, if her clear eyes and high coloring are any indication.

'You must be very close,' she says.

'Actually, no. I haven't really seen much of him in twenty-five years.'

'Oh . . . '

'I'm sorry. I didn't mean to embarrass you,' I say. 'He left when I was twelve.' I shrug, fake a smile.

'It's good of you to come.'

We both look at him, not quite sure what to say.

The hospital is quiet, almost no one in the hallways. A machine beeps, then hisses. My mother taught me to dance. She taught me the fox trot, the waltz, the rumba. I got quite good at it, a natural, she said. I could take hold of Margaret right now, sweep her into a nice, long-striding, three-step waltz. *Bum-ba-bum, bum-ba-bum, bum-ba-bum* . . .

'They say it helps to talk to them,' Margaret says, looking at my father, arms crossed tight across her chest. 'They hear your voice, somewhere inside.'

What about stabbing them?

She looks at me now, the benevolent nurse's smile. 'You could read him a story or a book. Music helps.' Now she shrugs. We're shruggers. We know nothing, really. We're all just guessing.

'Thank you,' I say. 'I'll give it a try.'

'Cafeteria's open until nine. It's not much but it's about the only thing you'll find open tonight.'

She smiles and walks away.

There is a window that looks out onto the back of the hospital, a small power plant of some kind, steam coming from one of the buildings, hospital vehicles parked, two men, janitors, smoking in the distance. I'm glad that I don't have to wear a uniform to work.

It seems to me that I must look exactly like a man should look in his dying father's room, standing by the window, pensively. It's the never-ending commercial again. You wouldn't even need to light this room. There's gorgeous light coming in from the powerful sodium

128

streetlight in the back parking lot, light coming in through the door. I want to share this idea with sturdy Margaret. But what's the product? How about Hallmark cards? A caring son visiting his douchebag father. Daddy's in a coma. The caring son reads the card aloud. The father wakes, brought back from the walk toward the light by his loving son's voice. The son then smothers the helpless father to death with a pillow.

Advertising often attempts the structure and devices of drama and film. And yet for the most part we are, I think, wildly disappointed when, after twenty-three deeply moving seconds of footage showing a grandmother trying to climb the stairs alone with her grocery bags, we see a Hallmark card awaiting her. *Happy Thursday, Nana. Just thinking of you. Love, Petey!*

I believe that if the story could somehow continue, in thirty-second installments, it would be more interesting. Not merely another Hallmark commercial, but another product. In the next spot, say, we might see Nana open the door and collapse, the victim of a massive heart attack (pharmaceutical industry). Where's the adorable grandson now?

Imagine it. Several advertisers, we'd never know which one until the end, pooling money, a kind of rolling, continuous TV commercial that never ends. The drama is constant. You don't ever know what it's for because it's constantly changing!

Death. It is one reality we refuse to face head-on in advertising. I think it's time to change that. The question is, can you move product with it? I broached this very topic with Boeing some years ago, late one evening after a day of shooting interior shots of a mock-up of a new 777–400 (their roomiest passenger jet) on a lot at Universal.

'What do you mean the plane *crashes?*' the client asked, his drink suddenly frozen midway to his lips. Hal? Herb? I could never remember.

'I mean it *crashes*, Hal,' I'd said, three-too-many scotches in. 'And we see it crash. We see all of it.'

'Let me see if I understand you,' he'd said, rather slowly if memory serves. 'You are proposing to make a television commercial wherein you *crash* one of our planes. One of our $400 million planes. On television.'

'That is *exactly* what I'm proposing,' I'd said, feeling the rush of the scotch, the heat of the gas fire in the lobby of the elegant Shutters hotel in Santa Monica, that heady feeling of power from talking to the client about an idea that, in this moment, seems to me genuinely brilliant.

'Let's take the gloves off of advertising. Let's see the luggage strewn on the runway. Let's see the random shoe, the eyeglasses that somehow survived the superheated flames. I want to do for advertising what Brando did for theater. Wake people up. Make them feel again. And, to a great extent, horrify them. There's no sound in the commercial. But then, a voice-over. Alan Rickman, maybe. English. Americans love the English. 'No one can guarantee your safety when you step onto an aircraft. But at Boeing, we're working harder than ever to make sure that you're as safe as you can be.' Something like that. We can tweak it. Herb? Your thoughts?'

Six weeks later we lost the account. I never mentioned the conversation to anyone.

★ ★ ★

Margaret returns with a doctor and another nurse.

'This is Dr. Benjamin, your father's doctor.'

He shakes my hand and winks at me.

'Mr. Dolan,' he says. 'I'm sorry I was unable to speak with you yesterday.'

'I didn't call yesterday,' I say, looking at Margaret and the other nurse for some reason. The other nurse is perhaps twenty-five and strikingly beautiful.

The doctor says, 'Your father is in what we call serious but stable condition.' Which makes me wonder if others call it something else. 'He's had a myocardial infarction.' He winks at me again. He enunciates these last two words, saying them slowly.

'Is that a real word?'

'Is what a real word?'

'*Infarction*,' I say.

'In common parlance, it means a heart attack,' Dr. Wink says. Double wink. Which is when I realize that it's not a wink, it's a tic. It's a tic that makes it difficult to concentrate on what he is saying about my dying father because it's like a video game, where you're waiting for the next wink. I have an expression on my face that suggests I am listening intently. I watch myself act intense. I think my look is the right one for this situation.

' . . . motor skills and speech,' he continues. Wink. I want to react, to pre-guess when the winks are going to come.

I nod slowly, as if understanding. Heather. The other nurse's name, according to her tag.

'So we wait,' he says. 'We watch.' Wink, wink. 'So often medicine is a matter of waiting for the body to heal itself.'

'Yes,' I say.

'You might want to try reading to him,' he says, and I look to Margaret, who smiles. 'It's been known to help.'

'Thank you,' I say.

He nods, with crisp, military precision, then winks twice and walks away.

Margaret, Heather, and I smile at one another and then they turn to leave.

I stand there looking at him. The change from what I remember is extraordinary and disturbing. He is smaller. His cheeks are hollowed and the skin appears thin, blue veins visible underneath. Were he to shave, blood would burst forth from his face. He is an old man.

But then, he was always old to me. He waited to get married. Perhaps it was a sign. Perhaps he never really wanted any of it. Who waited to get married back then, home from the war, aged by what they had done and seen? They were eager to get on with life, to marry and start a family. Not him. He waited almost ten years. And then they had trouble having children, my mother suffering two miscarriages before finally having Eddie in 1960. Kevin followed two years later. Maura four years after that. And that's how it was supposed to stay. Except I happened. *The little mistake*, he once called me. He was forty-four, an older dad back then.

There were times, after he left, when I would find my mother standing at the kitchen sink, water running, staring at a dish or the wall or the faucet. I wondered what she was thinking about in those long moments. Sometimes she'd be crying. People leave. People die. The secret no one tells us is that we don't get over it, ever.

When Kevin was sixteen and obviously gay, some neighborhood children caught him and another boy kissing in the woods near our home. My father heard the story — everyone in the neighborhood did — and he walked into Kevin's room that evening, the room Kevin shared with Eddie, and began beating him. My mother ran up from the kitchen, wondering what had crashed to the floor. Which is when she saw her husband beating her child, her sweet, kind son who helped her in the kitchen and with laundry and who liked to cook. I'd never heard her scream like that before. Kevin cowered on the floor. I don't know where Eddie came from — I just remember thinking he was moving very fast. And maybe he didn't realize that the person he was grabbing and throwing against the wall was our father. He probably knew when he grabbed fistfuls of my father's shirt, tearing it, pushing him against the wall so hard that my father's head bounced off the wall and for many years after there was an impression in the plaster. I was standing in the hallway, just outside the room. I had been on my way to go hang out with Kevin when my father marched by me and told me to stay out. I stood there and saw the whole thing. I saw as Kevin took his hands away from his face that they were bleeding. *He must have cut his hands*, I thought. And for just a moment I thought he'd put something in his mouth, some Halloween-like thing to make it seem like blood, only it wasn't a Halloween thing, and he spit up real blood on the floor, and he was shaking, and my mother went to him, held him, took the sleeve of her shirt and held it to his nose and she looked up, at me and Maura, and shouted for Maura to take me away. Only Maura couldn't pull me away. She stayed behind me and put her arms around me while Eddie's hand went to my father's throat and clutched it and squeezed it, so that my father winced in pain. Eddie was almost as big as my father then — not as wide, maybe, but strong and fit and angry. He and Kevin are two years apart in age. They rarely got along, rarely even spoke. And it was common knowledge in the neighborhood and at school, at the skating rink and the parks, that Kevin was a sissy and a fag and a homo and all the other words people used. But God help the person who dared harm Eddie Dolan's brother.

My father's hands went to his own throat. He couldn't breathe. Eddie's face was contorted in rage and he was biting his own tongue so hard that he had blood on his lips. He was throwing punches now, at my father's head and neck and

134

chest, hitting his own hand holding my father's throat. My mother looked up from the floor, from Kevin, holding him still, and screamed, 'Stop it!' Only Eddie didn't hear her. I think perhaps Eddie meant to kill our father, to finally stop him, stop the rage and outbursts — Eddie, even when he was smaller, standing up for my mother, taking the slapping and beatings because of it. The fear we all felt every moment our father was home.

Eddie pulled his hand away from my father's neck, which was pink and red. My father slumped a bit, breathing erratically. He looked around and must have seen the horror on my face and Maura's, too, and his bleeding, scrawny, harmless, lovely gay son, and his small wife crying, and his oldest boy, standing at the ready, sideways, right fist clenched so tight his knuckles were white, prepared to go again, wanting to go again, to beat him to death if need be.

My father left the next day for work and did not come home again.

★ ★ ★

I measure time in memories, fixed points, a street corner where a thing happened, where I will sometimes wonder, years later, why that same thing doesn't still exist every time I pass that street corner. Where did the event go?

Right now I am sitting in the kitchen of our house on Willow Road, eating a fried bologna sandwich because I have a slight fever and stayed home from school. Mostly I think my mother wanted the company. The table is Formica-topped with stainless steel legs, one of which wobbles, so we keep a folded napkin under it. There is a picture window looking out onto the backyard and the Carneys' house beyond. There's a radio tuned to a station that plays swing music, and my mother is smiling. And then it's gone. I run out of film.

We would hear about him from time to time. Occasionally we'd get a visit from one of the cops in his precinct. They'd take a collection and give my mother an envelope. Kevin told me that Eddie went looking for him after he left, waited for him outside the precinct house one night. There was a scuffle, some punches thrown. My mother heard about it. Kevin said she sat Eddie down and begged him to stop what he was doing. She said, 'You're becoming like him.'

It was strange after he left. We never spoke of it, but it hung in the air. His clothes remained in her closet, his coats on the hallway pegs. Until one day my mother gathered them up, with Maura's help, and drove them to Goodwill.

I thought she'd be happy with him gone. I thought things would get better. But they didn't. She changed. She spoke less, smiled rarely. I would walk in the back door and find her sitting at the kitchen table, looking out the window, a cigarette between her fingers, a long ash about to fall. As much as she wanted him to leave, something happened to her that day that I never fully understood. I didn't see what was so terrible. I didn't miss him. She died a little when he left. She went to church more. Maura and I

136

would go with her on Sundays. But then she started going on weekdays, too, early morning masses. In the evening, after dinner, the occasional Pall Mall and an Irish coffee, she'd retreat into her room, close the door. But after she died, it was different.

My father showed up at the wake. He walked in, knelt at the casket, his face a few feet from his dead ex-wife, her powdered lips sewn shut, the fluids drained out of her, pumped full of formaldehyde, bearing little resemblance to a living, breathing human being. That's how I saw it, anyway. I simply didn't believe that it was her, lying there. I wondered then, and sometimes now, what went through his mind during those few moments when everyone in the room at the James Gormley & Sons Funeral Home in Charlestown, Massachusetts, watched him walk in, felt the air leave the room, the hush that came over the place, looked to Eddie, watched him flush, saw the anger in his eyes. We all watched him as he blessed himself again, after maybe a minute, then he stood up and walked over to us. I stopped watching him because I turned to look at Eddie. And what I saw, as my father stood in front of his children, as we looked at him, was Kevin reach for Eddie's hand, palm open, as if to say, *Don't*.

He didn't speak for a time, and when he did, he spoke to a silent room. The booming, angry voice was gone.

'Your mother was a fine woman. She . . . she loved her children very much.'

He was looking down at a point on the carpet as he spoke.

'I'm terribly . . .'

The pants of his suit were too short. He didn't seem to know what to do with his hands. The four of us in a line. Eddie, Kevin, Maura, and me. I was looking at Maura and Maura was looking at the ceiling and Eddie was fast-breathing and I wondered if he was going to hit him.

The thing is that there were inconsistencies. That's what the police said. There was nothing wrong mechanically with her car, an old cream-colored Chevy Nova. No brake-line problem, no steering problem, none of the tires blew. A man from the life insurance company came to our house and asked if she'd been feeling depressed lately. That struck me as an odd question. Her husband walked out on her eighteen months earlier. It's a myth that time heals wounds. Not all wounds. Chemicals play a role. Then a nothing thing happens. You might look at, say, a Boston Bruins ashtray in the living room that he once used while watching the games. The sound of a lawn mower on a Saturday. The smell of aftershave on the man in front of you at the post office. A husband and wife in the distance laughing about something. The memories of the shouting recede. The early years return. One plans a life, writes a script, an outline at the very least. We will be different. We all think this. We shall deftly avoid the cancers and the premature death, the car accidents and job loss, the miscarriages and affairs. What was it like for her at night, late, alone, in bed?

I'd gotten home early from school. That day.

April 14. Our class had taken a field trip to the aquarium. She was on her way out to the car. We were standing outside.

I said, 'Where are you going?'

She looked at me for a time and then said, 'You're not supposed to be home.'

'We got back early. They let us go.'

'Petersen's,' she said. 'For milk. We need some things.' Petersen's Market. It was just down the street. Spring Street.

I turned to go into the house. She said, 'Finny.'

I stopped and looked back.

She reached her hand out, touched my face, my cheek, smoothed my hair. She looked like she wanted to say something. She looked tired. I watched her get in her car and back out, drive up the street. And I saw my bike, this crappy green bike that I had, lying on the grass next to the back stairs. I thought about moving it to the shed out back in case it rained but I didn't.

There are things you should never write down. For example, I think that it is not a good idea, for anyone involved, to get a large manila envelope in the mail a month or so after your mother's funeral addressed to *The Dolan Children* from your mother's best friend, Mary Downey. I think it is a mistake for Mary to write a short note: *Your mother asked me to send this to you. I am so sorry. Mary.* And I think that it is dangerous to send a one-page letter to your children telling them how much you loved them, talking of the *hole* in your heart, the *joy* that had gone out of your life, the *mistakes* and *sins* and

139

guilt, the *prayers* you had said for all of us, yet never saying the words *I am now going to drive my cream-colored Chevy Nova directly into the large elm tree at the bend in the road on Spring Street, the too-sharp bend, the site of so many accidents over the years, the tree just beyond the entrance to St. Joseph Cemetery.*

Eddie had told us to come to the kitchen. He read the letter. I don't remember much of it. I do remember that Maura held a dishtowel in her balled-up fists, her eyes wide, as if she were going insane. Kevin sobbed and said, 'Oh Jesus oh Jesus oh Jesus.' The muscles in Eddie's jaw moving, reading the letter with his teeth together, his voice cold and angry. As for myself, just as when my father left, I remember thinking that it wasn't real. I remember feeling as if it weren't happening to me. What I do remember very clearly is thinking this: What was going through her mind as she accelerated and turned the wheel toward the tree? I wondered if she was crying or mildly excited about doing something so dangerous or if she was scared. Was she smoking, as she often did in the car? Was the radio on? I remember watching them, my sister and brothers, that day. There was a tree in the backyard, the long, thin branches of which would scrape against the window when it was windy. It drove my father nuts. It scraped now, in the wind. They seemed far away and sad. I watched them, all four of them, me included. How could I tell them that it was okay, that it would be fine, that it wasn't true. That it couldn't be true.

I know that Eddie made a copy of her letter and mailed it to my father. I wonder what it was like to receive that.

Standing in front of his children, at his wife's wake, my father finally looked up.

He said, 'She deserved better than me. You all did.'

I stood closest to him. He seemed to be in so much pain. He seemed a stranger to me, a sad man in a bad suit. *Someone should help him*, I thought. I was going to say 'Dad.' I was going to put my arm out, touch him. That's what I thought. I could see it in my mind. But then he turned and walked out.

In the evenings, long before, when it was good, he would sit with a cup of tea, alone, after dinner, and leaf through the Sears catalog, humming.

My cell phone rings. I don't recognize the number.

'Hello?'

'Mr. Dolan?' I realize that I'm toying with my father's IV tube, flicking it with my index finger, causing small bubbles to form, which I don't think is a good thing.

'Mr. Dolan, Dwayne Nevis from American Express. Great news about your account. You're now Executive Platinum. Would you have a moment to talk about the benefits?'

IT'S THE MOST WONDERFUL TIME OF
THE YEAR

The woman behind the desk at the hotel says with a big grin, 'Are you here for Knockwurst Night?'

'I'm not sure how to respond to that, but no, I don't think I am.'

'Oh, okay, then.' The grin remains intact.

'Just a room, if you have one.'

She chuckles. 'Wide open tonight. Take your pick.'

'Something quiet, please.'

'You're on Cape Cod in the winter. Quiet is guaranteed. Let's see here. I'll put you in one of our nicest rooms, how about that?'

There's a hotel in Venice, Italy, called the Danieli that sits on the Grand Canal. There's a hotel in Bangkok called the Mandarin Oriental that serves high tea each afternoon. There's a hotel in Buenos Aires called the Alvear that has a butler on each floor. There's a hotel in Cape Cod where the room smells of mold and stale cigarette smoke and the TV is locked to the console, which is a pity because I was thinking of stealing it. The bedspread is a polyester paisley that looks like it's seen better days.

I dial Ian.

He says, 'I hate you. What's the temperature?'

I say, 'Eighty-one degrees. Sun's just set and

I'm on my second ice-cold Dos Equis.'

Ian says, 'You sound weird. You're lying. Where are you?'

'Cape Cod.'

'What? Why? What happened?'

'My father's dying.'

'Jesus. Fin. I'm sorry.' He pauses for a moment. 'Wait. I thought your father was dead. You told me he died years ago.'

'I might have said that. He's not, though. Not yet.'

My room looks out on the parking lot. A car pulls in and I watch as five men dressed as Santa get out of a car. They're laughing and talking loudly. They seem drunk. I lean my face against the window and exhale from my nose, watch the condensation form on the window, see that my left nostril is the one with the most air. I read once that it switches throughout the day, that it's never even.

I say, 'My brother called. Someone from the hospital called him. No one was going to come down. I just thought . . . ' I don't know what I'd thought.

I say, 'You wouldn't think it was so hard to take a vacation, ya know?'

'How is he?'

'Not good. Heart attack. A thousand years old. Smoker. Drinker. Ate red meat like M&Ms. They say it's a matter of time.'

'You want me to fly up? I'll come up in the morning. I'll bring Scott. We'll drive to P-Town, have dinner. We'll make a thing of it. I'm serious.'

I lean back from the window and I can just

make out, as if I'm almost not there, my own reflection. I can see that I have a slight smile on my face. Ian's got ten people coming to his apartment tomorrow and he would cancel it and get on a plane to be here with me. He is more like family to me than my family.

I say, 'You're a selfish prick, ya know that?'

'Seriously.'

'I'm fine. To be honest it's really not that different from the Yucatán Peninsula. Gorgeous, dark-skinned people, a very relaxed attitude.'

'Call me, okay?'

'I just saw five drunk Santas.'

'Is that a band?'

I'm about to hang up when I say, 'I don't know what I'm even doing here. I mean, I haven't seen him since I was twelve.'

'You're doing what you're supposed to do. He's your father.'

'In theory.'

Later, I turn on my computer, check e-mail, and for a moment consider working on Snugglies. But suddenly I am a camera on a crane outside this hotel looking through this window at me on my laptop on Christmas Eve. Alone. Time to go to a commercial break.

★ ★ ★

Sadly, I never spot the drunk Santas again. I sit at the bar and drink a beer and enjoy a knockwurst (as you do on Christmas Eve) and the musical stylings of Surf'n' Sand, a seventy-ish-year-old couple, he on piano, she holding a microphone

144

and making noise into it with her mouth. Some might call it singing.

Surf (Sand?) plays 'Moonlight in Vermont.'

I look over to see two women looking back at me. They look over and smile. Nothing good will come of this. And so I decide to say nothing. Which is when I open my mouth. 'Hi.'

'Hi,' they say, all smiles.

'Mind if we join you?' one of them asks.

'Please do.'

'You look lonesome over here all by your onesies,' one of them says. I have made a horrible mistake.

'Fin,' I say, extending my hand.

'Hi, Fin. That's Marta and I'm Janie.'

We shake hands, sit, and smile at one another for what seems like forty-five minutes.

'Are you staying at the hotel, Fin?' It's Marta.

'I am, Marta. Do I detect a slight accent?'

'You have good ears.'

'Marta, I'm going to guess Holland.'

'Germany.'

'That was my next guess.' I laugh out loud. They laugh with me. Marta points and raises her eyebrows as if to say, 'Good one!' I have glasses for distance, though I rarely wear them. Closer, I see that Marta and Janie are fifty if they are a day. Indeed, they may be closer to fifty-five. And yet, in their own way, in their St. John outfits, the hem of Janie's skirt a bit too high, Marta's black slacks a size too small, the blouses knowingly too snug, too revealing, they are remarkably well-preserved. Though, at some point, a grown woman should stop calling herself Janie.

'What brings you to Cape Cod on Christmas Eve?' I ask.

'Divorce and rotten kids,' Janie says, smiling. Marta laughs.

'Ha,' I say.

'No, really,' Janie says. 'We needed some me time. Some us time. Some time, I guess is what I mean.'

'I think that sounds great,' I say.

'We're driving to Provincetown tomorrow and staying at an inn.'

That doesn't sound sad at all.

'You know who he looks like,' Janie says to me, but I have to assume she is talking to Marta. 'He's the spitting image of a young Tommy Lee Jones.'

Marta has the blank look of a woman who grew up watching East German national TV and Franz Beckenbauer and lightly veiled anti-Semitic dramas (*'Das Juden Frau'*) featuring broad-shouldered, big-toothed, fondue-eating Germans who border on good-looking but are mostly just scary. She clearly has no idea who Tommy Lee Jones is. But she nods slowly. Janie looks at Marta.

'Marta, he's the one from, ya know, oh, what's that one where the prison bus falls over and Sela Ward gets her head smashed in?'

'*The Fugitive?*' I offer.

Janie snaps her fingers and points at me. 'That's the one.'

'Jaaaaaaa,' Marta says, realizing who Tommy Lee Jones is. 'But noooo,' she says. 'No, I don't zink zo.'

'Yes, Marta. He's the spitting image of a young Tommy Lee Jones. Look at his eyes.'

'Doesn't he have very bad skin?' I ask.

Janie nods. 'He does. But you don't. That's not what I mean. Facially. Bone structure.'

I take a big gulp of my beer.

'Ya know who I get a lot?' I ask.

'Who?' Janie wonders, leaning forward.

'Gandhi.'

You can almost hear the tumblers falling into place. The slight squint. Click.

'Gandhi,' Marta says, howling with laughter, turning to Janie. 'Gandhi. Yeah, yeah. Only he doesn't look like Gandhi, though.' Making the final ironic link for herself, desperately fighting her German DNA.

'You're a pistol,' Janie says, laughing. 'Marta, he's a pistol. That's funny. Gandhi. Very funny. Now which one was he?'

Janie catches me looking at her abundant cleavage and smiles.

'What is your line of work, Tim?' Marta asks.

'It's *Fin*, Marta,' Janie says, smiling but annoyed. 'Not Tim.'

They're both drunk. Marta keeps trying to make her eyes wider, as if trying to adjust the focus.

'I'm a freelance U-boat captain,' I say.

Janie says, 'That sounds interesting. Do you like it?'

Marta says, 'Did he say 'U-boat'?'

Janie says, 'Wait. What do you mean? Like . . . a submarine?'

'That's exactly right. I pilot German-made

147

submarines on a freelance basis.'

Janie, still smiling, though the smile is changing into a bad-smell confusion.

'I don't understand.'

A waitress comes over with a basket of buffalo wings, hot sauce, sour cream, and a porno-graphic knockwurst with a side of hot mustard. Both of them go at it like rabid animals, not taking their eyes from me as they eat, too drunk to know that their hands are covered in sauce.

'I think he's funning with us, Marta.'

'I am funning with you, Janie. No, I'm a copywriter at an ad agency,' I say.

'Oh my land!' Janie says. 'That sounds quite exciting. What does that mean exactly?'

'I write television commercials, Janie. I come up with the ideas for TV commercials.'

'Did you hear that, Marta? He writes television commercials. You know what one I like is that little dog for the taco place. He is so cute. I like the funny ones.'

'I wrote that commercial, Janie,' I lie.

She screams. Screams like she's won the lottery.

'You are a *famous* person.'

'In many ways I am. I travel only by private jet, if that's what you're wondering.'

'I find television commercials confusing,' Marta says to a buffalo wing.

Janie says, scooping a wing and dunking it in sour cream, up to her second knuckle, 'I once saw a commercial where they fired a gerbil out of the cannon and I laughed and laughed.'

'And why wouldn't you?' I say.

Janie's hand is on my knee. Her eyes are red, exploded blood vessels. Her breath smells of booze and soup.

'What's your room number?' she says, a grin on her face.

It's getting late.

★　★　★

I want to call Phoebe but it's late. I start to text her but stop. She thinks I'm in Mexico. Why worry her?

I flip through the channels. MTV and VH1 and Portuguese news and all-Arabic dramas and kickboxing and a Latvian documentary about a dairy farmer with one arm and a Hallmark special about a mentally challenged boy lost in the woods who finds the true meaning of friendship with an animal and a program on the History Channel about Nazis that they seem to play a lot and a thing on the Discovery Channel about gigantic equipment and the history of gigantic equipment and old footage of steam shovels and newer footage of trucks the size of ocean liners and there are movies, lots of movies, all of which I've seen before but I watch them nonetheless. And there are commercials. Foot odor and erectile dysfunction and toilet paper and tampons and cars, lots of cars, almost all on a road with no other cars, going fast, far too fast it seems, on winding, rain-slicked roads, leaves flying, and there are ones for beer, with a young guy doing something to get a young girl's attention but embarrassing himself in the process and his friends watching the entire time and laughing in the corner only the girl thinks it's cute and sits with him anyway and a line at the end, intoned by a cool-dude voice-over who says something like, 'Because life's worth living' or 'What it means to be a man' or 'Here's to good times,' jumbles of words that mean nothing, that merely sound like they mean something, words that were thought about by large groups of intelligent people for months at a time. Words that in some cases were written by me or my colleagues, there, on TV. If you only knew what went into it. The hours, the days, the weeks, the meetings, the stress, the deadlines, the money, the approvals, the casting, the flights, the hotels, the flare-ups, the drinking, the casual sex, the hope that it will mean something because at the time it certainly seemed to. It seemed to be important. And then you see it on TV. And it goes by so fast. A shot we spent half a day lighting is on the screen for eighteen frames — less than a second, a second being twenty-four frames, unless it's video and then it's thirty frames. The point is . . . what is the point? I look for *It's a Wonderful Life*, but can't find it anywhere.

⋆ ⋆ ⋆

I wake early and have no idea where I am. It's still dark, 7 A.M. I take a long, hot shower, make coffee in my room. It tastes like coffee I made in my room. I have two hours before visiting hours begin and I have to fight the regret of coming here. I turn on my phone and see a text message

150

from Phoebe. *Merry Christmas, mister! Wear sunblock!*

I walk through town, the deserted Main Street, the quaint shops with quaint names, The Grumpy Oyster, Clam Up, selling bric-a-brac like seashells and other crap you'll find at a yard sale in a few years. Lots of things with the words CAPE COD written on them. The outline of the Cape itself is permanently ruined for me after Ian once described it as looking like an erect penis with extreme curvature.

I keep walking, hoping to find a coffee shop. Near a rotary, mercifully, I find a Dunkin' Donuts that's open. I stop for a coffee and a plain donut. The woman behind the counter has bad skin and speaks with a heavy Brazilian accent. I know one word in Portuguese. Thank you. 'Obrigado,' I say. She looks up and smiles. 'Merry Christmas,' she says.

The road cuts behind the little airport and comes out onto the other side of the Cape, Route 6A. Here the feeling is of a very different place than the strip malls and fast food dumps of Hyannis. It looks like something out of an Edward Hopper painting. Small, neatly-kept wooden houses from the 1700s, stone walls worn smooth, slate roofs. I turn down a side road. You can smell the ocean, the salt air. There'd been a light wind but now it picks up, colder. The sun is up. The road opens up onto the water. I don't know the name of it, a harbor of some kind. There's a sandy spit of land across the water and an old lighthouse. It looks like a painting. It looks so beautiful.

On Sundays, in the winter, my mother and I would sometimes drive, just she and I, to New Hampshire, early, after breakfast, to watch the dog sled races. Bitterly cold. So much snow. A huge field, a blanketed farm, maybe a cornfield. People lined a track and waited for the dogs to come out into the open from the woods. Eight or nine times around the course they'd go. Beautiful Siberian huskies. Thick coats, Fresca-blue-green eyes, mouths open, plumes of steam, the condensation of their labored breath. 'Isn't this something?' she'd say, her eyes wide, a good clean feeling of joy and purpose, of being in the right place at the right time, at being away from a place of menial chores and quotidian tasks, being far from that man who shared her bed, who would never make this trip, who thought it foolish and said so. Of course it was something. It was the best thing. How could anything be better? I was alone with her, standing next to her, in our boots and hats, and later we'd walk to the shack at the edge of the field, near where people parked their cars, and get warm by the wood stove, drink a hot chocolate, eat a plain donut. When the dogs came around, out of the woods, people cheered and clapped, the sound of their hands muffled by gloves.

★　★　★

I'm surprised to find Margaret on duty. She says her kids are out of the house and that she likes to take a shift for one of the younger married girls. She says she'll be home by 3:00 P.M., anyway, and that she and her husband have a nice dinner and open presents then.

'Any improvement?' I ask.

'Still the same,' she says. 'These things can take time, especially with older folks.'

I sip my coffee. I read the newspaper. I occasionally look up at my father. It's really no different than waiting for a flight in an airport, if the airport has dying people in it and beeping machines and no planes.

The paper says that inflation is down and unemployment is holding steady.

The paper says that there is good news for life expectancy, up from 77.2 years to 77.4 years (lower for blacks and Hispanics, slightly higher for white women). The story says that last year, 2,417,797 people died in the U.S.

The paper says that yesterday's Dow Jones Industrial Average closed at 10,240.29, up 0.21 percent on a volume of two million shares, and that prices closed higher on the Nikkei in Tokyo. I have no idea what this means. I don't understand how the stock market works.

The paper says there's a chance of more snow Sunday night and that western Massachusetts reservoirs are at their highest point in over a decade.

I use the bathroom, wash my hands, scan my face in the mirror. Do I look like him? Hard to tell without a tube in my nose. His skin is ashen, his lips dry and cracked in places. He was a handsome man, with jet-black hair and a ruddy complexion, a man who worked outdoors in all kinds of weather. He took odd jobs, especially painting, between shifts at the police department. Will this be me someday? Will I look like this? Will anyone be in the room?

My cell phone rings. It's Phoebe.

I say, 'Merry Christmas from Meh-he-co.'

Phoebe says, 'How's your father? Ian called me.'

'He's great. We just played paddle tennis. I kicked his ass.'

'That's not funny. Okay, it's a little funny.'

'He's not good.'

'Where are you now?'

'The hospital. But I might as well be on a park bench for all the good it's doing.'

'I want you to do me a favor, okay?'

'Phoeb. I'm fine.'

'I want you to do me a favor. There's a bus from Hyannis to Boston. I want you to get on it and I'll come pick you up. You can have dinner with my family tonight.'

Phoeb, I can't. These are the words I want to say. But they don't quite make it out because the idea of staying in this room another minute, of going back to the hotel for what is sure to be Leftover Knockwurst Night, is too much. And for what? Why am I here? What would happen if he did regain consciousness? What if he wakes up and he's pissed? What if he says, 'Get the fuck out of my room'? Won't I feel like an asshole. Still, I'm going to say no. Because it's awkward. Because I'd be imposing. Because I don't know Phoebe's family.

'That sounds really nice,' I say.

★ ★ ★

I do the dishes and talk with Phoebe's mother, Judy.

Dinner was a rack of lamb and parmesan potatoes and green beans, followed by pumpkin and pecan pies for dessert with ice cream from Brigham's, a Boston institution. They talked and listened and laughed. No one said a single mean or sarcastic thing.

Phoebe and her father are in the living room. Her brothers and their wives have left. They hugged on their way out. Judy's putting away the dishes I wash. She says, 'But here's what I don't understand. I'm going to buy mayonnaise anyway. Why does someone need to go to all that trouble to advertise it? I've bought the same brand of mayonnaise for forty years and not once do I remember an ad for it.'

The dishes are old and can't go in the dishwasher. I take my time with them. The hot water and the soap and the sponge feel good. The window above the sink looks out onto the expansive backyard, mature trees, bare branches. It's the house Phoebe grew up in, a stately old pale yellow Victorian at the end of a wooded road in Brookline, a leafy town next door to Boston.

'Judy. You're calling into question my very existence.'

She grins and sips from her wineglass, moves clean cups and saucers back into the cupboards.

We had drinks in the living room. They opened presents. There was one for me, wrapped in today's newspaper. An old scarf that could not have been uglier. I smiled, they laughed. Her brother said, 'Everyone in this family has worn that scarf, Fin. And every one of us has tried to pawn it off on someone else.' I wrapped it around my neck.

Mr. Knowles stood and said, 'Fin, I seem to have accidentally spilled my drink down my throat. Getting a refresher. Top you off?'

He's clean-shaven with a gray crew cut. Phoebe told me that he saved a friend's life once when skating on a pond. The ice cracked, the friend fell in and disappeared. A deep pond. Mr. Knowles went in after him. This was a few years ago. Tonight he wears a sports coat and a tie.

They are a family of golfers and there was talk of the new greens-keeper at the club. He comes highly recommended — did Winged Foot, did Baltusrol, did Myopia. I have to assume that these are golf courses, though for all I know they could be Broadway shows. I merely nod.

Her brothers asked me questions about making TV commercials. They wanted to know about Gwyneth Paltrow. Phoebe's father said, 'Is she the one who adopts all the African children?' Judy said, 'No, Stu, that's Angelina Jolie.'

I watched her parents watch Phoebe. It is a lie that parents have no favorites among their children.

I'm on the last of the pots now and reach under the sink for a fresh Brillo Pad.

Judy says, 'Leave that. Come look at these.'

She sits down at the kitchen table and opens a photo album. She pours out two small glasses of wine.

I do a final wipe-down of the counter and sit down next to her. Judy leafs through the album and turns it toward me.

Pictures of Christmases past. Of birthdays. Of cookouts, vacations, weekends. Smiling people. Happy people. I could use these shots for ads. Baby pictures. Phoebe sitting in Stu's lap as a five-year-old, in her pajamas, while he reads her a story. Stu and Phoebe on the beach. Phoebe and her brothers on skis.

Judy says, 'I love that one. That's up in Woodstock.'

'New York?' I ask.

'Vermont,' she says. 'We have a small place up there. It was Stu's father's.'

A picture of Phoebe and Judy at a café in Paris.

A picture of Judy and Phoebe and a swarthy, handsome man at the same café, his arm around Phoebe. I feel a surprise twinge of jealousy.

Judy raises her eyebrows, rolls her eyes, and says, 'We won't talk about that.' She turns the page.

I scan each one, find Phoebe, page after page, watch as she grows up.

Judy turns another page and laughs. It's a picture of Phoebe with chicken pox, age fourteen. Pale, miserable, little bumps all over her face and neck and arms.

She keeps scanning, turning. She's smiling.

'This is in Wellfleet,' Judy says. 'Last year. Labor Day weekend.'

It's a picture of Phoebe, close up, three-quarter profile, just her face, lost in thought, late-afternoon light.

I stare, perhaps too long, and then turn to see Judy looking at me.

I say, 'Who took this?'

'I did.'

'It's amazing.'

'She's an easy subject.'

I nod, look at the picture again.

She removes it from the album and hands it to me.

She says, 'Take it. I have copies.'

I take it, say nothing, suddenly embarrassed.

Judy turns the pages and there's Phoebe in a wedding dress, which can't be right. But there she is. There's Phoebe in a wedding dress with bridesmaids, with her parents, with a man in a tuxedo, holding hands, kissing, cutting a large cake. It is strange to watch the feeling that comes over me, to step outside of my body slowly, the moment before impact in a car accident. My hands tingle and perspire, my eyes squint, the information unable to be fully processed. There's been a mistake.

Judy's looking at me. She says, 'You didn't know.'

I smile, but it's forced and weird. I could be wrong but I think Judy senses my discomfort.

She says, 'She was young. Right out of college. It was a mistake. Didn't last long.'

I'm nodding slowly, trying to understand it. That's wrong. I'm not trying to understand it. I'm trying to understand why I feel the way I do. Mildly nauseated.

'We all have our secrets,' I say, sounding like an idiot.

Judy says, 'Phoebe told us about your father, Fin. That must be very hard for you.'

She was married. How strange. How did I not know that about her?

'It is,' I lie. Then I say, 'I guess. I don't really know.'

She looks at me, cocks her head to one side.

I shrug. 'I haven't seen him in twenty-five years. He left a long time ago. And then my mother.' I never say these words out loud. The radio is on somewhere. Classical music very low.

I say, 'Yeah. My mother killed herself.'

I never use the word *suicide* when I think about what happened. It feels distant, academic. There's always *took her own life*, but that sounds odd and passive. Took her own life *where?* *Killed herself* is much more active. Killed herself is how I think of it, how I imagine it when I do imagine it.

Judy puts a hand to her cheek. She looks pained.

I say, 'I'm sorry. That came out very . . . I hope I didn't upset you.'

'No. I'm just so sorry. How old were you?'

'Twelve.'

'That must have been awful for you. For all of you.'

Phoebe has Judy's eyes, hazel, dabs of color, wide-set, almond-shaped. The lovely cheeks, high coloring, snow-white hair cut short. Phoebe said her mother cuts her own hair. I've always found it rude when people say of a woman of a certain age, 'She must have been beautiful when she was younger.' I can see how a man could fall in love with Judy Knowles.

I shrug and nod. 'It wasn't great.'

Images of Eddie's outbursts, of Kevin's leaving, of Maura's desperation to get away and start a new and very different life. You think you can walk away, leave it behind. It is amazing the lies you can tell yourself. I see the green bike again on its side on the grass by the back stairs. No kickstand. *You're not supposed to be home.* She drives away.

I want to tell her that for years I've told people that my father was dead, told them I was an only child. She watches me.

I say, 'Thank you for having me tonight. You have an amazing family.'

'Phoebe talks about you so often. She says she's learned so much from you.'

'Me? You've got the wrong guy.'

'You'd be surprised.'

'Well, I'll do my best to talk her out of advertising.'

'As long as she's happy, I don't mind what she does.'

I hear Phoebe and her father coming toward the kitchen.

Stu says, 'I'm heading up.' He shakes my hand. 'Fin. So great to meet you. Sleep well.' He kisses Phoebe's forehead.

Judy kisses Phoebe on the check, then she leans over and hugs me. Chanel No. 5.

★ ★ ★

Phoebe and I walk through the backyard, through a wooded area that opens onto the

160

fairway of a golf course and a field of snow. There is a partial moon and the sky is very clear and you can see stars in the black sky. There's no wind but it is very cold. I'm wearing my new old scarf. Phoebe has on her mother's Sorels and what looks like one of her brother's old coats. A wool hat her mother knit from old sweaters. Somehow Phoebe makes it look good. I follow her through the woods, watch the steam rise up over her. Our breathing is heavy, the snow crunching under our feet.

Phoebe says, 'We're going skiing tomorrow.'

I say, 'That's great. That'll be fun. I'm going to New York to work. Also fun.'

'Do you ski?'

'The name Franz Klammer mean anything to you? Alberto Tomba? I'd embarrass these guys.'

I can tell, even standing behind her, that she's smiling.

She says, 'You could come with for a few days. If you wanted.'

I look up, at her back, waiting for her to turn around. But she doesn't. She just keeps trudging through the snow,

'Thank you. That's really nice. Honestly. And I'd love to. Except for this thing.'

She says nothing for a time. Then, 'See that tree over there?'

I say, 'No.'

She says, 'Well, there's a tree over there and that's where Matt Simon gave me my first kiss.'

I say, 'I made out with him once. Guy's a pig.'

'Jackass.'

'Tongue?'

161

'It was so gross. He opened his mouth as wide as he could. Tongue going like he was searching for a filling.'

I'm walking alongside her now.

I say, 'Your mother's mean.'

She smiles. 'She likes you.'

'How do you know?'

'I know.'

I say, 'The hug. It was the hug, wasn't it?'

'She hugs everyone.'

'Then what?'

Phoebe says, 'The dishes.'

'What about them?'

'She let you do them. You volunteered for them. She likes that.'

'That's it? That's all you have to do? Do the dishes?'

'Not just the dishes. She likes you.'

'I like sleep. I like warmth. Why are we out here again?'

'Stop whining.'

'Where are we going?'

'Just trust me.'

A long, gradual rise. We don't speak. It's a struggle in the snow, the cold air in our lungs. Toward the top Phoebe starts to run. She reaches the top ahead of me.

Phoebe says, 'What d'ya think?'

There, laid out before us, is Boston, the city lights, the buildings, a plane in the distance on its approach to Logan. We're standing close. I can feel her against me, hear her labored breathing from the sprint up the hill. I'm looking at her profile when she turns and looks at me, smiling.

Did she stand here with him? Her husband? Did she look at him like this?

Unless you are married, unless you are in a relationship, unless you are at the dentist, it is very rare to see another person's face close up. Something happens in that small space. Fewer words, perhaps. A more fully realized understanding of the moment, of time, of vulnerability and fragility. Of breathing. You see them differently. When they do speak it's in a slightly different voice. Quieter. Intimate. There have been a few moments like that — a party, out with friends at night at a crowded bar, once on our way downtown on the subway — when I've been this close to Phoebe. And they have unnerved me.

Now, here, in my mind, I wrap my arms around her waist, gently pull her toward me, feel her body through the layers. She puts her arms around my shoulders, her face so close to mine. I can smell the Carmex she put on her lips before we left the house. What a thing, what an impossible gift. She leans into me before I have the chance and kisses me on the mouth, gently at first, then more intensely, more forcefully.

'Phoeb,' I whisper.

'Hi.'

Except that's not what happens. Only in my mind. I want to reach for her hand. I can't seem to do it. My mind races forward to *what if*. What if she rejects me? What if it doesn't work? What if the sun comes up and I want to run?

I'm looking at her and she's looking at the skyline.

Phoebe says, 'One beautiful thing.'

I say, 'World peace.'

She says, 'You're a moron. C'mon. One beautiful thing.'

I say, 'Your family.'

She turns and looks at me. 'That's a nice thing to say.'

'What about you?' I ask.

She looks out over Boston. 'That you came up.'

It's very cold. We stand there for a long time.

CAPTAIN UNDERPANTS

What a thing it is to live in New York City. To move here and not know a soul. A clean slate, a chance to walk away from the past and start anew.

Those first years were, for me, unlike anything I had ever known. The job paid very little. Most of my money went to rent. I'd often work late in part because they'd often order pizza or Chinese food and that meant dinner was free. On Thursday night the MoMA didn't charge admission after 6 P.M. I read *Here Is New York*. I traced the steps. I reread *The Catcher in the Rye* and did the same.

Everything seemed possible. *This* is your life, you think. I am alive in this place and I can do what I choose. I will go to a show at a museum and have no idea what I am looking at. But I will do it and think about it and talk about it. My mind will be different because of it. Better. I will take the flyer from the girl with the blue hair on the corner in the East Village and I will go to the show that starts at midnight in the basement of the building that looks like it might be condemned. I will do it because I have nothing else to do on Saturday night and because I don't know anyone. I will walk home at three in the morning after talking with the people in the show and making plans to get together the following weekend and I'll buy Sunday's newspaper that night, in a deli full of other people doing the same thing. People ordering a ham-and-cheese sandwich, in the middle of the night.

I will feign coolness. I will slowly learn the art of not showing that I am surprised or impressed or moved.

I will feel the elation that comes from anonymity.

I will feel the comfortable loneliness of wandering the avenues in the rush of humanity, the side streets by myself. Fort Tryon Park. The Cloisters. Fulton Street Fish Market. The view of midtown from Tenth Avenue near the Javits Center.

I will come upon the United Nations for the first time, thrill at what happens in this place.

I will, one snowy winter night, happen upon horse stables on the Upper West Side, a soft yellow light off the hay, three horses chewing, billows of condensed air streaming out of their distended nostrils, the snow falling silently around me, and be so moved by it that I will be frozen in place for minutes.

And I will eat at restaurants whose names I've heard and read about. I will eat there with clients and bottle after bottle of wine will be ordered and at the end of the meal I will simply get up from the table and leave, the dinner having been paid for. My mother would have shaken her head in wonder.

I will fly business class on an airplane to faraway places. London. Venice. Tokyo. I will try to look as bored as my fellow cabin-mates in my fully reclinable flatbed with in-seat DVD player, even though I want to shout, *Holy shit, I'm in business class!*

I will feel a great rush of pride at selling an idea to a multinational corporation, watch as they allocate huge sums of money to make my idea real. I will see it on television during a sporting event or a sitcom and friends, impressionable women, will say, 'You did that? That is *so* cool!'

I will compete (though I will not win) with colleagues to create an idea of such magnitude that it will be chosen to run during the Super Bowl. I will attend the Super Bowl and sit in a corporate box with gassy men eating meat and drinking beer, and later the client will want to go to a strip club. I will wonder where all the money comes from, as no one ever seems to pay for anything.

I will get into heated discussions with account people about the length of time a logo appears at the end of a spot. We will fight over thirty-six frames, which is the equivalent of one and a half seconds. Tempers will flare, e-mails will be exchanged, people will shout and curse.

I will thrill at the idea of creation. Of making something from nothing. Of making something funny or charming or poignant out of a mere product. Of transcending the product to a place of entertainment or insight.

I will begin a screenplay that I will never finish, having no idea how to write a screenplay, making the mistake 87 percent of all copywriters have made, thinking it's identical to a thirty-second commercial except much longer.

And then it will change. Slowly. It will become less . . . special. Less exciting, fulfilling.

I do not remember exactly when it went from being awe-inspiring having someone bring my breakfast to my room in an exceptional hotel to being mundane, and bordering on annoying when I asked for jam and not jelly.

From feeling guilt about taking something from the minibar to raiding it dry.

From feeling blessed to walk cross-town, in the shadow of these magnificent buildings, these storied streets and avenues, to cursing the cross-town traffic, which moves at an average speed of four miles an hour, I once read. 'I have a meeting at Palmolive!'

I will curse the stench and the humidity of August in New York. I will forget large chunks of time as I dedicate month after month to projects that are suddenly killed, put on the backburner, or cut because of budget concerns.

It will change. All of it. Imperceptibly at first. Then irrevocably. Thirty comes. Thirty-five surprises you. The prospect of forty stuns you. Once the money was a wonderful surprise. Now it is not enough. A restlessness creeps in. A wanting of something you cannot quite put your finger on. Stories of others people's lives fascinate you. The idea of many things — a career change, a sabbatical, graduate school, a tattoo — *seems* interesting but you never do any of them. Others somehow found time to marry, have babies. You hold them when they come to the office (the babies, not the adults). Round faces, absurd tooth-less smiles, soft and warm. Someone changed the clocks, pushed them ahead when you weren't looking. There is, occasionally (though more and more frequently), a small pit of anxiety in your stomach. You keep waiting for something to happen. And that is your mistake.

★   ★   ★

The subways are empty. It feels like everyone is out of town. The recession-proof rich are skiing in Killington, Aspen, Gstaad. They're sunning in Turks and Caicos, Miami Beach, Mustique. Others are enjoying the break with family, friends, catching up, making old bonds strong. They're talking and laughing. One wonders if others know a secret.

Ian and I sit in my office and try to come up with ideas for a revolutionary diaper. We visit the other teams, check on their progress, talk through their thinking. Sometimes we make the ideas better. Sometimes we make them worse. Sometimes we talk about how strange the circus is and why people would pay money to sit and watch clowns and elephants. We look at reels of award-winning commercials from Super Bowls past for inspiration, if by inspiration you mean ideas we can steal. In the afternoon I call the hospital and ask for Margaret. If she's not working she's told me to ask for the pretty one. Each day the news is the same.

★   ★   ★

I get an e-mail from Rachel Levin asking if we're still on for Tuesday night. Rachel is a friend of Stefano's. He's been trying to fix us up for a few months. I've been reluctant. In fact, I haven't gone out since we called off the wedding. I'm tempted to cancel, postpone, something. But I e-mail back, saying we're still on.

I receive an e-mail from Jill, cc'ing Ian, Alan, Frank, Dodge, Martin, and the teams. The subject heading is 'Revision to Brief. Important.' She says the client, at the urging of counsel, would like to remove the words *one-hundred percent non-toxic*.

★ ★ ★

Late afternoon, a gunmetal sky. A few days before New Year's Eve. Ian and I go out and bring Starbucks coffees and cakes and cookies back for everyone. We've decided to work as a group for a few hours, see what happens. We sit in my office. Paulie leafs through an advertising awards magazine. Stefano's head is back and his eyes are closed. Raj sits on the floor cross-legged. Malcolm is on the couch between Paulie and Stefano looking at his nails. He keeps sniffing them, which is bothering me, but I can't seem to look away. Ian sits at my desk. I have no chair.

Stefano says, 'I have an idea.'

I say, 'Fantastic. Tell us.'

Stefano says, 'The idea is that we get more time for this assignment.'

Ian says, 'That's not really an idea.'

Malcolm says, 'I like that idea.'

Paulie says, 'What's the worst that happens? We don't come up with anything.'

Ian says, 'The worst that happens is that we don't come up with anything, the client finds someone else to do it, and we all get fired.'

Stefano says, 'You have to admit, though. Very rushed. This is an American thing, I think. Rushing around. Always in a hurry. Do you mind if I smoke, Fin?'

'Yes,' I say.

He asks to smoke every time we get together as a group and try to come up with ideas, which almost never works. (The ideas. Or the smoking, for that matter.) But sitting in a group gives the appearance of work, despite the results of a recent study, which says that group brainstorming produces far fewer good ideas than people working on their own. The guys have brought half-written scripts, a line on a page, a half-baked idea, nothing. Rajit has an old issue of *National Geographic*.

Stefano says, 'Very fascist of you, Fin.'

Rajit mumbles something and he and Stefano and Malcolm laugh.

People tap their iPhones, their iPads, tweet, update a Facebook page, post a wall comment, browse Zappos. I stare out the window and imagine the reaction from the driver of the boat when someone first suggested waterskiing.

Stefano continues, 'I feel like we used to get much more time. Weeks. Now it's days. Am I alone here?'

Paulie says, 'Hey, ya know Captain Underpants, right?'

Ian says, 'You mean Dodge?'

Paulie says, 'No. Like Captain Underpants. The books.'

Malcolm says, 'Underpants. I don't understand.'

Paulie says, 'Underpants. Captain Underpants. Ya know.'

Ian has Googled *Captain Underpants* on his iPhone. 'I love this. I love his name.'

I say, 'Maybe he's a cartoon and everyone else is real.'

Paulie says, 'What if it's like, 'Be like Captain Underpants, don't crap your pants.''

Stefano says, without opening his eyes, 'I could have told you he was going to say that.'

Rajit's laughing. He's also in the process of lighting a cigarette.

I say, 'Raj. Could you please. Raj.' He just smiles and nods, lighting up. Stefano smells it, opens his eyes, and does the same. Smoke billows. I wave it away with my hand. No one else seems to mind.

Raj says something. Malcolm translates: 'Animate it. Everyone else is human except the diapers. They dissolve.'

Raj says, 'Pixar. Pixar.' Rajit holds his cigarette between his index finger and his thumb, as if he's about to throw a dart. When he inhales he turns his hand upside down and drags like he's smoking a bong. When he exhales, very little smoke comes out.

Ian types the ideas into my computer.

Paulie says, '*Up* was awesome. I cried.'

Malcom says, 'I cried like an infant. It could

172

be because I was adopted.'

Raj says something.

Malcolm says, 'He thinks celebrities with extremely large heads and tiny bodies are funny. Babies' bodies. Wearing diapers.'

Ian says, 'That's mental.' But he writes it down.

Malcolm says, 'Okay. Well, we had something. Use the song 'Under Pressure.' Queen and David Bowie. And we see landfills. All over the world. Getting fuller. Maybe. I don't know. Not sure you want to see trash.'

Raj says something. Malcolm says, 'He says maybe you reverse it. You see them getting less full, turning into fields again.'

Paulie says, 'Is that the right song, though?'

Malcolm says, 'Probably not. That's just the song we were listening to at the time.'

Paulie says, 'Ya know what could be kind of beautiful? Like, do you guys know Bach's *Cello Suites?* They're insane. The first one is my favorite.'

Ian's gone to iTunes and plays it. We listen and I wonder how someone can make that kind of sound. Everyone is quiet for the thirty seconds of free music iTunes gives us.

When it's done, Ian says, 'I kind of love that.' The others nod.

Ian writes it down as *under pressure idea/Bach.*

Paulie says, 'They used it on *The West Wing* a bunch of years ago. The episode where Josh has the flashbacks of being shot during the assassination attempt.'

173

Rajit says, 'I remember that one,' and we actually understand him.

Ian says, 'I loved that show.'

I say, 'I own it. The boxed set. I own it.'

People nod, drink their coffee, eat their unusually large Starbucks cookies.

Stefano says, 'Have your cake and eat it, too.'

We look at him.

He says, 'I was just thinking about that phrase. I don't understand it.'

Ian says, 'It's about greed, right?'

I say, 'I think that's right. Having cake, but being aware that you shouldn't eat it.'

Ian says, 'No. I think it's more like, you shouldn't want more than just your own cake.'

Stefano says, 'But why even have the cake in the first place, then? Why is it bad to have some delicious cake and eat it, too?'

Raj says, 'No, no,' and then something else.

Malcolm says, 'It's the idea of having cake but also eating it. Two things at once, yeah?'

Paulie says, 'Wait. Why would you have it and not eat it?'

Stefano says, 'You could be on a diet. Or maybe it's not a very good cake. The cake in the cafeteria is atrocious.'

Ian says, '*Cake*'s a funny word. Cake. Cupcake.'

Paulie says, 'That's what my wife calls her hoo-hoo.'

Ian says, 'Thanks for that.'

Stefano says, 'It's just odd to me, this notion that you would be served a piece of cake and then not eat it. What's the point? Is there coffee to go with it? Can I not drink that, too?'

Paulie says, 'I think it's like don't ask for too much.'

Malcolm says, 'Then why not have the saying be something like, 'Don't ask for a second piece of cake'?'

Stefano says, 'That works much better for me.'

Paulie says, 'Does a bear shit in the woods? Is the Pope Catholic?'

Stefano says, 'What's your point?'

Paulie says, 'People say that sometimes. Like, when something's obvious.'

Stefano says, 'Of course a bear shits in the woods. The Pope is the head of the Roman Catholic Church. I don't understand.'

Paulie says, 'We had a thing. I mean, you're gonna think it's like E-Trade but it's not E-Trade.'

E-Trade has for several years had wildly successful commercials during the Super Bowl where a baby talks like an adult.

Ian says, 'What is it?'

Paulie says, 'It's a baby who talks like an adult.'

Ian says, 'That's E-Trade.'

Paulie says, 'No. Listen. It's different. They're in a board room and they're talking about how to save the world.'

I say, 'With voices like adults or like babies?'

Paulie says, 'Adults.'

Ian says, 'Still E-Trade.'

Paulie says, 'Then they're talking like little kids. High baby voices. My daughter just turned three and she has the most awesome voice you've ever heard.'

175

Ian says, 'A kid's voice is okay. What else happens?'

Stefano says, 'That's as far as we got. Good, though, no?'

Ian says, 'Maybe work on it. People like babies.'

Malcolm stands, stretches, then shoves his hand down the back of his pants, scratching his ass aggressively. 'If I don't drink a beer soon, my head's going to burst into flames.'

The rest stand.

Paulie says, 'Who wants to buy me a drink?'

They all nod and shrug.

I say, 'I don't feel we've accomplished much. We don't have much time.'

Stefano says, 'This is what I've been saying.'

Paulie says, 'Fin D? Coming with us?'

I start to say something when Stefano says, 'Fin is predisposed this evening, Paulie. A romantic rendezvous.'

They all stop and turn.

Raj says, 'Fin. You dog.' Which sounds ridiculous in an Australian-Indian accent.

I say, 'Go away.'

They laugh and wander down the hall. I hear Stefano say something about cake.

★ ★ ★

Did I mention that I live in MORON?

MORON was the idiot brainchild of a small group of investors who, flush with money from the days before the Big Correction, were planning a new, very expensive, and exceptionally ugly high-rise on the edge of Little Italy. The building — on the corner and across the street from the 100-year-old building I live in — would in no way blend in with the neighborhood, a glass-and-steel monstrosity, Frank Gehry on acid. Huge, glossy posters went up around the proposed site, a sliver of a space surrounded by four-, five-, six-story buildings.

The developers wanted to create buzz. So they thought, *Why not create an entirely new neighborhood?!* It would be the new 'it' neighborhood. SoHo, TriBeCa, Nolita, DUMBO, MORON. It stands for Mott on Rim of Nolita. Which doesn't really mean anything. It's Little Italy. But they thought both its meaninglessness and its inanity played perfectly into the early-twenty-first-century zeitgeist of knowing sarcasm and idiocy. *We know it's stupid. We mean it to be stupid. That's what makes it funny. But we're also hoping you think that, within the open stupidity, it's cool.*

They blogged and tweeted, Facebooked and LinkedIn. They essentially campaigned for coolness. It never caught on. Part of the problem (besides inanity) was very bad PR. For the building to go ahead it would mean tearing down a small, family-owned shop that had sold fresh mozzarella and cream sauces for generations. A story appeared in *The New York Times*. People rallied for the shop. The investors hired a PR firm and an ad agency, as well as a Web design firm in Los Angeles. None of it worked. What did work was razing the mozzarella shop in the middle of the night and then constructing the building in six months. The *New York Post* headline said it best: MORONS LIVE HERE.

That was three years ago. Today the building is barely half full, the rents too high. I've heard the original developer defaulted, was indicted, and left the country. At some point every late afternoon, the new building blocks the sun and my apartment goes dark.

I go home to shower and change but instead head straight to the couch to review the many personal letters I've received in the mail that day. These include notes from my dear friends American Express and Con Ed. And a letter from Lady Gaga appealing for money (always an awkward subject between friends) for the children of Darfur. 'Dear Caring Friend,' Lady Gaga writes (and I can picture her writing it, too, longhand, no doubt). I read the first paragraph of the letter and am acutely aware of how the writing style engenders in me not empathy and sadness — as this subject most certainly should — but annoyance and laughter. Which then leads to sarcasm and mild anger. Which then leads to guilt and shame. Which then leads me to the refrigerator for a cold Sierra Nevada Pale Ale, which makes me remember the phrase *nancy boy*, a phrase my father reserved for men who drank beer that wasn't Miller. I'm an uncaring nancy boy who drinks fay beer and my father is laughing at me and bizarre Lady Gaga no longer wants to be my friend.

I briefly consider masturbating but decide I don't have the energy, so I shower instead.

I bought this apartment five years ago. In fact, the bathroom is one of the reasons I bought it. The toilet is in its own room. Like they do in

Europe. How great is that? I often say this to people upon showing them my toilet and they rarely react with the kind of excitement I hope for, the kind of excitement that I, myself, felt upon seeing it for the first time. The Realtor actually apologized for it. It's a small box with a window high up. In a separate room next door is the actual bathroom, sink and old tub with a wraparound curtain. It's got great charm and character, but it's a pain in the ass to actually shower in because the space is small and the curtain often clings to your body.

The apartment itself is a small one-bedroom, sixth-floor walk-up, top floor in the back. It's Connecticut quiet, except for the pipes in the winter. Uneven, wide plank floors, exposed brick wall on one side, old, drafty windows, a small working fireplace. Things break a lot but we have a great super on the ground floor — Ahmed — who is very fond of me, as I let him stay on my couch for two weeks last year when his wife briefly kicked him out. He was a dentist in Yemen.

It's sparse, clean, perhaps a bit monastic. I could pack and be out of here in half a day. Ian helped me buy some things, most of them at the Chelsea Flea Market on weekends, including a large, old leather chair that I don't really like and never sit in. There's a farm table that I do like and I use when I give my frequent lavish dinner parties (I've had two in five years). For the most part the walls are bare, which I like. Above the mantel, however, is something I'm quite fond of. It's an advertising poster from 1934 for a Swiss department store. It's a giant white button, 35″ by 50″, with the letters *PKZ* under it (the store's name). I can't say why I like it exactly.

I have plans to redo the kitchen, pages torn out from magazines as guides, notes and bad drawings about how I'll do it. But I haven't even started the process. These things take time.

I almost didn't buy the apartment. I panicked at the closing. I was putting down almost everything I had in the bank and began to have second thoughts. I realized I was happy renting. I liked the idea of impermanence. But I signed the many documents with a fake smile on my face. I convinced myself that it was the right thing to do. That it would make me happy. That it was a smart financial move. It's amazing how you can talk yourself into almost anything.

Now, I sit on the couch, my iPod on shuffle, and half watch TV with the sound off because I can't stand the commercials. Currently the iPod has chosen 'Worried About You' by The Rolling Stones, which is making a Pizza Hut commercial much better. I look at the pile of mail. Along with the catalogs from Crate & Barrel and L.L.Bean are two pieces addressed to Amy. One is a 1.9 percent introductory offer from Citibank and one is a yoga clothing catalog featuring remarkably fit women with lovely bums. I still get junk mail for her once in a while. We lived together here for nine months, during the engagement.

For a while after canceling the wedding, I tried to avoid the medicine cabinet or the top two drawers in the bureau (which I'd given her to use). Her prescriptions and lotions and face creams and lip balms and Lady Schick razors and Secret deodorant and underwear and bras and wonderfully formfitting Lululemon pants.

When she finally did come by, many weeks later, with her two best friends and a car to get her stuff — remaining furiously silent almost the entire time as she threw things into trash bags and a knapsack — I stood, slouched, afraid, regretful, sweaty, confused, ashamed, guilt-ridden in the middle of the living room with the smile of the village idiot on my face.

Finally she spoke as she was going through the books, packing hers, shoving mine back onto the shelf as if she wanted to hurt them.

Holding up a book, Amy said, 'I think this is my *Infinite Jest*.'

I laughed. The wrong response but it seemed funny to me. She laughed, too, for three seconds, then burst into tears.

Take your Infinite Jest, I wanted to say. Take my Infinite Jest. Take all of my jests and my infiniteness. Take the books, the plates, the glasses, the oddly large button poster. Take anything you want. Just please stop suffering because of me.

'Amy,' I said, but had no more to add.

I took a step to her, to hold her, perhaps, put a hand on her shoulder. It's how I would have directed the scene.

'Stop,' she said. She shook her head back and forth slowly. 'Do you know what you've done?' she said. 'To me? To my family? Do you have any idea?'

One of her friends — Barb? Mandy? Erin? — came to the door, panting, having gone up and down the six flights several times carrying the trash bags. 'All set, Amy. We'll be in the car.' Barb/Mandy/ Erin gave me a look as if to say, *I'd like to throw up in your mouth*, then walked out.

Amy started for the door and stopped.

She looked at me and said, 'Why did you ask me to marry you?'

There are basic questions in life that you need to have answers for.

Why do you do your job?

What can't you live without?

Who is the most important person in your life?

I do not have the answers to these questions yet. This is not good. Not on the eve of forty, alone, in an apartment whose most striking feature is a toilet in a boxed room.

Here's the answer: I have no idea why I asked her to marry me. Wishful thinking? That it was the right thing to do? That it was what she wanted me to do? That if I did it I would come around to agree with the idea of it? There are people who believe that life can be lived rationally, that we are in control of our deepest, most powerful emotions, that we can perhaps even escape the deep markers from the early days, the crucial days, where we learn it all. Those people are called crazy. In reality I was playing a part, doing what I imagined I was supposed to do. The words sounded right. That's why I asked her. How could I stand here and tell her that when I asked her to marry me I was imagining a scene, like in a commercial or a

182

movie, about how one would ask someone to marry them? That it was all distant and unreal to me? That ultimately I did it because it was safe, because I didn't love her?

Here's what I knew about myself when it came to Amy: I knew I couldn't be responsible for her happiness. She was too good, too kind, too loving, too giving. And it was only a matter of time before I let her down. But you cannot say that. Not out loud. Not when you've already hurt someone so badly.

I said, 'I wanted to make you happy.'

Amy's face contorted, as if she couldn't quite believe the words.

'But you *didn't* want to make me happy. You just liked the *idea* of making me happy.'

'Yes,' I said.

'You're so . . . you're so pathetic.'

I was running my tongue across the back of my teeth and my ears were hot. I was embarrassed and wounded and angry but ultimately I had no response because she was right.

★ ★ ★

I call Phoebe.

'Do you miss me?' I ask.

Phoebe says, 'No. Do you miss me?'

I say, 'Maybe. How are you? Where are you?'

'Skiing in Vermont. I told you like a thousand times.'

'I meant where are you this moment?'

'In front of a fire with a glass of wine the size of a Big Gulp.'

183

'How's the snow?'

'Amazing. Crazy cold, though. Do you smoke pot?'

'No. Maybe. Do you have any?'

'My brother got me stoned the other night. It was awesome. I haven't gotten stoned in so long. I can totally see how someone could become a pothead.'

'Like, totally, man.'

'Shut up. What are you up to?'

'Work.'

Phoebe says, 'How's it going?'

'Shitty.'

'That's a pun. I get it. If I were stoned I'd laugh my ass off. You doing anything fun?'

I'm about to say *I have a date tonight*, but decide against it.

'Me? Mr. Fun?'

'I'm sorry, who did you say you were?'

'I'm Mr. Fun. I'm all about fun. Finbar Good Times. That would be my mob name. Johnny the Gun, Guido Three Balls, Finbar Good Times.'

'The Frenchman called me,' she says.

On the TV obese people stand on a scale and compete to see who's lost more weight. Some of the obese people are crying. Some version of *Law & Order* is on four different channels. Far up the channels is a repeat of the women's college softball World Series from 2003 between Texas Tech and Cal State Fullerton. Phoebe has only mentioned the Frenchman to me once. We were talking about whether we'd ever had our hearts broken.

I say, 'You okay?'

'Yes. No.'

There's a silence.

Phoebe says, 'I was crushed when it ended. When he ended it. I'd call and leave long messages. I wrote him letters. God. I threw myself at him like a . . . ' She drifts off.

I don't know what to say. I'm tempted to say he's a selfish asshole but that's probably not what she wants to hear right now.

Phoebe says, 'It was a message. I didn't talk with him. Out of the blue. He left a message saying he was thinking of me, that he saw an old letter of mine and that he missed me and just wanted to say hi. I mean, you don't get to do that.'

'Maybe he does miss you,' I say.

'He cheated on me. Left me for someone. Maybe she left him. Maybe he's lonely. Maybe he's horny. I don't know. I don't know what the fuck men want sometimes. Some want sex and at least you know where you stand and some want a part-time connection and some want a mother and most are just boys and confused and they don't know their own minds. They don't tell the truth. They don't know what they want and it's tiring.'

Cal State Fullerton has brought in a new pitcher. She is short and stout and she looks exactly like the previous pitcher, to the point where I'm wondering if they are twins. I couldn't hit her pitching in a million years.

Phoebe sighs. 'Sorry.'

'I wish I knew what to say.'

'There's nothing to say.'

185

'Are you going to call him?' It's out before I can pull it back.

'I don't know. It's just . . . It's unfair to throw a little bomb from the past into someone's life, when they've worked so hard to lock it away.'

'Yes.'

'Where are you?'

'Home.'

'What are you watching?'

'Lesbian softball.'

Phoebe snorts. She snorts when she laughs. 'You're a moron.'

'What? It's not an insult. You should see these women. They're lesbian softballers. They'd look at me and say, 'There's a bland straight white man.''

'Moron.' But I can tell she's smiling. 'I gotta go help make dinner.'

'I'll talk to you later.'

'Okay.'

'Okay.'

I'm about to click off when I say, 'He was an idiot.'

'Whatever,' she says, then blows her nose.

'One more thing.'

'What?'

'You are my favorite lesbian softballer.'

She laughs. And hangs up.

★　★　★

The competing voices in my head vie for time.
Go out, Fin! Get laid, for Christ's sake.
Stay in, Fin, read a book, watch a Ken Burns

186

documentary, hang yourself as a result.

I arrive early and stand at the small bar. A place called Prune in the East Village. Couples wait for tables over drinks, wait for friends. Kiss, kiss, you look wonderful. The women in close, talking, making eye contact. The men at a distance, nodding, looking around the room. Rich, seductive scents, women in fitted skirts. Hips and thighs and long, milk-white necks.

A woman's voice says, 'You must be Fin.'

'Rachel,' I say. 'Hi.'

She kisses my cheek and I go to kiss hers, but she is moving too fast and pulls away so that I appear to be kissing nothing, a Chaplin moment. She is out of breath. She says, 'I need a drink, my lips are soooo chapped, I have to pee, I couldn't find a cab, where's the toilet? I'll have whatever you're having as long as that's Tanqueray and tonic on the rocks.' And then she is gone.

I order her drink and wait. It arrives as she returns from the ladies' room.

'How great is *that* timing?' Rachel says, nudging me, wide-eyed, laughing too hard.

Her coat and hat are off. She has an extraordinary mane of dark brown, tightly curled hair. For some reason it dawns on me that *pamplemousse* is one of the only words I know in French, and that I remember it only because it sounds ridiculous.

We are shown to a table. She organizes her coat on the back of her chair, bends to put her bag on the floor. I involuntarily look at her ass. She's talking, perhaps to her bag, possibly to me.

187

' . . . but that's the only time. So funny that you should pick this place,' she says.

'I know,' I say, smiling. 'I really like it.'

'So you know Stefano,' she says, sitting, exhaling.

'I do. A great guy.'

'*Such* a great guy. We worked together years ago. I used to be in advertising. Cheers.'

We both take big pulls from our drinks.

She has taken time to do her makeup, her hair, her outfit. I can tell. *Don't let him be another loser*, she has thought. She called a friend right before she walked in, for support. 'Call me as soon as it's over,' the friend said.

She says, 'These things make me tipsy.'

'That's the idea,' I say, smiling.

'Hey. No kidding,' she says and laughs hard.

Why are we talking like this?

'So you write for television,' I say. I make a conscious effort to stop bouncing my left leg. My hands are cold so I place them under my thighs.

She's talking but I am thinking of her hips, her marvelous round ass in that black, clingy skirt.

' . . . and then I hooked up with *Who's That Guy?* in its second season. It's been great. I love that we shoot in New York. Have you seen the show?'

'He's a sewer inspector who wants to be a poet?'

'That's the one,' she says, nodding.

'It's funny,' I lie. Stefano showed it to me online. It was awful. 'I like the goat,' I add.

'My idea. Thank you. I just thought it would be funny. Goats are funny.'

'They are funny.'

I don't know where to go from here. I sip my drink.

'That must be exciting, writing for TV,' I say.

'Fin, it's incredibly exciting at times, let me tell you, but there are days where I want to hack people to death with a machete. These stars' — she makes quote signs with her hands — 'are brutal. What a spectacular bunch of egotistical assholes, the lot of them, excuse my French.'

Pamplemousse.

' . . . wouldn't ever get involved with one of them again. *Huge* mistake. What does your father do?'

'My father?'

My father is dead. My father is almost dead. My father left us. My father beat my brothers and drove my mother to death.

'He's . . . retired. He was a police officer.'

'Ohmigod. *So* sexy. What *is* it about those guys?'

'I don't know. But I have to say that my father is incredibly sexy.'

Mid-drink, she spits an ice cube back into her glass as she laughs way too hard for it to be honest.

She says, 'My father's a podiatrist. His father sold sturgeon.'

I try to imagine that job.

' . . . and still runs three miles every single day of his *life*.'

'That's awesome.'

'I'm starved. You hungry? I could eat a dog. Let's split the calamari.'

We order food. We order wine. We watch the

189

absurd, awkward wine dance, the new glasses, the small pour, the taste, the search for the right words ('I'm getting a hint of . . . wine?'). She talks. About her grandmother, a Holocaust survivor, about her sister's divorce, about TV shows I don't watch, pilot season, the importance of the executive producer credit. I listen. I nod. I drift.

Will we have sex tonight? Will we click and find that animal magnetism that makes one person want to bite another? Will we say things in the night, feel a closeness? Is this the woman who will be my wife? *I love you, Rachel Levin.* Will I one day say these words? Will I send flowers to her office for no other reason than that I love her? Will she keep a photo of me, of us, from that time we went to the vineyard/Costa Rica/Taos, tanned, smiling, on her desk? Will I nurse her through a nasty bout of food poisoning, rampant diarrhea, where her hair is flat and greasy and smells like the inside of a ski hat after a long day, her face pale, her breath horrid? Will we have pet names, use baby talk? Will I sit in shops and watch her try on clothes? Will I meet her friends and family, try and impress them, make them like me? Will I find her friend Tracy, the yoga teacher, sexy? Will Rachel see me looking at her lustfully? Will we argue on our wedding night? Will she cry? Will this be the woman I go to sleep with every night of my life? Will I watch her grow pregnant? Will I watch our child emerge from her body, bloodied, crying, sweat on my wife's face? Will I comfort her when her father dies of a massive heart attack on the golf course? Will I be patient with her grief, months later? Will I say, instead, 'Get over it!' as I wonder what has happened to our marriage, each of us growing distant, building walls. Will I think of taking a rental car and driving to Phoenix, where I will hide inside a Best Western for months? Will she cheat on me on a business trip, with a man twelve years her junior named Chad? 'You really want to know? Yes, his penis was much larger than yours.' Will I cheat on her? Will she say, in the fight wc have in the kitchen, after the affair is found out about, during the long, drawn-out argument where things are said that can never be taken back, when all our energy is sapped, 'I wish I had never married you'? Will we sit in plastic folding chairs on the lawn of a university, exchange a look that cannot be put into words, one of deep connection and understanding, a pure human moment between two people who love and respect each other, a powerful cocktail of pride and melancholy and awe at time itself ('We were changing her diaper yesterday.') as our daughter accepts her diploma? Will I stand over my wife's grave and mourn, cry like a baby, wish myself dead? Will she do the same for me, if I die first? Will she remarry? Will anyone remember me twenty years after I die?

'Does it make me anti-Semitic if I don't want to date Jewish guys?' she asks through a mouthful of sea bass. I open my mouth, as if to answer, but she continues.

'I was seeing someone for a while. Not Jewish. Whatever. I told him he could have a Christmas

191

tree, a small one, but he wouldn't do the Chanukah thing. Can I try that creamed spinach? Another Jew hater, right? My curse in life, being attracted to Jew-hating men. What is it about Irish guys and Jewish girls? Have you ever been to Israel?'

'No,' I say. 'Have you?'

She nods, vigorously, gravely, over the lip of her wineglass. Big swallow.

'Mmm. Yeah. I've been. Every Jew *has* to go once, Fin. *Gorgeous*. The people, the country. *Gorgeous*. Paradise. If there were no Arabs. I'm kidding. Sort of. So angry, those people. Let's split a dessert.'

Then, the crucial moment that comes on every first date in New York. A litmus test. The post-dinner drink or coffee or walk. Neither of us suggests anything. It's over. I'm relieved. And I'm sure she is, too.

We leave and walk to the corner of First Avenue. The cold air feels good. I am not the kind of man she is looking for. I meet very few of the criteria on her checklist. She stamps her feet a few times to keep warm.

'Thank you for dinner. This was fun,' she lies.

'It was my pleasure,' I say. 'I enjoyed it.'

A cab sees us and honks. I raise my arm and it pulls to the curb.

'I'm sorry,' I say, without realizing that I was going to say it.

'For what?'

'I didn't try very hard.'

A smile spreads over her face. 'No. You didn't. Maybe I tried too hard. I hate these things.'

'Me, too.' We're both smiling. Finally, a real moment. She kisses my cheek. When she pulls back to look at me again, something clicks, a neuron fires. She needs to double-check something. She leans forward and kisses me on the mouth, puts her hand on my shoulder. It is a passionate kiss, sexy and deep. It surprises me, delights me, confuses me. I think of Phoebe. Why do I feel like I'm cheating?

'Okay, then,' she says.

'Okay,' I say, opening the door to the cab for her.

'I'll speak with you.'

'Definitely,' I say, then watch as the cab drives up First Avenue, knowing that we will never see each other again.

★ ★ ★

I wake early, lie on my side, and look out the window at the blanket of snow that covers the trees and the rooftops. It is still and quiet, except for the wind, the hiss of the radiator. I should go in to work. I should get an early start. Don't think of it as a diaper, Fin. Think of it as a thing that could save humanity. A superhero. A political message. A love story. A comedy. Let's get Jerry Seinfeld/Tina Fey/Al Roker/ someone-from-*The-Bachelor*-or-*Dancing-with-the-Stars*.

Excellent, Fin. Brilliant, Fin. Jackass, Fin.

From the next apartment I hear my neighbor's son, Henry, eighteen months, his muffled, high-pitched bird-of-a-boy voice, his parents laughing. I roll over and go back to sleep.

193

Later in the day. Ian comes into my office holding two coffees, puts one on my desk.

He says, 'What's the most famous Super Bowl spot ever?'

I say, ' 'Mean Joe' Greene.'

'Mean Joe' Greene was a football player known for his, well, meanness. In the spot, a beat-up, limping Mean Joe ambles down the corridor after the game, stadium empty except for a young boy, who is obviously in awe of Mean Joe. The kid holds a Coke. He gives it to Joe, who downs it. The kid turns to walk away, disappointed, and Joe says, 'Hey, kid.' And tosses him his filthy jersey, which he's been carrying over his shoulder.

Ian says, 'Bigger. The biggest ever. The commercial of commercials.'

I say, 'Apple 1984.'

He smiles and says, 'Apple 1984.'

He's grinning. It takes me a few seconds.

I say, 'Instead of the girl, it's a mother.'

He says, 'Instead of the sledgehammer, she hurls a huge doodie diaper at the screen.'

I say, 'It's babies in the seats instead of drones.'

He says, 'It's either really funny or incredibly dumb.'

The Apple 1984 spot is legend. It only ran once, during the Super Bowl. Some people say it started the big deal about Super Bowl commercials. It was directed by a young Ridley Scott, whose career largely petered out after that, except for directing *Blade Runner, Thelma & Louise, G.I. Jane*, and *Gladiator*, among others. In the spot, sixty seconds long, drone-ish people march in a gray futuristic world. A talking head — Big-Brother-meets-Stalin — speaks from a giant screen, a kind of indoctrination. Suddenly, something is wrong. A fit, blond-haired woman in red shorts is running with a sledgehammer. She's being chased by scary-looking guys in futuristic suits and helmets. Very Orwellian. This is early January 1984. Rows and rows of near brain-dead drones sit and watch a big screen. The fit blonde throws her hammer and destroys the screen. A voice-over says, 'On January such-and-such, Apple Computer will introduce Macintosh. And you'll see why 1984 won't be like *1984*.'

I call Paulie and ask him to come by. He's three offices away. When he gets to my doorway, I say, 'Apple 1984. For this.'

Paulie says, 'Dude, that's so stupid. I love it. Instead of the sledgehammer, it's a huge doodie diaper.'

I look at Ian.

Ian says, 'Great minds.'

I say, 'Great or sad?'

Ian says, 'Maybe sad.'

* * *

We order in from the diner, grilled cheese and soup.

Ian says, 'Maybe something serious.'

'Like what?'

195

'William McDonough.'

I say, 'Finbar Dolan.'

Ian says, 'No. William McDonough. Have you heard of him?'

'We went to junior high together. He tried to kiss me at prom.'

'You're a fool,' Ian says. 'He wrote a book called *Cradle to Cradle*.'

I say, 'A cradle is something a baby sleeps in. See? I know things.'

Ian says, 'There's a saying in the environmental design movement, 'cradle to grave.' It's about the life cycle of a product.'

'How do you know these things?'

'NPR. Anyway, William McDonough has this whole philosophy about how a product should be completely reusable. Cradle to cradle.'

'Make it a mini-documentary. Errol Morris.'

'Errol Morris.'

Errol Morris is an Academy Award-winning documentary filmmaker who also makes commercials. He made *Fog of War*, about Robert McNamara's experience as secretary of defense during the start of the Vietnam War. Ian and I have been trying to shoot with him for years. Like many creatives, we are keen to validate our work by making it *more* than merely a commercial. We want to make it a movement, a communication. But we've never had a script he was interested in shooting. No surprise there, though, as at the end of every Snugglies spot an animated diaper hugs itself and giggles. The last script we sent him to consider was a takeoff of the Broadway show *A Chorus Line* ('One . . .

196

singular sensation . . . every little time he makes . . . ' If you're sensing a theme of 'borrowing' other ideas and making them our own by putting the most minute twist on them, you're on to something.). His producer was very gracious, saying that as much as Errol loved the script — and musical theater in particular — he would have to pass, as 'Errol is on an extended holiday in India, where he's shooting a comedy with Adam Sandler.'

I say, 'Too serious, maybe?'

Ian says, 'Serious stuff, the environment.'

'Super Bowl audience, though. Straight guys. Drunk. Baseball caps on backwards. Guys who use the word *tits, boner*. Guys who use the word *party* as a verb.'

Ian says, 'It doesn't have to be super serious. Charming. Hopeful. Not unlike myself.'

I leave a message for Pam, asking her to get in touch with Errol Morris's production company and to see if William McDonough would be interested. I also ask her to get in touch with Ridley Scott's production company to see if he's available.

★ ★ ★

'Fin. How do you feel about fondue?'

It's Martin calling from Austria. A rough calculation says it's almost ten at night where he is. I'd e-mailed him scripts, paragraph write-ups of ideas from the guys earlier in the day, highlighting Captain Underpants, William McDonough, 1984, under pressure/Bach, and talking babies but not

197

E-Trade, as well as a couple other stragglers that weren't good but that added to the length of the Word doc I sent, making it seem like a lot of work.

I say, 'Warm stinky cheese?'

'You're a poet.'

'How's Austria?'

'Reminds me of Switzerland. Not far from the border, actually. What was that quote, Orson Welles's character in *The Third Man*. 'In Italy for thirty years under the Borgias they had warfare, terror, murder, and bloodshed, but they produced Michelangelo, Leonardo da Vinci, and the Renaissance. In Switzerland they had brotherly love — they had five hundred years of democracy and peace, and what did that produce? The cuckoo clock.''

I'm never bored listening to Martin. I hear a piano in the background, clinking glasses, silverware.

'You at dinner, Martin?'

'Friend has a place on the Gaschurn. I'm looking out over the valley, the lights, snow-capped Alps in the distance.'

I'm looking out over an avenue in midtown Manhattan, snow turned black. I have an intense pang of jealousy for Martin's life, his intelligence and success and cool.

Martin says, 'Captain Underpants could be interesting.'

'That's not a sentence I ever thought I'd hear you say, Martin.'

'Could be the altitude. And the wine.'

I hear a woman speak French. Martin replies

in kind, away from the phone.

Martin says, 'Bach. Could be nice. Talking babies. Tricky. E-Trade. If you can figure out a way to make it original, fine. But they can't talk like adults. William McDonough. Tell me.'

I start to explain who William McDonough is.

'I know *who* he is. What's the spot?'

'Maybe a mix of interview and beauty shots of the environment. Maybe just him talking to camera. Errol Morris.'

'Bit serious.'

'We watched clips of McDonough on TED. He's amazing. Great speaker, sense of humor. Won't feel too serious.'

I'm waiting for him to mention the 1984 idea, which I both love and hate. I love it because I think it could be funny. I hate it because it's someone else's idea and I can see it being mercilessly criticized. I worry that it's one of those ideas that you initially think is genius but that reveal themselves slowly to be idiotic.

He says, '1984.'

'Yes.'

'Has to be perfect. Shot for shot. Perfect but over the top. I don't hate it.'

Which means he likes it a lot. I hear the French woman again.

'I'm on a plane tomorrow. Be ready to show Frank and Dodge. *Tschüss.*'

★ ★ ★

The team gathers to share where we are. Ideas will be killed. Two or three might live for the eventual presentation, which is three days away, the day after New Year's.

Martin is back. He talks with Frank and another man I've never seen. Dodge is on vacation.

We sit at one of the conference room tables. Jill, Alan, me, Ian, Paulie, Stefano, Malcolm, Raj, Pam. Along the other side sit additional people I've only seen a few times and in some cases never at all.

Alan says, 'Frank? Shall we get started?' Alan becomes nervous around Frank.

I lean over to Ian. 'Who's the guy?'

The guy is perhaps thirty-five, Japanese, dressed in a bespoke Paul Smith suit that does not lend itself to his portly frame. A fat King George knot in his tie, London-style. The tie is also notable for its explosion of colors. He hasn't shaved in a few days, but the stubble is patchy fourteen-year-old goose down that looks like the result of a fight lost to a Flowbee. His black hair is a kind of buzz cut on the sides, creating a cupcake effect, the top frosting the recipient of a fair amount of mousse or gel or pomade or Brylcreem. His expression is severe. It could be my imagination but it looks to me like he's trying hard to keep from laughing.

Ian says, 'I don't know, but he looks familiar.'

Frank waits for silence and then says, smiling, 'What a group. I love you guys. Every one of you. To work over the holidays like this for one of the great brands in the world today.' He pauses and shakes his head slowly. 'I love your asses.'

The Japanese newcomer looks askance at Frank. Surely he's thinking, *Did he just say 'asses'?*

200

Martin jumps in. 'Well said as always, Frank. Before we look at the work, I'd like to introduce our good friend, Mr. Keita Nagori. He was in New York and was kind enough to drop by and join us for this review.'

Ian says, 'No. It can't be.'

I whisper, 'Is it me or does *Keita Nagori* sound like a California roll with salmon?'

Ian says, 'You make me cringe for you.'

Ian taps his iPhone a few times and holds it up to show me just exactly who Keita Nagori is. A quick Google search has Keita number twelve on the *Forbes* list of richest men in Japan. Keita's father bought the agency last year.

Ian says, still whispering, 'There's a billionaire in the room.'

Keita nods crisply.

Martin nods to me to begin. 'Fin. Please.'

I preface the ideas by saying we have a lot of good thinking on the table. I always say this. I say we've shared a lot of it with the account team already to make sure we were on the right track. I say, referring to the brief, that we feel we have a couple of ideas that could definitely be powerful, breakthrough, charming, funny, differentiating, memorable, groundbreaking, game-changing. I do not believe a word I am saying and am confident that no one else does either. They smile and nod politely, though. I notice that Keita is sitting forward, elbows on the table, leaning against his tented fingers. It looks awkward and uncomfortable, as if he is posing as a businessman at a meeting. He smiles briefly at me.

Each team shares their ideas.

Despite my initial excitement for the ideas, something often happens in the presentation phase where I am disappointed and slightly embarrassed by them. I make the mistake of assuming the flat expression on everyone's faces is boredom. I want them to look like children upon seeing puppies. My guess is that Martin, Alan, and Jill are thinking of every possible thing *wrong* with the idea. How will the client respond? Is it remotely like anything else out there? Who could we offend? Are there hidden messages the trade press could pick on? Ideally we should have had a month, not a week. Ideally we should have had another month to find the right director, location, and cast. The client sees the ideas in three days. They basically have to decide immediately. If this all happens — and I doubt it will as it's simply not a feasible schedule — we would need to be shooting in less than a week. Which is impossible. But we'll do it.

People like 1984 and William McDonough. But the idea they spark to is a new one. Ian came up with it this morning. Every baby we see in birthing rooms around the world — the U.S., Europe, China, Africa — has Al Gore's giant head on their tiny baby body. Proud Chinese fathers and grandfathers look at baby Al. An African mother and father hold baby Al. Swedes, Koreans, Mexicans, Filipinos. It's called 'An Inconvenient Poop.' Okay, that's not true. It's called 'Al Gore.' The voice-over would say, 'Now, with new Snugglies Planet Changers, the world's first disposable, biodegradable diapers, every time you change a diaper, you can help change the world.' Our online people are looking into change-a-diaper-change-the-world.com.

Frank says, 'Can we get Al Gore?'

Jill says, 'I saw him on *30 Rock*. He'll do TV. I have a friend at J. Walter Thompson and they were looking at him for something.' Frank nods.

Jill says, 'Should it just be newborns or should we show toddlers, too? Toddlers are a huge market for us.'

Ian says, 'Cleaner if it's newborns.'

Martin says, 'Pam. Any of these a production problem in the time allotted?'

Pam says, 'All of them. But with enough money you can do anything.'

Martin says, 'They'll put money against this. Alan. Your thoughts.'

Alan says, 'I think there's some great work on the table. Truly.'

Jill nods aggressively.

Alan says, 'It's original. It's ownable. I like that. They'll like that.'

Jill says, 'If I can speak to Alan's point, let's remember why we're here: to do nothing less than revolutionize the diaper industry.'

Alan says, 'That's who we are. As a company, and as a diaper maker. It's contemporary. It's now. I love the contextualization of it. Gritty, raw, on brand.'

He's lost the plot at this point and is just saying whatever pops into his mind.

Jill says, 'Definitely on brand.'

Alan says, 'We're saying something here that other diapers can't. Al Gore or the McDonough idea. Bold.'

Martin says, 'Let me have a think. Thank you, everyone.'

There is a brief, deflated pause and people gather their phones and papers and stand and stretch. Still seated at the end of the table, Keita smiles and says, 'I like Captain Underpants.'

⋆ ⋆ ⋆

Ian comes by my office.

He says, 'How do you think that went?'

I say, 'Good. I think it went well. You?'

'Not good.'

'No, me neither.'

Ian says, 'I need a night off. Do you mind?'

'Course not.'

'I'd like to stop thinking about revolutionary diapers for a bit.'

I say, 'Baby, you need to relax.'

'Please don't call me baby.'

'Baby, I know all about relaxing. Let me give you a piece of advice.'

'Please don't.'

'When the world is on your shoulders, gotta straighten up your act and boogie down.'

Ian says, 'Stop.'

I say, 'Livin' crazy, that's the only way.'

'You're not stopping.'

'Life ain't so bad at all if you live it off the wall.'

'You're the whitest, straightest man I know.'

'I'm about to stand up and dance.'

Ian says, 'I'm leaving.'

Later, I read disheartening stories online about

204

drug-related kidnapping, murder, and dismemberment in Mexico and how it's spreading to tourist communities.

The phone rings.

'Mr. Dolan? It's Margaret Nash, from Cape Cod Hospital.'

'Margaret. Hi.'

'I hope I'm not disturbing you.'

'Not at all.'

Margaret says, 'I'm calling because your father's vitals have taken a bit of a turn, and while we're not in a danger area, I did want to let you know. It's cause for some concern.'

I look up to see Keita standing at my door. I hold up an index finger and smile.

I say, 'What . . . what exactly does that mean?'

Margaret says, 'It means we're moving him to the ICU for a measure of precaution.'

I say, 'Okay. Well, that makes sense, I guess.'

'Yes. Well. I wanted to let you know.'

'Thank you. Honestly. That's very kind of you.'

I hang up and look at Keita.

'Keita,' I say. 'Hello.'

I stand up and he walks over and we shake hands.

Keita says, 'Fin. I like your presentation very much. Would you have time for one quick drink?'

Time to leave my nine to five up on a shelf.

★ ★ ★

Somehow it's late and I am drunk, in the back of a $350,000 Mercedes Maybach, with Keita and

205

a man and a woman whose names I do not know and who do not speak unless Keita speaks to them first.

Keita says, 'Tonight we have a party of epic proportions.' It's something he has said several times during the evening, a go-to line. (Mine's 'Hmm, that's interesting.')

Dinner was innocent enough. Gotham Bar and Grill. Then a series of bars on the West Side. The Standard, Pastis, Hotel Gansevoort, Soho House. The man and woman who are currently seated in the front of the Maybach secured entrée into each place and somehow whisked us past waiting crowds, got us seated at corner tables. Drinks appeared and were paid for without my ever seeing a bill or a wallet.

Keita says, 'Fin. You are super awesome. You are like Darrin Stephens.'

'I am like Darrin Stephens, Keita my friend.' A not particularly clever retort on my part, but the best I can do at the moment. Keita, however, finds this hilarious. All evening he seems to find everything I say either fascinating or hilarious.

Keita says, 'Fin. There were two Darrin Stephens. Why?'

'Well, Keita, that's tough to say. Dick York, the actor who played the first Darrin Stephens, left the show. Then came Dick Sargent. Two guys named Dick.'

Keita's torso hurls forward he laughs so hard. Loves a dick joke, apparently.

I say, 'Here's the best part.'

Keita's drink was three-quarters of the way to his mouth but is now suspended inches from his lips. His eyes go wide in anticipation.

I say, 'Dick Sargent was a fake name. His Hollywood name. His real name was Richard Cox.'

Keita squints. 'I don't understand.'

I say, 'In America, we sometimes call someone named Richard 'Dick.' Dick Cox.'

Keita's drink is airborne, brown liquid flying onto his pants, my pants, the floor of the car that costs more than the average American home.

I say, 'Keita, your English is quite good.'

'It is good and it is not so good. The more I drink the better it gets. I attended a British boarding school for three years as a boy. One of the worst experiences of my life.' He laughs. 'Do you speak another language, Fin?'

'No.'

'Of course not. You are American. But that is okay because you are super famous!'

'Yes, I am.'

'You have won many awards for your famous work.'

No, I haven't. 'Yes, I have.'

'And someday you will run the agency.'

Not a snowball's chance in hell. 'Absolutely.'

They'd lied to him. They told him I was the agency's best writer. They told him I'd been the lead on many new business wins. Frank was jiggling change in his pockets (or possibly playing with his balls), staring out the window of Martin's office. This was after this morning's meeting.

Frank had said, 'He shows up unannounced in the lobby. Thank God I was in New York. A sneak attack. It's Pearl Harbor all over again.'

Martin said, 'Don't be *daft*, Frank.'

Martin was in his chair, fingers tented, the jet lag surely kicking in.

'Fin,' Martin said. 'Keita has asked to meet our finest writer.'

I said, 'And he's on vacation.'

'The top *three* are on vacation,' Frank said to the window.

Martin said, 'Frank. For Christ's sake.' To me: 'He wants to see how a commercial is made.'

I say, 'Tell him to watch an old episode of *thirtysomething*.'

Martin says, 'He owns the company.'

Frank says, 'His *father* owns the company. I *run* the company.'

Martin, to Frank: 'We all know you run the company, Frank. Maybe go have lunch or buy some nice shirts.'

To me, 'Show him around. Let him sit with you and Ian. Take him to an edit session. He'll get bored and go home.'

Frank says, 'What exactly is a Rastafarian, anyway?'

Martin and I both look at him.

Frank says, 'My daughter says she's become one. She's at Dartmouth. Spoiled brat. Fifty grand a year. Every other week, it seems, she's home on school break. What the hell am I paying for? She used to be so sweet. Now she smokes marijuana in front of her mother.'

Martin says, 'A day or two. Tops. You don't mind being the best writer in the agency for a day or two, right? Nice work today, by the way.

There's a possibility Monday might not be a complete disaster.'

That was eight hours ago.

★ ★ ★

There is a bar in the back of the car and Keita is making drinks.

I say, 'Do you have any club soda or ginger ale?'

Keita says something in Japanese and the car pulls over and the woman in the front gets out and runs into a deli, returning in record time with a bottle of each. One could get used to this. I gulp down the club soda and check my voice mail messages on my home phone.

Keita says, 'We should go for a ride in a helicopter. See Manhattan at night.'

There's a message from Dr. Wink. 'There's been a change in your father's condition. You should come here now.'

I say, 'I'm not the best copywriter at the agency, Keita.'

'Fin! You are too modest.'

'No. I'm not. Martin and Frank lied to you. They didn't want to disappoint you. I'm just a guy who writes diaper commercials. I'm not even a creative director. And I'll never run the agency.'

He looks out the window, sips his drink.

'Fin. Maybe do you know what my title is?' He's still looking out the window.

'President?'

He turns. 'Special Assistant to the Chief Operating Officer of Lauderbeck, Kline &

Vanderhosen's parent company, Tomo, Japan's largest shipping company and third largest in the world.'

'What does that mean?'

'Nothing. It means I do nothing, am in charge of nothing. I am the only son, only child, and disappointment to my father. And I will never run my father's company because he thinks I am stupid. He buys the advertising firm to keep me busy. And then they don't let me do anything.'

I turn to look at him and he turns from the window.

'Fuck them,' I say.

'Who?'

'I don't know. Whoever told you that you couldn't do something. Fuck 'em. Course, I myself don't normally have the balls to say that, but I'm drunk and I'm riding in a Maybach.'

'Fin. I like you, even though you are not best writer.'

'I like you, too, even though your title means nothing. But I have to go home now. My father is dying.'

He turns to me, suddenly serious. 'Fin. This is a tragedy. He is a very great man, your father?'

'No. He's just a regular man.'

'You admire your father? You learn much from him?'

'I once whined to a therapist that my father never taught me anything. The therapist said, 'You're wrong. Your father taught you every-thing.''

Keita considers this a moment. Or not. He could be drifting. Although he seems to have a remarkable ability to remain reasonably sober.

'Fin,' Keita says in a stage whisper, 'my father is a very great man. Very great. He say to me, he say, 'You are weak and you must be strong. You are ordinary and you must be great.' He is a very great man, my father.'

He sounds like a dick.

Keita says, 'Fin. Do you love your father?'

'No. I hate him, actually.'

He smiles. 'Me, too.'

HAPPY NEW YEAR

I walk down the hall in the ICU toward the nurses station, where four of them are huddled together. I hear one nurse say, 'And the patient says, 'What's the *bad* news?' And the doctor says, 'I've been trying to *reach* you for twenty-four hours.'' They all laugh loudly.

One finally turns to me. Her expression suggests she's annoyed to find me standing there.

'What's the hardest part about rollerblading?' I say.

'Excuse me?'

The other three nurses have turned, the same mildly annoyed expressions.

'What's the hardest part about rollerblading?' Expressions that suggest confusion now.

I say, 'Telling your father you're gay.'

They think on it for a moment and one laughs.

'I'm here to see Edward Dolan,' I say.

The one who laughs shows me to his room. I ask if Margaret is on duty, but the nurse — Beverly — tells me that Margaret doesn't work the ICU. We look at my father, who has more machines around him that go beep and hiss. More tubes. There is a strip of white tape on either side of his mouth holding a tube in. There has to be a more dignified way to die.

'How bad is it?' I ask, thinking immediately

that I sound like someone in a TV show.

'He's not good.'

For some reason this annoys me. Give me facts. Give me data that I don't fully understand. Give me something.

'I understand that, but is there a time or . . . '

'We couldn't know that. I'm sorry. The doctor will be around later.'

The room is darker than the other room. Is it mood lighting, to suggest the severity of the situation? Is it to save money on the nearly dead? He looks helpless. He looks like a very old man. He looks like a baby. And just that fast, just that vividly, I remember the reject baseball glove.

My mother collected S&H Green Stamps, spending evenings after dinner and the dishes, a cup of tea, a Pall Mall, my father reading the *Record American* with the radio on — the Bruins game, the Red Sox — pasting in page after page of Green Stamps. Those rare times when it was good. I was starting Little League. She used the stamps to get me a glove. The model was called a Regent. Other kids had a Spalding or Wilson or Rawlings. Who'd ever heard of a Regent? I was only mildly disappointed, until Eddie Wyzbiki saw it and made fun of it. 'Look at Dolan's glove! It's a *Reeeee*-ject!' He pulled it out of my hand, ran around. 'Reject!' He was much bigger and I defended myself nicely by bursting into tears, red-faced, ears burning. I told my mother, who told my father. I was sitting in a chair at the kitchen table. I was terrified he'd scream, blame me for crying, being a little weasel. I was waiting for the explosion. In the evening he would shower and afterwards he smelled of Bay Rum.

He sat down opposite me.

'Look at me,' he said. My mother off to one side, biting a corner of her mouth.

I was trying hard not to cry. My ears ached.

He said, 'People say foolish things.' He shook his head. 'It means they don't like themselves. It's means they are afraid. That boy. He's just afraid. Feel sorry for people who say mean things.'

Later, we drove for an ice cream, just me and him, my father humming to the radio.

★ ★ ★

I call Eddie from the cafeteria, hoping it will go directly to voice mail. He answers.

I say, 'Hey. It's Fin.'

'Yeah. Hey. What's up?'

What's up? Gee, not much. What's up with you, asshole?

I say, 'They've transferred him to the ICU.'

I can hear children's voices in the background.

Eddie says, 'Has he said anything?'

Yes, Eddie. He said he's sorry. He said he loves you. He said you're a good person and he's proud of you. No, Eddie. He hasn't. He never said he's sorry and he never said he loves us and he's never going to.

You are always a certain age in your family. I am twelve forever. It's annoying.

I say, 'No. Not that I know of. I was here Christmas Eve, part of Christmas Day.'

214

'I have the kids. Tonight and tomorrow.'

'Okay.'

I'm running my thumbnail back and forth across a packet of sugar.

'Do you know if Maura has any intention of coming down?' The words are polite but the sound of my voice suggests a mild annoyance.

Eddie says, 'You'd have to ask her that, Fin.' The subtitle would read 'Fuck you, Fin.'

I say, 'But she knows he's in here, right?' The subtitle would read 'Why am I the only one here, you selfish, sad prick?'

'Yeah.'

I say, 'She knows he's . . . '

But I stop. What more is there to say? Why fight it? Why let it get to me? But it does.

Eddie says, 'Of course she *knows*, Fin. We all *know*. We've all made our choices. Just like he made his.' He turns from the phone and shouts. 'Kara! Turn that *down*!'

I'm tempted to tell Eddie that he sounds exactly like our father. But I don't.

★　★　★

Phoebe calls.

'Hi,' she says.

'Hi.'

I'm still at the hotel. No Knockwurst Night tonight. Not much of anything. I had a beer and two bites of a disgusting cheeseburger. I ordered another beer and took it back to my room. I'm watching *The Shawshank Redemption*. I've seen it maybe five times.

'Where are you?' I ask.

'Friends of the family. They have a party on New Year's every year.'

'Sounds fun.'

'Lots of cute boys. Ski instructors. Snow-boarders. Why are boys who ski so hot?'

'I've been asking myself this question for years. You've had some wine, I think.'

'Maybe I have. Your date wasn't good, huh?'

'How do you know I was on a date?'

'Ian told me. Is she there now? Is she hot? Are you guys in love?'

'We're totally in love.' I pause. 'I need to be younger and hotter and a skier, maybe.'

'You're not that old.'

'Thank you.'

'And you're not hideous.' She laughs.

'I'm so glad we talked.'

'What are you doing?'

I say, 'I'm back up on Cape Cod.'

'What?' Her voice softens. 'Why didn't you tell me?'

'I got a call yesterday. There's been a change in his condition.'

'I'm so sorry. God.'

I have no line. I don't know what to say or feel or do. I'm simply watching myself, as if waiting to write my own dialogue.

I flip around the channels and see poor Dick Clark for the eleven seconds they let him speak before cutting to Ryan Seacrest. They keep saying it's the greatest party in the world, while showing shots of people standing in the bitter cold of Times Square looking around, bored.

There's a clock in the corner. Twenty-one minutes until midnight.

I say, 'It's an awful thing to die alone. How does that sound, by the way, because I'm not sure I believe it. I want it to sound like an episode of *ER*.'

There's a long silence before Phoebe says, 'You're a good man, Fin.'

It is strange the effect those words have on me. It's something my mother used to say to Eddie. It is a thing I feel I have not remotely achieved, as if it may be beyond my reach. Fathers on their way to the park with their kids on Sunday morning, when I'm on my way to get coffee and the paper. These are good men. Men in meetings who look tired because they were up half the night comforting a colicky baby. These are good men. Men who know themselves, who commit to a thing greater than themselves: a wife, a family. These are good men. How does one get there?

I watch part of a commercial our agency did for a drug for type 2 diabetes that has an unusually high incidence of death. The creative team on it told me that during the fair balance — the reading of the long list of possible side effects — they had had a week's worth of meetings about what shot to show when the voice-over says, 'May cause death.' Ultimately they decided upon a man clapping for himself at his own birthday party. I asked them why. They said they had no idea. They thought it was absurd and pointless. But they told the client they did it because it was a metaphor for the celebration of life. The client loved it.

217

'No. I'm not. I'm not a good man.'

Phoebe says, 'You showed up when it would have been easy not to. No one else did. That's called being a good man. You're touching your scar.'

'How do you know that?'

'Because I know you. Who are you going to kiss at midnight?'

'Myself. I'm going to make out with myself ferociously. Probably get to second. What about you?'

'No one.'

I start to say, 'Okay, then,' but Phoebe starts to say, 'If you were here,' only I don't fully hear what she says.

I say, 'What?'

She says, 'Nothing.'

I say, 'Okay.'

She says, 'Wait. One beautiful thing.'

I say, 'You go first.'

She says, 'A one-legged man skiing.'

I say, 'See, that sounds like a punch line.'

'Shut up. You should have seen it. It wasn't like those commercials for people with disabilities where everyone's an Olympian. This guy wasn't good. He kept falling. But he was trying so hard.'

'Sounds like an episode of *Curb Your Enthusiasm*.'

'What's yours?' she asks.

I say, 'It's nothing. You'll laugh.'

She says, 'I won't laugh. Okay, maybe I'll laugh.'

'No.'

Phoebe says, 'Tell me.'

I say, 'This couple at the hospital. I was coming to see my father and I passed a room and I saw this old man sitting in a chair next to his wife's bed and he was reading to her. Later, when I left, I walked by and she was asleep and he was still there, but he was holding her hand.'

I think the phone's gone dead.

I say, 'You're not laughing.'

'No.'

Three, four seconds.

I say, 'Okay, then. Go kiss someone.' I don't know why I say it. I feel foolish for saying it.

Phoebe says, 'I'd kiss you if you were here. On the cheek.'

'I'd let you,' I say.

★   ★   ★

The phone rings at 4:12 A.M. That's how you know your father is dead.

I dress slowly, call a cab.

At the hospital, I am led into his room by two nurses and the doctor. He looks old and gray and dead and his mouth is slightly open and there is what appears to be white mucus around his mouth.

I reach out to touch his arm. I do it with my index finger, not really wanting to touch him, his deadness, but unable to stop myself. His arm is hard and dry and does not feel like skin. I did the same thing to my mother when she died, only I held her hand. This was when Eddie and Kevin and Maura and I were led into the room where my mother's casket was. Now, I am

219

convinced for a moment that he will react, pull away. I snort thinking about it, thinking it would be funny. The nurse mistakes this for crying and hands me a Kleenex.

I don't know why but I imagine him atop my mother, having sex. I imagine him as a child. I imagine him as a seventeen-year-old who lied about his age to sign up for the war. I imagine him on the toilet. I imagine him driving a car and laughing. I imagine him opening a medicine cabinet, looking for aspirins, a razor, a Band-Aid. I imagine him opening an umbrella. I imagine him asleep. I imagine his parents looking at him as an infant, imagine what they themselves thought, felt. I see them smiling and cooing. I imagine him at twenty-five or thirty thinking that his entire life was ahead of him, excited, perhaps, by the possibility of it all, how wonderful it could be. I imagine him years later, somewhere in Florida, alone on Cape Cod, a stranger to his family, wondering how it had all come to be, impotent to change it, a constant refrain of sadness and regret. Where once time seemed to me to move slowly, languidly, now life seems to move so much faster, a speed that frightens me at times. One day, someone will stand over me like this and do the same.

Later, I sign several documents, all of which I am supposed to be given copies of but the copier is broken. The only thing I notice is the time of death: Friday, January 1, 3:42 A.M.

We've spoken very little, the nurses and I.

'Okay, then,' I say, unsure of what to do. I have no idea what happens to him now. Where does he go? Has anyone made arrangements for a funeral?

'I'm sorry,' I say to the nurse. 'What happens now?'

'Your father wished to be cremated. It's on the admitting form.'

'Then what?' I ask.

'I don't know. That would be in his will, if he left one.'

Another nurse comes over — SIMONE, it says on her nametag — and puts a clear plastic bag on the counter of the nurses station where we are standing.

'This is for you,' she says. 'Your father's things. His . . . personal effects.' She wants to sound professional. 'Clothes, wallet.' She pauses. She can't think of any more nouns. 'Shoes.' Except his shoes aren't in the bag.

In the plastic bag I see his wallet and an opened pack of Lucky Strikes. The logo used to be green, he told me when I was little, but during the war the army needed the dye for everything and so they switched to red. *Lucky Strike went to war*, the ads said. In movies where the art director does his or her homework, he said, you can see that the logo is green. And an old silver cigarette lighter, heavy, with his initials engraved on one side and on the other these names: DUTCH HARBOR, ATTU, PEARL HARBOR, MIDWAY, ADMIRALTY ISLAND, BRISBANE, SYDNEY, BIAK, ESPIRITU SANTO. I put it to my nose and smell it. The hint of lighter fluid. He always smelled of cigarettes. And there are brown corduroy pants with the belt still in the loops and black socks that I imagine smell bad and a handkerchief. Who carries a handkerchief anymore? And a plaid flannel shirt and a pilly dark green sweater. I reach in for the wallet, open it, and find $41. A twenty, four fives, and a one. Bills arranged front to back, high to low.

Margaret appears, fresh-faced, clear-eyed, starting her shift. We look at each other for a time and I think how wonderful it must be to share a life with her.

'Oh, for heaven's sake,' my mother would say when someone told her something interesting, something mildly surprising. *Oh, for heaven's sake. Is that right?* She loved him and held him and planned a life. I have their wedding album in my closet in my apartment on a shelf underneath a couple of old boxes. For a time, on occasion, usually late, a glass of wine in hand, I would bring it down and leaf through it. On page after page, her pretty dress, her lovely hair, the tiny flowers, baby's breath, long white gloves, her broad smile. And him, smiling, too, closed-mouthed, forever embarrassed of his bad teeth. So much possibility. So much hope. We will have children. We will laugh. We will build a life and a family, fill it with rich memories, and nothing, *nothing*, so help us God, will ever pull us apart. What do we really get in life besides family, besides people whose job it is to look out for us? Whose blood oath is that they must never forget that? I would look at the pictures and think, *They knew nothing of what was to come.* I stopped looking after a while because it was like knowing an accident was going to happen but not being able to do anything to stop it.

How does it come to this? Not death, but this . . . this empty, nothing thing. A wallet, a bag of clothes. A half-empty pack of cigarettes. A Social Security card in laminate and a pension card for the Boston Police Department and a pick-up slip for a dry cleaner's dated two years ago and there, tattered at the edges, almost stuck to the leather, is a photo, in black and white, of Eddie and Kevin and Maura and me, sitting in a row, in matching sweaters, me a fat-faced three-year-old and on the back the date and the imprint SEARS ROEBUCK & CO. PHOTO LAB. MAKE THE MEMORIES LAST.

Oh, for heaven's sake.

Margaret says, 'Mr. Dolan?'

I look up and smile at her.

'I'm fine, Margaret. Honestly.'

I put the wallet back into the bag.

'We're so sorry,' Simone says suddenly.

'Thank you,' I say, nodding. 'Thank you.'

Milky light outside. New Year's Day.

'Happy New Year,' I say.

They force a smile. It's time to go. Except I don't move. And Margaret, sweet Margaret, knower of secrets, of the right way to live, early morning walker, maker of homemade soups, understands far sooner than I the simple truth that however far you drift from your family, however much pain they've caused you, however hard you try to run, at some point, perhaps without knowing it, you end up running back. Even if it's too late. Which is why she comes over and puts her arms around me, a light embrace,

223

gently patting my back.

I pick up the plastic bag, what is left of my father, and walk out into the blue-gray dawn. I need to call my family.

MAKE THE MEMORIES LAST

The train heads north hugging the Connecticut coast for a time. Late-afternoon light. I'm going to Boston. Tomorrow we are going to sit in a room — the Dolans — and listen to our father's last will and testament. Tonight, we will have dinner.

Now, though, sitting in the café car on the Acela, I wait for the conference call. The presentation is today. I told Ian I'd prefer to go to the meeting and call in to the reading of the will, but he wouldn't have it. I told Ian about my father when I got back to New York from Cape Cod. It was early, in the office. He'd come in with coffees. We were going to crack it. We were going to best the lame ideas we had. This was the Super Bowl and we were going to make a name for ourselves with this spot.

I say, 'My father died.'

Ian says, 'Is this a joke?'

'No. Real this time.'

'Jesus, Fin. I'm so sorry. You okay?'

'I'm fine. I'm tired.'

'What happened?'

'He stopped breathing,' I say.

'Cut the shit.'

'He was old.'

'Who else was there?'

'Where?'

Ian says, 'In the room. When he died.'

'No one. He died in the middle of the night. Then I went over.'

'It's sad, man.'

'Yeah.'

Ian says, 'Why don't you take a few days off. I'll tell Martin. He'll understand.'

'It's fine. It's nothing.'

'Nothing?'

'How long have you known me? How many times have I mentioned my father?'

'Twice,' he says. 'Both times to tell me he was dead.'

'Exactly. So. He wasn't really a part of my life.'

'I don't know what to say. Have you told Phoebe?'

'No. I will, though.'

We didn't crack it. In the end, after two dozen more ideas from all of us, Martin narrowed it down to Al Gore and William McDonough, with 1984 as a distant safety. We were eager to sell Al Gore. Big shoot, lots of travel, great computer-generated graphics, work for two weeks in L.A., which would largely involve Ian and me playing Ping-Pong at the post-production facility and eating expensive dinners. And then we would win awards for our spot. That's how we scripted it.

I stopped by Ian's office before I left for Penn Station. 'I'm off.'

'Good luck up there.'

'Yeah. Thanks.'

I waited by the door.

I said, 'The Al Gore idea is good.'

226

Ian said, 'Al Gore is good.'

I said, 'The others kind of suck, huh?'

Ian said, 'They're not great.'

'Is the Al Gore idea good?'

Ian said, 'Not really.'

'Why is that?'

'Well, we're not that good.'

I said, 'That sounds about right.'

I turned to go but stopped.

I said, 'It's a good job, isn't it?'

Ian said, 'Yes.'

I said, 'And we're lucky to have it. Especially these days.'

'Yes.'

'But we don't really like it anymore.'

'No.'

'And yet we don't leave.'

'Nope.'

'Why is that?'

Ian said, 'Fear. Laziness. Complacency. Mostly we don't know what to do.'

I said, 'We die, ya know. One day. We die.'

Ian said, 'I know.'

Silence.

Ian said, 'Listen, thanks for stopping by, this has been great.'

I said, 'The ideas.'

Ian said, 'Don't worry. It's no big deal. It's just the Super Bowl.'

* * *

The train hits a straightaway and ramps up speed. Time for the conference call.

Martin, Ian, Alan, Jill, and Keita will be with the client. Several other clients from offices around the globe will call in.

I dial the number, say my name, hit pound.

Someone says, 'Hi. Who was that who just joined?'

I say, 'It's Fin.'

The voice says, 'Hey, Fin, we're just waiting on a couple of others.'

I hear muffled talk as people gather, the beep as others join the call, their recorded name announced.

Perhaps my father has left us millions of dollars, money we never knew he had. Perhaps he has left us stocks that he bought in IBM decades ago, a nest egg, an apology. 'I was looking out for you. I just had anger issues.' Maybe there are home movies, a box of Super 8 film that he secretly took, edited together, making a short film of our young lives, one he narrated, explaining everything.

Someone says, 'Hey, everyone. I'm Carole. Some of you might not know me. I wanted to thank you all for calling in. It's much appreciated. I know we have a lot of ground to cover and I hope everyone has the agenda, but I'd also like today to be informal enough for people to jump in. The other thing is confidentiality. What we're talking about here is serious and proprietary and potentially huge for this company. You wouldn't be on this call if you weren't vital to this project. So what's said here stays here. Who'd like to start us out?'

There's silence and then laughing.

I'm wondering if Martin or Alan is going to do any setup but perhaps there's no need since we all know why we're here.

I decide to jump in.

I say, 'Hey, everyone. It's Fin Dolan in New York. Well, on a train from New York to Boston.'

Carole says, 'Hey, Fin.'

'I thought I'd say a few words about our thinking.'

'Great,' Carole says. 'Exactly what we were hoping for.'

Perhaps it's the three cups of Amtrak high-octane coffee and the Sara Lee crumb cake I've had, but I'm feeling good. I want to lay the groundwork for the Al Gore idea. I want them to see the genius.

I say, 'I think what makes this product so great is that it will have such an impact on the planet. On landfills and oceans. And I think we need to align ourselves with the environmental movement. Diapers can be green. That's an amazing thought. You think of what a diaper is and does . . . and here we have something that won't harm the environment . . . How remarkable is that?'

There's an unusually long silence and I worry that I've hit a bad cell zone.

It's Carole. 'I'm sorry. Who did you say you were again?'

'It's Fin.'

'I'm sorry, I don't see that name on our call sheet. You're in Gentron's New York office?'

'Gentron? This isn't Snugglies?'

'Get off this call *now* or we will hunt you down and sue you!'

I check into a hotel using our company's rate and take a long shower. Eddie has e-mailed us the name of a restaurant near where he works. It's not far from the hotel.

Ian calls.

'Why didn't you call in?'

'I did. Just to the wrong call. I was seconds away from being a tech billionaire. How'd it go?'

'Tough to say. Might have liked Al Gore.'

'Did they buy anything?'

'They're having a think, getting back to us in a couple of days.'

'Was I missed?'

'No. There were half-a-dozen people on the phone and at least twenty in the room. You okay?'

'Fine. Why?'

'When's the last time you guys were all together?'

'The first Clinton administration. We'll be fine. We're just like a family. Except for the caring part.'

★ ★ ★

There's a sparse crowd, lots of seats at the bar, a few people sitting in the lounge area. A bitterly cold night a few nights into the New Year. I'm nervous.

The bartender is Grace Kelly. She's Grace Kelly when Grace Kelly was twenty-five, a vision, the porcelain skin and the ice-blue eyes, the honest-to-God blond hair, a smile and a beauty that unnerves your internal monologue. Then she speaks. And what comes out is the world's heaviest Boston accent.

'How ahh ya?' she says, which can also be pronounced *How are you?*

'I'm good. How are you?'

'Me? I'm supah. What can I get ya?'

'Beer would be great.'

'Sam Adams?' Except it comes out 'See-aaaaam Adams.' Long soft vowels. It makes me love her more.

She draws the beer from the tap and I watch her. She is used to being watched.

'In town on business?' she asks as she puts the glass down in front of me.

I nod, do a kind of bobblehead doll move, back and forth. 'Well, it's certainly a *kind* of business.'

'That sounds intriguing,' she says with a flirty smile that makes my insides turn to jelly. 'What do you do?'

Me? What do I do? I'm a fighter pilot. I'm a rescue diver. I'm a stunt man. I do stunt work. Hanging off cliffs, that kind of thing. Did you see the opening of *Mission: Impossible III?* That was me hanging off that rock. No. I'm with Oxfam America. I'm back in the U.S. to drum up money for a new project I'm working on. It will bring video games . . . I mean, water . . . to a village. I'm a vascular surgeon. No . . . don't. Just tell the truth. I'm a copywriter and I'm in town because my father died. He died and we were estranged and now my family and I will

231

hear his last will and testament. Say it.

'I'm in town to try to buy the New England Patriots.'

'You're kiddin'!'

'I'm not. I represent a man, a very wealthy man, who has his eyes on them.'

'Wow. That's amazing. You're not going to take them away, are you? We love our Pats.'

I say, 'No, no. We'd never do that.'

A couple has sat down at the far end of the bar.

She smiles and says, 'Don't go anywhere.'

Don't go anywhere? What does that mean? Is she flirting? Is that possible? Or is she just being friendly? Is she propositioning me? What does she look like naked? Someone taps me. I look up and see a guy, late fifties, suit, tie undone, sitting a few stools away. He's had a few drinks. He says, 'James Dean dying in a Porsche accident?'

I smile. 'Yes.'

He says, 'Who cares, besides maybe Mrs. Dean and the guy's agent? He made three movies and they were lousy. *Rebel Without a Cause?* How about rebel without a friggin' clue? What a little girl in that red windbreaker. Brando read for that role.'

He nods. Grace Kelly is back and rolls her eyes and smiles.

'And what about Duane Allman?' he says. 'The day he crashed his Harley-Davidson Sportster a few months after the release of *Live at the Filmore East . . .* '

He turns quickly to face me. 'What day was that?'

'I have no idea.'

He says, 'October 29, 1971. Where was it?'

'Belgium,' I say, though he's not really listening.

'Macon, Georgia. The day he . . . well, something ended in this country. For me, anyway.'

He sips his drink. Brown liquid. He sings softly, in a not unpleasant voice.

'Lord, I was born a ramblin' man, tryin' to make a livin' and doin' the best I can . . . '

He's looking straight ahead now. 'Ever notice no one talks about Scope anymore?'

'The mouthwash?'

'Scope, Boraxo, wax paper, paper lunch bags, Colgate Tooth Powder. Came in a red tin with a little plastic cap. What happened to that stuff?'

'I guess people just stopped using it.'

'That makes no sense to me. How can you just one day stop using something like Scope?'

I shrug. Grace Kelly puts a fresh beer in front of me and winks.

He checks his BlackBerry. He types quickly with his thumbs. This is a man with a job. Perhaps he runs a company, is responsible for other people's jobs. He makes decisions, determines what kind of ad agency is chosen. I fear he's going to remove his pants. He puts the Black-Berry down.

He says, 'I mean, *seat* belts, for Christ's sake.'

He looks at me, as if those two words explain it all, as if they are a kind of genius answer to Fermat's theorem.

'Seat belts,' I say, as if I understand what he's talking about.

233

'Right?' he says. 'I mean, we used to crawl around the station wagon like cosmonauts in a weightless environment. Adults would literally blow cigarette smoke in your face for fun. We drank whole milk with five tablespoons of Bosco in it. We ate Chips Ahoy like kids eat vitamins now. And look at us. We're fine. Aren't we fine?'

'I certainly think so.'

He picks up his glass, smiles, and clinks it against mine. He drinks.

He says, 'I've gotta take a piss. Be right back.'

I say, 'I can't wait.'

And then I turn and look toward the door and see my sister walk in. How bizarre, I think. I am related to her. We have the same parents. We grew up in the same house. And yet she is a stranger to me. I read once that 99.9 percent of one person's DNA is identical to another's. I walk over as Maura hands her coat to the hostess. I watch her undo her scarf, stuff it in the arm of the coat, fix her hair by rolling it back behind her ears. I have watched her do these things a thousand times. The youngest always watches his brothers and sisters more than they ever know.

'Hi,' I say.

My voice jerks her head up.

'Fin. I didn't see you there. Am I late? Hi.' A fast blinker, often nervous, high-strung. We hug, the awkward hug of strangers, the flat hand pat, slow repeat, on the back.

'Not at all. I just got here.'

The hostess seats us at a table for four and hands both of us an array of enormous menus

— daily specials, wine lists — as if we're taking part in a food-and-beverage convention. Maura has put on lipstick for this. She has done her hair, which she wears in the chin-length bob of a Boston suburban mom, sensible, non-sexual, kind-of-cute. She wears a canary-yellow sweater set with black pants. Her shoes are round-toed, comfortable slip-ons. She rubs her hands.

'This is nice,' she says, looking around.

I nod and smile. Our mother called her Honey Bee. She read me stories when I was little. She said, 'Don't ever let Mum see you cry.'

The waitress takes her drink order.

'Did you drive in?' I ask, though I had no knowledge that these words were going to come out of my mouth. I have a smile on my face like a game-show host. I want to slap myself.

'No. No, I took the commuter rail. Paul didn't want me driving. Supposed to get three to six inches tonight. I hope Kevin's flight lands.'

Maura has four kids. They have names and ages and she stays at home, having left a job in something or other at Fidelity. She used to go to church a lot. We talked about it once, a long time ago. She felt a connection. She used to go with my mother. Then the monsignor of her church was sentenced to prison for molesting dozens of young boys over the course of thirty years. Now she cleans obsessively. She loathes newspapers in the house, she told me. Her husband, Paul, is an engineer or a scientist or a programmer or a hedge-fund guy who invented a software program. He made a lot of money. They live in a house slightly larger than Finland.

'You look good,' I say, though this is a lie. She looks tired and stressed, older than I remember, a woman in deep need of yoga and a massage and a beach and sexual healing.

She rolls her eyes. 'I look old. There's Eddie.' She waves toward the front of the restaurant and I look to see my oldest brother, the man who knows everything. I stand and shake his hand. He leans over for a perfunctory kiss on Maura's cheek, both of them turning away, skin barely touching. The waitress brings Maura's drink.

Eddie says, 'Grey Goose rocks, olives, please.'

It is striking to me how much Eddie looks like our father, though I would never say that out loud. He would be insulted, as if that were a criticism, as if somehow he and not his DNA were at fault. Eddie is a real estate lawyer. Three kids, separated last I'd heard. I don't think he's looked either of us in the eye yet.

Maura sips her wine, puts it down. I smile at the salt shaker. Maura picks up her drink and sips again. Eddie looks around.

Maura says, 'How are the kids, Eddie?'

Eddie nods to the table. 'Good. Good.'

Check, please.

Eddie says, 'Where's Kevin?'

Maura says, 'On his way, I guess. If his flight landed.'

Or if he ever got on it in the first place. It is hard to say who took the worst from our father. Certainly not me. And he left Maura alone for the most part. It was Eddie or Kevin or my mother. My mother, though, could calm him sometimes. And Eddie was tough. Kevin

. . . Kevin was mostly just confused that his father would treat him like that, that his own father seemed to hate him. He applied only to schools on the West Coast after high school. He just wanted to get away. He studied graphic design, somehow got a job at Apple. Now he has his own firm. He lives with his boyfriend. I get a card from them at Christmas. He used to call me Finneus.

The waitress brings Eddie's drink. He eats an olive off the pick, sips the drink, clears his throat. *Who are you? Where's the person I knew? Where did he go? And am I different to him, as well? To Maura?*

Eddie says to Maura, 'How's Paul? The kids?'

Maura says, 'Good. All good.'

Eddie looks down at his drink and says, 'Did he say anything?' Then he looks up at me. It hits me that I've not seen him in a long time.

'No. He never regained consciousness.'

Eddie nods.

Maura and I are looking at Eddie, waiting for him to say something. The same dynamic for as long as I can remember. He's the oldest. We watch and wait and follow his lead.

Eddie says, 'Were you there when he died? In the room?'

Maura exhales loudly, looks away, sips deeply from her drink.

I say, 'No. It was late. I was asleep at the hotel. They called me.'

'And you went there?'

'No. I went to the hotel gym at three in the morning, did the Stairmaster.'

'Don't be a wise ass.'

'Don't ask me stupid questions.' It comes out too loud.

He glares at me across the table.

Eddie says, 'Whatever. I don't really give a fuck.'

Maura says, 'Language.'

I form my response and then tell myself not to say it but I say it anyway, as if I'm out of control, on a bad adrenaline rush. I'm running my tongue against the back of my lower teeth like I'm on coke. My neck is hot.

I say, 'You're asking a lot of questions for someone who doesn't care.'

I can smell booze on Eddie's breath, even from where I sit. He stopped for one on the way, perhaps the only way to face us, to face this. I'm four seconds away from walking out. *This* is why we never see each other. Because every time we do we revisit the past and sit in it, unable to do anything but flail and scream and injure ourselves. So much of our conversation is unsaid, spoken so long ago. We have nothing in common but a last name and a history that won't let us go.

Again, I say the words without thinking. 'Why weren't *you* there? Why weren't *either* of you there?'

They look at me like the witnesses must have looked at Eichmann on trial. Eddie, leaning across the table, face contorted. 'Because he was a *fucking* prick, that's why. Because he killed . . . '

'*Stop* it.' Maura.

238

If you dropped the ambient noise you'd hear the three of us breathing heavily.

The waiter has a smile like he's trying out for a Broadway show.

'How are we all this evening? I'm Gareth and I would love to tell you about our specials . . . '

I cut him off. 'Hi. Sorry. We're actually waiting on one more person. Maybe we could hear those in a bit.'

We sit in silence, waiting for the night to be over. I'm staring at the ceiling, so I don't see Kevin walk in. He looks at the three of us, reads our faces.

'I see we've already begun.'

★　★　★

I oversleep and have to walk quickly to the lawyer's office for the reading of the will. I pass a bank clock on the way and the readout says it is twenty-one degrees. The bellhop says I can get there faster on foot than by cab at this time of morning in this part of town. I get lost. The streets are a labyrinth in the old part of the city and I end up at the water twice. I'm frozen and stop in at a coffee shop, a pre-Starbucks time capsule.

There's a Formica counter at which sits a handful of men who look like they've worked a nightshift, drinking bottles of Miller High Life. There is an older woman wearing two overcoats stirring her coffee and putting packet after packet of sugar into it. She has a newspaper folded to the crossword puzzle. 'I read two hundred books a year,' she says to the newspaper. 'I'm a writer and a poet and I've had my books published. In Israel. A rose is a rose is a rose. Who said that?'

I order a coffee to go for warmth more than anything else, and my cell phone rings. The display reads *Amy Deacon*.

'Amy,' I say rather cleverly. I'm in a mild state of shock. We've spoken once in eight months. That call did not go well. A call initiated by me, 'checking in.' A mistake, having done what I did. I did it to assuage my guilt, she said.

Also, I'm not sure if it's a general low-grade nervousness in my gut or the particularly potent coffee I gulped in the lobby of the hotel on my way out, but yet again my lower intestinal tract is warming up for what appears to be an Irish jig and I fear a Four Seasons-like toilet at this establishment is out of the question. The men laugh and one says, 'Sully, you're such an asshole.' Only 'asshole' comes out 'ahhs-hole.'

Amy says, 'Hi, Fin.' I smile at the high pitch, the kindness in her voice. The older woman with two coats now seems to be staring at my crotch. I make a quick tactile examination of the area to make sure my fly is up and I've not accidentally urinated on myself, though to be frank, in my current state of lower intestinal agitation, I sense my penis retracting like wheels after takeoff.

'How are you?' she says.

We'd met on a plane. I was on my way to Cincinnati for a client meeting. Amy was headed to a conference on trauma therapy. A storm was over eastern Pennsylvania. We sat on the tarmac

240

at LaGuardia for three and a half hours before the flight was canceled (foreshadowing?). We exchanged numbers. This was two years ago. Amy asked what my feelings were about children on the third date. I lied and said I'd always wanted them. It seemed the right thing to say. It seemed the thing normal people do: get married, have children, mow the lawn.

We started dating. We went to dinner. We went for drinks with friends (hers mostly). We went to weddings (also her friends). And during those Saturday-night weddings, dancing, too much champagne, I could see so clearly that she wanted me to ask her. And yet it was as if I were watching myself from across the room.

'What are you doing, Fin?' my alter ego would ask. This Fin is leaning casually against a tent pole, sipping a gin-and-tonic, wearing a white dinner jacket. This Fin is really good-looking and I wish I were more like him.

'What am I doing? I'm doing what people do. I'm at a wedding. I'm thinking about proposing to Amy, who I almost love.'

'You *almost* love her?' my other self asks doubtfully.

'Yes. Almost. That's the best I can do. Real love? Movie love? That doesn't exist, handsome Fin.'

'I'm not sure I agree with you, normal-looking Fin.'

'But this is what one does. I want to be a normal person. I want to do normal things.'

'You are in love with the idea of love.'

'That's terrible, terrible dialogue.'

'You're in love with the *idea* of romance, with the *idea* of Amy.'

And, of course, handsome Fin was right. Love is not the feeling you get at a friend's wedding on Martha's Vineyard on a perfect summer evening, you in a tux, Amy in a sexy dress. That's called a buzz. Love is something else.

Always, deep down, in a place I rarely ventured, I felt anything but normal. I felt damaged and wrong. I felt hollow and different. I felt I was acting all the time. We look for family. If we have none, if people scatter and die, we look for family in other forms — friends, in-laws, coworkers. I'd found that in advertising, albeit in a slightly twisted way, in New York City. Now I thought I could find it in Amy and her family, that the being-in-love-with-her part would eventually come.

That first winter together, on the sidewalk at Central Park West and Sixty-third. That's when she first told me she loved me. It was cold. We'd gone skating. We were waiting for the light to change. We were trying to figure out what to do for dinner. I'd taken her glove off and was holding her hand, blowing warm air on it, putting it to my face.

'I love you,' she said, looking at her hand.

I stopped blowing on her hands. My expression must have changed. *And I like you very much!* I wanted to say.

I had what I'm sure was an inane smile on my face. I knew I was expected to say something in return. I'd seen the movies, read the books. My mind searched for the words, unable to simply utter *I love you, too*.

What came out instead, though somehow she didn't find it odd, was, 'I have love for you, too.' Like a bad Russian translation. Though what may have saved me was the fact that I hugged her as I was saying it and my voice was muffled by the furry hood on her winter coat. What a terrible thing it is to not love someone who loves you. Far worse is acting as if you do.

I went through with it, never questioning any of it, convinced that if I simply kept taking steps forward I'd be okay, that I was doing the right thing.

In bed, deep into the night, I would wake and go and sit in the kitchen, in the dark, stare out the window, hold my breath, try not to make a sound, as the escape plan hatched itself. I had money in the bank. I could pack a small bag, a knapsack, be on a flight by midday, to Poland or Morocco or Vietnam, places where a person could live for long periods of time on little money. I had researched this. The złoty. Polish money is called the złoty. In Vietnam, the dong (unfortunate). I sat there in the dark, cold coming through the windowpane, the small rattle when the wind blew, shaking, my heart racing and a strange rash under my arms. And yet I was a willing participant in this entire charade. I made this happen, me, the person who's supposed to be immune to false narratives, the person who creates false narratives for a living. 'You make her happy,' Amy's mother had said. Yes, and then I made her very unhappy.

With six weeks to go until the wedding, she

found me in the kitchen one night, sitting on a chair by the window, converting dollars to złoty on a pad of paper.

'Honey?' she said, the slightly confused, mildly frightened voice one uses to speak to the insane. 'What are you doing?'

I hadn't known she was there and I looked up, terrified, a feral animal cornered.

'I'm fine,' I'd said, too loudly — and certainly not convincingly — considering the fact that I was naked, wide-eyed, and shivering.

Amy said, 'You're scaring me.'

I had to say it. I felt like I might vomit. My palms were sweating and my heart was racing, like I'd had eleven cups of coffee.

'I'm not sure I can do this,' I said, looking at the figures on the paper in front of me.

'Do what?'

I could take it back. I could dance around it. But she knew.

The light from the streetlamp was the only light in the kitchen.

She was staring at me, her arms folded tightly across her chest. I could feel it. But I couldn't quite bring myself to look at her. Finally I said it again, slower this time, a dare to myself, to what tiny amount of courage I had left. 'I'm not sure I can do this.'

She said, 'Honey. People get cold feet sometimes. It's . . . it's a huge thing. It's natural to be a little scared.'

'No,' I said. 'It's more than that.'

And perhaps it's the way I said it, the tone of my voice. That's the thing about a play. They're

244

not meant to be read. You read them in high school and in college, but often they don't mean as much as when you see them on stage. You hear the actor's voice, their inflection. It's all about how we say a thing.

She stared at me, a woman looking at an accident on the highway, at a dead body, only to realize she knows the person lying there.

'What!?'

I said nothing, just looked at her. I'd hoped that she would understand what I myself didn't quite understand; that I liked her a lot but that the idea of marrying her and being responsible for her happiness when lately, for some time, I had been unable to find any myself, well, that was just a little too much at the moment.

She'll understand, I thought. It is one of the things that drew me to her, her empathy. This is her job, really, as a social worker, to listen and put herself in the shoes of other people, to help them help themselves.

Her face began to crinkle. She winced. Her hand went to her mouth and I realized, as she leaned back on the stove for support, repeating 'Oh my God' through muffled sobs, that what she understood was that I was calling off the wedding.

That was eight months ago.

★ ★ ★

'I'm good,' I say now. 'Yeah. I'm okay. I'm in Boston, actually.'

'Really? Why's that?'

And here a memory comes to me clear and fast. I once told Amy my father was dead.

'We're pitching Legal Sea Food. Do you know it? Amazing sea food restaurant. How are you?'

The old woman is sniffing the backs of her hands like a maniac, like she's lost a scent.

'I'm great. Do you have a minute?'

Maybe we could have a coffee or a drink, I think to myself. Maybe we could have crazy dirty monkey sex. Maybe that's why she's calling, like she once did, to describe the color and satiny texture of her bra, the demi-cup, the fullness of her gorgeous breasts. Is it possible she's been thinking about me? *So what he backed out on the wedding. Other than that he was a catch.*

She says, 'I've actually been meaning to call you.'

There is a tenderness to her voice. The sadness and anger of the break-up long forgotten now. She is the kind of person who will only remember the good things — a far better, more nuanced, more emotionally mature person than I. She once said, 'Fin, we all have an emotional toolbox. Our parents give us these toolboxes on our eighteenth birthday after years and years of filling them with all the wonderful tools we'll need. Compassion, patience, empathy, courage, optimism, determination, confidence, altruism. Some of us have one of those big, red, shiny ones, like you find in the pit stop area of NASCAR races. And some have a good-sized household one. You have a little one, like a child might have. And inside there's almost nothing. Maybe just like a ball-peen hammer and a broken measuring tape. But it's not your fault, sweetie.'

I have giant words in my head when I think of certain people. For Ian it's SECURE. For Martin it's CONFIDENT. For Phoebe it's LOVELY. With Amy the word KIND appears in big letters, maybe a strong, clean Helvetica. And I threw that away. And in this moment, like so many others, I regret everything and in the exact same moment wonder if maybe we could get back together, if only for tonight. And the mere thought of that floods me with a comfort that is palpable. My mood lifts. I can see her bright, warm, clean apartment, the working fireplace, the big bed with far too many pillows. Her tidy kitchen filled with All-Clad pots and pans and complete sets of dishes, glasses that match, place settings. A refrigerator with food in it. She buys flowers for no other reason than they look pretty on the table. And I think yes, perhaps we could talk all night in front of the fireplace and drink wine and order food. I could tell her the whole story, the story even I don't understand, about how I've gotten here, to this distant, empty, emotionless place. I would purge my soul to her and she would listen, nod, comfort and affirm me. 'Life is a process, Fin,' she would say, slowly, nodding. 'You're doing fine. Just a little slower than most.' And later, after much sex, we would sleep for many hours. And then I would leave, run screaming into the morning, wanting nothing more than to escape again.

'I wanted to call because . . . this is a bit awkward . . . '

I knew it. She wants to get together. I could be on a shuttle flight at five and in her apartment by seven.

She says, 'I wanted to call because my boyfriend proposed to me New Year's Eve and we're getting married in a month. We're flying to Paris. He's rented the restaurant at the Crillon. He's bringing my family and his family, some of whom live over there and . . . I'm rambling, I know, but I'm just so happy. And I wanted you to know that because I know how upset it made you to make me as unhappy as you did. I was really angry at you for a while, but I'm over that now. I wanted you to not feel bad about it anymore because looking back, not marrying you was the best thing that ever happened to me. And I wanted to thank you for that.'

It's as if someone has just handed me a different script to my life. As if the one I was working from was the wrong one. In the old one I was someone with time, with a great job, with possibility ahead of him. It was a rollicking good comedy. This new one is a sad drama. The hero is almost forty, which means he's almost fifty, which means his life is basically over and any chance of success long gone. And the truly sad part is that it's his own fault. He thought he could live a life where you blamed fate for your lot. Father left. Mother died. Poor me. What he failed to realize is that there is no fate. There is only how hard you are willing to work to be happy. And in this new script, he's a fool.

In the end all I can manage is, 'I'm very happy for you, Aim. Honest.'

We hang up and I stand there, thinking I may shit myself. I see a door that says TOILET but underneath is a sign that says OUT OF ORDER.

I turn to see the old woman staring at me. She squints and says, 'Did you hear the one about the most optimistic man in the world? He jumped off the Empire State Building and halfway down the window washers hear him say, 'So far, so good.''

She cackles and turns away.

★　★　★

We are in a small conference room at the law office. Sullivan, O'Neil & Levy is a working man's law firm. From the looks of it the offices haven't changed much in forty years. Beiges and browns on the walls, the furniture. Cheaply framed posters of Cape Cod, the Freedom Trail, the Boston skyline.

Tom Hanley introduces himself as my father's attorney, shakes hands, smiles, looks us in the eye. A full head of snow-white hair, stocky, broad-shouldered, fat fingers. Two rings. One a large class ring. Boston College. The other a gold Claddagh ring with a diamond on his wedding finger. He keeps smoothing his tie over his belly, a nervous tic maybe. His tone is more like that of a parish priest about to say a funeral mass.

'Coffee? Water? Something stronger? The restrooms are just down the hall if anyone needs one before we start.'

He's saying, *I'm sorry. I know this is painful. I want to make it a little easier.* Boston Irish.

Don't say what you're feeling. Find another way to say it.

We take our seats. A woman who Tom Hanley introduces as Rosemary sits with a stenograph at the end of the table. And there, on the table in front of Tom Hanley, to the left of his yellow legal pad and gold Cross pen, sit the remains of our father.

'Okay,' Tom Hanley says. 'This is the reading of the Last Will and Testament of Edward Lawrence Dolan, Senior. Present at the reading are Thomas Hanley, attorney at law representing the deceased, Rosemary Kelleher, stenographer, and the children of Edward Lawrence Dolan, Senior, Edward Lawrence Dolan, Junior, Kevin Francis Dolan, Maura Ann Dolan-Macaphee, and Finbar Thomsen Dolan.'

He pauses. It feels like church. Why do I keep needing a toilet?

''I, Edward Lawrence Dolan, a resident of Bradenton, Florida, and Hyannis, Massachusetts, hereby make this Will and revoke all prior Wills and Codicils. I was born May 17, 1926, in Portsmouth, New Hampshire. I am not currently married but I was previously married to Emily Kelleher Dolan from October 1955 to 1980 and the marriage ended by the Commonwealth of Massachusetts in 1982. I have four living children.''

Eddie is looking out the window. Kevin is looking at his iPhone. Maura is examining her nails.

It takes only a few blurred minutes to read through the will itself because there was nothing to bequeath. No money, no houses, no antiques, no art, no cars, no stocks or bonds. Except the letter.

Tom Hanley removes the letter from a binder and lays it out in front of him on the table. He sips from a glass of water. He looks at us. 'We good?' No one says anything.

He reads. ''My dear children.''

Eddie, stage whisper: 'Oh, give me a break.'

Kevin says, in a voice a bit too loud, 'Eddie.'

Eddie shakes his head back and forth, stands, and goes to the window, hands in his pockets, back to us. Tom Hanley is unfazed. How many times has he sat in this room, read these kinds of documents to families? Hurt families, fractured families, loving families. Every time drawn back into the past, to the beauty of a memory, the pain, the ongoing tragedy of family. He seems like the kind of guy who'd be a great neighbor.

Tom Hanley continues. ''My dear children.''

He pauses, as if a small scold to Eddie, as if to say, *You dumb asshole, you still don't get it, do you?*

One day you will sit down and write out something that you know will be read after you die. If you've done it all wrong, they will be the words you hope will replace the actions of your life. I wasn't a very good father. And I wasn't a very good husband. If you think it is easy for me to write these words you are wrong. I tried. I swear to God Almighty I did. What I tell you now I tell you not as an excuse but so you might understand. Your mother and I grew apart.

*She stopped being in love with me years
before I left. I couldn't be the man she
wanted or needed. I couldn't get a handle
on my anger or, for a long time, my drinking. But just so you know, I did not
choose to leave. Though I believe it was
for the best in the end, your mother asked
me to leave. Your mother had met someone else.*

Tom Hanley is channeling Anthony Hopkins
because he knows to pause here, the perfect
dramatic beat, not too long. He's ready for this.
He's read the letter before today and knows the
effect these words will have on us.

'He's a *liar*!' It's Maura.

'This is bullshit.' Eddie, turning from the
window.

'Let him finish.' Kevin.

Tom Hanley sips from a glass of water and
continues.

*It doesn't matter who, as he's long dead.
He was married at the time. It was not
something that was ever going to be. But
she did love him. Your mother was a good
woman and a good Catholic and the guilt
and shame of it was very hard for her. She
told me. She told me I had ruined her life.
She said that I had taken her for granted
and that the children are afraid of me. She
said things I will never forget and I sat
there and took them because they were
true. She asked me to leave and to leave*

252

you all alone. There are things that you do that you cannot change no matter how hard you try. The rest of my life is of little consequence to you now. I met people, they saw me as a good man. I liked that. But know this. There are things I did that were good. There are memories I have, as clear to me now as if they happened this morning. I can picture each of you as small children. I can feel you, in the middle of the night, holding you as you cried, feeding you a bottle, sitting in that chair in the den rocking you back to sleep. Hundreds of times over the years. And what do they count for? To you nothing. To me so much more than you can know. I do not ask that you forgive me. I wouldn't if I was in your place. But I would ask that you try to understand that a person can make terrible mistakes. No one in this room is free of sin. You asked me to be more than I was capable of. I ask only one thing and it is of all of you. Or any one of you. I would like my ashes spread at sea, in the Pacific, 12 nautical miles from Pearl Harbor, latitude 21 degrees, 23 minutes north longitude −158 degrees, 57 minutes west. That's where I was the day the war ended. I would say I'm sorry but I don't think it would mean much. Your father, Edward Dolan.

Rosemary, the stenographer, has stopped typing but she continues staring at the machine.

Tom Hanley stands. 'I'll leave you alone.' He and Rosemary leave.

I have an odd capacity to escape reality. It makes life much more pleasant. Now, in this moment, I realize I have no intention of ever spreading my father's ashes off the coast of Hawaii or the coast of Coney Island, for that matter. A Buddhist might say that I wasn't living in the moment. I would reply to my saffron-robe-wearing meditator that with rare exceptions there are few moments I want to live in. I like escape. I like my made-up world.

No one says anything for a long time. Until Kevin says, 'I was hoping for cash.'

★ ★ ★

How do you see the world? Is there music underscoring scenes of your life? Do you slow things down for intensity and drama? Speed them up for comedy? Do you rewrite dialogue, if, say, you've had a fight with your boss or your wife or some jackass who cut the line at Dunkin' Donuts? In these rewrites are you wittier, more bold? I do and I am. It makes life more interesting for me, gives me a wonderful sense of false empowerment.

And yet I know I miss the far more interesting narratives, the narratives I will never know, of strangers. Because you can't possibly know what's going through someone's mind when you pass them on the street, see them standing at a traffic light, looking around in front of an office building in downtown Boston, looking left,

254

looking right, wondering where to go. I wonder what the four of us look like as we walk out of the building. Do we look like lost tourists? What do passersby see? Does anyone notice Maura's fast blinking or Eddie's slightly shaking right hand as he smokes a cigarette or Kevin's near-constant text messaging to God-only-knows who. Does anyone notice my heart palpitations and sweating palms in the twenty-degree weather, holding a cardboard-beige box with several pounds of human ash, searching out a cab to Logan for the next shuttle to LaGuardia?

In a near-perfect example of Dolan family dynamics, we all walked out of the conference room without the box containing my father's ashes before I returned for my gloves and saw it sitting there.

I say, 'That was fun. We should do that again soon.'

Maura says, 'I'm freezing. Can we get a coffee or something?'

There is a Starbucks across the street. We go in and eat cold sandwiches. We drink burnt, awful-tasting, nuclear-hot, overpriced coffee. The Carpenters sing, '*I'm on the . . . top of the world lookin' . . . down on creation . . .* '

Eddie says, 'He's a liar. It's not true.'

Maura says, 'What if it is?'

Eddie says, 'It's not.'

Maura says, 'But what if it is?'

It's strange how it didn't come as a shock to me. Strange how once I heard Tom Hanley say the words — 'Your mother had met someone else' — it unearthed a vague memory, the seemingly chance encounter in the supermarket or the dry cleaner's. 'Oh you remember Mr. So-and-so, Finny.' A brief chat. I could sense her awkwardness with me standing there. I watched him watch her, thought nothing of it, but somehow, in the memory, I can see it differently, see the intensity with which he looked at her. Later, after my father left, there would be phone calls, a man's voice. She would take the calls in her room. Not often. But enough for me — for all of us, is my guess — to remember, to sense at the time that something was happening.

Kevin says, 'What does it change? He was still an asshole. He still left. And good for her, by the way. I hope it is true. I hope she did find love.'

Maura says, 'What about the ashes?'

I look at Kevin for some reason. He and Maura are looking at Eddie, waiting. I notice, in the cold light of Starbucks, the small scar near Kevin's left eye. My father wore a ring, Golden Gloves. He'd been a boxer as a teenager.

Kevin says, 'It's insane.'

Maura says, 'Even dead he never fails to disappoint. The gall. Eddie?'

Eddie says, 'What? Are you asking me if I'm going to buy an airplane ticket to Hawaii and rent a boat and find this spot and spread my father's ashes and say a few thoughtful words about what a great guy he was?'

I say, 'So what do we do?'

Eddie says, 'This is pretty common.' He was in the Marines. He knows about these things. 'World War Two vets. Korean War vets. They ask that their ashes be spread, ask for burial at sea. If

256

they saw combat, they're entitled to a full military burial. I know a guy at the VA. He's in veterans affairs.'

I say, 'See, now to me, that sounds like a new drama on ABC. 'Soldiers. Heroes. Lovers. It's all part of Veterans Affairs. Thursdays following *Everybody Loves Raymond.*''

Kevin snorts and sips his giant latte. Maura shakes her head and nibbles on a premade sandwich. Eddie looks at me like I have snot on my face. It's like we're strangers stuck on an elevator, waiting for help.

What happened was this. We stopped caring. I don't know when, exactly. We were all hurt, suffering. Eddie, our legal guardian. Maura, our emotional guardian. Neighbors checked in, but we drifted inward, to our own worlds, needing no one. We crossed paths in the house occasionally, left a note when we went out, then left nothing. Then simply left. Eddie enlisted in the Marine Corps (feeling the need to prove himself a man, angry, instantly regretting his three-year stint), Kevin went to college in California, Maura to God. But not happy, all-encompassing God. Boston-Catholic God. Feel-bad-about-yourself God. I read, watched a lot of television, and learned to make up stories. We sold the house when I left for college. The occasional phone call turned into the rare phone call. Maura's wedding was an excuse to get drunk. So was Eddie's. Our friends became our new family, untainted by the Dolan history. Each of us tried to distance ourselves from our common past. From his leaving, from her sadness. Until what you end up with is four

257

strangers with the same last name who look a bit alike sitting in a coffee shop counting the minutes until they leave each other.

A woman, mid-forties, long dark hair, sits alone, looking at the door. A man walks in. She stands and they hold each other as if no one else is in the room. They sit across from each other, leaning across the small table, faces close. She touches his face.

Kevin says, 'I think that's a good idea.'

Maura says, 'Sounds good to me. Unless someone wants to get on a plane. Finny?'

Before I can answer, Maura says, 'Why wouldn't he want to be buried with his wife?'

Eddie shakes his head. 'No. I wouldn't have allowed that.'

Maura says, 'It wouldn't be your call, Eddie. Like it or not, they were married.'

A little too much edge. Eddie raises his eyebrows.

Sip the crappy coffee, look at the couple. What are they saying?

Maura says, 'I'm just saying, okay?' She shakes her head slowly and looks away, annoyed.

It wasn't always like this. And that's what I don't understand about time. Where did we go as a family? Because for a short period of time, after she died, we came together.

This one time. Not long after we buried our mother, Eddie got tickets to a Bruce Springsteen concert at the old Boston Garden. I remember I had a test the next day. 'What are you going to remember in fifty years, my little man?' Eddie had said with a smile. The old Eddie. I'd never been in the Garden — never been to a concert for that matter — but I loved hockey, loved the Bruins. When we walked in, when the place opened up in front of me, what a thing that was. Those Stanley Cup banners hanging from the rafters, the Celtics World Champion banners, the energy of the crowd, the heat and the lights. It was gorgeous. We made our way up to the front. I couldn't stop looking around.

'You stay by me, right?' Eddie said. Maura was holding my hand. Kevin was on one end and he'd somehow managed to get a couple of cans of beer in his coat. He and Maura snuck sips. He hated Bruce Springsteen. He was into Echo & the Bunnymen, The Clash, Joy Division. It was winter. Eddie was leaning over to say something to me when then the lights went down. The crowd went wild. Eddie had bought the album and listened to it pretty much nonstop. He loved 'Thunder Road,' loved the song 'Born to Run.' I loved 'Meeting Across the River,' this sad song about a guy named Eddie. The lights came up on the stage as the music kicked in. Loud, fast, intense. 'Born to Run.' Those drums, that horn. And Springsteen screaming into the mic. Everyone dancing in place, mouthing the lyrics. We all knew them. It felt incredible. I felt so alive. I turned to look at Eddie, to look at Maura and Kevin, to see if they were feeling this, too. Maura's beautiful wide-eyed smile, those big green eyes, Eddie's squint-eyed grin, just like our mother's, slow nodding. Even Kevin's face lit up. We didn't need to say a thing. It had been a long, horrible few months. But here we were, together. Kevin draped his arm around Maura's shoulder and Eddie put his arm around me and Maura wrapped her arm around my waist. We'd never done anything like that before and wouldn't again. We weren't huggers. We weren't touchers. But in that one moment we were a family, together, the Dolans. And I remember thinking, *If we could just stay like this.*

I lean back in my chair now, the memory so sharp. I feel my eyes begin to well so I look to the ceiling, realize I'm touching my scar and quickly stop. I'd gotten it that day, the day my mother died. Did I mention that? I should have mentioned that. When I came home, Maura stared at me. She was smoking, which she never did in the house. Mother would kill her, I thought. She didn't seem to notice the blood on my chin, my shirt.

'Finny,' she said. 'There was an accident. Mum's dead.'

She sat down on the kitchen floor. Dropped to the floor, really, sobbing. I sat down next to her. I didn't want to get blood on her. I didn't cry.

Now, at Starbucks, I put my hands inside the pockets of my coat and feel the plastic bag. I take it out and put it on the table.

I say, 'They gave me this at the hospital. It's what he had on him.'

I take the wallet out of the bag and empty the contents on the table. I take the picture out last. No one says anything. Not even Eddie has anything to say this time.

Kevin goes first, looks for a time, says, 'Jesus.'

Maura takes it and stares and I can see her

trying hard not to cry. She hands it to Eddie. He takes it and puts it down without looking at it, then can't help himself and stares at it for several seconds.

Everyone wants to leave, to go back to their families, the families they chose.

I slide the box across the table to Eddie. 'He's all yours.'

★   ★   ★

Outside the plane window, Manhattan from three thousand feet. Silent and clear and a partial moon. The weather says it's twenty-three degrees. We bank left at the Brooklyn Bridge, make our approach to LaGuardia. I made the last Delta shuttle.

The cab driver asks where to, and at first I'm not sure. Work comes to mind. Home. But neither is very appealing. I am suddenly hungry and in need of three glasses of wine. I give him the address of a place in SoHo, a small French place called Jean-Claude.

I have texts from Ian and Phoebe and a voice mail message from Keita.

'Fin. I hope your father's better. I am here if you need me. Maybe we could have a drink or dinner. Tell me please and I will help. This is Keita, by the way.'

I call Phoebe.

'How are you?' she says.

'I'm sorry I haven't called.'

'I'm so sorry about your dad. Are you okay?'

'Not really.'

She waits, the good listener.
I say, 'Have you had dinner?'
'Fin, it's ten-thirty.'

★ ★ ★

There are two other couples in the place, a bitterly cold Tuesday night in January. The tables, maybe twenty of them, are small, with squares of brown grocer-bag paper held down by silver clips at their edges. A candle on each table. A small zinc bar, the two waiters speaking French. One pours two glasses of wine.

Cornish game hen and risotto and for Phoebe a bowl of potato leek soup and very good bread and we're on our second glasses of Bordeaux. She's windburned from skiing and her hair is down and a mess and lovely and she has her glasses on because she'd taken her contacts out for the night. They were her father's frames, dorky, forty years old. Bad imitations are available now at Barneys for $350.

I'm watching the waiters and she's watching the beautiful couple in the corner and we're close enough, the place small enough, to hear goodly parts of their conversation.

The music is low, Chet Baker, I think. I hear the gentle scrape of fork and knife against plate, of a chair moving against the wood floor as someone adjusts their position. I smell Phoebe's perfume, faint at the end of the day. She's leaning forward, arms splayed out on the table, head tilted a bit to one side, face open and inviting, flushed from the cold, the wine. I am intensely aware of this moment. Here I am, in New York City, in a restaurant, on a winter's night, eating this food and drinking this wine, and I am alive and for a moment, just a moment, before it flits away, I am happy, feel, in fact, an overwhelming joy. And then, just that fast, as I try to hold on to it, to stay in it, the noise of thought pushes it away, like coffee spilled on a table, spreading out, covering everything. What have I been doing, why have I never been to Morocco, why don't I speak Spanish, why can't I kickbox, why didn't I take a night course in philosophy/art history/ Euclidean geometry, how is it that Eddie and Kevin and Maura are strangers to me? I watch my mind come back to the moment, unable to pick up the thread from before, the feeling from before. But right before it ends I want to touch her face, put my hand to her cheek, feel her lean into my hand. I need to tell her about the ashes. I need to tell her that my mother met another man, had an affair. I need to explain my confusion and anger. She'll help me put it into perspective. I have heard that people can talk like this.

I say, 'It was all a hoax. My father was there. We all laughed and hugged and then went to Olive Garden, whose new tagline is 'When you're here, you've made a horrible mistake.''

Phoebe waits. I swirl wine in my glass, watching myself, a suave man in a restaurant swirling wine in a glass at dinner with a beautiful woman. Except I do it too fast and a small amount of wine jumps the rim and spills onto the table.

Phoebe says, 'I'm sorry. That must have been awful. Especially the Olive Garden part.'

I smile. She listens to what I mean, not what I say.

The waiter comes by, wipes at my small spill, tops off our glasses without saying a word.

The beautiful couple nearby have been eating while also doing things with their iPhones. Now, the beautiful man says to the beautiful woman, 'If you could be any animal, what would you be?'

The beautiful woman looks up from her phone and says, 'I don't know. Like, a deer, I guess?'

He nods. 'That's cool.'

He clearly wants her to ask him but she's back to looking down at her iPhone.

He says, 'You know what I'd be?'

'What?' she says, still looking at her phone.

'A plum.'

She looks up and stares at him, then nods and says, 'Totally.'

They both go back to their phones.

Phoebe stares out the window and I yawn.

I say, 'Do you ever think about dying?'

Phoebe says, 'This is fun. I'm glad you called.'

I say, 'Isn't it funny that we all know that we're going to die?'

Phoebe says, 'Hilarious.'

The waiter brings a dessert, a crème brûlée. It's a thing they do for people who eat there a lot. I go to take a bite but Phoebe knocks my spoon away and goes first.

I say, 'Amy called me today.'

Phoebe says, 'Your fiancée?'

'Former fiancée.'

'Why?'

'To tell me she's getting married. To thank me for not marrying her.'

'Seriously?'

I nod and Phoebe tries, unsuccessfully, not to laugh.

She says, 'I'm sorry. It's just . . . you had a bad day, pumpkin.'

I say, 'There was a moment . . . ' But I stop.

Phoebe says, 'What?'

'Nothing.'

'Tell me.'

'It's stupid. It's pathetic.'

'Tell me.'

'There was a moment when . . . I thought . . . this is stupid . . . when I thought she was calling to get back together. And there was this part of me that was actually a little excited about it. Not that I want to be with Amy. That's not it. More just the idea that maybe I could . . . that I could get a second chance.'

'It's not stupid. It's a tiny bit sad and pathetic, but it's not stupid.'

I think of her wedding photos. I take a spoonful of dessert.

Phoebe says, 'Okay. If tomorrow were your last day to live, what would you want to do?'

'That's easy. Work on a diaper account. You?'

Phoebe says, 'C'mon. Last day on earth. You die at midnight. What would you do?'

I look to the beautiful people. No help there. The waiters. Nothing. The window. Nada. To Phoebe. 'I don't know.'

She reaches over, gently removes my hand

from my face. I was touching my scar. I hadn't realized.

She says, 'You do that when you're nervous.'

I'm embarrassed. I say, 'What about you?'

Phoebe says, 'I'm doing it. Hang out with my friends, my family. Wine would be involved. Possibly pot. And an eighteen-year-old Spanish bullfighter.'

She sips her wine and says, ''I think that life would suddenly seem wonderful to us if we were threatened to die. Just think of all the projects, travels, love affairs, studies, it — our life — hides from us, made invisible by our laziness, which, certain of a future, delays them incessantly.''

'Who said that?'

Phoebe says, 'Frank.' She smiles. 'Marcel Proust.'

I say, 'How do you remember that?'

She says, 'I printed it out, had it on my desk at work in Paris. I used to look at it all the time.'

'We'll blow it up big, put it in the lobby. Except people would walk in, read it, and run screaming from the building.' I pause. 'You still thinking about leaving?'

She nods.

I say, 'That's probably a good idea. I would if I wasn't so insanely happy in my work. Any ideas about what you're going to do?'

'No. Just thinking about it.'

A tidal wave of regret and fear sweeps over me. I have done it all wrong. I understand nothing. My stomach roils and my palms tingle and Phoebe is young and I imagine her life laid out before her. The real marriage this time. The one she wanted. With the right man. Fulfilling work, children, a home, me a distant memory. She'll run into Ian in a restaurant/airport/Grand Central. They'll talk, catch up. The older child will hold Phoebe's hand, the little one on her hip. Pretty dresses. They'll look like their mother. Ian will have left the agency years before, moved on, started his own design firm, gotten married in Massachusetts, spend August at his new place in Provincetown. Friends. Love. Joy. Fulfillment. And you, Phoebe? he'll ask. Three children, she'll say. A boy, the oldest, with his father, who we're on our way to meet. He's a former model turned yachtsman turned novelist. Just sold his second book to Hollywood. We live up on the Park at Seventy-ninth Street. Mostly we're at our place in Maine. Do you ever hear from Fin? she'll ask. Really? Cocaine? Wow. Without his pants? In a restaurant? Yikes. And still single? Still at that agency? Wow. That's . . . horribly sad and pathetic.

I say, 'You were married once.'

It comes out more like an accusation than a statement. I didn't mean to say it out loud. The reaction is like a slap. She looks at me, trying to figure out how I know.

I say, 'Christmas night. Looking through photo albums with your mother. It's not a big deal. I mean . . . it's none of my business.'

Phoebe says, 'Yeah. I was married. What's your point?'

Her voice is cold. I've never heard her like that before. She looks down at her wine, smoothes the table, takes a sip, looks away.

I say, 'I'm sorry. I didn't . . . I didn't mean to be rude.'

She looks up, stares at me unblinking for what feels like a long time, as if she's trying to decide something.

Phoebe says, 'Our families knew each other. Had for years. We knew the same people, the same friends. It was comfortable. I thought I was in love.'

She hasn't taken her eyes from mine and I'm afraid to take mine from hers.

Phoebe says, 'I got pregnant right away. It was a mistake. We weren't trying. That wasn't the plan. Not then, anyway. We were twenty-four. But he was so excited. Nate. That was his name. This was all he ever wanted. But I was . . . I was terrified. And I just thought, 'Ohmigod. What have I done?' And then, right before I was three months pregnant, I lost the baby. And ya know. That word . . . *miscarriage* . . . I used to think, 'Oh, how awful,' of course. But it didn't have real meaning to me before. Then you think you're going to have a baby, even if you aren't ready or are scared shitless, so when they . . . when they die . . . you change. You change a little.'

She drinks her water.

She says, 'We went on for a bit, but he knew something was wrong. He took me on vacation. St. John. He thought it would cheer me up. That's when I said I wanted a divorce. He fell apart. It was ugly. His family was angry. It was fucking horrible.'

She takes a long drink from her wine.

'When it was done, I left for Paris. The

Frenchman was perfect. He treated me like shit, which felt pretty good at the time.'

I say, 'I'm sorry.'

Phoebe says, 'It's late. Maybe let's call it a night.'

There's so much more I want to say but I can't seem to find the words.

* * *

We walk to the corner of Houston and Sullivan. The wind blows in gusts, cuts through your clothes. Phoebe has on one of those Russian hats, all fake fur and flaps. No one's out. She puts her arm up and a cab cuts over two lanes and pulls to the sidewalk. The driver is talking animatedly on a Bluetooth and picking his nose. I open the door to the cab, smiling, lean over and give her a half hug, say, 'Thank you for coming out tonight. I really needed it and your friendship means the world to me.' Close the door, watch the cab drive away, walk home, secure in the knowledge that while my father is dead and his ashes will be taken care of, I have good friends who care about me and I them.

But that's not what I do. That's not what happens.

She puts her arm up and a cab cuts over two lanes and pulls to the sidewalk. The driver is talking animatedly on a Bluetooth and picking his nose. She turns to give me a half hug and I lean in too fast, misjudging the distance, thinking she was farther away, and kiss her on the mouth, hard, awkward, horrible, getting part

269

of her cheek along with lips and somehow smelling my own breath, a steamy potpourri of hen, wine, and airplane.

'Ow!' Phoebe says, covering her mouth, pulling away.

'I'm sorry. I'm so sorry.'

I put a gloved hand to my lip, thinking I may be bleeding.

She puts a hand to her forehead, confused, annoyed, and takes a deep breath.

I say, 'I'm sorry. I'm so sorry.'

'Fin. You should go home.'

'I'm sorry.'

'It's okay. Just . . . it's late.'

HOW ARE YOU ENJOYING THE PARTY?

There is a plaque above the entrance to our office building, the names Lauderbeck, Kline & Vanderhosen writ large in crisp Futura. There was a time when it thrilled me to see those words, to walk under them and into this place. The year I started, the agency had been voted Agency of the Year by one of the trade publications. Like most institutions when viewed from the outside — other people's families, other careers — it appeared to be a wonderful place.

Now I am simply part of the crowd that daily streams in through the revolving doors, shows their ID, waits for one of six elevators, quick fake smile, nods, reads the paper, stares at the coffee cup, the feet, sniffles, listens to the iPod, presses the elevator button over and over and over.

The days meld together. Moments of lightness, of meetings, walks down a hallway and nods and smiles to coworkers of five years, eight years. Wasn't I taking this exact shower at this exact time yesterday morning? Or was it a week ago? What day is it? The subway and the coffee cart and the gym, the copier, the men's room, the cafeteria, the void of time lost. We settle into a life. Maybe we made this life or maybe it simply happened. People get promoted. They get married. They have children. She's how old now? Holy cow. Where does the time go? They leave

271

for another company. They come back three years later. They get divorced. They move to a larger home. They take a trip to Africa. They have chemo. They have an affair. They lose a parent. They find their way, are blessed with good fortune, win the club doubles tournament. They travel to Detroit for business. They drive through an intersection, are hit by a drunk driver, live in a nursing home the rest of their days. I don't know where time goes. This seems like a good tagline for something.

The holiday party starts at 10:00 A.M. and the office is dead, people taking the morning off.

The paper says the war in Iraq is not going well.

The paper says the war in Afghanistan is not going well.

The paper says the man whose ex-wife cut off his penis years ago and threw it out of a car window is in talks with Fox to start his own reality TV show called *How Bad Is Your Ex?*

I stand and look out the window, watch as two men unload sacks of what looks like flour. Each time one of the bags hits the two-wheeled cart, a puff of white mist comes out of the corner of the bag. The job seems appealing from this distance. They wear work boots and heavy cloth jackets and there is physical labor involved. They're talking and laughing as they do it. Has one of them told the other a filthy joke, using words like *tits* or *pussy?* Is that snobbish of me? How the hell do I know who they really are? Maybe both are trying to get their master's in writing at Columbia. Maybe one just told the other the story of Sisyphus, of rolling the rock up the hill, only to have it fall down and start again, how it's a metaphor for life, for work. Are they classical scholars, Larry Darrell — like from W. Somerset Maugham's *The Razor's Edge?* Seekers of truth, of God in the everyday, the every detail? A woman in a formfitting skirt walks by and I see one of them mouth something. The woman turns and gives them the finger. The men laugh.

Smash cut to opening credits of *Oprah*. Camera dollies in over the heads of applauding audience members. Cut to Oprah, clapping (for herself?).

Oprah says, 'Finbar Dolan. My last show and there was only one guest I wanted and that was you.'

'Thank you, Oprah.'

Oprah says, 'Wouldn't commercials be funnier if you were allowed to swear?'

'Absolutely.'

'If every spot were like something on HBO.'

'Volvo. Drive fucking safely.'

The audience laughs.

I say, 'And brought to you by McDonald's. I'm fucking loving it.'

Oprah laughs. 'Hahahahaha!'

I laugh and jump up and down like Tom Cruise. The audience is hysterical, applauding. Oprah's laughing.

Oprah says, 'You're awesome.'

I say, 'No, you're awesome.'

The audience applauds both of us and our awesomeness.

Oprah says, 'Why aren't you more famous, more successful?'

'I don't know. I don't know what others are missing.'

'Your father was a police officer.'

'Yes.'

'He went into harm's way to protect people. He stood between us and danger.'

'Yes.'

'And yet you . . . you do nothing for others.'

'No.'

'Do you volunteer?'

'No.'

'Do you give money away?'

'Once in a while but not much.'

'Do you give blood?'

'God, no. Can't stand needles.' I laugh and turn to the audience, but it's an entirely different audience of somber, disappointed people who loathe me.

Oprah says, 'What do you do for others?'

I say, 'What do you mean?'

'Your father was a volunteer during World War Two, saw combat, sat in the pitch black for hours with a dead man on him. Yet you can't even bring yourself to honor a dying man's request.'

'You have no idea what you're talking about. He hit my brothers. He left my mother.'

'Your mother had an affair.'

'No.'

'Your mother had sex with someone who wasn't her husband.'

'Shut your goddamned mouth.'

Oprah says, 'It's your a-ha moment.'

'It's not true.'

'Why do you lie?'

'Why do you put yourself on the cover of every issue of your magazine?'

'We're talking about you.'

I say, 'I've never watched your show.'

'You even lie to yourself. You're like one of those birds that skim across the water, looking barely below the surface, unable to engage in anything lasting or meaningful.'

I say, 'Let's go to a commercial.'

★ ★ ★

Keita is standing at my door.

He says, 'Fin. I am so sorry for you.'

It's begun to rain outside and though it's still early, dark clouds make it seem like dusk.

'Keita,' I say. 'Thank you. And thank you for your very kind message last night.' It's only then that I notice his expression. 'Is something wrong?'

'Fin. Have I offended you?'

'Offended? No. God, no. Why?'

'Did I do something wrong?'

'Absolutely not. Why? What happened?'

'My father's office call me. I must go back. I am told I am impeding business.'

'What? No. There's very little business that happens here to begin with.'

'I wanted to see the TV commercial. Go to Hollywood.'

The math comes slowly to me, but when it does, it's clear. Someone called. Frank, Martin, Dodge. Most likely Frank. He'd push a Girl Scout down to win a race. I would prefer that

275

Keita fly home, truth be told. I'm deeply tired and don't feel like babysitting. But there's something about his expression, the wounded, childlike look that says he simply wants to belong, that somehow opens a small empathic window. He's also wearing suede Converse All Stars with his dark suit, a nod to this morning's party, perhaps. I say, 'Then come to the shoot with me. Please. As my guest. Put me on the phone with your father.'

A wide-eyed grin. 'You would do this?'

'Absolutely. We're buds, right?'

I've strayed too far into jargon.

I say, 'Buddies. Friends.'

He likes this word. 'Buddies. Yes. Buddies. Okay.'

He pulls up a chair next to mine and we sit uncomfortably close as Keita dials his Vertu cell phone (base price, $4,000) and speaks Japanese, his personality changing, his voice rising, his tone more severe. He waits, puts his hand over the phone. 'One of his three assistants. She does not like me. Fin. Your father. He is better?'

Maybe all conversations should take place from a few inches away, where you are almost touching the other person, where you are looking each other in the eye. Perhaps there would be less lying.

'No,' I say. 'He died.'

Keita puts his hand to his head. It's the hand that's holding the phone and his forehead hits the speaker button. I know this because I hear someone speaking in Japanese on the other end of the phone.

Keita ignores it. 'Buddy,' Keita says to me, putting his other hand on my shoulder. There is something about his pain, the gesture, that moves me to the point where I find a hitch in my throat. The voice speaking Japanese becomes louder, angrier.

Keita whispers, 'My father,' and rolls his eyes.

Keita takes the phone off speaker and talks to his father in Japanese. I hear his father respond, watch Keita's bad-dog expression. I understand it all too well. Anger sweeps over me, a kind of chemical response that surprises me. Keita hands me the phone and I lie my face off to Keita's father, telling him that we need Keita for the shoot, that he provided valuable input during the early stages of the creative process and during the internal review and that the client met him and asked for him to be there. And that we know he's needed in Japan but he's needed here as well. Keita's round face smiling the entire time. And who knows. It never hurts to have a billionaire around.

★ ★ ★

We're gathered in a massive room in a hotel in midtown Manhattan with stained carpeting. There are no decorations, nothing to suggest Christmas. The feeling is less festive and more of a mandatory conference on ethics in the workplace. I stand at the back, having arrived late. The anxiety pit in my stomach has returned. I feel as if I've not done the homework and am trying not to be called upon. Also, I want a clear line of sight to the men's room. I'm still having digestive issues.

At present Frank is speaking. He has been speaking for some time. Dodge stands at his side. 'When you take away the bricks and mortar, the computers, the copiers, the faxes, and phones, all the paper and the soda and stuff, you, our people, are our most important resource. I love you guys. And no, I don't mean in that way. Although some of you, I'd be open to it.' He laughs, though no one joins him. People make disgusted faces. Someone says, a little too loud, 'Asshole,' and causes a small commotion. Frank seems unfazed.

Later, promotions are announced. New partners, awards. Outstanding Employee. Best Attitude. Person Who Makes the Workplace Better. Outstanding Account Service Person, Outstanding Copywriter, Art Director. The magic of the AV Department flashing a giant photo on the huge screen at the front. To look around in these moments is to see something rich. When a name is announced for a promotion or partnership or an award, I see, in the faces of my coworkers, the happiness they feel for this person, hear the genuine applause as the embarrassed recipient returns to his or her seat, red-faced, swarmed by their seatmates. The older women in accounting — from Brooklyn and Queens and the Bronx — have changed from their work clothes into pretty dresses, nicer shoes. People look around in their chairs, wave to friends, a kind of instant regression to high school. The women giggle. The men push one

278

another on the shoulder. We look for something deeper than merely a paycheck.

After the buffet and polite chat, the mixing and socializing, the music is turned up and the lights are dimmed and the line at the open bars set up around the perimeter of the enormous, hideous, curious-smelling room begins to grow. People react with lunatic delight when a Kool and the Gang song is played. 'Celllllllll-e-brate good times, come on . . . da-da-da-dut-dut-dut-da-da . . . waa-who!'

The music gets louder, the dance floor gets more crowded, women remove those pretty party shoes as they pit out with sweat and take large gulps off of their sixteen-ounce plastic cup of Bud Light (regular Bud was the only other choice). Odd pairings, both on the dance floor and in the room itself. People begin to touch one another when explaining a point. Or hug one another for no reason. 'You're the best!' God was bored with the humans, so he invented alcohol.

It is one-thirty in the afternoon.

I see some of the young copywriters and art directors talking with some of the young account and media girls. *Will you remember this day, any of you, years from now?* I see Ian talking with two older, heavy-set women who work in human resources and for some reason it breaks my heart. He is a person who cares about other people, wants them to feel welcome, as if he, himself, is throwing the party.

'Helen,' he'll say. 'Are you having a good time? You look gorgeous in that dress. Why don't you wear your hair like that more often?'

I see Phoebe in a cluster of people across the room. She smiles, but something's different. I've made a horrible mistake.

I see Martin talking with Frank and Dodge. He sees me, motions me over.

Frank says, 'Fin. You can fix this, right? You can make your mark with this one. Merry Christmas, by the way. Even though it's January.' It's something Frank says. *Make your mark.* Every assignment, every ad, every spot could be the thing that will vault you to . . . what? Fame, I guess. I'm not really sure what he's talking about.

Before I can respond Dodge puts his arms around me and holds me. 'Of course he can fix it. This is the prince of diapers. And what a handsome prince he is. What an opportunity. The Super Bowl. And yes, Merry Christmas in a completely nondenominational way,' he says. 'And *I* can say that because I'm a Dutch Jew, okay?' Forced laugh. The hug goes on several seconds too long. Boozy breath. I'm holding my drink and am not sure what to do with my other hand, so they both hang suspended. This must look strange. He releases me and wipes something off my lapel as he says, 'It's a marvelous party. Promise you'll save me a dance.'

I say, 'I promise.' I turn to Martin. 'Fix what?'

Frank says, 'How was your evening with Keita? Did he mention me?'

I say, 'He did, Frank. He likes you very much. He said his father admires you.'

Frank turns to Dodge. 'I told you the old man

wasn't offended by the *Lost in Translation* joke.'

Martin says, 'Excuse us.'

We walk to the bar.

Martin says to the bartender, 'Johnnie Walker Blue. Neat. In a glass, not a plastic cup.'

The bartender says, 'Bud Light, undrinkable white wine, shitty vodka.'

I say, 'Fix what?'

Martin turns to me and says, 'The account. Your account. The world's greatest diaper, my good chap. Not a good meeting yesterday, I'm afraid.' He turns back to the bartender and says, 'There is a bag marked MARTIN CARLSON, EXECUTIVE CREATIVE DIRECTOR under the table behind you. Open it.' We watch as the bartender opens the bag and produces a bottle of Johnnie Walker Blue.

Martin says to me, 'Sent Emma 'round this morning.' To the barman, 'Make it two, please.' Martin drops a twenty in the tip cup and we take our drinks, turn and look at the crowd. We see Keita dancing with several women.

'What happened?' I ask.

'They were underwhelmed. My fault. I should have put more resources on it.'

I feel my face flush, an open embarrassment.

He clinks my glass with his. 'Cheers.'

We drink. It tastes like ash to me.

'I thought they liked Al Gore. I thought you liked Al Gore.'

'I did. They didn't.'

I say, 'Did they buy anything?'

'1984.'

'You seem disappointed.'

'I am. I think it's mediocre at best. It's someone else's idea. I don't like doing other people's ideas. That's not how I got where I am.' There's an edge to his voice.

Then he says, 'Can you do this? Because if you can't — and I understand if your head is elsewhere — I need someone else on it.'

He turns and looks at me and I think, *I don't know this guy at all*. He's the kind of person who would fire me now and never think twice about it. In other words, a boss.

I'm tempted to say *fuck you*. But I don't. Would never. I'll rescript this whole conversation later in my mind and I will sound bold and strong and turn and walk away after a biting, insightful comment. Martin will follow me and say how right I am and how he was testing me and I passed and also here's a raise and a promotion. But here, now, my current feelings are a jumble of fear, embarrassment, and a pathetic need to please. Also, I need the job.

The DJ plays The Isley Brothers' 'Shout.' 'Don't forget to say yeah yeah yeah yeah . . . say you will . . . '

We watch as Keita lays down on the floor and does the worm, clearly a fan of the movie *Animal House*. He urges others to join him, though no one does.

Martin says, 'How's your father, by the way?'

There are times in life when you can, if you choose, truly connect with another human being. You simply have to tell the truth.

I say, 'He's doing much better. Thank you.'

'Is it?' asks one of the young creatives.

'Is it what?' I ask.

The party has broken up and cabloads of people have made their way to a dive bar just north of Houston, which, until we arrived, was nearly empty. The Clash song 'Train in Vain' keeps playing on the jukebox. It's not a large place, and we've packed dozens of people in. Much drinking. The windows are fogged up. Someone breaks a glass and screams. Others laugh. The bartender doesn't react. I saw Ian and Phoebe earlier but lost them in the crowd. I stand against the wall of the bar, drinking a stale draft beer, and watch Mike Carroll talk very closely with Karen Simpson. He touches her arm to make a point. She nods deeply in agreement. In the next moment they are kissing passionately, comically, the kind of kiss where the woman wraps one of her legs around the man's leg. They are married. But not to each other. No one seems to notice or care. Two young creatives are talking to me but I'm not listening to what they're saying. They keep buying me beers, saying I'm 'awesome' and that it must be 'awesome' to go on big shoots and work with A-list directors like Raphael and huge stars like Gwyneth Paltrow. I make out the occasional word in what they're saying, here and there, like I do if someone's speaking French to me very, very slowly. I see Phoebe's profile. She's talking with two other guys from the creative department. She's laughing.

'Awesome,' he says, a big innocent smile on his unlined face. 'Is it awesome?'

I've read that for an average-size adult, cremation takes from two to three hours at a normal operating temperature between 1,500 and 2,000 degrees Fahrenheit. And that afterwards any remaining bone fragments are processed in a machine to a consistent size and placed into an urn selected by the family. Awesome? Depends on the day, the hour, the moment. Yes. No. It depends on what you want from a job. Although international business class on a new British Airways 747 upper deck is pretty great.

I say, 'It *is* awesome. It's completely awesome.'

They look at each other and high five.

'Awesome,' one of them says.

I shake hands with the two young creatives and make my way to the men's room, wash my hands, throw cold water on my face. I look tired. I should go home. I should go home and take a hot shower, read a book. I'm breathing heavily. I lean against the dirty basin, look at my face, turn and look at my scar, run my finger over it.

We had a great assignment. A Super Bowl spot. And we blew it.

To the bar, smiling, nodding, pointing. At the bar I order another beer.

'Signore,' I hear next to me.

'Stefano. What's new?'

'Not bad.'

His English gets confused, especially when he's been drinking.

Stefano says, 'I heard that Tom Pope vomited in public.'

'I heard something about that.'

My beer arrives. His scotch. We clink glasses, sip, look around the room at our life.

'You look tired, Fin.'

'I am tired,' I say.

He smiles. 'Do you know what you need?' he asks, the hint of mischief on his face. 'You need a woman. Not a girl,' he says, frowning comically, drawing out the word *girl* as if it were somehow below his European sensibilities.

'These little, these little *minxes* here, the, the Jennifers and the Kims and the Jills and the Courtneys and the Alexandras. My God. These little Botticellis running around with their lovely round bottoms. But so clueless. Fun, of course. Yes. Why not. But a woman. A good woman. This is a different thing.'

One of the young creatives has his arm around Phoebe's shoulder. She has on a black cashmere sweater with buttons up the front. A long skirt. Boots. No makeup. Her lips are glossy. She's talking and her teeth are very white.

'Fin. I would like to say a name to you and ask if you know who it is, please.'

'Okay.'

'Mr. Roger Bannister,' he says, nodding slowly, a slight grin on his stubbled face.

'Roger Bannister,' I say. 'Did he break the four-minute mile?'

'That is exactly correct.' He says this with great pride, as if Bannister were his father.

Stefano says, 'May I tell you about that day?'

'Please do.'

'It was a windy day in Oxford, Fin. We are

talking about May 5, 1954. England. He almost called the attempt off, you see, because of the wind.' Stefano is looking off into the distance, telling the story as if he was there that day, as if he'd reported upon it for the BBC.

'He was a medical doctor, Mr. Roger Bannister was. Imagine that. It is late afternoon, by the way. Five o'clock when this takes place. The wind had died down.'

He turns to look at me now, suddenly. 'He almost canceled the attempt, Fin.' A look of dismay on his face.

'Because of the wind,' I say.

'Exactly right. Because of the wind.'

He turns back to the movie that is playing in his mind. He nods slowly.

'But he did not cancel, Fin. No. On this day, he ran. He ran like no man had run before. On this day he became immortal. The first man to run a mile in under four minutes. Three fifty-nine point four. He was twenty-five years old that day. My God, what a thing.'

He sips his drink.

'He would go on, of course, to a very successful career in medicine. Neurology.' He turns to say this last word to me, a secret between men.

'He married, raised a family. Fin, he was knighted by the Queen of England in 1975. This once meant something, to be knighted. Not like now, where they knight the Spice Girls or George Michael.'

He says, 'Do you know what Roger Bannister wrote of that day? He said, 'I felt at that moment that it was my chance to do one thing supremely well.'' '

Stefano raises his glass to mine, gently taps it against the lip, the quietest click amid the conversations and music, and takes a slow sip off the old-farm-table-colored scotch.

'Fin, I turn forty soon. This is a milestone. Most surely the end of any hint of youth. This is a sobering thought for a man. One's erection will never quite be the same. I read this in a magazine. Tragic to me, this is. Of course, as an Italian I am very different.' He winks. 'Fin, would it surprise you to learn that I intend to break the four-minute mile on my birthday?'

'It would, yes.'

'Do you think it's possible? Do you think by sheer force of will a man can transcend his shortcomings and do this great thing?'

Several thoughts go through my head.

Depends upon the man.

Absolutely not.

It would be lovely to think so.

And then I say what he wants to hear. 'Definitely.'

★   ★   ★

I'm thinking about leaving without saying good-bye to anyone when Phoebe comes up behind me.

'Hi,' she says.

'Hi.'

We both look around.

Phoebe says, 'Last night was weird, right?'

'I'm a fan of pretending things never happened.' I'm wincing.

She nods, a fake smile. 'I know. I'm not, though.'

The words sting.

I say, 'I'm sorry. It was dumb and selfish and . . . I'm sorry.'

'Yeah. You confused me a bit there.'

'I said I was sorry.' A little too much edge.

'Don't get mad. It'd been a weird day for me. I mean, I know you'd been through a lot in Boston and that's why I came out to meet you. It's just that . . . the Frenchman sent me a ticket to Paris. And it was just . . . it was a weird day and it's not like . . . '

Ian comes over and puts his arm around each of us. He's had a few drinks.

He says, 'My favorites. My Scott and Zelda. My Nick and Nora. My Sacco and Vanzetti. How are we?'

I say, 'Good. All good.'

Phoebe says, 'Did you hear that Stefano wants to run a mile in four minutes?'

Ian says, 'You said 'run.' You mean 'drive,' right?'

I say to Ian, 'Martin said the meeting didn't go so good.'

Ian says, 'Not so much. Who cares. How are you? How was yesterday?'

I say, 'Fine. It's all fine. Did I mention the ashes?'

Ian says, 'What ashes?'

'In my father's will.' To Phoebe: 'I didn't mention this last night.' To both of them: 'This lawyer reads a letter. My father wants to be cremated. And he wants his ashes spread out over the Pacific near Pearl Harbor. And he wants one of us to do it.'

I say this to them with an attitude in my voice, a tone that suggests, *Can you believe he's asked for that?* I hear my voice. I hear it as if I am someone else listening to me. And I think, *That guy's an asshole.*

Ian says, 'So wait. Are you going? I'm confused.'

'No. No.' I want to say more, but that's all that comes out.

Phoebe says, 'So what happens to the ashes?'

I say, 'We're sending them to the VA. They take care of it.'

Ian says nothing but I know his expressions. Phoebe's, too.

'What?' I ask.

'Nothing,' he says. 'It's sad.'

'What's so sad about it?'

'It's just sad.'

I say, 'It's not sad so much as insane.'

Phoebe says, 'Why is it insane?'

I say, 'Because . . . it's . . . he was . . . '

The knot in my stomach has grown tighter and there's something about the condescension in Phoebe's voice. Or am I putting the condescension there, the way you do with sarcasm in an e-mail that wasn't meant to be sarcastic? I'm suddenly very tired and drunk. Who the hell is he, after all these years, to tell us we have to do this thing for him? Why the fuck should any of us bring his ashes to the middle of the goddamned Pacific Ocean?

One of the young creatives comes up to Phoebe. He is younger than I am and probably more talented and certainly better looking and he was making Phoebe laugh earlier.

He says to Ian and me, 'What up, dawgs?' Then to her: 'A bunch of us are heading over to this place in the East Village. Thought you might want to come along.'

I want to punch his handsome face, his confidence, his straight white teeth. He probably knows karate. Someday, not all that many years away, I will be dead.

Phoebe smiles. 'That sounds great.' I hate that she smiles.

He smiles, too. I know what he's thinking. I know exactly what he is thinking. And I want to punch him again. He turns to leave, flashing a peace sign as he does.

Phoebe says, 'So you're really not going to do it?'

It is almost impossible to explain family behavior to someone outside the family. What seems normal, acceptable, within the circle can seem selfish, foolish, absurd outside of it. The simple truth is that I don't want to do it. Can't be bothered. To do it is to deal with it, think about it, face it. Eddie chose anger, Maura chose a bizarrely clean house, Kevin chose leaving. I chose made-up stories about diapers. And yet it is unsettling to have a mirror held up to your selfishness in the cold, ugly light of day. It embarrasses me. It pisses me off.

'No,' I say a little too forcefully. 'I'm not. And

he didn't ask just me. He asked all of us.'

'But none of the others are going to do it, you said. They didn't even come to the hospital.'

It's as if she's found the pain point and keeps pressing on it. I realize in a moment how angry I am that Maura and Eddie couldn't drive the seventy-five miles from Boston to Hyannis to see their dying father, how I agree with Phoebe 100 percent. And in the same moment how Phoebe doesn't get to criticize my family and how angry she makes me by being right.

'No . . . no.' I can't seem to get the words out.

She says, 'So maybe you should. I think it would be a nice gesture.'

I'm shaking my head back and forth. 'No. No, it wouldn't be a nice gesture. I'm not sure you understand. This person's a *stranger* to me.'

Phoebe says, 'But it's not about you.'

It triggers something, some Eddie-like place that I rarely go, a pathetic, dangerous place where you pity yourself, gather up all the hurts, the slights, the disappointments, the anger. I read something once that said the harder you argue a point, the less sure you are of how you feel about it. I want her to take my side, to understand me, validate me. Even though I know I'm wrong.

'What the fuck does *that* mean?' I say, too loud, channeling my father.

I feel Ian look at me. 'Easy, Fin.'

Phoebe's face, genuine surprise. 'It means forgive him.'

I gulp my beer. The last thing I need. I should order a glass of water.

I say, 'You don't know what you're talking about.'

I've never spoken to her like that before. I can see the hurt. I need to stop this but can't. She takes one step too many.

'I'm sorry,' she says. 'It just . . . it seems a little sad. It's a dying man's wish. I mean, do it for your mother.'

★　★　★

'You're not supposed to be home,' she'd said.

'Finny,' she'd said.

'I'll be back,' she'd said.

I saw it. That's the part I always leave out in the retelling. Especially to myself. I followed her. On my bike. Did I mention that? I probably should have mentioned that. Back streets. One-ways she couldn't go down. I'd thought it would be funny. Show up at the store at the same time. Slow motion. The bike and pedaling fast and the breeze. Cloudy sky. Streets I knew so well. The way a boy rides a bicycle, the second nature of it, the assurance and joy. He's smiling, this boy. Me. I see him as someone else, though, in the memory. It's a game to him. He'll catch her. She'll be surprised and they'll laugh. Except, she didn't turn into the store parking lot. He almost shouted. She kept going and didn't make the bend in the road farther on. Big old trees. The car rockets forward, up over the curb, airborne — he sees it rise up — and hit the tree. A car horn as he careens across the road, still following, forgetting now that he's on a bicycle, knowing only that he has to get to the car. If he can just get to it everything will be okay. The noise of the car hitting the tree a tremendous thing. But it's not happening. It can't be happening. He's across the road and off his bike before it stops. You can know a thing before it happens. There is, still, deep within us, primal, acute instincts that sense danger. He'd never followed her to the store before on his bike. Why today? *You're not supposed to be home.* Why touch his face? We weren't physical. We didn't hug. It's a trick. It's a joke. It can't be happening. The hood bent up like a tent and fluid running from the car and steam hissing and the windshield on the driver's side shattered and her head on the dash at an unnatural angle, black blood — see, it's fake, blood is usually red — pouring in a thick stream down her forehead, nose, mouth, chin. He tries the door. It's stuck. He's a boy, a skinny boy, no strength. The driver's side window is cracked with a space big enough to push his head in, which is hard because he's shaking so badly now it's difficult to move but move he does and puts his head in and the moment before he touches her — no, pushes her, pushes her to see if she is alive, his last hope — he pulls his head out fast and cuts his jaw on the jagged glass. If he doesn't push her, she can still be alive. Men are running from Petersen's, from the market. He sees a woman standing by her car with her hands over her mouth and nose, eyes wide. *It's fine,* he wants to say. *It's fine. It's not happening. It didn't happen.* He just needs to get on his bike, get home, beat her home. *It's a game. She's going to the store for milk. She's coming home. We needed some things.* He got on his bike and pedaled. When he came home Maura stared at him. She was smoking, which she never did in the house. Our mother would kill her. She didn't seem to notice the blood on his chin, his shirt.

'Finny,' she said. 'There was an accident. Mum's dead.'

She sat down on the kitchen floor. Dropped to the kitchen floor, really. She sobbed and sobbed. He sat down next to her. He didn't want to get blood on her. He didn't cry. 'Never let Mum see you cry,' Maura had told him.

They took him for stitches that evening when the cut wouldn't stop bleeding. Four stitches.

The thing is, I never told anyone.

Now, here, in the bar, I feel shaky, light-headed, like my blood sugar is low. Someone is shouting. It's very loud and I would turn to look but I'm the one shouting.

'You don't know what the *fuck* you're talking about! That *dying* man left his *family*! He left his wife! She committed suicide! Do you know *that* about the dying man?! Forgiveness!? She drove into a fucking *tree*!'

Massive amounts of information in a tiny space of time. Mick Jagger singing. 'I can almost hear ya sigh . . . ' The *Steel Wheels* album. Someone — a man's voice — says under his breath, 'What the fuck, dude?' People murmur. The squeak of the door at the front of the bar. Someone scrapes a barstool back. My ears are hot and my throat hurts. Ian's strength, taking

294

my hand from Phoebe's arm. Ian's voice. 'Fin. Calm down.' No, that can't be. Wait. My hand wasn't holding her forearm, squeezing too hard. The expression on her face, eyes wide, genuinely scared. Phoebe pushing her tongue up against the back of her top teeth, trying hard not to cry, the tears welling in her eyes, the last image I remember before I grab my jacket and find the door as fast as I can.

★ ★ ★

There is a package.

Tom Hanley sent it from Boston with a note. 'Your father asked that I give this to you, but not in front of the others.' He also wishes me the very best and that if I'm ever in need of legal services to please consider him.

Consider him? Absolutely. But perhaps you, Tom, could consider the effect of getting a package from your dead father. Consider this, my portly Boston Irishman. You walk in the door of your apartment. It's late. You've had a bit to drink. Perhaps you kick off your shoes. Perhaps in doing so you trip, stub your toe, and say filthy swear words out loud, surprising yourself at the volume of your own voice. Perhaps you take your coat off and drop the mail on the floor as you make your way to the refrigerator, noticing along the way that you can't seem to catch your breath. This could be in part because you ran from a bar for several blocks before throwing up in a dirty snowbank, a group of passing college kids laughing and calling you a dick-head. You drink deeply from a bottle of club soda, some of it spilling down your shirt front. Small flashbacks, what Ian calls 'Oh, shit' movies. You screamed at a friend. No. Not possible. You grabbed her shoulders. You shook her. Again, not possible. You've never done anything like that in your life. Before tonight. And she is not any person. She's your best friend. No. More than that. You reach into the refrigerator and grab leftover vegetable lo mein, wondering whether to use a fork or eat it with your hands when you see her face in your mind, the horrified expression on her face as you shouted at her. You opt for the fork. You sit down on the floor, back against the wall, and look at the mail you've dropped, splayed out, and realize that you look like an ad for . . . what? Maybe for a guy who's an asshole and is sitting on the floor? No product there. Maybe for 'Refreshing Canada Dry Club Soda,' a drink so refreshing that you're forced to drop your mail and sit down to enjoy it? Very bad. Your cell phone rings and you hope it's her so you can beg forgiveness but you see it's Ian and you don't feel like talking. Maybe for Pine-Sol, floors so clean you actually prefer not to sit on a chair. There's an American Express bill, a Crate & Barrel catalog, a New Yorker magazine that will join an unread pile of others, a Con Ed bill, and a manila envelope from Sullivan, O'Neil & Levy, Attorneys-at-Law, in Boston. Inside is a separate envelope. I decide that it would be a good idea to floss my teeth.

I stand up, with difficulty, and walk into the bathroom, turn on the hot water, though it will be some time before it arrives, as I'm on the sixth floor of an old building and it takes minutes for the hot water to make its way up. I brush my teeth and then floss, digging into my gums by accident several times, causing my mouth to bleed. I make the mistake of gargling with Listerine and am forced to spit it out immediately, as it stings my now-open gum wounds. I wash my face and the soap gets in my eyes. I look up, lean against the basin, my face inches from the mirror, and stare. I stare at the pores on my nose, the tiny, almost invisible hairs on the ball of my nose, the lines around my eyes when I squint, lines I've not really noticed before. Out loud I say, 'You are Finbar Dolan.' I say it again, slowly. 'You. Are. Fin. Bar. Do. Lan.' I say it again. And again. And again. Slower each time, trying hard to understand what the words mean. But the more I say it, the less it means, the more confused I am as to who the man in the mirror is, as if he's a total stranger. And not in a Michael Jackson way. In a meaningless way.

It's a nine-by-twelve manila envelope and it has my name on it, Catholic-school cursive, blue-ink pen. Inside, two sheets on white notebook paper, blue lined, unfolded. Where was he when he wrote it? What time of day? Was he wearing a robe? Did he have a cup of coffee in front of him?

Dear Finbar,
In early 1945 I was on a submarine that did patrols out of Pearl Harbor. We sailed north to the Aleutians, south to Australia.

For over a year we never saw combat. In February, we were on our way back from a two-week patrol when we were hit by a Japanese destroyer. There was an explosion. Then another. And another. I was in the tiller room with signalman second-class Ralph Thomsen. We were both thrown. The sub rocked side to side with each new explosion. Ralph screamed. He screamed like I've never heard a man scream. The lights had gone out. I made my way to him, felt around, and realized that he'd been caught in the rudder ram and it was crushing his chest. He kept screaming. Please, dear God, help me. Help me. There was nothing I could do. I couldn't see. I had blood coming from a gash on my forehead. He just kept screaming. The door to the tiller room was jammed. He grabbed my hand and held it. He wouldn't let go. I don't know how long we were in there. Several hours. And I'm not sure when he died.

The rest of the war was different for me. I was terrified every day until the war ended. And then one day, on maneuvers an hour away from Pearl Harbor, we surfaced. I was the first man up. Another boat was signaling like crazy: 'War is over.' All you think about when you're in the service is getting out. But then I was out, standing in front of the Fargo Building in Boston, still in uniform, and didn't know what to do, didn't know where to go. Some guys, they got out of the service and they felt like they had a new lease on life. I never felt that. I just felt like I didn't deserve to live. I felt guilt at being alive. Can you understand that?

I am not sure you can point to a single incident in your life and say, 'I am the way I am because of this.' I don't know. Maybe you can. My point is I take full responsibility for who I was. I am not proud of it.

I never blamed your mother for what happened with that man. It was a relief in a way. It's not that I didn't love her or you kids. As God is my witness. I was just different, after the war. I was afraid. That's why I went on the police department. I needed to prove to myself that I wasn't.

Sometimes, at the scene of an accident, I would watch the people who survived. They would sit with their head in their hands with this look on their face. And the look was always the same. It said, 'Just make things go back to how they were before this happened.'

I heard about your mother's death. I felt responsible. When I came to the wake and saw you kids, I knew it was over. I knew there was nothing I could ever do to make it right. I thought it would be easier for all of you if I stayed away. I was dead to the four of you. I was dead to myself. All I can tell you is that I wish I had it to do over again. I am not proud of the life I have lived.

Why you?

Because Eddie would have thrown the envelope away without opening it. Kevin would have read it and thrown it away. Maura's more like me than her mother. So it will be you. If anyone does this thing, it will be you.

You owe me nothing. I know that.

I am not looking for forgiveness. I've been to confession. All I am saying is that I was changed by the war. I tried. I did try. But I failed, I don't know what else to say. Except that there is a part of me that wished it was me and not Ralph who died that day.

Your father,
Edward Dolan, Sr.

YOUR FATHER IS IN DÜSSELDORF

The plane lunges forward, gains speed. The power pushes me back in my seat. A small thrill. Kennedy has the third longest runway in the United States at 14,752 feet. Faster now. I place my feet flat on the carpet, sit up straight, as if at attention. It is a thing I do on planes at takeoff and landing. I am not sure why. A nod to humility, perhaps, to something greater than myself at a moment when humans transcend their limitations. The pilot eases back the yoke as he hits a ground speed of at least 150 miles per hour, thereby deflecting the horizontal control surface elevator on the tail. Up faster now, a steep climb over the water, over Queens, as he pushes out the engines, in the case of this plane twin Pratt & Whitney 4062s, engines with a maximum thrust capacity of 63,300 lbs. As I mentioned, we had the Boeing account awhile back.

The shoot starts tomorrow. I'm on the 7 A.M. flight to Los Angeles, flying back in time. I like the idea of gaining time, as if I could undo or change or keep something from happening.

★ ★ ★

Today we have the pre-production meeting, a largely ceremonial gathering where all of the

301

principals on the shoot — the director, producers, agency, and client — eat expensive, catered food and review the pre-production booklet, which includes the script, the locations, and the casting, as well as the name and phone number of every crew member, catering, and insurance company. None of it is news to anyone. It's the equivalent of that part during a wedding ceremony where the minister asks if anyone has a reason why these people should not be wed.

I take a cab to the production company's office in Santa Monica. A young assistant leads me through the cavernous space. It must have been a warehouse or storage facility at one point. A one-story cinder-block structure, a few blocks back from the beach. In a far corner is a glassed-in conference room. Alan, Jill, Ian, Pam, Jan, and Jan's team of perhaps six people. Ian and Pam flew out to L.A. two days ago to begin casting, wardrobe, set design. Alan and Jill arrived last night with the client. They have the underappreciated job of shadowing the client, Secret Service-like, throughout the process. Account service, to my mind, is the hardest job at an agency. Much of the blame when things go wrong, none of the credit when they go right. All of them appear to be listening to Keita, fake smiles plastered on their faces. He's wearing old-fashioned board shorts, a white dress shirt under a seersucker jacket, and Vans. He must have seen a Beach Boys album cover fairly recently. He waves to me and smiles. On a table at one end are sandwiches and bottles of water

— sparkling and flat — from a natural spring in Iceland. I can't shake the bubble of tension in my abdomen. I'm sneezing and my nose is running.

Jan makes her way to me.

'Jan,' I say with a fake smile, kiss-kiss.

'Fin. How are you? How's your father?'

What if I went in for it, full tongue? I think that Jan is far more sexual than I give her credit for. Then I notice her shoes.

Ian told Jan my father was ill. I'd suggested it, as I thought it would create sympathy and make her more amenable during the shoot.

'He's much better,' I say. 'Thank you. Would you believe he asked for a Philly cheesesteak when he woke up?' I smile and fake a laugh. Jan smiles awkwardly.

'Is he from Philadelphia?'

'No.'

'Strange. Are you close, Fin?'

'How do you define close?'

'We're all going through it, aren't we?'

'Yes.' I nod, though I'm not sure what she means.

'We think we're here for ourselves but we're really here for our children, aren't we? We're placeholders for the next generation,' she says with the head-tilted earnestness of a daytime TV talk-show host.

I'm nodding like a Hasid at the Wailing Wall. 'I think that's right,' I say, though I have no idea what she's talking about. I think it's about dying and making room for others.

Jan says, 'Fin, I had no idea Keita Nagori

would be here. Did you see the *Fortune* story about him last year? 'Samurai or Sap?''

'I missed it.'

Jan tells me about the article, how Keita insisted that every office of Tomo shipping, advertising, and PR have Ping-Pong tables and half-day Fridays in the summer, apparently a very un-Japanese thing to do. An e-mail written to Keita by his father was leaked to the Japanese press (the story intimated that his father leaked it) savaging Keita, calling him stupid and incompetent, a spoiled playboy who didn't deserve to inherit a great company. The fallout was a massive public embarrassment for Keita.

Jan continues, her thin, glossy lips moving fast while I dial down the volume to almost nothing, the faintest sound of her voice in the distance. My own personal camera has zoomed in on Jan's mouth. I read a book awhile ago. It was by a Buddhist monk and it talked about how all you had to do — the secret to happiness in life — was to live in the moment. And the way to do that was to breathe and to focus on what you were doing. I'm breathing and I'm washing a dish. I'm breathing and I'm walking down the street. I'm breathing and I'm staring at a woman's breasts. And I tried this, breathing and focusing on the moment. But for the most part it never worked for me (which, let me just emphasize, is far more of an indictment of me that any shortcoming of Buddhism or meditation). Except this one thing did happen. The handful of times I tried, in that close-to-immeasurably small space of time when I was

304

almost in the moment, all I felt was . . . afraid. I could see myself, as if at a great distance, completely alone in the world, and I could imagine my own death. Now, it may seem obvious by this point that perhaps I wasn't even close to being in the moment. But I was in *something*.

The headmaster of my high school used to give talks every couple of weeks, before classes would start for the day. For some reason I always remember them taking place in the winter, when it was really cold and the sun hadn't fully come up yet on a raw, gray New England January morning. And he would say things like, 'You are a speck upon a speck upon a vast speck.' Dust in the wind and how no one would remember us in one hundred years' time. But he said despite all that, we mattered, and that what we did mattered, that there was beauty in the small thing, the little achievement, even if we are destined to end up as ashes.

Jan's mouth continues to move silently, hands gesturing.

So why wouldn't I do it? Why wouldn't I find a way to get on a plane and bring his ashes to Pearl Harbor? What's the big deal? Because I don't want to? Because it isn't convenient? Because he disappeared? Because he drove my mother to suicide? But what does that have to do with now? With one hundred years from now? And yet my anger — when I let myself think about him, about what he left in his wake — is crippling. Again and again he hurts me, hurts us. Which is why I choose not to think about him.

In the nights before I left for L.A., the nights when I half watched reality television, waiting for Phoebe to call back, waiting for sleep to come at 3 A.M., 4 A.M., 5 A.M., and instead getting up and showering and walking to work, where I sat and stared out the window, the nagging, guilt-addled comeback was always the same. *Do it.*

I had called Eddie the night before I left and asked him to FedEx the ashes to Los Angeles. It was around nine in the evening when I called.

I'd said, 'I was wondering if you've called your guy yet. The VA guy.'

He snorted, a not-so-funny laugh. Mean-spirited Boston sarcasm. It's only funny if it hurts someone's feelings. He'd been drinking.

Eddie said, 'There is no guy. I made that up. There's no *guy.*'

I said, 'What are you talking about?'

'Do you know where they are now? His ashes? They're in the trunk of my car. I can't bring myself to bring them into my home, I'm *that* sickened by the man. Can you understand that?'

'Eddie.'

'His ashes are going where they belong. In the garbage or out the window as I'm driving over the Tobin Bridge or into a dumpster behind a Denny's.'

'Eddie. What are you talking about?'

'He *killed* her. He drove her to her death as much as if he was in the driver's seat of that goddamned Chevy Nova.'

Then he mumbled something about *ashes* and the *fucking Navy.*

I said, 'Eddie.'

No response. Tinkling ice cubes.

'Eddie,' I'd said. 'I hate him, too. But you're better than this. I need you to send them to me.'

Still no response. And now he has left me no choice. Eddie's Kryptonite.

'Ed.'

'What!'

'Mum wouldn't want this.'

'Fuck you. Fuck *you* for saying that to me.'

I heard a Zippo lighter open. It must have been close to the phone. Heard the tobacco burn as he inhaled. Heard the click of the lighter close. All one-handed, I'd bet.

He said, suddenly sober as morning, 'I can't believe you're going to do this for him.'

I couldn't quite believe it myself.

Eddie said, 'Why? Why do it?'

Until the moment he asked me I didn't have an answer.

I said, 'Because I can think of twenty really good reasons not to but I still feel guilty. Because he was a sad, angry man but he was my father and our mother loved him once. Because he asked me. Because you're convinced it's the wrong thing to do. Because I'm tired of the way people treat each other in this family, especially when they're alive.'

The phone was quiet for a time and I thought he'd hung up until I heard what I realized was clapping.

'Bravo,' he said. 'Spoken like the toilet-paper salesman you are.'

'Fuck you. Diapers.'

'Sorry. Huge difference.'

'What happened to you? What happened to this family?'

He said, 'You know nothing. You were a child. You didn't live through what we lived through. You think I *want* to feel this way, that I *choose* to feel this way?'

I said, 'How long do you hold on to this?'

'Till I die.'

Then he hung up.

I called Pam, who was already in LA. with Ian.

'I need to ship something,' I said. 'Out to L.A. To the hotel. Can you give me the FedEx number?'

'Don't tell me it's your luggage, Dolan. Creatives who do that drive me nuts. We're on a tight budget on this one and I can't do shit like that.'

'It's not my luggage . . . '

'Because if it is . . . '

'Pam, it's not my fucking luggage.'

I don't talk like this to her.

I said, 'I'm sorry. I just . . . I've got a situation here and I just need the FedEx number, please.'

I told her the basics. She asked for Eddie's address. She said she'd take care of everything, that the ashes would be waiting for me at the hotel. If you are lucky you have a friend or two who understand what you mean, not what you say.

Now, here in L.A., I want to run from the room. I feel wildly alone. Then the thought comes so fast and so clear it's startling. *Without her I am lost.*

308

Standing here with Jan, I find myself still nodding. I'm nodding only because Jan is nodding. She's nodding gravely. She's making a serious point that I am agreeing with, though I have no idea what the point is as I haven't heard a thing she's said for the past several minutes. The volume returns and Jan says, 'I've just returned from Diaper World.' She says this with the gravitas of someone who's just returned from a life-altering trip to Machu Picchu or Angkor Wat.

'Wow,' I say. 'How was it?'

Diaper World, despite its name, is not a theme park with rides on giant diapers. It's an annual diaper convention for the industry to show off its latest offerings. I have been to two Diaper World conventions, one in Cincinnati and one in Phoenix. The one in Phoenix I attended not one moment of, sitting instead by the pool, where I read, drank beer, and sustained a savage sunburn.

Jan says, 'Fin, it was inspiring. A diaper convention, right? But I mean, amazing things are happening in diapers right now' — to my mind an unfortunate sentence construction.

She plows ahead. 'It was in Montevideo, Uruguay. Have you been? Of course not. No one has. Amazing city. Who knew, right?' (Well, the Montevideans, certainly.)

I see Ian and Pam talking with a man, late fifties/early sixties, with a wispy gray ponytail and a kaffiyeh around his neck.

'Are you excited about the spot?' I ask.

'Excited? I think it's interesting. I worry that

309

it's too serious and maybe not serious enough. Does that make sense?'

No.

'Absolutely,' I say, a nodding, sycophantic jackass. Three loud sneezes.

'Bless you,' she says. 'I want to strike the right tone with this. I want to be serious, of course. We're a serious brand, it's a serious product. But I want to communicate *revolutionary*. Revolutionary meets breakthrough. Meets intense. But funny. We're a funny brand, Fin. As you well know. Funny but not laugh-out-loud funny. That's not what we're about. Light. I think that's the right word. A wink. The kind of thing that makes you smile more than laugh. Like many of your ideas. I want people watching to turn and elbow each other . . . '

She elbows me to prove her point and I spill club soda from my cup. Jan remains oblivious.

' . . . and say, '*That* was amazing. I want to buy those, And even if I don't have children and I don't *actually* want to buy those, I admire that company and see it at the *forefront* of eco-think. Like Apple or Google or GE. Or DuPont, post-Bhopal.' You got the e-mail about removing *non-toxic* and *biodegradable?*'

'What? No.'

'Might have just been to the account team. We'll talk about it.'

Ian, Pam, and Ponytail are making their way toward us.

Pam says, 'I'm sorry to interrupt. Jan, I wanted to introduce our director, Flonz Kemp.'

Jan extends her hand but Flonz embraces her

310

like a former girlfriend you bump into in a bar, both of you single, and think, *You look good.*

Jan lets out an involuntary, 'Ohh.'

Flonz lets go and looks Jan up and down. Jan is suddenly a flummoxed teenager in the presence of a star.

Jan says, 'Okay. I just have to say I loved *Scrambled Eggs at Midnight.*'

Flonz says, 'It was very good, wasn't it? You're an attractive woman, Jane.'

'Jan.'

Flonz laughs like a character from an episode of *Barnaby Jones*. 'What is the actual product we're shooting tomorrow?'

Jan laughs. Pam doesn't, as she knows he's serious.

Flonz is tying and retying his kaffiyeh. 'I just got back from six months in Morocco. Any of you speak Arabic? Because I do.'

Flonz Kemp was a legend, at one time the most famous commercial director in the United States. He shot most every great spot, won every big award. During his runaway success, when agencies would beg him to shoot their work, he had, one hears, great disdain for the business. He threw fits on the set, screamed at agency people, at clients. Yet they continued to hire him. He made vast sums, threw it around on fancy cars, houses in Europe. But what he was really looking for was validation, proof that he was better than commercials. He wanted to direct movies, take Hollywood by storm. He got his chance when he co-wrote a comic thriller about a night watchman (Flonz's job before he became a director)

311

who wants to direct movies who foils a real jewelry heist by filming it all as if it were a thriller. He catches the thieves, sells the movie, and moves to Hollywood, where he takes a part-time job as a night watchman. For his 'lunch' each night he ate scrambled eggs. *Scrambled Eggs at Midnight*. The film was a summer hit. Flonz was hailed as the next Spielberg. He was given huge money for his next film, for which he insisted upon rewriting the script, much to the annoyance of the Academy Award-winning screen-writer, who quit after Flonz began tinkering. It was a comedy about people during the ice age. Flonz didn't see it entirely as a comedy and felt adamant about shooting in the Swiss Alps in winter. And also about having the actors sing their lines. Conditions for cast and crew were apparently horrendous, shooting at times nearly impossible. He came in a year late and wildly over budget. The film was laughed out of the-aters, and not in a good way. 'Flonz Flop,' they called him. He tried to get back into commercials but he'd made too many enemies in the ad world. He was our sixth choice.

People find a seat at the large table. Pam leans over and says to me, 'We need to talk about the package.'

Jan says, 'Why don't we get started.'

Talk? About what? About the possibility of FedEx losing my dead father? Did Eddie not drop the ashes off at the FedEx office in Boston?

Alan says a few words, welcomes everyone. Jill sits next to him, nodding vigorously at everything he says.

Pam takes charge. She is eloquent but all business. She makes special mention of Keita, as I have asked her to.

Pam says, 'We are honored that Keita Nagori, special assistant to the chief operating officer of Lauderbeck, Kline & Vanderhosen's parent company, Tomo, Japan's largest shipping company and third largest in the world, has joined us today.'

We go around the room and introduce ourselves, say what we do.

I text Pam, who sits two seats away. *Package lost?*

Pam texts back, *Not now!*

Ian texts, *What's the problem?*

I text him back, *Ashes. Might be lost.*

Ian texts back, *OMG.*

Pam walks everyone through the pre-pro book, talks about locations, wardrobe, casting. None of it is news to anyone in the room. We've all seen the location pictures, the casting, the wardrobe. At some point on each page Pam politely turns to Flonz in the hope that this person our client is paying $25,000 a day will have directorial input. He smiles vacantly, like the weird uncle at Thanksgiving dinner. It is unlikely he's looked at the locations, casting, or wardrobe. All of which bodes well for a great shoot.

Slow nodding along the way. All good. Until we come to the casting of the hero. Who will play the role of the woman from the original spot, who was young, lithe, blond? Pam has, as always, found a broad range of choices. Our recommendation is someone yoga-fit and gorgeous. It's advertising, not a Michael Moore documentary.

Jan turns to one of her people. 'Karen. You had some concerns here, yes?' Which means Jan had concerns but will voice them through Karen.

'I do, Jan. Thanks.' Karen's voice, wardrobe, and demeanor suggest she might have been a local cable anchor in Tulsa.

Karen says, 'Your recommendations don't fit the psycho-graphic.'

Flonz is laughing. 'What the hell is that? Is that even a word?'

Karen is taken aback. 'Well, that's a pretty important litmus test for us at the brand level.'

Flonz is making a face like Karen has started speaking Hebrew.

Karen continues. 'We feel some of your gals are a bit thin. We'd like someone who represents our mommies a bit better.' She sorts through some of the casting headshots on the table and produces a photo of a woman who is easily a size sixteen.

Eyebrows raise. Even Flonz is too politically correct to say anything.

Ian says, 'I wonder if, considering the running part of the spot, we look at someone who, while representing the demographic, might also represent the aspirational nature of the demographic.'

Jan trusts Ian. She's looking at the headshot and the additional shots of the actress we've chosen; now in shorts, now in a bathing suit, now bulging out of yoga clothes.

Jan says, 'Who else do we have?'

Pam is ready for this and puts out two other, noticeably svelter choices.

314

'I like her,' Flonz says, pointing at one of the headshots. 'Interesting face. Let's go with her.'

Jan thinks on it a moment and nods.

Karen (herself a woman you might describe as on the large side) seems annoyed.

Pam says, 'Good. That leaves the script and I believe we're locked on that.'

The clients look at one another.

Jan says, 'Not quite.'

Ian looks at me. News to both of us. We look to Jill and Alan, for whom it is clearly *not* news.

The script (if you can call it that) is the exact line from the Apple 1984 spot, except for the name and date change. *On January 27th, Snugglies will introduce Planet Changers. The first non-toxic, one-hundred-percent biodegradable flushable diaper. And you'll see why 2010 won't be like 2010.*

Granted, this doesn't make any sense, as 2010 wasn't expected to *be* anything, unlike 1984, Big Brother, blah blah blah. My great hope was that no one would notice that it doesn't make sense. And that it's a joke. Granted, not a funny joke, but I was pressed for time.

A client, I don't know her name, says, 'We're concerned that the 2010 part doesn't make any sense.'

I'm ready for this. I'm nodding, smiling. 'It's meant as a joke.'

She says, 'I'm not sure I get it.'

Nor I. Sneeze. Pam tosses a packet of Kleenex at me. I use them as I formulate my response.

I say, 'Well, ya know. 2010 won't be like . . . 2010.'

Heads tilt, eyes squint. Even Flonz.

Flonz chuckles. 'I know Ridley. He's a prick. So wait. What do you mean, 2010? Have people been talking about 2010 being bad?'

Ian says, 'I think we mean that it's a just spoof of the 1984 spot. No one's saying anything about 2010 per se.'

Jill, eager to be part of the conversation and help, adds, 'I don't think the words are meant to be taken literally.'

Jan says, 'But that's what the script says.'

One of the clients says, 'Could we change the year?'

Karen says, 'So it would say, 'And you'll see why 2010 won't be like the future''?

Someone says, 'No. It would say, 'You'll see why the future won't be like the future.''

Flonz says, 'That makes no sense.'

Jan says, 'I'm not sure that's the answer.'

Someone says, 'Why couldn't it say, 'And you'll see why the future won't be so scary'?'

Ian looks at me with a face that suggests he's being strangled.

Someone says, 'Is there a year people talk about like 1984?'

Someone else says, 'There's talk in the Bible of 2012 being the end of the world.'

Ian says, 'I think you're thinking of the Mayan calendar.'

Karen says, 'That strikes me as very negative, the end of the world. Do we want to be associated with that?'

Jill says, 'That's not part of the brand at all.'

Client heads turn toward one another. *No,*

definitely not. Right?

I write down *Could mark the beginning of a new world* on a piece of paper and slide it to Ian. He nods. I say, 'How about this: 'And you'll see why 2010 will mark the beginning of a new world.''

Heads nod. Flonz says, 'That's not bad. At least it makes sense.'

Jan says, 'Say it again, please, Fin.'

I say it again, in my best voice-over voice. Imagine if people actually spoke like a voice-over. You'd never stop slapping them.

Karen says, 'New world? How about a *better* world?'

I say, 'How about a *cleaner* world?'

Jan says, 'I like *cleaner*.' Others nod aggressively.

I'm tempted to say that the average adult will weigh about six pounds after cremation and that on average, for every pound the person weighed when alive, they'll produce about one cubic inch of ash after cremation. Do we want to be associated with that?

Pam says, 'Okay, just so I'm clear on the Magna Carta here: *On January 27th, Snugglies will introduce Planet Changers. The first non-toxic, one-hundred-percent biodegradable flushable diaper. And you'll see why 2010 will mark the beginning of a cleaner world.*'

Karen says, '*Could.*'

Pam says, 'Excuse me?'

Jan says, '*Could* mark the beginning of a cleaner world. Legally we can't say they will for sure.'

317

Jan looks to Karen. Karen says, 'Let's talk about the N.T.B. issue.'

I say, 'N.T.B.?'

Jill says, 'Non-toxic biodegradable.'

Ian says, 'I didn't know there was an issue. Or an acronym.'

Jan says, all smiles, 'In all likelihood, there isn't.'

Karen says, 'But there may be.'

Ian says, 'What would the problem be?'

Karen says, 'Whether or not they're non-toxic or biodegradable.'

I say, 'But isn't that the whole point? Wasn't that the revolutionary part?'

Jan says, 'Absolutely. And we believe that they're still very much a revolutionary product.'

Karen says, 'They're just not one-hundred-percent biodegradable.'

'Or non-toxic,' adds the client I don't know.

Ian says, 'I thought you didn't know for sure.'

The client with no name says, 'It's almost impossible to ever know these things for sure. It's science.'

Karen says, 'We're hearing rumors of new results. Mind you, this is one result in a series of tests.'

Ian says, 'Did the other tests come back negative?'

The nameless client. 'No, no. Very positive.'

Ian says, 'That's great. You mean positive in a good way, not positive in a test-result-bad way.'

Nameless client. 'Oh, I see what you were asking. No. Positive in a bad way.'

'Do they do anything different than a regular diaper?' I ask.

Karen says, 'Very much so. We're confident they will, once in the ocean, break down.'

Jan says, '*Could*. Confident they *could* break down.'

'At some point,' the nameless client says. 'Though it's impossible to know when. Or if.'

More nodding.

Ian says, 'Is it flushable?'

Karen says, 'Not in any standard toilet, no.'

I look at Jill, who's taking notes and smiling. Alan shrugs.

I say, 'I'm confused.' More sneezing.

Jan says, 'New data. It's not a problem. The ship has sailed. We need to make sure the advertising works and that the wording is correct.'

I say, 'How about this: *On January 27th, Snugglies will introduce Planet Enders. A possibly toxic biohazard that will clog toilets and destroy the sea. And you'll see why 2010 will be Armageddon.*'

Ian says, 'Could be Armageddon.'

Long pause.

Keita — God love him — starts laughing his ass off.

★　★　★

Later, Pam and I sit at a table in the bar of The Four Seasons. Faux elegance, preternaturally good-looking people looking at one another, looking for famous people, known people, a model, an actress, so-and-so's boyfriend/girlfriend/ex-friend. Tori Spelling is at the bar. It's 10:00 P.M. and the high-priced call girls have slowly begun their nightly prowl, sidling up to lonely rich white men, striking up casual conversations, things in common. *Ohmigod, you like tits!?! I have tits!*

We're halfway through our second drink and tired and bored and it was time to go to bed an hour ago. I'm sneezing and feel mildly feverish. I bought Sudafed at the hotel shop and have taken two of them, along with that many beers. The effect is not unpleasant. Ian and Keita bowed out after one drink.

After the pre-pro we took the client to dinner at The Ivy, where the clients drank too much and Flonz talked about himself and Hollywood and famous people he knows. (Keanu Reeves is a 'close friend.' Mel Gibson is an 'old friend.' They used to shoot rats after a night of drinking with pistols Mel kept in his car. 'Maniac. But I honestly never heard him bad-mouth the Jews.')

It was on the way back that Pam told me. 'FedEx fucked up. Your father is in Düsseldorf. They think. Or Hong Kong. They're not sure. I'm working on it.'

Hitchcock did a thing in the movie *Vertigo*. It's called a dolly zoom. Apparently a Paramount cameraman came up with it. To simulate vertigo, put the camera on a track — or dolly — and pull back fast, the camera resetting its focal point. Zoom in, pull back. The result made your stomach flip. Pam's news is my own personal dolly zoom.

'A dying man's request,' Phoebe had said.

'He deserves to be in the garbage,' Eddie had said.

No, he doesn't. Nor in Düsseldorf, for that matter.

There is a minor commotion as a man and a woman and their entourage walk in.

Pam says, 'You know who that is?'

I say, 'The guy is Nikita Khrushchev. The woman is the great female athlete of the 1920s, 'Babe' Didrikson Zaharias.'

'Close. The guy is Cam Kendrick and the woman is Cindy Steel. They're the hosts of *Inappropriate Candid Camera*.'

'You're making that up.'

'I'm not. You've never seen it? It's huge. They put cameras in toilets, in dressing rooms, bedrooms, confessionals, therapist offices. People masturbate. People screw. They pixelate the screen. It makes *The Howard Stern Show* look like *MacNeil/Lehrer*. But people watch. I watch. I don't know why. They call it entertainment. It is the end of civilization. Of any modicum of decency. It's on MTV but Fox owns it. Right after *Jersey Shore*.'

'What do the hosts do?'

'They comment. They set up. They flirt with each other. She wears whore-ish outfits. He has a massive bulge in his jeans. Cartoon arrows appear on the screen from time to time and point at her breasts, her snatch. They point to his dick. The camera zooms in and out and they put in stock noises. *Boing*. Humping noises. Fart sounds. The crew laugh. Her nipples stick out. She says with a giggle, 'You *guys*! Who turned the AC on?!''

'Who's worse: us or them?'

Pam says, 'Us. Much worse. At least they're entertaining.'

'We have the wrong director, don't we?'

'We have the wrong director and the wrong script.'

'What are the chances this will be good?'

'Oh, Dolan. You poor boy.'

We watch an unnaturally beautiful woman take a seat alone at the bar, look around, take in the male crowd like an MI-6 agent in Berlin during the Cold War. She's wearing what appears to be a vacuum-sealed dress that someone didn't quite finish making, because it's missing a lot of material that might cover the thighs. She crosses her legs and even Pam stares. It's a show, after all. It's been three days since I've talked with Phoebe, the longest stretch we've gone in two years.

Pam gets up. 'I'm done.'

I say, 'What if they can't find them?'

She pushes the side of my head. 'Get some rest. Meet in the lobby at six. And don't fuck a hooker.'

I'm tempted to close my eyes for a moment. The Sudafed and beer have thrown a light blanket over me, muted the rough edges, lowered the extraneous noise. I watch as the sex bomb marks me, a bleary-eyed man sitting alone at a bar, surely a look that suggests *lost*, because otherwise why wouldn't this guy be in bed, where any normal person is. Easy target, she thinks. She smiles and it's so good that for a moment I'm convinced she actually likes me. I break the stare and then notice that my parents have walked in.

My father is wearing what he almost always wore, dark blue work pants — Dickies was the brand — and a matching blue work shirt, like a guy from a filling station in the fifties. His uniform on his days off, work clothes. His fingernails are dirty. He was always fixing something. Anything to get him out of the house. The lawn mower was upside down and he was readjusting the blade or cleaning the gutter or pouring concrete into the back of the rusty swing set, which he put in wrong and which came out of the ground if you swung too high. It had fallen when Eddie was on it. Six stitches in the back of his head.

They do this at some point on every shoot I've ever been on, every business class flight I've ever taken, every fancy restaurant I've ever eaten in. And they ruin it. They sit down, look around at the crowd, the swank of it all, the money. They never stayed at a hotel like this in their lives. My mother is wearing a simple skirt and a sleeveless white blouse and a pair of faded red Keds, with a small hole cut out of the fabric to allow for her bunions.

'What a nice place,' my mother says, pulling a wide-eyed face as if to say, Wow.

My father smiles. He always smiles at first. 'So they sent you on a business trip, huh?'

My mother's still making the wow face, the I'm so impressed and proud of you face.

'It's no big deal,' I say. But I want them to think it's a big deal.

'I should say it is, mister,' my mother says.

My father says, 'They fly a man across the

country, pay for his flight, put him up in a swish hotel. Says something about how that company thinks of a man.'

'Do you remember the government cheese?' my mother asks, smiling.

I nod. We got government assistance after he left. Large blocks of cheese in a plain cardboard box. CHEESE, it said on the side. Not Kraft. Not a name brand. FLAKES, too. A plain box that said FLAKES. Not Kellogg's Corn Flakes. Not Frosted Mini-Wheats or Cap'n Crunch or Post Raisin Bran. Flakes. I was aware of it, knew that we needed help, that we had very little money. I was embarrassed by it. Worse, I was ashamed that I was embarrassed. My mother knew it and I knew it made her feel worse.

'I didn't mind the cheese, Mum. I swear I didn't.'

She smiles and says, 'Yes you did. It hurt my feelings.'

'Please don't say that. I was stupid. I just . . . I didn't know. I will buy you anything you want. I will put you up here. Please.'

I say 'Please' out loud. I hear myself say it out loud. The people at the next table look at me and laugh.

The waitress is looking at me funny. 'Maybe it's time for the check?' she says.

'Yes,' I say. 'Thank you.'

When I turn back my mother is on the verge of crying.

'What happened?' I ask.

My father says, 'None of your goddamned business.'

324

That's how it would happen. That's how fast his mood would change.

'Don't talk to the boy like that,' my mother says.

'He lost my ashes,' my father says. 'I asked him for a favor. I said I was sorry. But goddamnit. I was a soldier. I volunteered for my country. I was given *nothing*. I was a cop. I protected people. What do *you* do? What have *you* done? You whining, white-collar waste. You pussy. You have it so easy you have no idea. Has a man ever died in your lap? What have you ever done?'

I say, 'Dad, please. What did I do wrong? Please tell me.'

My mother says, 'Leave the boy alone.' To me, 'You didn't do anything wrong, Finny.'

My father stands and turns. I can no longer see his face.

She stands and looks at me. She looked at me before she left to go to the store that day. She stared.

I say, 'Please don't go. Please.'

But she simply walks away.

A few years ago the agency invited a professor from the University of Chicago whose area of expertise was the social sciences to give a talk. It was called 'Understanding the Consumer's Psyche.' I remember nothing of what she said, except this. She said that our interior monologue, our little Gary voice that narrates our lives, is largely responsible for whether we are happy or not. Where does it originate? How do we change it?

While I consider this the sex bomb decides to

make her move. Liquid hips and thighs. A practiced walk. She smiles, doe-eyed, leans over, a free sample of her abundant décolletage, which she knowingly puts at eye level, and says, 'Looking for a date?'

I stare at her breasts for a time but I'm not sure I'm really seeing them. I look up and say, 'I'm looking for my dead father, actually.'

She says, 'I don't do threesomes.'

THE CLEAVERS AREN'T HOME

I read somewhere that on average each of us is exposed to something like five thousand advertising messages a day. If you sleep for eight hours that's something like 312 messages — commercials, print ads, Web banners, T-shirt logos, coffee-cup sleeves, sneaker swooshes — an hour. Where once you simply ran an ad in the local newspaper or on one of the three networks, now teams of people sit in corporations with their advertising and marketing and PR counterparts and talk earnestly about 360-degree branding. 'Let's surround the consumer.' I have been in meetings where people have suggested buying the space in urinals, in toilets — hotel toilets, airline toilets, the toilets at Yankee Stadium — for a Snugglies ad. We had someone mock up a board of both a toilet bowl and a urinal. We realized there was vastly more space to play with on the inside wall of a urinal. But then someone from the account group pointed out that our target was largely female and that 'she'd be left out of the urinal creative.' (Should I ever start my own agency, I've found my name for the company.) Mine is a business wherein we — in the service of our clients — are fighting for every inch of emotional space available in a consumer's increasingly crowded mind. Our brand managers and media strategists speak boldly of the *new* media, of *guerrilla* marketing. No physical or digital space is off limits. Sure, nature is beautiful, but couldn't it be made lucrative with, say, a giant ad wrapped around the Grand Canyon? (*You think this interior is roomy? Wait until you step inside the new Cadillac Escalade.*)

Logos everywhere. What do they mean? Is anyone listening? While you're thinking about that, have a Coke and a smile.

★　★　★

Day one goes off without a hitch. Okay, perhaps that's a slight exaggeration. There were problems from well before the opening shot. In the pre-pro meeting, for example, Flonz had said, 'We're going to do this old school. Film, none of this digital rubbish. We're filmmakers, not digital makers. Digital is something a proctologist does to an old man. We'll shoot thirty-five millimeter. We'll cut it by hand on a Movieola. Who needs a computer to edit?'

Super. Why not just have the Amish do a flip-book?

Shoots are highly organized events. Every detail has been thought out and planned ahead of time by the hierarchy: director, first assistant director, line producer, agency producer. Every hour of the twelve-hour shoot day is accounted for. When you have a film camera and fifty union crew members working, you are spending large sums of money, so structure is crucial. There are only four things that can endanger that structure: solipsistic stars, insecure directors,

328

animals, and, the most dangerous of all, babies.

Ours is a three-day shoot. And during almost every minute of those three days, we are shooting babies. To recap, the spot opens with our drone-babies walking through a hallway in a futuristic setting. We then see an auditorium where babies sit and watch a screen. Then our hero-mom comes running into the hall and throws a doodie diaper at the screen. Very simple.

At the moment we are trying to shoot the mothers sitting with their babies, all of whom are supposed to be mesmerized by the Big Brother — like character on the screen, who's talking about the welfare of the planet and who — per the client's in-house legal department — will not be Big Brother-like at all, as that's A) legally far too close to the original Apple spot, and B) too scary for the babies. So Big Brother instead will be a she and she will be a bunny. Flonz felt strongly that we needed to shoot with as many babies as possible. 'I want real. I want a thousand babies and their mothers. I want to feel it, smell it, and taste it on the film.'

Pam, on the other hand, did not want to feel it or smell it and especially did not want to taste it. She said we were asking for trouble, that surely we could shoot ten, maybe twenty babies tops and replicate them in post-production, much the same way crowd scenes are shot now, where you simply cut and paste a small crowd to fill a stadium. Pam had raised this concern again to Flonz's producer as the pre-pro meeting was breaking up and all of us were headed to dinner.

Flonz had made the terrible mistake of being both condescending and sexist to Pam in the same sentence.

'Don't worry, sweetheart,' he began, retying his kaffiyeh around his neck. 'I've been doing this awhile, okay?' He chuckled but there was a hint of nastiness to his comment.

Pam had paused and then nodded a lot. Never a good sign with Pam.

'Grampa. You haven't made a commercial since the Internet was dial-up, but if this is how you want to play it, be my guest. Also, call me sweetheart again and I'll pull the hair off your balls.' (They were seated at opposite ends of the long table at dinner.)

But Flonz got his babies.

We arrive at a soundstage at Universal at 7:00 A.M., Pam, Ian, Keita, myself. A wide-eyed production assistant greets us, smiling.

'Lot of babies,' he says.

'Excuse me?' I say.

'Lot of babies. Never seen so many babies in my life. You'll see.'

He asks if we want to get breakfast first or go to the set. We opt for the set. We have an hour before Jan and her team arrive and want to make sure everything is ready for the first shot. The plan is for Alan and Jill to escort them here from the hotel.

Keita says to me, 'This is very exciting. I love Hollywood.'

The PA brings us to the set, a replication of the set from the 1984 commercial — auditorium-like, chairs facing a large movie screen.

And it is there that my good energy begins leaking like a baby's wee from a Snugglie. It's not the set itself. It's the sound, and, to a great extent, the smell. Babies. Everywhere. Smiling, happy, screaming, crying, wailing, teething, crawling, toddling, running, falling. Who's to say how many. A million, perhaps? A huge section away from the set in the cavernous soundstage is dedicated to tables with baby formula, diapers, clothes, and rows of chairs for the moms. Makeup people try to tend to the mothers, who are also in the spot.

I look at Ian and Ian looks at Pam and Pam is shaking her head slowly. 'This will not end well,' she says.

Keita is smiling. 'So many babies!'

Ian says, 'This is gay man hell.'

And then we all happen to notice our director, the once-famous Flonz Kemp, the man in charge, the man with the vision, the man who is responsible for our Super Bowl spot, our chance for greatness, a man who is earning $25,000 a day for the next three days. He looks confused. This is not the look you hope to see on your director's face on the first day.

Unfortunately, the client arrives early. Jan walks up to me and says, 'I don't understand what's happening.'

We are scheduled to roll film at 8:30 A.M. Our first shot is slated to be the babies walking through the hallway to get to the auditorium to watch the Big Brother-like character. By ten-thirty we are still setting up, as the babies keep falling or walking in the wrong direction.

Some boycotted the idea of walking altogether and simply sat, looking around. A decision was made to reduce the number of babies, which helped a great deal.

By late afternoon we get the shots of the babies toddling, though some of them are crawling, and we all agree, after a twenty-five-minute discussion among the group, that this is adorable and, as Flonz says, 'exactly the reason I love working with babies. You never know what you're going to get.' His smile is not met with other smiles.

Not surprisingly, the shoot ran late. The overages cost the agency tens of thousands of dollars. Ian and I are supposed to be in charge. Martin will hear about this. Moods soured. A dinner had been planned and we all agreed that perhaps it would be best to postpone until the following evening. Everyone wants to go to their rooms, order room service, and hope to find *Tommy Boy* on Pay-Per-View.

Throughout the day I looked to Pam each time her iPhone buzzed. Is it my father, who never traveled to Europe or China during his life but managed to visit both shortly after his death? Have the gods of logistics — these movers of cargo and packages, toilet paper and salmon, legal documents and illegal drugs, and, occasionally, the remains of a World War II veteran from Boston — finally rerouted him the 7,254 miles from HKG to LAX, deep within the cargo hold, ashes class, 30,000 feet above sea level, one last time?

Each time Pam looks over, shakes her head.

My cold is getting worse and I stand in a hot shower for a long time. I can't seem to get warm. L.A. is unusually cold, even for January. The news says something about strange winds from the North Pacific. The heat in my room doesn't seem to be working, so I put on both bathrobes hanging in the bathroom, thinking I might be able to sweat out my illness. I've ordered a bowl of spaghetti from room service. I've also opened a half-bottle of red wine and a $15 can of peanuts, which I'm confident the finance department will reject. I'm lying in bed clicking through the channels on TV.

Ian calls.

I say, 'I'm wearing two robes.'

Ian says, 'Paulie just called me. Phoebe quit.'

The Mighty Ducks are playing the Toronto Maple Leafs on TV. A commercial comes on and it's Snugglies' main competitor. A guy with long hair plays guitar and sings a song called 'Do the Potty Dance.' Toddlers dance. The man sings. 'Let's all wear our big-kid pants.' I feel jealous. Why didn't we come up with that? I hate it but admire the thinking.

I say, 'When?'

'This afternoon, late. She gave two weeks' notice. Have you talked to her recently?'

The next spot is for soda, done by our agency. I press mute and watch with the sound off. The cool instantly dissipates and the spot without sound looks absurd.

Ian says, 'Fin.'

'Yeah.'

'Have you talked with her?'

'No. I left her a couple of messages.'

Ian says, 'You should call her.'

I'm not hungry and I regret ordering the $25 bowl of pasta. For a moment I think about taking a red-eye home to New York. I flip the channel and watch as a man puts petroleum jelly on his nose, dips his nose into a bowl of cotton balls, and then runs to another bowl, where he shakes the cotton ball off with some struggle. He then repeats this task several times as a clock counts to sixty seconds. I have the TV on mute but watch as the audience shrieks with delight; whether this is an honest reaction or the result of aggressive, unseen prompting by flashing signs and eager producers, one can't know. The host, a fleshy man with dyed, spiky hair and who, if he hadn't landed this job, looks like he might be tending bar at a convention, watches with a smirk. It comes out quietly and surprises me, a private thought expressed out loud.

I say, 'I think I'm in love with her.'

Ian says, 'I know. Everyone knows.'

'Why didn't I know?'

'You really want to hear this?'

'Yes.'

'Because you lie to yourself. Because you keep everyone and everything at arm's length. What happened to you as a kid . . . I wouldn't wish on anyone. But at some point . . . '

He stops. Then says, 'Look. What the hell do I know. I just want you to be happy. She makes you happy.'

It's past midnight in New York. Too late to call. A text message seems weird. She's not responded to my e-mail yet. The doorbell to my room rings.

I say, 'My room service is here.'

Ian says, 'I'll see you in the lobby at six.'

'My father's ashes are lost,' I say, not wanting to hang up quite yet.

'What? What happened?'

'FedEx lost them. They were supposed to arrive yesterday. They're in Düsseldorf. Or Hong Kong. Maybe.'

'Jesus. So wait. Does that mean you're going to do it? If you find them?'

It's strange and embarrassing to admit, but I hadn't really thought that far. I just knew I didn't want Eddie to hurl them off the Tobin Bridge or into a dumpster. But actually getting on a plane to Hawaii, finding a boat, spreading the ashes . . . I hadn't thought that far. The doorbell rings again.

'Yes,' I say. 'I am.' The words surprise me.

Ian says, 'Okay.'

I say, 'Okay. See you at six.'

I open the door and can't figure out why the room service waiter is looking at me strangely. Until I remember that I'm wearing two bathrobes.

★   ★   ★

This is the forty-second commercial I've made in my career. I know this because I keep the pre-production books from each shoot and number them. There's a name for that and that

335

name is 'sad.' You have to understand that I never thought I'd get to go on a shoot. A shoot was what you strived for, it was achievement and success. When I started out I was mostly working on direct mail letters, coupons, and in-store banners. I took it seriously. I would fight the client hard on the use of exclamation points (they pro, me con). I worked the copy to death, convinced, somehow, that despite the fact that it might have been for diapers, the likes of Aaron Sorkin and Jeffrey Katzenberg would see it and demand to know who wrote it. Sorkin: 'There's a voice beneath the mail-in rebate copy that feels very fresh to me. Who is this guy?'

Those first few times on a set are unforgettable. The crew and the energy and the actors and the little magic that happens when the camera rolls, when the light hits the film and leaves a perfect inverse image. *I wrote this*, I would think. *Millions of people will see this on TV.*

I wanted to be great.

So you try. You throw yourself into it. You learn. You learn the difference between writing and shooting. You learn the difference between how you hear a line of dialogue and how an actor says a line of dialogue. The line you thought was so funny turns out to be hackneyed and expected. Later, in the edit room, the takes you thought were great turn out to be not so great. You try harder next time, work longer on the script, on cutting the superfluous, on saying it better, funnier, more . . . real. You read plays and screenplays. You study them. You try to understand how they work. You take a writing class at the 92nd Street Y. You see plays at an off-Broadway theater. You read the scripts of award-winning commercials. You realize that advertising, at its best, tells a story. It closes the gap between the thing being sold and the person watching. The really good work, done by the best people, makes you feel something. It tells the truth. It elevates the business, transcends a mere ad to something better, more valuable. It connects with another human being, breaks through the inanity and noise to find something essential and real and lasting. Like art. Not always. Not often. But sometimes. You have seen it done. You have admired the people who do it. And you have come to the realization, in spot after mediocre spot, that you are not that good.

★ ★ ★

Day two.

The rain has stopped but it is overcast and cold. Still dark on our way to the set. Pam gets a call while we're in the van. Jan wants to meet before we roll. Probably not a great sign.

My phone rings. I hold it up for Pam, Ian, and Keita to see.

I answer. 'Martin.'

'What's going on?'

'Well, we had a good day yesterday . . . '

'That's not what I heard. Jan called last night. Had concerns, she said. Worried, she said. Too big to screw up, she said. What the hell is going on?'

His voice is low, angry.

I revert immediately to my go-to mode when confronted by angry, displeased superiors: frightened child. Pam, Ian, and Keita are watching me. We pull into the Universal lot, past security, to our soundstage.

I say, 'We can handle this. Yesterday was a little rough, but . . .'

We come to a stop.

Martin says, 'Listen carefully, Fin. Don't fuck this up.'

I say, 'I won't.' But he's already hung up.

We get out of the car and there, standing at the door to the soundstage, is Martin.

★ ★ ★

More babies.

We're shooting the wide shot of all the moms and babies sitting in the auditorium, facing the screen. Try getting one hundred babies to look at the same place at the same time. I dare you.

Martin's anger has turned to endearing British charm as he air-kisses Jan, Euro-style, both cheeks.

'Martin.' Jan beams. 'What a lovely surprise. You didn't have to do this, but thank you.'

Ian and I don't look at each other. But I feel him not looking at me.

'I have a meeting here tomorrow but figured I'd come out a day early and observe,' Martin lies. 'Pretend I'm not here.'

'I'd certainly like to,' Pam says.

Karen comes over. 'Jan? Sorry to interrupt.

338

But we need to get on that call.'

Jan excuses herself. Martin says, 'Come with me.'

Pam, Ian, Keita, and I follow him to the camera, where Flonz is looking through the lens.

Martin says, 'Mr. Kemp. Martin Carlson. A great honor. Fan of your work.'

Flonz smiles, 'Hey, Marty. Glad you could make it out.'

They're shaking hands but Martin's not letting go.

Martin, still smiling. 'I'm not sure what kind of arseholes you're used to working with but if the next two days don't go flawlessly, and I mean flawlessly, I'll see to it no one ever wants to work with you again. Clear?' Still smiling. 'And it's Martin, not Marty.' He takes his hand back.

You can see remnants of the old Flonz temper. His eyes narrow, his cheeks color. But his fame and power are long gone. He needs the job. Welcome to the new world, Flonz old boy.

Flonz says, 'We're going to be fine.'

'So glad we had this little chat.' Martin turns and walks away.

Pam, looking at Martin walk away, says, 'Wow, I like him so much more now.'

* * *

Martin sits in video village with Jan. Ian, Pam, Keita, and I stand a few yards back from the camera, watching on a monitor. Martin's chat with Flonz seems to have inspired him. He's moving faster, the shots coming more smoothly.

The baby gods are kind to us and we get the wide shot as well as several tighter shots on moms and babies looking to the screen. Now we're shooting extreme close-ups of moms and babies, just babies, just moms. Everyone on the set with access to a monitor can't help smiling. The perfect little faces fill the frame in close-up, wide-eyed and gorgeous.

There's a break as they reset. The moms stand and stretch. Some change their babies.

Ian and Pam find a space to sit and open Pam's laptop to log on to the website of a digital design company in New York. They're the ones who will create the not-Big-Brother — like bunny figure on the screen. We will then fill that image in during post-production. It's art-related, which means Ian's in charge. Keita mingles with the crew.

One of the moms comes over. She says, 'What do you do?'

'I'm the writer.'

'Oh, wow. That's cool. Seems like a neat spot. I'm Cindy.'

'Fin. Thanks. We'll see how it turns out. Do you remember the original?'

'Original what?'

'The original spot. Apple 1984?' I'm speaking Russian, if her expression is any indication. 'This is a spoof,' I add, instantly ashamed at using a word I loathe, sounding like something from *A Prairie Home Companion.*

Cindy says, 'Oh. No. I didn't know that.'

She's smiley, maybe thirty, thirty-one. Athletic looking. She's cradling her son — I think it's a boy — on her chest, his back to her, her arm across him like a seat belt, holding him under his well-padded crotch. He's staring at me.

I say, 'What's his name?'

'Nathan.'

'How old?'

'Ten months next week. Do you have kids?'

'I don't.' I feel I should say more, explain why a man of almost forty doesn't have children. The hair and makeup woman comes over.

She says to Cindy, 'Excuse me. Hi. Sorry. You're up soon and I just need to do a touch-up.'

Cindy turns and holds the baby out toward me. 'Would you hold him for a sec? I don't want the powder to get on him.'

Before I have time to answer she hands him to me and then focuses on the makeup woman.

He's lighter than I imagined, despite his pudginess. His face is close to mine. He takes his hands and grabs fistfuls of my cheeks, which does not feel great. A primal noise emanates from him.

I say, 'Hi.'

He opens his mouth and puts it on my nose, leaving a great deal of slobber in the process.

I pull back. 'What are you doing? You can't eat a nose. Who eats a nose?'

He laughs.

I say it again. 'Who eats a nose?'

He laughs again.

He doesn't blink. He just stares and waits, smiles.

Pam comes up next to me.

She says, 'What are you doing?'

'Holding a baby.'

'I can see that. I guess I meant why are you holding a baby?'

I say, 'I'm helping. His name is Nathan. He likes me.'

Nathan puts his mouth on my nose again. I could get used to it. His breath is remarkably pleasant.

Cindy says 'Thanks,' as she takes him back and heads back for her close-up.

I watch them walk away and turn to see Pam looking at me.

I say, 'What?'

'What am I going to do with you, Dolan?' She shakes her head and walks away.

★ ★ ★

Later, a major problem arises when one of the junior clients notices that the industrial-size box of diapers made available for the baby changings throughout the day is the leading competitor and not Snugglies. This caused no small amount of consternation and a trip by two PAs to the nearest Ralph's. A small uproar in response by the moms, fully seventy-five percent of whom complained that they preferred the leading competitor's brand and refused to use Snugglies. This provoked a call to the Snugglies legal department, asking if a baby not wearing a Snugglies diaper, but a competitor's, could legally appear in the spot. Several lawyers were consulted and a conference call was scheduled thirty minutes later, wherein four in-house attorneys, Jan and her team, and several team members back at the New York headquarters took forty-five minutes to decide that the babies had to be wearing Snugglies, even if you couldn't see them. The moms were told to change their babies or forfeit their day-rate and residuals. Every one changed their own baby's diaper.

★ ★ ★

My cell phone is buzzing. I must have fallen asleep.

I answer.

Pam says, 'They're here. They landed at LAX thirty minutes ago.'

It takes me a second. It's just after midnight and I'd only gone to bed a half hour ago. Keita arranged a dinner at Matsuhisa, a well-known sushi restaurant in Beverly Hills. Jan, Pam, Ian, Martin, Alan, Jill, Flonz. Keita was a star, the perfect host, ordering, translating. Somehow we were all friends. Flonz made Jan the center of attention. Flonz and Martin were fast buddies after the first bottle of wine. By the third they were praising each other's greatness.

'You're kidding,' I say to Pam.

'When it absolutely positively has to be there.'

'Jesus.'

Pam says, 'FedEx wanted me to let you know they're profoundly sorry and as a gesture of their appreciation of your business would like to offer you free shipping next time you send internationally.'

'I'll keep that in mind for the next relative who dies.'

Pam says, 'They'll be at the hotel soon.'

She made calls. She lit into people, people's managers, shift supervisors. She spoke with people in Boston and Memphis and Düsseldorf and Hong Kong. She made it her mission. Of this I am sure. Just as I am sure she would never, ever admit it to me or share the back-story. She forces you to read between the lines. Who knows, maybe she's a distant Dolan relative.

'Thank you,' I say.

'Good luck with this, Fin.'

'You never call me Fin. Are you falling for me?'

'Fuck off.' She laughs and hangs up.

I call the front desk and ask if they could send the package up as soon as it arrives. Thirty minutes later, after a knock on my door, I accept a squat, surprisingly heavy well-handled FedEx box with my father's remains — Boston to Los Angeles with stops in Memphis, Düsseldorf, Kuala Lumpur, and Hong Kong — handing the kid who brought them up $20. Then, for the first time in twenty-five years, my father and I sleep under the same roof.

★   ★   ★

Day three.

It's early and the crew is setting up for the first shot — our hero-mom running from the guards. It's our last big shot. The remainder of the day will be used for shooting the green screen — that is, the movie screen at the front of the auditorium that the mom/babies are looking at

344

so that the image can be put in by the computer artists later. A minor legal issue derailed us briefly late yesterday when the Snugglies lawyers urged us to avoid shorts and thus any potential infringement issues. Working together with several members of the marketing team back in New York, they drafted a memo (subject heading 'Shorts v. pants issue') reminding us that 'our target audience is, according to research, *very* uncomfortable with their thighs.' Their italics, not mine. The marketing team, with the lawyers' blessing, went on to strongly suggest that we consider 'a nice pair of beige-colored slacks.'

Jan told us to ignore the memo and stay with the loose-fitting Snugglie-blue shorts-cum-gauchos.

One senses a change on the set. The excitement of day one, the camaraderie of day two have evaporated, been replaced by something heavier, more fatigued. People want to go home.

For me — and I sense for Ian — a mild panic has set in, expressed through moist palms, a mildly upset stomach, an all-encompassing fatigue. My career (such as it is) could use help. Indeed, I could use a significant boost to my fortunes at the agency, a Best-of-Super-Bowl spot, a much-deserved promotion, a new account. It would change my life and make it better. I would achieve happiness. In theory, anyway. I have believed this same thing for many years, that each commercial I made would somehow change my life, catapult me to the next level, whatever that level is. A happier level. Of this I am sure.

Some of that nervousness could be due to the fact that I'm carrying around my father's ashes. I stared at the box as I was about to leave my room this morning and paranoia overtook me. What if the exceptionally efficient Four Seasons housekeeping staff mistook the FedEx box for an outgoing parcel? What if they mistook it for trash? What if they stole it, thinking it was drugs or money or jewelry? What if it disappeared again? I arrived in the lobby to meet Pam, Ian, and Keita. They looked at the box.

Ian said, 'Bring Your Father to Work Day?'

I said, 'He's never been on a shoot.'

Keita said, 'This will be fun.'

Pam said, 'I still intend to smoke and yes, there will be ashes and no, I'm not going to feel bad about it. Let's go.'

We shoot our hero-mom, who's carrying a comically (one hopes) large doodie diaper. Initially there are problems with that as well. Some of the toddlers saw the guards (all female, by the way) don their masks, which we tried hard — with the production company's art department — not to make scary in any way. But some of the kids screamed, setting off a chain reaction of screaming. It took forty-five minutes to calm everyone down (graham crackers, juice boxes, Elmo movie).

Flonz began to trust Ian to the point where he relied on him. Ian knows lenses, focal length, understands what we'll need in the edit room. We shoot hero-mom in close-up and in a wide shot. We shoot her rounding corners and on straightaways. We shoot the drone-guards chasing her. We shoot her at twenty-four frames per second — the way your eye sees the world

— and we shoot her at forty-eight frames per second — slow motion.

At some point during every shoot the moment comes when I see the idea as dog shit. On this shoot that moment comes when Flonz shouts, 'Cut!' — a huge smile on his face — having just watched our hero-mom throw a giant doodie diaper (we used dozens of Baggies full of chocolate Jell-O pudding for heft) at the screen. I video the woman running and throwing the diaper with my phone and send it to Phoebe. No answer. Normally she'd text back right away.

I imagine the post-Super Bowl Monday-morning reviews online, in the trade magazines. *'Lauderbeck, Kline & Vanderhosen strike out again.'* *'Pooperbowl losers.'* *'Derivative. And mind-numbingly stupid. Finbar Dolan should be shot.'*

* * *

I have little to do so I walk to video village, check on the team of clients surrounding Jan. We're in between shots so no one watches the monitors. They're typing on laptops, tapping on phones, speaking into headsets. There's a table set up with snacks, coffee, bottles of water. There is a gravitas to their expressions, their tone of voice, their frantic typing and texting. I stand there holding my box. Everyone is working. There can be no stopping in the new world. We take pride in our busy-ness, our relentless workiness. You hear it every day.

I'm swamped. I'm incredibly busy. I've never been busier. Work's insane.

347

It validates us. Helps us feel important. Helps us feel alive. If we were to stop, stand still, not do anything, we'd burst into flames.

'Dad,' I say to the box. 'This is my client, Jan, and her team, whose names I forget, except for Karen, who's pacing near the snacks table talking into a headset and who last smiled in 1987. This is my job. I come up with ideas, most of which are killed, and once in a great while one is made into a TV commercial and then we stand around and watch as they are filmed. You would think it would be more fun. I'd introduce you but they're busy and you're dead.'

No one has noticed my father and me. We turn and walk away.

* * *

Martin asks me to walk with him. He's spent the morning on calls, occasionally checking in with Flonz and making sure Jan was happy.

He says, 'I'm off. You're back in New York tomorrow, yes?'

'Yes,' I lie.

'I'll see you at the editor. I told Jan she can come by as well. What's in the box?' he asks.

I'm tempted to tell him. 'Nothing. Candy. It's a gift. For a friend. Late Christmas gift. Candy and wine. Small bottle. See you in New York.'

* * *

After lunch, Ian and Pam oversee the green screen shots. There's little for me to do so I walk outside. The sky is still overcast. It feels like rain. Two PAs sit in matching golf carts watching a movie on one of their iPhones, sharing the headset. I ask if I can use one of the golf carts.

Beyond the soundstages, in the backlot, sits a seemingly real world without human beings. Streets you know, houses you've seen hundreds of times. There's the pond where they filmed the close-up shots of *Jaws*. There's the street where *Leave It to Beaver* lived. There's the *Munsters* house. There's a corner of Greenwich Village and Little Italy.

Up and down each street, the all-American homes, the manicured lawns, the driveways, not a soul, not a car, not a sound. I've stepped out of our soundstage of make-believe and into a neighborhood of make-believe.

I park and get out of the golf cart, walk to the Cleavers' front door, peer inside. It is a shell of a home, pure façade. I shout, 'June! I'm home! And I'm not wearing pants!' It comes out louder than I thought it would and I am sure Universal security will arrive any minute.

There was a boy on my street growing up, Bobby Sullivan. We went to grade school together. One day, his older brother, Phil, told us a joke. He said, 'What was the first dirty joke ever on television?' We had no idea, boys of eight, nine, ten years old. Phil said, ' 'Ward, you were awfully rough on The Beaver last night.' ' Phil laughed. We laughed. We had no idea what he was talking about.

I sit down on the steps and call Phoebe, desperate for her to answer but surprised when she does.

I say, 'Guess where I am.'

'I don't know.' Her voice is different. Flatter, trying, polite. She means, *I don't care.*

'*Leave It to Beaver*'s house.'

'Tell the Cleavers I said hello. How's the shoot going?'

'Okay. I hear you have some news.'

'Yeah. I was going to call you.'

'You got my messages?'

'I did. Yes. Thank you.'

Silence.

I say, 'So what are you going to do?'

'I'm not sure. I was thinking about maybe going back to school. Photography.'

'That'd be great.'

'Or maybe teaching,' she says.

'You have no plan, do you?'

'Not a clue.' She forces a small laugh. 'I just know I don't see myself in advertising.'

'I can understand that.'

Phoebe says, 'Why is that? Why are there so few people who seem to enjoy working in advertising?'

'I don't know. But it seems to be that way.'

More silence.

I say, 'What are you up to today?'

'Going to see a movie.'

'What movie?'

'*Grey Gardens.*'

'Fun. Is that the one with Steven Seagal?'

'Yeah.' She fakes a laugh. 'I actually should head out soon.'

'Oh. Okay. Well, I won't keep you.'

My breathing comes in short, uncomfortable

breaths. It begins to rain very lightly and I slide back, against the front door, under an eave.

She says, 'The Frenchman asked me to marry him.'

Dolly zoom. Vertigo. Hand to forehead involuntarily. Panic.

Why wasn't there an episode where June Cleaver left the house to go to the market for milk and turned and looked at The Beav for an unusually long time and then got in her car and drove into a tree? *That* would have made for interesting TV.

I say, 'Are you going to . . . what are you going . . . ' I'm unable to form a full sentence.

Everything slows down. The sound goes away. I watch myself. *Look at him*, I think. *Look at Fin*. I do a quick flashback of his life, watch from overhead as he wanders through the maze, making wrong turns, wanting to turn back, sitting down, unable to go forward. Running in circles. I want to help him. From high up I can see it all so clearly. I want to steer him in the right direction. But I know he won't listen. He doesn't have the courage to listen. He just wants to keep moving. If he keeps moving he's safe.

'No,' she says.

I'm not sure how much time passes. And maybe it's all my imagination, my particular narrative and view of the world. But in that 'no' I hear the greatest hope I've heard in a long time.

I say, 'It's raining here.'

'It's snowing here. And windy. It's snowing up outside my window.'

'I'm sorry.'

'It's okay.'

'It's not. It's really not,' I say. And then I say, without knowing I was going to, 'I saw her.'

'Saw who?'

I'm reaching the point in life where a door is about to close.

'I saw her. I mean, I was there. My mother. I saw her . . . It's not an excuse. I'm just. I'm so sorry.'

'What?'

The slow-motion film again. Long stretches in my life where it didn't run. Then stretches where it ran all the time. And always I found a distance from it. The boy. The boy on the bike. I wrote a spot just like it once. Except it's a girl and her father. Very clever change, I thought. It was for tampons and I had it as a flashback at the now grown girl's wedding and it was complicated. In fact, it made no sense. The creative director said, 'What does this have to do with tampons?'

I've never told anyone before. But now it tumbles out. I tell her the whole story. I tell it as if it happened to someone else. I tell it like a narrator, like I have always told it to myself.

'Fin.' Her voice low, intense, so pained.

I say, 'That's how I got the scar.'

It's colder now, the rain steadier. How lovely it would be to walk into the Cleaver home right now, their clean, warm, loving home. June would have something in the oven, cookies or a cake, a roast for dinner. The boys would be doing their homework, reading a comic book. Maybe The

Beav would be up to his usual wacky shenanigans; glueing the cat to the chimney, masturbating outside the window of a female neighbor, attaching a scope to a high-powered rifle and lying in wait for Eddie Haskell. Crazy kids.

I say, 'I'm just so sorry. I'm not sure . . . I mean, I'm not sure you understand how much you mean to me.'

'Then tell me.'

★ ★ ★

Flonz turns to his first AD and says, 'Call it.' The first AD says, 'That's a wrap. Thank you, everyone.' It's a thing that happens at the end of every shoot. Everyone applauds.

Within thirty minutes the energy of the shoot has dissipated. Pizza and beer arrive for the crew, but they're eager to break the set down and go home. Flonz hugs everyone and tells Ian he's wasting his time as an art director and gives him his cell phone number. Everyone hugs everyone else. Flonz's entourage whisks him away, the clients hop into a waiting van and head to the airport to catch the red-eye. Ian and Pam will do the same. But not before stopping for dinner at Chez Jay in Santa Monica. The plan is to meet at the editor in New York tomorrow.

'It was genius on paper,' I say to Ian.

He smiles and hugs me.

'You good?' he asks.

'I'm good.'

'Call me.'

Keita and I watch as the world that we created is quickly and easily dismantled and put away. Outside, the skies are clearer. Wispy clouds move fast in the high winds.

★ ★ ★

Keita and I walk back to the hotel from dinner, an overpriced Italian place on Robertson. He'd asked at dinner when I was going and I told him I was on a morning flight to Honolulu. He asked how I was going to do it and I told him I hadn't thought that far ahead, that I'd probably just rent a boat. He smiled, as he almost always does, and changed the subject.

We walk through the driveway to the hotel. Instead of walking in, Keita walks over to the life-size statue of Marilyn Monroe, frozen in her famous skirt-billowing moment from *The Seven Year Itch*. A vintage Aston Martin, a Porsche, and the cleanest Range Rover in the world are waiting for their owners.

Keita says, 'Would you take her life and fame for being dead at thirty-seven?'

'No. I like being no one. Plus I wouldn't date a Kennedy.'

'Can I ask you one question?'

'Sure.'

'Why are you doing it?'

He's looking at the fake grill that Marilyn is standing on and I'm looking at Marilyn's breasts.

I say, 'Because the others won't.'

He looks at me and says, 'I do not think that's

true. I think you go because it makes you feel better than them.'

I say nothing. But he knows he's right.

He says, 'I hope you are not offended.'

'No. I'm not offended.'

'I think maybe it is not enough, your reason.'

'So why should I go?' I ask.

'Because he is your father. Because this is what we do as sons. Even when they hurt us and ruin us.'

Shame and embarrassment wash over me. Such an obvious thing. I know nothing.

I say, 'Yes.'

Keita smiles.

A man and woman walk out of the hotel to the Aston Martin. Both are on their cell phones, the man wearing a headset. He points to Keita, then points to the door of his car. My adrenaline goes nuclear and I'm on the verge of telling him to go fuck himself when Keita opens the car door as the man slides in. Keita closes the door and the man hands Keita a five-dollar bill.

The man says, 'Save up. Maybe someday you'll be able to afford one.' He winks and drives off.

The calm smile still there, Keita says, 'Our family actually has two.'

In the lobby we shake hands and Keita bows deeply. We agree to keep in touch. He looks like he wants to say something but then turns and gets in the elevator.

★ ★ ★

I'm in bed, having foregone brushing my teeth or doing anything with my clothes except stepping out of them. I'm so tired I can't sleep. The fan clicks on and off in an attempt to keep the room at a constant temperature.

The little voice is Katie Couric. No. It's Joan Rivers. No, wait. It's Barbara Walters.

The voice says, 'You thought it would be different by now.'

I say, 'Yes.'

She says, 'You thought things would be clearer at this point in your life. But you're just more confused.'

I say, 'Yes.'

She says, 'You thought with age would come a sense of security, of knowledge about how life works. But you still don't know anything. You haven't figured anything out yet.'

'No.'

She says, 'You don't know what you want.'

'No.'

'You live in New York City and yet you almost never go to museums or theater, to hear music. You might as well live in Houston. Do you find that very sad?'

'I find your blouse sad.'

'Are you a happy person?'

'Yes.'

'What makes you happy?'

'My work.'

'Is that a true statement?'

'No.'

'Why don't you quit, find another job?'

'I can't.'

'You can't or you won't? Are you afraid?'

'I choose not to. And no, not out of fear.'

'Are you afraid?'

'No.'

'Are you afraid of what might happen if you quit?'

'Who wouldn't be?'

'A courageous person.'

'I'm not afraid.'

'What would happen if you quit?'

'I don't know. I'm not very good at a lot of things.'

'Well, at least we know that's true.'

'There's no reason to turn to the camera and wink.'

'Are you happy?'

'You asked me that already. Yes. I'm happy. I'm very happy.'

'Are you happy?'

'You *asked* me that already.'

'But you didn't answer me. You lied. What makes you happy?'

'My friends.'

'Who? What friends? You don't really have friends. You have acquaintances. You don't let people in.'

'I have almost two hundred friends on Facebook. How many do you have?'

'Over three thousand. Are you happy?'

'Stop!'

'You had plans when you first moved to New York, didn't you? You were going to try new things. You wrote that the first New Year's Eve you were here, didn't you?'

357

'Don't read my journal.'

'You've written it every year since, haven't you? '*Try new things. Be fearless. Take a class in something. Change careers.*' You wrote those words. You've written those words every New Year's Eve for seven years. And yet you've done none of it. Why?'

'I don't know. Time slips away.'

'Do you have regrets?'

'Not using Brian Williams for this dialogue.'

'Are you a happy person?'

'I'm begging you. Please leave me alone.'

'You name me Barbara Walters.'

'Yes.'

'You name me Oprah or Terry Gross.'

Yes.'

'You give me names and let me savage you.'

'Yes.'

'And yet you know who I really am.'

'Yes.'

'So answer me. Are you a happy person?'

'No.'

'Then change that.'

'I don't know how.'

'Yes, you do.'

'No, I don't.'

'Let me go.'

'I can't.'

'Stop crying, Finny. Let me go. Forgive me.'

'Why did you do it?'

'Pain. Guilt. Shame.'

'You ruined me. How could you do that to us?'

'Don't say that. You know it's not true.'

'I'm nothing. I'm a fake person. We're not a family anymore.'

'You have a chance, every day, to change. If you want. One beautiful thing.'

'I don't know how.'

'Yes, you do. Let me go. Forgive me. Because if you don't let go, then *this* is it. *This* is your life. Are you happy?'

'I've never been happy.'

'Okay, then. Let me go. Both of us. Your father and me. Let us go, Finny. Please.'

I stare at the ceiling, the hot tears streaming down the sides of my face, into my ears.

ONE BEAUTIFUL THING

They called it a boat, not a submarine, and it was 260 feet long and back then it ran submerged during the day and surfaced at night to recharge the batteries, which needed air to operate. Bow to stern: the forward torpedoes and the forward battery, which was a bank, five feet high, of forty batteries. Then came the control room, the after-battery, and the engine room, which consisted of twin twelve-cylinder Nelsico engines. Then came the motor room. I read this online. It's the kind of thing he might have told me about if we'd been close, if he'd stayed. Perhaps he told Eddie. Perhaps he shared it with my mother on one of their early dates. 'What was life like on a submarine?' she might have asked. It was an all-volunteer service. There was extra pay. Better food. There was also diesel rash, when fumes from the engines caused your skin to break out. You couldn't sit up in your bunk; you had to slide in and out. Four years in a submarine. At night in the dark, at war, bombs going off, locked in the motor room with a dead man in your lap. Fascists wanted to take over the world. Young men, teenagers, said, *Fuck you. Over my dead body*. My father was one of those men. He served. Not for himself but for a principle. He was also angry and hit Eddie, hit Kevin, verbally abused my mother, abandoned his family, left us ruined people. What narrative do we choose to live by?

⋆   ⋆   ⋆

The plane is half full, an early morning flight to Hawaii. Keita has the window seat. He was waiting in the lobby when I came down at 6 A.M. Our seats are in the back, by the toilets. I hold the FedEx box on my lap.

'You can't do that,' the flight attendant had said, pointing at the box. She hated us on sight for some reason. You could feel her bad mood. A fight with her husband or boyfriend, her surly teenage daughter who now can't stand her mother, where once they sat close, watching *Sesame Street* together. How painful that must be. Her makeup was too heavy and it looked as if she hadn't slept well.

I smiled. 'I'm sorry?'

She didn't smile. 'You have to put that package in the overhead.'

It seemed logical enough. But I had visions of a section of the roof popping off and the FedEx box being sucked out into the thin cold air, falling into the Pacific. I'd read just a few weeks ago of a similar incident on a flight from Tucson, horrified passengers looking up into open sky, fierce wind and noise. No one was hurt. The pilot made an emergency landing. The story did not say whether anyone's ashes were lost.

I said, 'If it's okay, I'd really prefer to hold on to it.'

She said, 'Federal regulations.'

I was about to hand it over when Keita said, 'Inside the box is his dead father. His ashes.'

She looked at each of us, one to the other, slammed the overhead, and walked away.

Keita opened a large Four Seasons bag he'd brought on the plane and spread out the breakfast that he'd had them prepare. Bagels, lox, capers, croissant, and jam.

Keita said, 'You're a good son, Fin. Maybe I think your mother would be proud.'

There was something about the way he said it. I looked at him and smiled, saw small flakes of croissant around his mouth, a dab of jam on his chin.

I said, 'Would you do it for your father?'

He reclined his chair and closed his eyes. He said, 'My father once told me I was biggest disappointment of his life. He said these words to me. Because I wasn't like him.'

Then he opened his eyes and looked at me. 'Would I do it? Yes. Because I always hope that one day he likes me.'

He closed his eyes. I stared out the window until I fell asleep.

★ ★ ★

Later, after a cab from the airport, we stand at the railing, looking out over the water at the remains of the USS *Arizona*, and I wonder if we look like a bad print ad for the Pearl Harbor Museum, with politically correct casting. Below us the souls of a thousand men, trapped on the *Arizona* that day. Another 1,300 killed that

362

Sunday morning. I wonder what went through their minds as the bombs started exploding around them. Did they simply react as trained soldiers or did they panic, fear for their lives? Do you know, in the flash moment before your own death, that you are going to die?

I've watched the footage from that day and the days after. Movie-tone newsreels. Sixteen-millimeter film, a handheld camera that reporters used called a Bolex. No sound. We use them on shoots sometimes for their grainy quality. 'A day that will live in infamy.' Except that wasn't what Roosevelt originally wrote. He wrote, 'A day which will live in world history.' I saw a story about it once in the newspaper. It stayed with me, how carefully he chose his words.

My father was here. He saw what I am seeing now. He walked here, a boy of sixteen who lied about his age. I have seen photos. I remember finding an envelope in my mother's room, in a box in a closet behind shoes. Photos of him in his police department uniform, in a sailor's uniform. I remember one clearly. He is standing alone looking at the camera, so skinny, more a boy than a soldier. Dress whites, no hat. His arms hanging down by his sides, as if he didn't quite know what to do with them. He is smiling.

Keita says, 'I feel that I should apologize. On behalf of the Japanese people. For this.' He extends his arm, palm up. There is a moment when I think he is making some kind of horrible joke. But then I look at his face and he looks like he might cry.

I say, 'Then I should apologize, on behalf of

363

the American people, for Hiroshima and Nagasaki.'

He nods and thinks about this. Then says, 'Thank you.'

It begins to rain sideways.

★ ★ ★

Keita made a call to his assistant. Calls were made on his behalf. A boat was found. A taxi takes us across the island, my father in the FedEx box between us. I roll down the window, the brief shower over, and the humidity hits me in the face, soft and warm, the smell of flowers and ocean.

We drive through roads cut through hills, the occasional breathtaking view of an inlet. I write and produce television commercials for diapers. I have a good job with a good wage. I use my brain. I am successful. This is the story I have been telling myself for many years. Why is it that I have always thought that I was a better person than my father, when, in truth, I've done very little with my life, certainly nothing that took courage?

My phone rings. It's Martin. I am supposed to be in New York at the edit house. Jan is scheduled to come by tomorrow. We have a deadline to make. Super Bowl spot. Make your mark. Sorry, Martin. I'm running a little late this morning.

★ ★ ★

One imagines things, one plays out scenarios, populates them with people, things, colors, sounds. When I imagined this playing out, I saw clear Hawaiian skies, soft breezes, sun. I imagined a spotless, white pleasure boat, thirty feet long, with the only crew member a beautiful, dark-skinned woman of twenty-three. Cut to one mile out. Cut to me nodding gravely, dumping the ashes over the side, shrugging. Cut to my Polynesian friend fixing me a drink with dark rum, massaging my shoulders. Cut to a wide shot of us slowly heading back to shore.

Our cab drives through a shipyard that opens on massive, industrial piers. Most of the berths are empty, save for two, one an exceptionally large cargo ship, one smaller but still an awe-inspiring sight.

'Where's our boat?' I ask Keita.

'There,' he says.

'I don't understand.'

Our boat is different than I had imagined. It's black, first of all. It's also five hundred feet long and nine stories high. I learn that it is one of Keita's father's and that it's scheduled to leave next week for Anchorage, via the ports of Los Angeles and Seattle. It will carry hundreds of tractor-trailer-sized containers holding many tons of pineapples, limes, flash-frozen mahi-mahi, macadamia nuts, and brown sugar. Today, empty, its only cargo will be the six-pound remains of Edward Lawrence Dolan, Sr.

Keita says, 'What do you think?'

I say, 'Do you have anything bigger?'

Keita says, 'Short notice, Fin. If we wait until Wednesday there's a 1,600-foot tanker coming in from Dubai.'

There are rooms with carpeting and bunks built into the wall. There is a dining room with a bar area. Tables bolted to the floor. We are offered coffee that is surprisingly good. My forearms ache from switching the box back and forth. Four to six pounds, the average remains. Anywhere from two to three hours at normal operating temperature between 1,500 and 2,000 degrees Fahrenheit. I can't seem to put the box down.

Keita and I stand just below the bridge at a railing watching the pier recede.

Keita says, 'Fin. There are many types of ships. Do you understand?'

I smile and nod. No, I don't understand.

Keita says, 'This. This is small ship. This is called Handy Size, up to 40,000 deadweight tons. Then there is Handymax, up to 50,000 deadweight tons. Then Aframax, up to 115,000 deadweight tons. Suezmax, the largest ship that can pass through the Suez Canal. Panamax, the Panama Canal. Malaccamax, the Malacca Strait.'

He turns and looks at the water. 'Look, Fin. Seals.'

I turn and see a herd of seals, maybe eight, swimming off the right of the ship. Sleek and fast. They look like they're playing.

Keita says, 'Okay. Now we mention the big ships. VLCC, Very Large Crude Carrier, up to 320,000 deadweight tons. And the ULCC, Ultra Large Crude Carrier, up to 550,000 deadweight tons. Over 1,500 feet long. Okay. Maybe this is a big boat, Fin. Too big for our needs today.'

He turns to me. 'I work at my father's company for twenty-five years, since I was ten years old. He make me read everything, make me travel on them for months. I throw up. I miss home. I hate ships.'

★ ★ ★

We were met by a representative of the company, a Japanese man named Aki, early thirties, who is clearly in awe of being around Keita, son to the famous Nagori-San. Aki gives us a brief tour that ends on the bridge, high above the main deck, 360-degree views. Aki introduces Keita and me to the ship's captain. His name is Swede Walker and he's 6′ 3″ and has more hair on his forearms than I have on my head. He's late fifties, tall, military bearing, brush cut, clean shaven, all business. From the few words he's said I'd guess he's from Oklahoma or Texas. I'd also guess that he hates me. Two other men are on the bridge with him, punching numbers into a computer. Both are quiet, deferential. One is Japanese and works for Keita's father's company and I don't get his name. He's training on the boat for a year. The other is named Larry, early thirties, James Taylor's twin brother. He laughs a lot and looks like someone who might follow The Grateful Dead from city to city as a hobby.

Keita says something to the Japanese sailor and Aki, in Japanese, and the three of them laugh. He turns to us and says, 'I do not mean to be rude, speaking Japanese. I say to them that it is strange that the son of a Japanese shipping empire gets seasick.'

Larry smiles. Swede Walker stares out the window.

Keita leans over to me. 'Fin. I do not feel very good. I must lie down.'

He and Aki leave the bridge. I feel awkward, sense that the captain wants me to leave.

I ask Larry how he likes working on a cargo ship.

'Awesome, sir.' He laughs. 'Ya know. The people. The quiet. Like, the ocean, right?'

I ask him where he's from.

'Nova Scotia. So I kind of *have* to be around the ocean, sir.'

I ask him if he sees himself doing this for a while. He laughs.

'No big plan. Just kind of working my way around the world. Have you seen the aurora borealis?'

I shake my head no.

'You have to see it.'

I envy his easygoing nature, his ease with the unknown future.

The Japanese sailor excuses himself. It's just Swede Walker and James Taylor now. Swede stands behind a large chair looking at a bank of computer screens, arms folded.

Swede says to the computer monitors, 'So what is this shit show?'

Larry says nothing, knows that Swede isn't talking to him.

I say, 'What do you mean?'

368

I know exactly what he means but I ask to annoy him. He reminds me of my father at his worst, of temperamental bosses who like to instill fear, who operate by intimidation. My reaction to that is always the same; to be intimidated and then to feel profoundly unmanly for feeling intimidated, to feel that I have done something wrong.

He says, 'What the hell are we doing out here?'

I say, 'My father died. He wanted his ashes scattered here.'

Larry turns, surprised, and says, 'Did you consider a smaller boat, sir? There are fishing charters.'

Swede is looking at me — the disgust palpable — but turns back now, looking ahead, out the window. He says, under his breath but clearly audible, 'Un-fucking-believable. If you're rich enough you get to do anything.'

My stomach tightens and I turn to leave. He's someone who thrives on confrontation and anger. But I don't leave. Instead I stop, turn back around, and say, 'He wasn't rich.' It's the way I say it. *You know nothing. Go to hell*.

Swede, excitement in his voice now. He turns and stares at me. 'What did you say?' He's looking for a fight. And he's much better at intimidation than I am.

But I'm not backing down. Not today.

'I said he wasn't rich. And you don't know what you're talking about, pal.'

'Who the fuck do you think you're talking to? This is my ship and — '

I don't know where the anger comes from, on

those rare occasions when it does come. I have always been afraid of anger, seen it as a weakness, a fault. I saw so much of it in my father, in Eddie, saw the result. I have tried to pretend it didn't exist in me. But all that has done is bury it deep, letting it fester over time, until it erupts in strange, unexpected ways. I cut him off at the knees.

I say, 'Fuck *you*. It's *not* your ship. It's Keita Nagori's *father*'s ship. And I needed a favor. And I have no idea what I've done to ruin your day, but my guess is most of your days are ruined by someone. So I don't know what your fucking problem is with me, but I don't have time for it today. And don't assume you know anything about me or my father.'

It's the last line that surprises me. I feel drained and tired, as I always do after it happens. I looked it up once. The body releases adrenaline. A turbo charge, then a crash.

He looks at me and I think he's going to come over and kick my teeth down my throat.

I say, 'And he wasn't rich. He was a cop. He was in submarines in World War Two. His sub was here. The day the war ended. He was here.'

He stares at me. 'Your old man was in subs?'

I just stare, eager to leave because for some reason I suddenly feel like crying.

I'm waiting for the line but it doesn't come. He just looks at me. Then he says, 'You ever been in a World War Two sub?'

I shake my head.

He says, 'I have. Took a tour at Groton. Wouldn't wish it on anyone.'

370

No one says anything for a time. I start to leave when he says, 'What was his name?'

'What?'

'Your father. What was his name?'

'Ed Dolan.'

'Was he a good man?'

I'm surprised by the question, the personal nature of it, the intensity with which he asks it. James Taylor's twin has turned and is looking at me, waiting for my answer.

Let me go, Finny, she said. *Let us go.*

'Not really,' I say. 'But he tried like hell.'

★　★　★

I have searched online, late into the night. I have found the crappy-looking websites put together by liver-spotted old men. Sullystributetosubmarines.com; heroesofthesilentservice.org. I can picture them, these old men, shoeboxes of old photos, pristine memories of their war years, trying somehow to work the damned computer, peering over their glasses, looking around the screen, trying desperately to figure out how to make a website, put up facts, grainy old black-and-white photos. Their granddaughter/grandson/nurse's aide helping guide them. HTML, not Flash, not interactive and cool like the Snugglies site that has music and movies and funny interviews with toddlers. *How is it I am eighty-seven years old?* they wonder alone, at night, widowed now. *How will I be remembered? We fought in a war. We risked our lives for a cause. It mattered. We mattered. Didn't we?*

371

And so they share their history, their story, their moment in time.

The United States submarine service sustained the highest mortality rate of all branches of the U.S. military during WWII.

One out of every five U.S. Navy submariners was killed in WWII.

Take a steel tube, put it three hundred feet underwater, take away its sight except for the most rudimentary sonar, send it out into a war. But before you do, fill it with teenagers and tell them not to be afraid.

Would you go to work if you had a twenty percent chance of dying?

★ ★ ★

You are a camera with a fish-eye lens on a helicopter moving high and fast over a wide-open expanse of ocean. No land in sight. The fish-eye rounds the edges of the lens, giving a sense of curve to the shot. There, on the horizon, is a tiny dot. Closer now and you see that it is a ship, a large ship dwarfed by the sea. And on the side of the ship, being lowered down by motorized winch, is a lifeboat.

It was Swede Walker who suggested the lifeboat.

He said, 'The ship can't exactly stop on a dime and at this height it's not really the ideal ashes dispersal vehicle. Also, there is the small matter of reversing course, which will take us an hour. Plus we need to conduct our monthly lifeboat training exercise anyway.'

His tone was different. He didn't look at me, but he was trying. Later, James Taylor would tell us that Swede spent twenty years in the Navy on a Tender.

It is a new and terrifying experience, hanging sixty feet above the water. The lifeboat has a plexiglass top and is completely enclosed and rolls us in our seats when it hits water level, which changes with every swell. We motor away from the ship. The captain told James Taylor to go five minutes east, that that would be, approximately, the coordinates.

The ride is rough as we motor away from the ship and I can tell from Keita's expression that this is hell on his stomach. The engine is loud and makes talking hard. After about ten minutes, James Taylor cuts the engines, the boat bobs to a stop, moves gently back and forth in the swells. He unhinges two of the plexiglass plates, rolls them back. There are no man-made sounds. We can't hear the engines of the cargo ship at this distance. What I hear instead is the soft slap of swells against the lifeboat. Above, patches of blue sky, high clouds, seemingly still, and lower, faster moving, wispy clouds. The air is so clean. The wind comes in gusts, and sea spray flies in my face. I'm tempted to call Eddie or Maura or Kevin, some connection to family, some sense of ceremony, of meaning.

Keita says, 'Maybe it is time, Fin.'

Once, a submarine broke the surface, here, near here, right here, and the hatch opened and my father climbed up and signaled to another ship during a training exercise and learned that the war was over. There was so much possibility for him then, everything in front of him.

Keita holds up his iPhone. 'I will record it for you, yes?'

I nod.

I open the FedEx box. Inside is another box. I open that one and remove what I thought would be an urn. But it is, instead, a plastic container with a hinged snap-lock. It's the kind of container you might keep leftovers in. Tomato sauce, or stuffing, or maybe bolts and screws in a basement tool room. I assumed it would be an urn, the kind one might see in a movie. Silver and cylindrical, with a thick screw top. Something one could place atop a mantel. Instead he sits in a fucking piece of Tupperware. Inside the Tupperware is a plastic bag holding my father's remains. My hands shake slightly and my stomach tenses and here I realize, in a moment of embarrassment and sadness and regret, that our family would have needed to have had the foresight, the concern, the love, the tenderness, the forgiveness, to buy a proper urn, the way one does with a casket, with funeral arrangements. I'm overwhelmed by the sadness of this, the apathy. There isn't a jury in the world, presented with the evidence against Edward Dolan, Sr., that wouldn't find for his wife and family. But what would be their judgment against his surviving children in this moment, in this piece of hard plastic Tupperware, in this nothing thing? Perhaps he deserved better from us, too.

The side of the boat — surely there's a name

for that — is high, to the middle of my chest. I press myself against it. I try to gauge the wind. For some reason I stretch my hand out, try to touch the water. A swell comes up, washes over my arm. The water is far colder than I imagined it would be. I smell my arm, turn, and see Keita and James Taylor looking at me.

'Okay,' I say to Keita.

Should I say a prayer? Give a eulogy?

I hold the container out over the edge, nervous that I am somehow doing it wrong, and turn it upside down, watch as a surprising quantity of ash flies, watch as my father's incinerated body — this body that once held me, held my siblings, made love to my mother, smoked a cigarette, raised a beer to his lips, threw a ball with Eddie, climbed the ladder of a submarine, struck his children, tilted his head back on a summer's day and wondered, knelt in church and prayed to God — rides the wind, dissipates in the distance, disappears into the water. I watch for a long time. I want to feel something, know something has changed. But I'm not sure it works that way.

I turn to see Keita, tears streaming down his cheeks. He reaches his hand out, holds my shoulder.

'Fin. Do you believe in reincarnation? In the possibility that maybe we come back as something better?'

I don't know what I believe. But I don't see why not.

I shrug. 'Sure.'

'You have ash on your face, Fin. Maybe this a good sign. Maybe someone lives inside you who want to be better.' He smiles.

'Let's hope so.'

James Taylor starts the engines and ferries us back to the ship, where we are hoisted up and made safe.

★   ★   ★

Henry David Thoreau wrote that 'the mass of men lead lives of quiet desperation.' I can clearly remember reading that in college and thinking, *Wow. He is so right.* Now, I think, *Wow. What a pompous asshole.* This from a guy whose idea of a sojourn to the deep woods took him all of a mile from his home. Quiet desperation? *Most* men? Who among us can say that? Who can know what goes on in someone else's life? In their worries and fears and hopes. Their history and pain. Who knows the quiet joy that one might feel in the quotidian thing, the nothing thing; a child's evening bath, volunteering at a soup kitchen, walking the dog when the family is asleep, the neighborhood quiet, a cigarette smoked alone. Lunch with a favorite coworker. Who can know the little worlds of beauty we try desperately to guard during the onslaught: watching your wife go through chemo; your father waste away from Alzheimer's; your sister relapse into alcoholism. The simple truth is that we know nothing about the inner life of the person sitting next to us on the plane, in the subway, the car behind us in traffic. We know nothing unless we choose to listen. Quiet desperation? What about quiet resilience. Quiet courage. Quiet hope.

Keita's flight leaves first.

'Thank you,' I say.

'For what? I did nothing.'

'You commandeered a container ship.'

Keita laughs. 'It was easy. I just paid for the gas.'

'How much was that?'

'$125,000.' He laughs again when he sees my expression.

Keita says, 'It's just money, Fin. Also business travel. Tax deductible.'

I wish he wasn't leaving.

He says, 'Maybe instead I think that life is about having a passion.'

'What's your passion?'

'This depends on the day. Today, it is helping you.'

'Why?'

'Because you are my friend. Because today you needed help.'

'What if you don't have a passion?'

'Everyone has a passion. I say to you, okay, there is something you can't do tomorrow, forever. Someone you can't see, talk to. A place you can't go. A food you can't eat. What comes to mind? What are your passions? What can't you live without?'

He extends his hand and we shake and he bows to me, smiling the whole time.

Except the formal Japanese good-bye isn't quite cutting it for him today.

'I will miss you,' he says.

'I'll miss you, too.'

He nods. And standing there, in his diminutive Converse sneakers, he looks suddenly to me like a boy of ten. A quick hand wave and he turns and walks to the mouth of the jetway, hands the agent his boarding pass, and disappears.

★   ★   ★

Before I board my flight I transcribe the letter my father wrote to me into an e-mail. I send it, along with the video of today, to Eddie, Maura, and Kevin.

> *Dear family,*
>
> *At 3:51 P.M., I spread our father's ashes over the Pacific Ocean. It was windy and overcast and colder than you might have imagined. I wish you'd been there with me.*

It's the closing I pause with. How do I sign off?

Your friend?

Your brother?

That's the news, I'm Katie Couric?

Fondly?

All best?

In the end I opt for what I wished was true, what was once true, what could be true again if only we would try.

> *Much love,*
> *Finbar*

378

I call Phoebe but get her voice mail.

'Hey. I'm at the airport. In Hawaii. I just . . . I just spread his ashes. My father's ashes. Keita borrowed one of his father's container ships. It's a long story.'

I say to her voice mail, 'Okay, then. Good message. Beautifully conceived and delivered, I think. It's Fin, by the way. I miss my friend.'

The flight attendant has asked us to turn off all electronic devices.

It's time to go home.

★　★　★

There are fifty-four countries in Africa. There are over two thousand languages spoken. There is a country called Mayotte. Its capital is Mamoudzou. Four billion people live in Asia. In India alone they speak over eight hundred languages. The Sahara Desert is roughly the size of the United States. There are sand dunes six hundred feet high. It's said that beyond the Atlas Mountains of Morocco, when the wind dies down, there is no sound of any kind, neither man-made or natural. There is a country snug between India and China called Bhutan, the only country in the world whose king insists that they measure the nation's Gross National Happiness. I have two first-class tickets anywhere in the world.

I land at JFK in the late afternoon, having lost a day on my twelve-hour flight, with a stop in L.A., and it's already dark. I want to go home and sleep for a day but I ask the cab to take me to the editorial house in SoHo. The driver clips his fingernails as he drives, speaking one of the eight hundred languages of India on a headset. Five thousand miles away, my father floats in peace, at last. The war is over.

PREPARE FOR DEPARTURE

'Welcome to Lazy Weasel,' the twenty-five-year-old receptionist says. She may or may not also be a heroin addict from her appearance. Lazy Weasel is not a saloon in Wyoming but rather an editorial company on the sixth floor of an old building that once housed a printer's shop, south of Grand Street.

The receptionist leads me back to a large, dimly lit room.

I checked my messages on the way in from the airport. Four from Martin and three from Emma. None of them sounded like they wanted to give me a raise or a promotion.

Ian and Pam stand and greet me with a hug.

Pam says, 'You look like ass. You okay?' Pam-speak for *I care about you*.

'I'm fine, thanks.'

'Good. Settle in, relax, get your bearings. Take your time. You have five seconds.'

'What happened?' I ask.

Ian says, 'My advice would have been to stay in Hawaii. Martin's been looking for you. Not in a good way.'

I say, 'I'll talk with him.'

Ian says, 'You could do worse than tell him the truth.'

Pam and Ian have the pasty, red-eyed, fatigued look that comes from having sat in a darkened editorial room, looking at footage for the past forty-eight hours.

Pam gestures to the man in the chair at the control board. 'Biz, say hello to Fin Dolan, Ian's partner.'

Biz is famous. Biz is cool. Biz has guitars in his office. He plays in a band. He has tattoos. Biz edits the famous commercials and also one movie with Brad Pitt. Biz was the top editor at Foolish Braggart in New York (also an editorial company) before parting ways with his business partner (and taking the business partner's wife) and starting Lazy Weasel. He has the laid-back demeanor of a rock star. We were lucky he agreed to do this.

'Fiiiiiiiiin,' Biz says in a way that suggests that he's stoned or recently ingested five Tylenol PMs. 'Heeeeeey, maaaaan,' he says as he hugs me.

Biz's head is shaved and he sports a beard that would give a grizzly bear an inferiority complex.

I say, 'Hey, Biz. Thanks so much for doing this.'

'Pleasure, man.'

'How's it looking?'

'Well. Ya know. Work in progress.'

After each shoot day in Los Angeles, the day's film was processed and sent to Biz. He then went through every minute of it, choosing the best takes, building our commercial. Biz's languid speech stands in direct contrast to his editing speed. He already has several cuts to look at. Ian and Pam have been going over the cuts, looking for additional takes. The editing process can be a pleasant experience if the footage is right and enough time is built into the schedule. It can also be a maze of confusion, trying to figure out which minutely different take is better. Much of it is about trying to convince yourself how good it is. At this I excel.

Ian says, 'You want the good news or the bad news first?'

'Good.'

Ian says, 'Scott and I are going to Paris in the spring.'

'Is that good news for me?'

'No. But it's good news for me.'

'What's the bad news?' I ask.

'Client's coming into the agency tomorrow. They want to see a cut.'

'How is that possible? We're supposed to have three more days.'

Ian says, 'Jan said something about the CEO. He wants to see it.'

I say, 'I wanted to go home. I wanted to unpack, unwind, bathe, sleep for twelve hours.'

The receptionist brings in a bottle of wine and three wineglasses.

Pam pours and says, 'You can do all of it except unpack, unwind, bathe, and sleep. Settle in. It's going to be a long night.'

★ ★ ★

Throughout the evening we post cuts for Martin. He reviews them and calls in changes.

He asks to speak to me.

'Martin,' I say. 'I've been meaning to call you.'

'We need to talk. Tomorrow. After the meeting.'

He hangs up.

★　★　★

Most people have no idea how hard it is to create something good on film. Why would they? Easier to sit in front of your TV or in a movie theater and critique. You imagine it, write, rewrite it, plan it, see it, cast it, shoot it, reshoot it, edit it, re-edit it. You colorize it, find the right music, mix the sound. Months of work under normal circumstances. And yet most times, for most commercials — indeed, most movies — the result is simply . . . okay. But it's not great.

But somehow, something remarkable has happened with our spot. It's certainly not the writing. It's Flonz Kemp and his babies. It's Biz and his pacing: tight cuts, followed by unexpected long shots, followed by super close-ups of the babies looking at the screen, the mom hurling the diaper. He's found the perfect balance between serious and absurd. It's not terrible. In fact, it may be the best thing Ian and I have ever done. The sad thing is we're not quite sure how. We look at one another, Ian, Pam, and I. Perhaps it's the fatigue. But we're surprised that it works. Even Biz gives it his blessing.

'I have to be honest, my dudes. No offense, but when I saw the storyboard for this I thought, 'Oh, shit. Gotta pass on this job.' But it's awright.'

We post a final cut for Martin a little after

3 A.M. He responds two minutes later. *Like it. Show this tomorrow. Nicely done.*

We go to shake hands, but Biz is a hugger. We tell him we'll call him tomorrow after the meeting.

★ ★ ★

Ian and I put Pam in a cab, then walk for a block or two. It's closing in on 4 A.M. Pent-up energy from sitting. Too tired to sleep just yet. We walk down Grand, right on West Broadway. Past John Varvatos and James Perse, the Hästens store selling $50,000 mattresses, the Maserati dealership, the shops selling artisanal jams, past the adorable bakeries, purveyors of eight-dollar cupcakes. I stop in front of the Ralph Lauren Double RL, not sure I even understand the name of the store. In the window are vintage-looking clothes from the 1940s, a mix of industrial worker and military. Chinos and old boots and rucksacks. There's an attache case with the seal of the United States Navy and it looks like it might be the real deal and it's $595. There's a Navy Watchman's Cap for $145. I don't know if the cap is vintage or not. I don't know if a sailor in World War II wore it. I don't know if it was taken from his dead head by Ralph's grandfather, who thought, *Now this is a cap. With this my son will start the definitive empire of all-American, blue-blood WASP clothing and style, despite the fact that we're Jews from the Bronx named Lifshitz.*

Branding. Myth. What would my father make

of this? Of a wool hat, made for pennies by the thousands, probably in China by fourteen-year-olds, once worn by nineteen-year-olds who would have done anything *not* to wear it, *not* to be on night watch on a sub or a battleship, freezing their asses off, thinking God-knows-what; now here in SoHo selling for more than he made in a month? Would he be able to wrap his head around it? Would my mother? Why are there no protests in front of this store? Why aren't people smashing the windows and burning the bullshit merchandise that's cashing in on a time of depression and war and sacrifice and poverty and death? Where is the mention, Ralphie boy, of that less fashionable part of the story? Of the sixty million dead from World War II. More than 2.5 percent of the world's population. Almost half a million in this country. Where is the copy on the ad with the beautiful people in the manor house with the horses reminding us that of all U.S. World War II battle casualties, the Navy lost one in 118, the Army one in 44, the Marines one in 36, but submarines . . . submarines lost one in five. *Dutch Harbor, Attu, Pearl Harbor, Midway, Admiralty Island, Brisbane, Sydney, Biak, Espiritu Santo.* Where is the story of Ralph Thomsen dying in my father's arms, of the effect that had on a seventeen-year-old? Where is the story of what it is like to think you are going to die in the dark in a submarine, deep below the surface, with a dead friend on your lap? Brand that, my fashionable friend. Call it the 'One-in-Five' campaign.

Ian says, 'What?'

I turn and look at him. He's looking at me strangely. 'What?' I ask.

Ian says, 'You said 'one in five.'

'I did?'

'That's not scary at all.'

'I need to sleep.'

'You okay? The thing. The ashes. It went okay?'

I nod. He looks at me, trying to make sure.

Ian says, 'Okay, then. See you in . . . six hours.'

★ ★ ★

I sleep for a few hours, then shower, shave, pick out a decent shirt, a sports coat. The meeting is a big deal. I stop for coffees for Ian and Pam and myself.

The agency is buzzing, post-holiday work. Phoebe's empty desk throws me. All gone, no photos, nothing. Pam is in Ian's office. She's wearing a black skirt, black boots, white shirt, and black sweater. Ian, of course, looks like he's ready for an Armani shoot.

I hand them the coffees. I say to Pam, 'You look pretty.'

Pam says, 'Shut up.'

I say, 'Ian, you look pretty.'

Ian says, 'I feel pretty.'

We walk to the main conference room. Someone has ordered catering, a large breakfast spread. The room's been neatened up, agency stationery and pens at each seat. Pam sets up the computer and brings up the spot on the screen at the front of the room, tests the audio levels.

Jill comes in. 'Hi, guys!'

Ian says, 'How are you, Jilly?'

She says, 'I hear the spot is brilliant.'

I say, 'Who told you?'

She says, 'Well . . . no one. I was just assuming.'

Ian says, 'Where's Alan?'

Jill says, 'On a call.'

Paulie and Stefano come in.

Stefano says, 'Signore Dolan. *Come sta?*'

We shake hands. Stefano says, 'We heard there was food.'

Jill says, 'You guys, seriously, this is for the meeting. You can't touch it.'

Stefano pours coffee and Paulie makes a bagel.

Paulie says, 'They won't even know it's gone, Jill. We were never here.'

Malcolm and Raj come in. Malcolm says, 'We heard there was food.'

Jill says, 'You guys!'

Pam has the spot cued up. I turn and say to the guys, 'Take a look.' Pam hits play.

We watch it play through once. Pam plays it again before anyone says anything.

When it finishes Paulie says, 'Nice. Really nice, you guys.'

Stefano says, 'I must say I am surprised. It's not terrible.'

Rajit is shaking his head 'no' but that's a good sign as he's Indian.

Malcolm says, 'Well done.' He pours himself some coffee and makes a bagel.

Jill says, 'You're messing up the lox.' Her phone rings. We watch her answer it. We watch her listen and hang up.

She says, 'They want us in Martin's.'

★ ★ ★

Alan is sitting in Martin's office when we arrive. Emma says to go right in. Frank is standing at the window, his back to us, but the sky is a gunmetal gray and with the lights on in the office we can see his reflection and his thumb plumbing for something deep in one nostril.

You can tell by the way they look at us, by their stillness.

Martin says, 'Have a seat.'

Alan says, 'Hey, guys.'

Martin says, 'Bad news, I'm afraid. Spot's dead. Alan's just had a call from Jan, our trusted friend at Snugglies. Alan. Why don't you share her thoughts.'

I look at Ian, he at me. Pam stares straight ahead.

Alan says, 'Their legal department is worried about the claims they're making for the diaper. There's new research. It basically doesn't work. So it's dead.'

They keep saying 'dead.' But it's not dead. It's just not alive. It's a project for a diaper and diapers don't die, especially Snugglies Planet Changers. My mother is dead. My father is dead. The project just isn't happening anymore. There's a difference. Words matter. A day that will live in world history . . . in infamy.

389

Alan says, 'We were able to unload the media slot, which was $3.2 million. Sold it to Skippy. First time for a peanut butter on the Super Bowl. So that's good.'

They seem to be waiting for one of the three of us to say something. But none of us says anything. Perhaps it's the windowless editing room we've spent the night in, the January darkness, the jet lag, the missed holiday vacations, the waste of time.

And then Frank turns, Cheshire-cat grin, and says, 'Tell them the good news.'

Martin says, 'We've been . . . '

But Frank cuts him off, school-boy excited. 'We've been invited to pitch Petroleon. Just us and Saatchi, and we know they hate Saatchi. Ours for the taking. Massive billings, *Fortune* top ten company. The pitch is next week.'

Jill says, 'We're briefing tomorrow.'

Ian says, 'Tomorrow's Saturday.'

Frank says, 'There are no Saturdays anymore. Every day is Monday.' He laughs, but he's not kidding.

I look at Martin, who's slowly massaging his temples. I look at Jill, who's furiously texting on her BlackBerry. Alan looks like a man waiting for a bus. I'm waiting for someone to say something, to laugh, to scream, to set the room on fire.

Frank says, 'There are other teams, of course, not just you. But this could be a career-maker. You could make your mark with this one.'

It's a warm feeling that comes over me, the kind you experience in the moments before sleep, a lovely calm. But right behind it is a line

390

of cocaine. I'm suddenly shaky and the words fall out before I've had time to think about them.

'My mark?' I say. 'My mark?' I'm chuckling, but not in a happy-funny way. I also want to say more than 'My mark' but don't quite know how.

Frank looks confused.

'My mark?' I say again. My eyes go wide. 'Oh! I know! It'll be the thing I have carved on my tombstone! That's what you mean by mark. You mean like a life's work, like Mother Teresa of Calcutta or Gandhi or Neil Armstrong. You mean the thing I will be known for, the thing that people on the streets or in airports stop me about, recognize me for. They'll say, 'You're the guy who won Petroleon, aren't you? You did that campaign that made that big, repulsive oil company look good.' Wait. I know! I could have my mark tattooed on my body; on my ass, my balls. I could have it tattooed on my scrotum. Better yet, I could have one of my balls removed, have my mark etched on it, have it bronzed, put in Lucite, and put it on my desk. People would come into my office and say, 'Ohmigod! Is that one of your balls?!' And I'd say, 'No. That's my mark.' Is that what you mean, Frank, you clueless, soulless douchebag?!'

Jill's mouth is open, her fingers frozen in mid-text. Alan looks like a wax version of himself. Frank has a look that suggests I've been speaking French. It's Martin who has the slightest hint of something that suggests pleasure.

Pam breaks the silence. 'Dolan, I would fuck you right now.' She laughs and walks out.

391

I stand and walk out and hear Frank say to Martin, 'Wait. Was he talking to me?'

★　★　★

Ian and Pam come by my office.

Ian says, 'Well, that was interesting.'

I say, 'Did I just quit?'

Pam says, '*Quit* isn't the right word. But I think you went a long way toward getting yourself fired.'

Ian nods. 'I'll quit, too. A symbol of my loyalty. We're a team. We'll freelance. Even though there is no freelance. Or we'll get great jobs at another agency. Even though there are no jobs anywhere. Maybe I won't quit. You're on your own. I wish you the best.'

Pam stands. 'I've got shit to do. But one of you is buying me dinner.'

Ian says, 'Raoul's. Seven tonight. On Fin.'

★　★　★

I leave the office and go for a walk. I watch the skaters at Bryant Park. Are they tourists? New Yorkers taking the day off? They seem happy, skating on a Friday in the middle of the day. I walk across Forty-second Street and take a left on Fifth, make my way over to Grand Central. I go for a walk inside, I stand on the stairs and watch the crowds hustle through. Most walk while looking at their phones. Some wait by the information booth, by the famous clock. I watch them wait, watch as they look around, look at the

392

ceiling. I watch as their friends or coworkers or ex-wife or brother-in-law arrives and says their name. I watch their faces change as they look up and see another human being they know. Watch their faces soften and animate. I watch a woman with a scarf on her head. It's not fashion, this scarf. It's something else. She is thin, pale. After a time I see another woman approach. They look to be about the same age, same height, similar features. They could be friends, but I get the sense that they are sisters. They hug and the woman wearing the scarf lays her head on the other woman's shoulder, the other woman gently holding her scarved head. They stand there like this for some time. I have to look away. It is too much. It is the opposite of quiet desperation. It is connection.

I keep walking.

On Fifty-second near Lex I pass an open garage. Men pull shiny silver carts out onto the street. BEST COFFEE it says on some. The wind picks up. Farther north I pass a homeless woman pushing a baby carriage with two dachshunds in it.

Up Madison Avenue to Sixty-fifth and then over to the park. I walk down the stairs, and sit on a bench in front of the zoo.

I have worked in the same office, in the same building, noticing the same stains on the carpet, using the same bathroom, with the same people, talking about the same things, for eight years of my life. And yet I remember next to nothing of the *detail* of that time. Eight years. That's 2,922 days. I recall a handful. Why is that? Why do we forget so much of our life? Of the morning shower and the subway ride, the coffee cart and the meetings, the slow, steady slippage of time? And as you're going through the motions, picking up a few things at the market on the way home, unlocking the mailbox door, pulling on the refrigerator door that sticks, you wonder, *Wasn't it just last night/last week/last year/five years ago that I did this very thing, felt this very same way?*

It's cold but sunny, and when the wind dies down it's pleasant to sit on a bench in the sun. I could fall asleep. I could sit here all day. I close my eyes, play the film. I play it slowly, watch every detail. I don't try to push it from my mind this time. I don't try to rewrite it. I don't wince. I welcome the pain, a man who doesn't put his arms out as he's falling. I don't watch *the boy* this time. I watch me follow her on my bike. I watch the car speed up, turn sharply, rocket up over the curb, and hit the tree. I hear the noise, the sharp, fast crack. Time stops. Waits. I watch as I ride through traffic, watch, out of the corner of my eye, the car that had to skid to keep from hitting me. Watch as I run to the driver's-side door, try to open it. Watch as I stick my head in the opening of the shattered glass. Watch as I say . . . no . . . as I screamed *Mum, Mum, Mum!* Watch as I pull my head out fast, the small cut, the drops of blood, the woman with her hands over her mouth and nose. The cars stopping. The men running. The sirens. I wait for reality to begin again. But it is already far ahead of me. It's not all right. I won't beat her home.

I open my eyes and see a black woman pushing an older man in a wheelchair. He smiles at me. A toddler waddles past, looking like he will fall with every step, his mother a step behind him, arms wide, just in case. Two teenagers, maybe sixteen, a boy and a girl, sit a bench away, talking closely, making out.

This is it, then. Right here. This moment.

Let me go, Finny. Let us go.

I call Phoebe. She lives across the park, on the Upper West Side.

'Hi,' she says.

'Hi.'

'You're back.'

'I'm back.'

'How's the spot?'

'Have you ever been to the petting zoo?'

'What?'

'The petting zoo. In the park. They have a petting zoo. You can feed the animals. I was wondering, if you're not doing anything, if you wanted to go to the zoo.'

'It's thirty-nine degrees outside.'

'Wear a warm coat.'

She meets me at the entrance to the children's zoo and we feed quarters into a gumball machine that dispenses pellet food for goats. If you lay your hand flat, the goats lick the pellet off your hand. There's also a Purell dispenser.

We look at the pigs, the llama, the cow. The goats are the only ones that seem happy.

We leave and walk through the park, wander past frozen ball fields, bundled joggers. I tell her about the meeting, about blowing up. I tell her they'll probably fire me later today, when I go back. Near the Great Lawn there's a café and I buy two coffees. We keep walking.

'What are you going to do?' she asks.

'No idea.'

'Does Martin know? About your father?'

I say, 'No.'

She nods.

'You seem okay,' she says.

'Could be sleep deprivation. I'll probably wake up in a massive panic attack tonight. I've got enough money to live for about a year. If I move to Angola.'

'Why are you smiling?'

'I don't know. I feel good.'

She nods.

I say, 'I'm sorry.'

'You already apologized.'

'I know. But I'm sorry.'

'You scared me.'

'I know.'

Clouds have moved in and covered the sun. It's getting colder.

Phoebe says, 'Anyway. I think I'm going to head back now.'

I say, 'Do you want to come on vacation with me?'

'Fin.'

'We could go someplace.'

She looks at me.

She says, 'Give me a reason.'

I say, 'Because I've got these two tickets. These two first-class tickets.'

'Not good enough.'

Two kids on skateboards go by. On the road, a hansom carriage pulled by a sad old horse clops along. I take a deep breath. It's not that I don't have the words. I do. I've had them for a long time. I just couldn't quite bring myself to say them.

Finally I say, 'Because there's only you. Because I want to make you happy. Because I want to show you that I'm worthy of you.'

I'm looking at a tree and Phoebe is looking at me. I look at her now.

Phoebe, her voice different, says, 'Why couldn't you have just said that in the first place?'

I step closer and take my glove off and put my hand on her face, her cheek. I lean in farther, put my face against hers.

I say, 'I thought you knew.'

★ ★ ★

Time to get fired.

I walk back into the office, going through the revolving doors as others are leaving. I need my bag. There is a FedEx package on my desk. I am instantly unnerved. I open it and inside there is a small box and a note.

Fin. Time is what you make of it. I hope what I mean is coming out with my words. Also, I bought one for myself so we both have the same one. Like brothers. Your tomodachi. Keita.

Inside the box is a Rolex Submariner watch.

The office is quiet. I grab my bag and leave. I step off the elevator and walk through the lobby. Martin is on his cell phone. He ends the call and looks at me for what feels like a long time.

He says, 'There are four hours every lunar cycle when I am not an egotistical, heartless jackass. You happen to be catching me on the last hour. So I'm going to ask you this once, and only once, and, no matter what your answer, I'm then going to walk out of this building, get into a new Jaguar XJ, drive to Per Se, have dinner with a twenty-eight-year-old woman of mind-altering beauty, and, by my second sake, forget you exist. Do you want this job?'

Yes. No. I don't know. I don't know the answer. I do know I wish I'd studied harder in college. I wish I had a calling. I wish I was remarkably good at one thing. Just one thing that I could point to and say, 'I am superb at this. I know this.' Badminton. The violin. Carpentry. Organic farming. Litigation. Geology. Animal husbandry. The Hula-Hoop. Something. But I am not good at anything. And the little voice reminds me of that every chance he gets. 'Hey, Gary. Gary? You suck.' And always, for so long, I have believed him. It's habit. It's easier. There are times in my life when I look for experiences I can be proud of, things that might define me: the winning goal senior year, the acceptance letter from Harvard, the big account win, the wedding, the house, the first-born, the good father, the good husband, the good brother, volunteering at the hospice, jumping onto the tracks to rescue the fainting victim as the subway car pulls in. The stories of a life well lived. Little monuments we all need to sustain us during those long stretches where nothing quite so memorable occurs, when life simply passes by. I scan my memory for something to hold on to. I can find almost nothing. And then I think of the ashes. *Hey, little voice. Fuck you. I did that.*

I say, 'Is it enough? What we do?'

Martin stares for a time. 'No. It's not enough. Relative to a trauma surgeon or special ed teacher or UN AIDS worker in Uganda, no. It's not nearly enough. But I'm not any of those things. And I'm okay with that. I like what I do. I think what we do has value. Good companies matter to people. Their products matter to people. Do they make a difference in their lives? Probably not. But it does matter. By the way, in the time I've been here, this agency has worked on campaigns to get teenagers to stop smoking, bring inner-city children to camp for the summer, a battered women's shelter in Queens, and the New York chapter of the American Red Cross. For free. And we've changed people's lives as a result. I think that's a pretty good way to make a living.'

I'm waiting for him to fire me, waiting to be humiliated because I do not understand basic things sometimes.

'Do you know how many portfolios we receive each day? Copywriters, art directors, people who want to make their living here? And yet here I stand with you, a person who wants to throw a good job away. I mean, if I could show you a photo of the woman I'm dining with . . . and yet here I stand. Why? It's rhetorical, so don't try to answer. I stand here because although I have thought about firing you many times with great relish, I don't. I don't because I think you could be good. But you have to want it. People like you, Fin. That's not a small thing in this business. You want to hug me now, I know. I have that effect on people.'

Then he says, 'I'm sorry about your father. And although it's none of my business, I was very sorry to hear what happened to your mother. I know it was a long time ago but . . . '

I feel myself color, feel instantly uncomfortable.

Martin says, 'I had an older brother. A god to me. He died twenty-four years ago, November seventh. Drunk driver. Not a day goes by that . . . well . . . you know.'

He looks beyond me, out the windows onto the street. I assume he's seen someone or something, but he doesn't react for several seconds.

He looks back at me. 'So, I'm sorry. The job gets in the way sometimes. But that's life, isn't it? Come by the office sometime and I'll show you the rejection letters I received from London's finest publishing houses in regard to my book of poetry sixteen years ago. I keep them in a drawer. A reminder of who I am. We can be many people, you see. Good to keep in mind in this business.'

'Thank you.'

'Take a vacation. Think about what you want. The job's still yours if you want it. Maybe you've been in diapers too long. Time for a change.'

'You can't have just said that.'

'I'm not proud of it.'

I say, 'What about Frank?'

'I'll handle Frank. 'Clueless, soulless douchebag.' One of your better lines, actually. Maybe there's hope for you as a writer.'

He walks away. Then stops and turns back.

'Your friend Phoebe stopped by my office yesterday afternoon. Lucky man to have a friend like that.'

He looks at me and does something he's never done in the eighteen months I've known him. He smiles. An honest-to-God smile. And I find that I'm smiling, too.

I shout to him, 'I feel like we should make out.'

Over his shoulder, 'Dodge says that to me all the time.'

$\star$ $\star$ $\star$

We held a funeral mass for my father in Boston and we all cried and hugged and told wonderful stories about the past, stories we'd all forgotten but that were now rendered clear in our collective memories. It was cathartic and I was deeply changed because of it. We promised to rent a house together next summer on Nantucket.

That is a lie, of course. Life doesn't work that way, except in commercials and adorable Jennifer Aniston movies. It's just that I can *see* that ending so clearly. The wide shot at the cemetery. Pan down from the gray sky to the leafless trees. Cut to a shot of the man (me, I guess) looking at the wind in the trees and the shapes that the fast-moving clouds make on the lawn and the gravestones. Cut to hands grabbing fistfuls of the chocolate-brown dirt that the gravediggers have placed in a pile atop a large square of Astroturf. Cut to the diggers leaning on their shovels. Inevitably one of them must wipe his nose with the back of his gloved hand. Note: Have a wind machine ready if it's not a windy day. Shoot in New York to make it look like Boston. Less travel. If you want blue sky we can color correct it in post, no problem. We can do it in twenty-seven seconds with three seconds left for a VO and a logo. Just tell me what the product is.

The annoying thing about life is that it screws up the production. It's rarely neat and tidy. And yet sometimes it can surprise you.

Maura called me awhile ago, one night at home, out of the blue. She wanted to know the story of the ashes. She told me she wished she'd been there. We talked for forty-five minutes. She told me about her children, how one of them reminds her of me at times. He makes up stories and makes his parents laugh. I promised to visit. They have a summer place in Maine. She said maybe we could all get together there sometime.

Kevin called and we spoke. I'm going to San Francisco in the spring. I've never met his partner.

F. Scott Fitzgerald said that there are no

second acts in American lives. I have no idea what that means but I believe that in quoting him I appear far more intelligent than I am. I don't know about second acts, but I do think we get second chances, fifth chances, eighteenth chances. Every day we get a fresh chance to live the way we want. We get a chance to do one amazing thing, one scary thing, one difficult thing, one beautiful thing. We get a chance to make a difference.

I tell Phoebe that I'm going to be at the American Airlines international departures terminal at JFK. I tell her I'll have a passport and a suitcase. I tell her I have these two first-class tickets anywhere in the world.

★ ★ ★

Thirty yards away, a bobbing mass of lovely energy walking down the wide corridor. I watch her and realize I'm smiling. She pulls a wheelie suitcase behind her. Her long dark coat is open and she wears blue jeans and her tall brown boots and cashmere sweater her mother gave her for Christmas. Her cheeks are flushed and her hair is down and she is wearing her glasses. How strange to see her differently. The eye doctor does the test and says, 'Better or worse?' A slight alteration in the curve of the glass can change the acuity, change your vision. And in the flick of his wrist things come into view.

'You certainly do a good first date,' she says, smiling. I can smell her shampoo and it smells like grapefruit.

I take her by the shoulders and move her so that her back is to the large board with the long list of departure destinations.

I say, 'Pick a number.'

Phoebe says, 'One million nine.'

I say, 'There are twenty lines on the departure board behind you. The number you pick is the place we're flying to tonight.'

People say, if you could do anything, if money were no object, what would you do? I've never known the answer to that question. I've never had a passion, a hobby, a calling. Except now. Money no object. I want to be with her. I want to tell her everything. To tell her the truth.

Phoebe says, 'Can I look?'

'No.'

'I think I saw Cape Town. I think I saw Rome. I think I saw Mumbai.'

'Pick a number.'

'Oh, God.' She's grinning. 'Nine. No. Wait. Yes. Nine.'

I look up at the board, count nine lines down. Marrakech.

Phoebe says, 'Where is it?'

I have been waiting for my life to begin.

It takes me a while to find the words. I say, 'I don't know how to do this.'

She moves my hand from my face, from my scar.

She says, 'You want to know how to do this?'

'Yes.'

'There are two steps. Give me your hands.'

I extend my arms and she takes hold of my hands.

She says, 'You just learned the first step.'
'What's the second?' I ask.
'Don't let go.'

★ ★ ★

I remember the day I bought the tickets. I was going to get married and go on a honeymoon in Italy with my wife. People did this all the time. I used miles. First class. But they still cost more than I'd ever thought I'd spend on airplane tickets. Or a used car for that matter. The big trip. They were my fear-of-flying tickets. My fear-of-life tickets.

Phoebe and I walked to the ticketing window at JFK. Just after 2 P.M. I figured we'd get our tickets, have lunch, book a hotel online, sit in the Admirals Club until our flight.

The agent typed in the reservation number. You can sense a thing before you know it, in the details: a slight squint, a small tilt of the head, eyes blinking faster.

'Mr. Dolan,' she said. 'I think there's been a mistake. These tickets have expired, sir.'

'That's not possible,' I said.

'I'm sorry, sir. Here, look.'

I looked, half listened. I'd waited a year for this. We have luggage. We have passports. Phoebe started laughing. 'So what's our second date?'

Which is how it came to be that instead of boarding the first-class cabin on an American Airlines Boeing 777–400 to Marrakech, we boarded the AirTrain from JFK to the A train at Howard Beach, transferring at Atlantic Avenue

405

for the N train, making all local stops to Coney Island. And there, at Nathan's, in a gray, misty, half-light of dusk, is where we dined on wrinkled frankfurters, soggy fries, and watery beer. It's where, sitting on a stool looking out the window at the old wooden rollercoaster, with a homeless man asleep two tables away, I told Phoebe I loved her.

It wasn't the big trip. But it was a trip. I took ten days off, slept in. We drank coffee, wandered the city like tourists. Skating at Bryant Park, an afternoon at the Frick, rode the Staten Island Ferry. I had never walked across the Brooklyn Bridge. The weather was terrible. Cold and windy, freezing rain. It was perfect.

★ ★ ★

And then one day I went back.

Martin had told Frank and Dodge about my father, the ashes. I have to say they were very kind, considering how easy it would have been to fire me.

There is a part of me that would like to say that I did quit. It seems so much more heroic. But I do not think that's how it works. Not today. Not in a good job, with high unemployment and real pain out there. I do not think we up and leave our lives. We don't make huge changes for the most part. Subtle shifts, small adjustments in perspective.

If you are one of the lucky ones who know what they want to do for a living — who've always known and who love it — God bless you.

If you are a doctor, a priest, a boat builder, a teacher, a firefighter — a person with a calling — consider yourself fortunate. And if you are like me, someone who simply found themselves doing a job they never imagined doing, I'm not sure what to say.

Except this. I will live and I will die and when I do there might be a few lines in the newspaper about the job I did and the children I made, about the wife I left behind and how long we were married. Perhaps some will cry and there will be a get-together at my home after my dead body is placed in the cold ground. Sandwiches will be eaten and coffee drunk and conversation will be had about me and hopefully what a decent guy I was but also about lawn care and insurance and movies and children and the weather and sports teams and politics and whether or not there's more chicken salad. Later, people will go home with a renewed intensity and appreciation of their world, of how precious and fleeting it all is. They'll hold their children a little longer, the kids not sure what's going on with mom or dad as they try to squirm away to watch TV. A husband and wife will make love in the night as a result of the closeness of death. And then, in the morning, there will be lunches to make and dentist appointments to keep, meetings to attend, ideas to share with clients, leaves to rake, dry cleaning to drop off. The car needs a tune-up.

So there is life. The quiet routine of every day. I read the newspaper, take the subway, go to a meeting. I get a haircut, have dinner with friends, help a woman with a baby carriage up the subway stairs. I get frustrated at a coworker, annoyed by humidity, depressed at the sight of people eating alone. I try to be human. It rains. I go to bed wondering how another day, another week, another year has passed so quickly. It scares me. It makes me want to do better.

We make dinner during these long, cold, dead-of-winter nights. We listen to music and talk and Phoebe teaches me how to cook. We watch movies on my computer. We read in bed. Spring is coming.

Long after Phoebe is asleep I watch the snow fall outside the window, listen to the wind, the rattle of the old glass panes, her hip a touch away. In that moment I think, *This is my life.* This, here and now. This is as close as I am ever going to get to that elusive thing called happiness. How could I ask for more?

* * *

Life is best viewed from a distance. The long lens. This has been my guiding principle. If you step back and watch, well, it's just easier. Because if you don't, if instead you pull others close — if you *need* them — you will never want to let go.

Eddie called to say he was in New York for work. He was taking a flight back that evening, but did I have time for a coffee? We met at a Starbucks in midtown, sat for a time, made small talk. I told him about the shoot, about Keita. He listened but didn't say much.

He started to put his coat on and stopped. He said, 'I'm getting a divorce.'

'Jesus. Eddie. I'm sorry.'

'Yeah. She met someone.'

I didn't know what to say.

He said, 'You know what my biggest fear in life has always been? The thing I've tried so hard to avoid?'

I waited for the answer, but I knew what it was.

Eddie said, 'Being like him.'

'You're not him,' I said. 'You're not even close.'

'Really? I'm leaving my wife, my kids hate me, and I'm angry.'

The old anger was gone, a spent shell. He seemed lost and wounded.

'Ever see *Apollo 13?*' he asked.

'The movie?'

'No. The Broadway musical. Yeah, the movie.'

'Yeah, I've seen it.'

'Well, it's like that,' he said.

'What's like that?'

'Life.' He looked at me as if I should understand.

He said, 'They're coming back through space. At the end. Trying to get home. They have these coordinates and if they don't get them just right, if they're off by even a little bit, it's magnified huge and they slip off the curvature of the earth and shoot out into space, lost.'

He looked out the window and then said, 'We got it wrong. The four of us.'

'Yes,' I said.

He kept looking out the window. 'Still time, though, maybe.'

'Still time.'

He looked at me. You can grow away from your family. You can run away from your family. You can choose to not talk to them. You can be hurt by them, estranged from them. But then, in a Starbucks off Bryant Park, you can be made whole by them. He smiled, my mother's smile, the little squint.

I don't know why the memory comes now. I've not thought of it in many years. This was after she died. Eddie was waiting for me outside school. He had a Ford Galaxie 500 that he somehow managed to keep running.

'C'mon. Got a surprise,' he'd said.

We drove for a while, south of Boston. It was April. Still cool. Halfway there I knew where we were going. Paragon Park. An old amusement park whose best days were long past. The rollercoaster was wood and it creaked and wobbled, a thick, heavy greased chain whipping the cars around. The first hill was so steep that when you went over it felt as if you were going to fall out. The park was across the street from Nantasket Beach. We went there a lot as kids. Blue-collar Riviera. The sand was like concrete, the water painfully, wonderfully cold. On an August day, my mother would make tuna sandwiches and wrap tinfoil around cans of Clicquot Club orange soda. The road out there from the highway had a bend and there was a point where the top of the rollercoaster came into view. Past what used to be Howard

410

Johnsons, faded and abandoned now. Past an old motel. VACANCY. AIR CONDITIONING! COLOR TV! The bend in the road to the left, the beach opening out to the right. Sand blown over onto the road. We pulled into the parking lot near the entrance and saw a hand-painted sign. OPEN MEMORIAL DAY WEEKEND. SEE YOU THEN!

I laughed, more out of embarrassment than anything else. Then I turned and saw Eddie's face, saw how disappointed he was, staring at the closed sign.

'That's okay,' I said.

He mumbled, 'Christ, Finny. I should have called. Dumb ass.'

We got out of the car and stood there, Eddie looking around.

'C'mon,' he said.

We walked toward a shack up the road, near the beach. A fish market with a takeout window on the side. There was no way in hell it would be open. But it was. And it was like Christmas morning to Eddie.

'Look at this, will ya?' he said, all grins.

We ordered fried clams and french fries and Eddie got a beer and I got a Coke and we found a spot beside the shack, out of the wind, in the sun. I don't know what we talked about. I just remember how good it felt being there with him. I felt safe. That was the thing about being around Eddie when I was young. I always felt safe.

We walked outside the Starbucks and stood at the corner looking for a taxi, Eddie's arm up like an out-of-towner, waving to the off-duty cabs. He put his arm down and stared at the traffic.

I said, 'Do you think about her much?'

He was still looking at the traffic. Cars were honking as a fire truck made its way through a block away. It passed.

He said, 'Every day.'

'Me, too.'

He looked around, like he was searching for a landmark, a familiar corner. Anywhere but at me.

Eddie said, 'I thought it would get better. As I got older. I thought it would get easier.'

'Yeah.'

He looked down and said something to the sidewalk. I couldn't hear him. He looked at me.

'What?' I said.

'I'm sorry,' he said.

It was rush hour. Throngs of people on the sidewalk, traffic, horns.

He said, 'I just . . . I'm so sorry.'

His eyes were red rimmed and he looked tired and he was blinking quickly. His voice, though. The old Eddie. My best friend.

How many times could I have called or written a letter, taken the train to Boston? How many times could I have made an effort but didn't?

I said, 'I'm sorry, too.'

I reached out my hand and he took it and we were in an awkward handshake, except we weren't shaking hands, we were just holding hands in a handshake position, which is not what I'd meant to do.

Eddie said, 'It wasn't supposed to be like this, the four of us.'

I nodded and reached my left hand out and

held his forearm. Also not what I'd meant to do.

'I was supposed to take care of everyone. I mean . . . it's not like I don't worry about you guys.'

Boston Irish: *I miss you. I care about you. I love you.* You just have to listen.

He said, 'It's just been a lousy . . . twenty years.'

A taxi pulled up and a woman got out. Eddie tossed his bag into the backseat and held the door. He took a deep breath. I thought of that moment at my mother's wake when I almost reached out for my father but didn't.

'Anyway,' he said.

I moved before I realized I was going to, wrapped my arms around him, felt him go slack, heard his sobs into my jacket, the painful lump in my throat.

'Fuck,' he mumbled.

I said, 'You're a good man, Eddie Dolan. Don't forget that.'

He got into the cab and in the moment before it pulled away, he turned and gave me a little head nod, a half smile, the smallest wave. And I waved, too.

I'd put it in a commercial, but no one would believe it.

ACKNOWLEDGMENTS

This is my second first novel. The previous first novel was, to my (and I'm confident to your) great good fortune, not published. If this novel is good, it is in no small part due to a handful of people who believed in me.

Sally Kim, my editor at Touchstone. She bought something imperfect and in need of help. She guided me, pushed me, helped me find the story. I don't have words to express how I feel about her. But if I did, they would probably be the wrong words and she would then be able to help me find the right ones.

Stacy Creamer, David Falk, Marcia Burch, Wendy Sheanin, Michael Croy, and everyone else at Touchstone. Passionate readers and champions of the unknown writer.

Susan Morrison and David Remnick at *The New Yorker* have been running my Shouts & Murmurs pieces since 1999.

David Kuhn helped make the book a reality, as did Billy Kingsland, Maree Hamilton, Grant Ginder, Nicole Tourtelot, and Jessie Borkan.

At *The New York Times*, Scott Shane, Nora Krug, Michael Newman, Carmel McCoubrey, and David Shipley. At the *Los Angeles Times*, Nick Goldberg and Susan Brennenman.

Rick Knief, unparalleled friend and godfather to my daughter, read draft after draft. His relentless optimism and honesty buoyed me at many turns.

Deirdre Dolan added many insightful comments and encouragement.

Richard Syvanen, screenwriter extraordinaire, dear friend since college, who died at age thirty-five and who, upon reading my first screenplay, urged me to pursue novel writing.

My father, Charles Kenney, and my brothers, Charlie, Michael, Tom, Patrick, and Tim. Good men all. And to the memory of my mother, Anne Barry.

I have no intention of thanking the people at the MacArthur Foundation, as I found their note on my returned application for a genius grant ('HA-HA!') not very funny.

I wrote half of this book in the main reading room of the New York Public Library. I was surrounded each day by scores of people writing what I can only imagine were books, poems, dissertations, job applications, screenplays, wills, and that one guy who just kept writing swear words over and over. It is an awe-inspiring thing to sit among people trying to create something day after day. It's a quiet extended family who respects silence and devotion and one another's belongings during bathroom breaks. So thank you to my fellow writers and to the city of New York and its benefactors for making that space possible.

The other half I wrote at a coffee shop on Sullivan Street in SoHo called Once Upon a Tart. Jerome Audureau, the owner, kindly let me sit all day over one or two coffees, taking up a table, using his electrical outlets. Some of the people who work there — Josie Canseco, Cleo Rivera, Samina Naz, and Anna Marcell — took care of me, fed me, had a smile ready.

My daughter and son, Lulu and Hewitt, who came along and showed me what mattered.

And finally, my wife, Lissa. Our daughter was three months old when I came home one day and said, 'I just got laid off. And they're canceling our health insurance tomorrow. I was thinking I might try novel writing.' Throughout this long, confidence-sapping process, Lissa guided me, believed in me, encouraged me. She listened in the evenings as I read the day's work. She corrected the falseness, the overwriting, the bad dialogue. She taught me, and continues to teach me, what it means to love and be loved.

We do hope that you have enjoyed reading this large print book.

Did you know that all of our titles are available for purchase?

We publish a wide range of high quality large print books including:
Romances, Mysteries, Classics
General Fiction
Non Fiction and Westerns

Special interest titles available in large print are:
The Little Oxford Dictionary
Music Book
Song Book
Hymn Book
Service Book

Also available from us courtesy of Oxford University Press:
Young Readers' Dictionary
(large print edition)
Young Readers' Thesaurus
(large print edition)

For further information or a free brochure, please contact us at:
Ulverscroft Large Print Books Ltd.,
The Green, Bradgate Road, Anstey,
Leicester, LE7 7FU, England.
Tel: (00 44) 0116 236 4325
Fax: (00 44) 0116 234 0205

Other titles published by Ulverscroft:

PILLOW MAN

Nick Coleman

William has a good, steady job in retail. He works in the bedlinen department of an Oxford Street store. He knows everything there is to know about comfy. Lucy has a portfolio career which, in her view, is no kind of career at all. Her life is in a mess; her love life even more unsatisfactory than that. She wouldn't be comfortable if she sat on a sofa in Heal's. Unable to sleep, she thinks a new pillow might be the answer. William and Lucy are not connected. Yet the pair of them share a terrible memory from the past — the sort of joint recollection that changes with the light, depending on who you were and where you were standing at the time. The question is: what to do with it?

THE WAY WE WERE

Maeve Haran

Rachel is a promising A-level student — until she falls for sexy, dangerous Marko (Heathcliff with a nose stud). Her mother, Catherine, is trying to be a good parent and work colleague — but wishes the attentions of her attractive boss didn't suddenly seeming so alluring. Grandmother Lavinia is certain of her values, protecting the country village she loves from change — until the return of a long-lost love reminds her that life moves on, for people as well as places. Is it too late for her to embrace change and find happiness? After all these years — and a lifetime divided by convention — could they really throw other people's expectations to the wind and be the way they were?

THE HORSEMAN

Tim Pears

1911: In a forgotten valley on the Devon-Somerset border, the seasons unfold, marked only by the rituals of the farming calendar. Twelve-year-old Leopold Sercombe skips school to help his father, a carter. Skinny and pale, with eyes the colour of blackberries, Leo dreams of a job on the master's stud farm. As ploughs furrow the hard January fields, the master's daughter, young Miss Charlotte, shocks the estate's tenants by wielding a gun at the annual shoot. One day Leo is breaking a colt for his father when a boy in breeches and riding boots appears — and peering under the stranger's hat, Leo discovers Charlotte. So a friendship begins, bound by a deep love of horses, but divided by rigid social boundaries — boundaries that become increasingly difficult to navigate as the couple approach adolescence.

THE STRANGER

Saskia Sarginson

We all have our secrets. Eleanor Rathmell has kept one her whole life. But when her husband dies and a stranger arrives at her door, her safe life in the idyllic English village she's chosen as her home begins to topple. Everyone is suspicious of this stranger — except for Eleanor; and her trust in him will put her life in danger. Nothing is as it seems — not her dead husband, the man who claims to love her, or the inscrutable outsider to whom she's opened her home and her heart . . .

LEAVING LUCY PEAR

Anna Solomon

One night in 1917, Beatrice Haven creeps out of her uncle's house on Cape Ann, Massachusetts, and leaves her newborn baby at the foot of a pear tree, then watches as another woman claims the child as her own. The unwed daughter of wealthy Jewish industrialists and a gifted pianist bound for Radcliffe, Bea plans to leave her shameful secret behind and make a fresh start . . . Ten years later, Bea's hopes for her future remain unfulfilled. When she returns to her uncle's house, seeking a refuge from her unhappiness, she discovers far more when the rum-running manager of the local quarry inadvertently unites her with Emma Murphy, the headstrong Irish Catholic woman who has been raising her abandoned child — now a bright, bold, cross-dressing girl named Lucy Pear, with secrets of her own.